"A lovely, quirky novel about misfits across the generations . . . There is humor as well as hope." — *Daily Mail* (UK)

"A beguiling, heart-wrenching, and funny book about families, and how they come undone and are remade in unexpected ways . . . Absolutely gorgeous." — *Psychologies* (UK)

"Wood's prose sparkles with lyrical descriptions and sharp observations." — *Irish Examiner*

"If you're looking for a book that entertains and is thought-provoking at the same time, *The One-in-a-Million Boy* by Monica Wood has that wrapped up in a bright red package . . . Beautifully written . . . I loved this book." — *Blurb Magazine* (Australia)

"A bittersweet page-turner that celebrates the everyday soul." — *Sunday Times* (South Africa)

"At the heart of [*The One-in-a-Million Boy*] is the very idea of human connection and its nature—all the joy, suffering, and hope it comes with, and [the novel] reiterates the possibility of finding these connections in the oddest and least expected places." — *The Hindu* (India)

"A simultaneously sad and joyous story . . . peopled by endearing characters." — *Booklist* (US)

"To say I loved this wonderful, wonderful book would be a serious understatement. More like I imprinted on it. I still find myself thinking about these characters. This lovely, sweet story of a boy, his estranged father, and his 104-year-old friend will stay with you for a long time." — Liberty Hardy, *Book Riot* (US)

"In *The One-in-a-Million Boy*, Monica Wood tells a magical, beautifully written story about the healing power of friendship, music, and unexpected, generation-spanning connections. As emotionally resonant as *The Curious Incident of the Dog in the Night-Time*, this novel hums with energy, warmth, wisdom, humor, and soul."

— Christina Baker Kline, author of *Orphan Train* (US)

THE ONE-
IN-A-MILLION
BOY

Monica Wood

MARINER

An Imprint of HarperCollins*Publishers*
Boston   New York

First Mariner Books edition 2017

marinerbooks.com

Library of Congress Cataloging-in-Publication Data
Wood, Monica.
The one-in-a-million boy / Monica Wood.
pages ; cm
ISBN 978-0-544-61707-0 (hardcover)—
ISBN 978-0-544-94721-4 (pbk.)—
ISBN 978-0-544-61844-2 (ebook)
I. Title.
PS3573.O5948O54 2015
813'.54—dc23
2015004345

Book design by Greta D. Sibley

Printed in the United States of America
23 24 25 26 27 LBC 16 15 14 13 12

For

Joe Sirois,

who completed our family,

and

Gail Hochman,

who made the whole journey

Contents

Author's Note

The One-in-a-Million Boy includes lists of world records, most of them assembled from various editions of the Guinness World Records series. Except for four obvious exceptions, the names and feats are real, and a matter of public record; however, they, and the Guinness World Records brand, are used here to embroider a world that exists only in my imagination. Some of the records will likely have been broken by more current contenders in the time between the writing and publication of this book. I also consulted the website of the Gerontology Research Group, an organization that keeps track of the world's oldest people. The real-life musician David Crosby makes a brief appearance in the story, and he, too, is used fictionally.

PART ONE

Brolis (Brother)

* * *

This is Miss Ona Vitkus. This is her life story on tape. This is Part One.

Is it on?
. . .
I can't answer all these. We'll be here till doomsday.
. . .
I'll answer the first one, but that's it.
. . .
I was born in Lithuania. In the year nineteen hundred. I don't recall the place. I might have, oh, the vaguest recollection of some farm animals. A horse, or some other large beast. White, with spots.
. . .
Maybe a cow.
. . .
I have no idea what type of cows live in Lithuania. But I seem to recollect—you know those spotted dairy-type cows you see everywhere?
. . .
Holsteins. Thank you. Oh, and cherry trees. Lovely cherry trees that looked like soapsuds in the spring. Big, frothy, flowering things.
. . .
Then there was a long trip, and a ship's crossing. I remember that in pieces. You've got a million questions on that sheet—
. . .
Fifty, yes. Fine. I'm just saying, you don't have to ask them in order.
. . .
Because the story of your life never starts at the beginning. Don't they teach you anything in school?

Chapter 1

She was waiting for him—or someone—though he had not phoned ahead. "Where's the boy?" she called from her porch.

"Couldn't make it," he said. "You Mrs. Vitkus?" He'd come to fill her bird feeders and put out her trash and tender sixty minutes to the care of her property. He could do at least that.

She regarded him peevishly, her face a collapsed apple, drained of color but for the small, unsettling, seed-bright eyes. "My birds went hungry," she said. "I can't manage the ladder." Her voice suggested mashed glass.

"Mrs. Ona Vitkus? Forty-two Sibley Ave.?" He checked the address again; he'd taken two buses across town to get here. The green bungalow sat at the woodsy edge of a dead-end street, two blocks from a Lowe's and a few strides from a hiking trail. Standing in the driveway, Quinn could hear birds and traffic in equal measure.

"It's 'Miss,'" she said haughtily. He caught the faintest trace of an accent. The boy hadn't mentioned it. She'd probably staggered through Ellis Island with the huddled masses. "He didn't come last week, either," she said. "These boys don't stick to things."

"I can't help that," Quinn said, suddenly wary. He'd been led to expect a pink-cheeked charmer. The house resembled a witch's hovel, with its dreary flower beds and sharply pitched dormers and shingles the color of thatch.

"They're supposed to be teaching these boys about obedience. Prepared and kind and obedient . . . kind and obedient and . . ." She rapped herself lightly on the forehead.

"Clean," Quinn offered.

The boy was gone: clean gone. But Quinn couldn't bring himself to say it.

"Clean and reverent," the woman said. "That's what they promise. They pledge. I thought this one was the real McCoy." Another weak echo of accent: something brushy in the consonants, nothing an ordinary ear would pick up.

"I'm his father," Quinn said.

"I figured." She shifted inside her quilted parka. She also wore a hat with pompoms, though it was fifty-five degrees, late May, the sun beading down. "Is he sick?"

"No," Quinn said. "Where's the birdseed?"

The old woman shivered. Her stockinged legs looked like rake handles jammed into small black shoes. "Out back in the shed," she said. "Next to the door, unless the boy moved it. He gets his little notions. There's a ladder there, too. You're tall. You might not need it." She sized Quinn up as if considering a run at his clothes.

"If I lowered the feeders," he suggested, "you could fill them yourself."

She dug her fists into her hips. "I'm quite put out about this," she said. All at once she sounded near tears, an unexpected key change that sped things up on Quinn's end.

"Let me get to it," he said.

"I'll be inside." She aimed a knuckly finger toward her door. "I can supervise just as well through the window." She spoke with a zeal at odds with her physical frailty, and Quinn doubted for the first time Belle's word that Ona Vitkus was 104 years old. Since the boy's death, Belle's view of reality had gone somewhat gluey. Quinn was awed by her grief, cowed by its power to alter her. He wanted to save her but had no talent for anything more interpersonally complicated than to obey commands as a form of atonement. Which was how he'd wound up here, under orders from his twice-ex-wife, to complete their son's good deed.

The shed had peeling double doors that opened easily. The hinges looked recently oiled. Inside, he found a stepladder with a broken rung. The place reeked of animal—not dog or cat, something grainier; mice, maybe. Or skinny, balding, fanged rats. Garden implements, seized with rust, hung in a diagonal line on the far wall, points and prongs and blades facing out. He considered the ways the boy could have been hurt on this weekly mission of mercy: ambushed by falling timber, gnawed by vermin—Troop 23's version of bait and switch.

But the boy had not been hurt. He had been, in his words, "inspired."

Quinn found the birdseed in a plastic bucket that he recognized. It had once held the five gallons of joint compound with which he'd repaired the walls of Belle's garage—before their final parting, before she returned his rehearsal space to a repository for paint thinner and plant poisons and spare tires. Inside the bucket Quinn found a king-size scoop, shiny and cherry red, jolly as a prop in a Christmas play. On a nearby shelf he spotted nine more scoops, identical. The boy was a hoarder. He kept things that could not be explained. On the day before the funeral, Belle had opened the door to the boy's room, instructing Quinn to look around if he wanted, but to remove nothing, touch nothing. So, he counted. Bird nests: 10; copies of *Old Yeller*: 10; flashlights: 10; piggy banks: 10; Boy Scout manuals: 10. He had Popsicle sticks, acorns, miniature spools of the sort found in ladies' sewing kits, everything corralled into tidy ten-count groupings. One computer, ten mouse pads. One desk, ten pencil cases. Hoarding, Belle maintained, was a reasonable response to a father whose attentions dribbled like water from a broken spigot. "Figure it out," she had once told him. "Why would an eleven-year-old child insist on all this backup for the things he needs?"

Because there's something wrong with him, went Quinn's silent answer. But on that solemn day they'd observed the room in silence. As Belle preceded Quinn out the door, Quinn palmed the boy's diary—a single notebook, spiral-bound, five by seven, basic black—and shoved it inside his jacket. Nine others remained, still sealed in shrink-wrap.

As Quinn lugged the birdseed out to Miss Vitkus's feeders, he pictured the rest of Troop 23 happily do-gooding for more appealing charity cases, the type who knitted pink afghans. The scoutmaster, Ted Ledbetter, a middle-school teacher and single father who claimed to love woodland hikes, had likely foisted Miss Vitkus on the one kid least likely to complain. Now she was tapping on the window, motioning for Quinn to get cracking.

Between the house and a massive birch, Miss Vitkus had strung a thirty-foot clothesline festooned with bird feeders. At six-two, he didn't require the ladder, though the boy would have, small as he was, elfin and fine-boned. Quinn had also been small at eleven, shooting up the following summer in a growth spurt that left him literally aching and out of clothes. Perhaps the boy would have been tall. A tall hoarder. A tall counter of mysterious things.

Quinn began at the tree end, and as he uncapped the first feeder, birds began to light, foliating the shivering branches. Chickadees, he guessed. Everything new he'd learned in the last two weeks had come from the cautious, well-formed, old-mannish handwriting of his son. A future Eagle Scout, the mysterious fruit of Quinn's feckless loins, the boy had, according to the diary, set his sights on a merit badge in bird identification.

Miss Vitkus lifted her window. "They think you're the boy," she called to him as the birds flittered down. "Same jacket." Fresh air tunneled into his lungs, blunt and merciless. Miss Vitkus watched him, her sweater bunched across her deflated chest. When he didn't respond, she snapped the window down.

After dispatching the feeders and running a push mower over her lawn, Quinn returned to the house, where Miss Vitkus stood at the door, waiting for him. No hair to speak of, just a few whitish hanks that put him in mind of dandelions. She said, "I give him cookies after."

"No, thanks."

"It's part of the duty."

So he went in, leaving his jacket on. It was, as Miss Vitkus had pointed out, exactly like the one the boy wore: a leather bomber with rivets, which made Quinn look like a rock-and-roll man and the boy like a meerkat struggling out of a trap. Belle had buried him in it.

He expected cats and doilies, but Miss Vitkus's house was pleasant and airy. Her kitchen counter, though crowded at one end with stacked newspapers, shone whitely in the unmolested places. The sink taps gleamed. The exterior must once have looked like the other houses on the street — straight and well appointed and framed by precise green lawns — but she'd obviously lost her ability to keep up.

Her table had been whisked clean but for two mismatched plates, a box of animal crackers, a deck of cards, and a pair of ugly drugstore reading glasses. The chairs smelled of lemon polish. He could see how the boy might have liked it here.

"I heard you're a hundred and four," Quinn ventured, mostly to fill up space.

"Plus one hundred thirty-three days." She divided the animal crackers, one to each plate, over and over, like dealing cards. Apparently there would be no milk.

"I'm forty-two," he said. "That's eighty-four in musician years."

"You look older." Her greenish eyes glimmered over him. The boy had written, in his faultless spelling: *Miss Vitkus is EXTREMELY inspiring in her magic powers and AMAZING life events!!!* The diary was twenty-nine pages long, a chronicle of lists interrupted by brief, breathless transcriptions from the world of Miss Vitkus, his new friend.

"Do you have help?" he asked. "Besides the Scouts?"

"I get Meals on Wheels," she said. "I have to take the food apart and recook it, but it saves me on groceries." She held up a cookie dinosaur. "This is their idea of dessert." She looked him over again. "Your boy told me you're famous. Are you?"

He laughed. "In my dreams."

"What style of music do you play?"

"Anything except jazz. Jazz you have to be born with."

"Elvis?"

"Sure."

"Cowboy songs?"

"If you ask me nice."

"I always liked Gene Autry. Perry Como?"

"Perry Como or Gene Autry or Led Zeppelin or a cat-food commercial. As long as they pay me."

"I've never heard of Ed Zeppelin but I've seen my share of cat-food commercials." She blinked a few times. "So, a jack of all trades."

"A journeyman," he said. "That's how you stay working."

She considered him anew. "You must be quite talented, then."

"I'm okay." What had the boy told her? He felt like a bug on a pin. "I've been working steady since I was seventeen."

To this she had nothing to say.

"As a guitar player, I mean. I've been working mainly as a guitar player."

Again, nothing; so Quinn switched gears. "Your English is excellent."

"Why wouldn't it be? I've lived in this country for a hundred years. I'll have you know I was a headmaster's secretary. Lester Academy. Have you heard of it?"

"No."

"Dr. Mason Valentine? Brilliant man."

"I went to public schools."

She fumbled with her sweater, a relic from the forties with big glass buttons. "These boys don't stick to anything. We had ongoing business." She glared at him.

Quinn said, "I guess I should go."

"Suit yourself." She drummed her fingers on the well-used cards, which looked a little smaller than regulation.

"My son says you do tricks," he said, unable to resist.

"Not for free I don't."

"You charge him?"

"Not him. He's a child." She slipped the glasses on—they were too big for her face—and inspected the deck.

The boy had written: *Miss Vitkus is* EXTREMELY *talented. She makes cards and quarters* DISAPPEAR. *Then they* APPEAR *again!!! She smiles well.*

This was exactly the way he had talked in real life.

Quinn said, "How much?"

She shuffled her cards, her mood changing. "I shall regale you," she said, a magician's misdirection. Quinn had run into all manner of flimflammery over the years, and this old bird was a champ.

"Just the trick would be fine," he said, glancing at her kitchen clock.

"You're in a hurry," she said. "Everybody's in a hurry." She was accordioning the cards now, hand to hand, less impressively than she seemed to think, but impressive enough. "I ran off with a midway show in the summer of 1914 and learned the art of prestidigitation." Her eyes lifted, as if the word itself produced magic. "Three months later, I came back home and for the rest of my days lived the most conventional life imaginable." Her expression was intense but ambiguous. "I do this to remind myself that I was once a girl." Reddening, she added, "I told your boy a lot of stories. Too many, possibly."

He'd been right to fear coming here: the boy was everywhere. Quinn had never wanted children, had been an awkward, largely absent father; and now, in the wake of the boy's death, he was left with neither the ice-smooth paralysis of shock, nor the crystalline focus of grief, but rather with a heart-swelling package of murky and miserable ironies.

Miss Vitkus fanned the cards and waited. Her teeth were long, squarish, still white enough, her bumpy fingers remarkably nimble, her nails shiny and ridgeless.

"Five bucks," Quinn said, taking out his wallet.

"You read my mind." She took the bill and stowed it in her sweater.

After a moment, Quinn said, "Where's the trick?"

She leaned across the table and gathered up the cards. "Five gets you inside the tent." He saw what was in her eyes now: anger. "Five more, you get the show."

"That's extortion."

"I wasn't born yesterday," she said. "Next time, bring the boy."

* * *

This is Miss Ona Vitkus. This is her life story on tape. This is also
Part One.

Eighty-eight more minutes? On that little gizmo?
. . .
I'll take your word for it. Fire away.
. . .
Well, there was radio. That was a good one. And copy machines.
Velcro. The electric mixer. Oh, and some marvelous improvements
in ladies' underthings. It's hard to pick just one.
. . .
Then I'll go with the automatic washer. Definitely the automatic
washer. I don't recall just when I made the changeover. One minute
you're drubbing petticoats on a washboard, the next minute you've
got two teenagers and a brand-new Maytag. The in-between goes
kind of blinky.
. . .
That's it. That's all I have for you.

Chapter 2

Quinn left Miss Vitkus's house five dollars poorer and deprived of magic. He took the bus all the way to Belle's neighborhood of North Deering, where he found her raking a tulip bed behind a cliché of a fence—all those smiling pickets. He'd always thought of the house as Belle's place—which it was, legally speaking—despite the five and a half nonconsecutive years he himself had lived there. The bay windows reminded him of the sitcoms of the sixties, which the boy had ardently watched, one after the other, on a TV channel lousy with proper husbands and fathers, stand-up guys who stayed home nights to anchor the home vessel.

"So?" she asked. Even her voice had thinned, its layered notes erased.

"It's out near Westbrook," he said. "Her yard's a mess."

"He committed till mid-July. I told Ted we'd take care of it."

"She's got like twenty feeders, hung way too high. He had his work cut out for him."

Belle checked the street. "You on foot?"

"I sold the Honda." He slipped a check from his pocket and gave it to her. He'd mailed her a child-support check every Saturday since their second divorce and had yet to miss a payment.

She regarded him woodenly. "I told you, Quinn. There's no more—need."

He wondered, not for the first time, if a person could literally die of grief. She was wearing a pink shirt so desperately wrinkled it looked as if it had been filched from a washer at a public laundry.

"Belle," he said. "Let me."

She didn't let him, not at first, but he stood there with the proffered check, blood sloshing in his temples, the check lifting in the weak breeze, until he made clear his intention to outlast her. She relented, took the check, said nothing, and his head calmed.

The place looked deceptively renewed. Late-May flowers popping up everywhere, windows a-twinkle, and another collection of things set out for the trash man.

"Cleaning out again?" he asked.

"Just the things I can't bear."

What she meant remained a mystery. He took stock of the rejects: a stuffed chair, a blender, a table lamp, some flatware. Then he caught it, sitting apart from the rest: his first amplifier, two watts, a present from his thirteenth birthday.

"Isn't that my Marvel?"

They stared at it, together, as they might inspect a dead animal. It was a cheap Japanese import in a case so heavily lacquered it appeared wet even under a three-decade layer of grime.

"It's ugly," Belle said, "and it doesn't work. Nobody wants it."

"My mother gave me that." Six-inch speaker, three knobs; junk, pretty much, the sole surviving relic of his adolescence. And of his mother, for that matter.

"It still works," he said, defensive now. He'd loved that amp. It had meant something.

"How about if you remove your junk from my house once and for all? There isn't a damn thing to hold you here now."

"Belle," he said, wounded. "Don't." He had missed his last two custody visits and there would be no forgiving him. Certain things, examined in the frozen light of retrospect, were simply unforgivable.

He looked around. For two weeks Belle's family had swarmed like a gang of hornets, led by Amy, Belle's sister. Also Ted Ledbetter, another matter entirely. But today the house was quiet, the driveway empty.

"Is Ted here?"

"No. And how is that your business?"

"Sorry. Where's everyone else?"

"The aunts went home. Amy's out mailing thank-you cards. I pretend to need things to get four seconds of peace." She set the rake against a tree and stuttered out a breath that reminded him of childbirth exercises. He followed her inside, where she seemed surprised to see him.

"Can I have some water?" he asked.

She went into the kitchen and poured him a glass. The house was a tidy Cape, a suburban classic, though technically they were inside Portland's city limits. Lawns stamped into the once-bumpy landscape. Swing sets, treehouses, dog runs aplenty. Belle's parents had owned the house and passed it to Belle under condition that Quinn's name be omitted from the paperwork.

"Did she mention him? The old woman?"

He shook his head. "She cheated me out of five bucks."

"They had charming conversations," she said. "I'm quoting."

"I don't know how he put up with her." He meant to sound lighthearted but lately everything landed with the weighted thud of trying-too-hard.

"Did *you* mention him?"

He drained the glass. The animal crackers had made him thirsty. "To her?"

"Yes, to her. Who else, Quinn?"

"I didn't." He added, "Couldn't."

The icy surface of her anger—she was encased in it—thawed incrementally. "It's not a strike against his character that he put up with her," she said at last. "She's absurdly old."

"I took that into consideration."

She laid her fingers on his arm. "It's the one thing I asked you to do. He made a commitment, and to him the word means something. I'd do it myself, but this"—she searched the air for some words—"this is the job of the father."

Quinn said nothing. What was there to say? He'd left when the boy was three, returned when the boy was eight. Five years willingly hacked from the fragile core of fatherhood. She could call him on it now, but didn't. Boston, New York, and finally Chicago, until it came to him that he was living the same life he'd left, only lonelier. After that, a long, humiliating bus ride home. He'd made a decent living—had always made a decent living, his one source of pride—but still he dreaded facing his former bandmates and day-job shift supervisors with the predictable news that no, ha-ha, he hadn't Made It, and yeah, he was back for good.

"I didn't say I was quitting. All I said is that she's no twinkly old gal in a gingham apron."

"Poor you," Belle said. "What else have you got to do today?"

"A wedding at five."

"You always have a wedding at five. Mr. In-Demand."

This was their old struggle, and her willingness to unearth it now made him feel less alone. Belle had once compared his chronic gigging to the daily requirements of a maintenance alcoholic. To Quinn, for whom alcohol was a touchy simile, the truth was this: playing guitar was the single occasion in his slight and baffling life when he had the power to deliver exactly the thing another human being wanted.

He trailed Belle into the living room but was not asked to sit. He looked around, sensing a false note, and then it came to him: she'd put her books away. A profligate reader, she usually had four or five going at once, leaving them everywhere, spines flattened by her passion. How many nights had she spent with him recounting plots as he pleaded with her, laughing, not to give it all away? But she always did; when she loved a story she gave it to him whole. Now those same books were stacked by size into a bookcase that looked freshly washed.

"It's only a few more Saturdays," she said now.

"Seven, actually."

"Seven, then. It takes, what, two hours out of your busy day?"

"Yeah, but then you have to eat poisoned cookies."

She laughed, a brief bark that startled them both. He took her hands and held them; his sympathy filled him to bursting. It was bottomless, this sympathy.

"Can I see his room again? Just for a minute?" He hoped to return the diary before she missed it. He couldn't imagine her not knowing of the diary's existence, she who had observed the boy's life as if in the belief he would need a biographer someday.

She withdrew her hands. "Not now."

She was punishing him, this fierce and lovely woman, his truest friend. He deserved it; but he knew her well, knew she didn't have the juice to sustain her rage.

"I've got cards to write out," she said. "Your father sent a note. And Allan called, all the way from Hong Kong." She waited. "Allan didn't know about our divorce. Probably he didn't even know about our first one."

He shrugged. "You know us." His father was in Florida year-round now, his brother on the other side of the world. They rarely spoke.

It was ten o'clock. He had hours to fill. He asked, "Are you eating?"

The question seemed to confuse her. "Probably," she said. "I guess I must be."

"Do you need anything?"

"Quinn," she said gently. "There's nothing you can do for me now."

The truth of this hurt him like a soft, blue bruise. Belle walked him outside, all the way to the sidewalk, as if he had a car waiting there. "I'm somebody else now," she said, and if there had ever been a time in his life when he knew what to do with this kind of information, that time had long passed. He locked eyes with her until she released him with a slow shake of her head.

He picked up the amp—it weighed nothing—and carried it out of his former neighborhood and all the way down Washington Avenue and around the Boulevard and up the long slope of State Street to the Peninsula and finally to Brackett Street and up the three dark flights to his apartment, which held beautifully tended music equipment, a few sticks of secondhand furniture, and a framed photo of the boy in his Scout uniform, his short teeth bared in earnest cooperation. Someone had told him to smile, and he'd done the best he could.

BIRDS

1. Smallest bird. Bee hummingbird. 2.24 inches and 0.056 ounces.
2. Fastest bird over land. Ostrich. 45 miles per hour.
3. Highest-flying bird. Ruppell's griffon vulture. 37,000 feet.
4. Most talkative bird. Prudie. African gray parrot. 800 words.
5. Most feathers on bird. Whistling swan. 25,216 feathers.
6. Least feathers on bird. Ruby-throated hummingbird. 940 feathers.
7. Slowest-flying bird. American woodcock. 5 miles per hour.
8. Longest bill on bird. 18.5 inches. Australian pelican.
9. Nicest bird. In my opinion. Black-capped chickadee.
10. Longest bird flight. Common tern. 16,210 miles.

Chapter 3

On that first Saturday, at the beginning of the early March thaw, the boy arrived in a gray van commandeered by a well-constructed scoutmaster in a pressed uniform. Water dripped off Ona's gutters, her porch rails, her bird feeders, and the van's sideview mirrors. The scoutmaster disconnected the boy from the rest of the troop—all of them larger and lunkier than the boy—and marched (literally, it seemed) up the steps. He introduced himself as Ted Ledbetter, then presented the slender, crewcutted boy, whose air of willing restraint instantly unsettled her.

The first word plinked into her conscious mind, odd as a stray hailstone: *brolis*. She blinked hard, as if the word had literally hit her on the head.

Brother.

Eleven, he was, though small enough to pass for eight. Over his uniform he wore a ludicrous, water-stained leather jacket from which his neck rose, skinny and naked, an unearthly white. He looked open to wounding. The scoutmaster left the boy with several well-turned instructions and promised a pickup, two hours hence, expressed in military time.

After the van lumbered off, the boy stood wordless and waiting, as reedy and guileless as a grasshopper. "It's a pleasure to meet you," he said.

"Hmm," Ona said.

The boy stared. "How old are you?"

The second word dropped: *šimtas.*

He blinked once. "What?"

"One hundred."

"What language is that?"

"I don't know," Ona said, mystified. "Lithuanian, I surmise. I'm one hundred *four,* not one hundred. One-oh-*four.*"

They stood together in the dripping world, sizing each other up, the boy appearing to marvel at the weight of a century-plus, Ona wondering how in hell she'd unearthed two unrelated words in a tongue she couldn't remember ever speaking.

"Come in, then," she said, and he did, staying politely on the mat in his trickling shoes.

"I have several jobs for you," she said, "and if you can't do them, or don't want to, I'd just as soon know now."

"I can do them."

"I haven't told you what they are."

"I can do them anyway." He enunciated beautifully, though his diction contained barely perceptible pauses in the wrong places, as if he were a foreigner, or short of breath.

But he proved a good worker, willing and persistent and agreeably thorough. Saturday was trash day; he rolled her big trash can all the way from the curb to the shed, which she expected, then replaced the bungee cord over the lid, which she did not expect. He removed all the bird feeders, filled them to brimming, then rehung them with the assiduous care of a window dresser. He cleared straggling blots of snow from the edges of her walk. By the time she got around to offering him a cookie, the scoutmaster had returned.

Ona agreed to take the boy on. Mr. Ledbetter looked relieved; she'd sent the others back on day one.

On the second Saturday—after he'd cleaned and filled the feeders in so precise an imitation of the previous week that she suspected he'd written instructions on his hand—the boy confided his passion for world records. They were sitting at her table, eating animal crackers, which the boy did in stages: tail, legs, head, body. Each one exactly the same.

"Not sports-type records," he assured her. "Records like . . . One, how long can you spin a coin. Two, largest collection of golf pencils. Three, longest ear hair." He took a short breath. "Four—"

"Guinness records," she said. She had no trouble hearing him, which delighted her.

"You've heard of it!" He looked absurdly pleased. "It's harder to get in than people think."

Normally, Scouts bored her, with their Game Boy stats and soccer scores and lazy, shortcutting ways. This one, though, brought a literal sense of second childhood: she felt as if she were speaking to a child she might have known when she herself was eleven. How easily she placed him at McGovern's, installed at the white marble soda fountain, sipping a chocolate phosphate. She could see him amid the white-shirted boys playing stickball on Wald Street, tagging the door of Joe Preble's black REO. There was something vaguely wrong with him that made him seem like a visitor from another time and place.

He reminded her that she'd once found people fascinating. That she'd lived more than one life.

She pulled a quarter from her pocket. After a few fumbling tries, she got it to spin. "Five seconds plus," she said, after it wobbled free and succumbed to gravity. "What's the record?"

"Nineteen-point-three-seven seconds," the boy said. "Mr. Scott Day, country of Great Britain. Your table isn't smooth enough."

She eyed the sash he wore across his chest, bedecked with shiny patches. "Do you hold the record for merit badges?"

"Mr. John Stanford, country of USA, earned one hundred forty-two merit badges." He looked out the window. "There's a badge for bird study."

"Really?" She pointed. "That's a goldfinch." She had learned the basics from Louise back when life still held its little surprises. She'd kept a list for about ten years but couldn't now recall the last time she'd actually *observed* a bird. She fed them out of pity.

"I already know some regular ones," he said. "One, crow. Two, robin. Three, cardinal. Four, chickadee. But one, you have to know twenty birds to get a badge. Two, you have to build a birdhouse. Three, you have to name five birds by their song." His soft mouth slackened. "I'm bad at music."

"Really? Because of my husband, Howard, who was a failed and frustrated songster, I'm somewhat ambivalent about music myself." Ona patted her ear. "Birdsong is different, but I've lost the high-pitched ones. Last time I heard a warbler I was seventy-two. Even the robins drop out at times, like a broken radio."

"That's too bad," he said. His entire body stilled in a way that telegraphed his sympathy, and she began to feel fully, truly sorry to have lost all those birds, whose fluting notes had apparently escaped for good down a decrepitating hatch in her inner ear. After nursing Louise through the final dregs of cancer, Ona couldn't relocate her former pastimes and believed they had quite literally fled with Louise into the Great Unknowable Somewhere. *Don't turn into an old crab,* Louise warned her in those final days. *It's too predictable.* But that's exactly what Ona *had* turned into: an old crab.

"Mr. John Reznikoff, country of USA, got into Guinness World Records by collecting hair," the boy said. "One, hair from Abraham Lincoln. Two, hair from Marilyn Monroe. Three, hair from Albert Einstein. Four . . ."

This list was very long, and she waited for him to complete it. His eyes never moved from her face. He'd committed a stunning number of records to memory, all of them of the hair-collecting/coin-spinning variety. He, too, collected things—unsuccessfully, he confessed. Serious collecting apparently took a measure of money and opportunity not readily available to the average fifth-grader. "Mr. John Reznikoff buys his hair," he informed her. "It's not like he dug up Lincoln's grave."

"Oh. I wondered."

"Mr. Ashrita Furman, country of USA, walked eighty-point-nine-six miles with a glass milk bottle balanced on his head."

"All at once?" Ona asked, incredulous.

"Mr. Ashrita Furman also holds the record for number of records." He stopped. "One, where would I get a glass milk bottle? Two, how would I measure eighty miles? Three, my mother wouldn't let me walk eighty miles with a bottle on my head even if I wanted to." He paused again. "Which I sort of do."

Though he offered little more about himself, Ona gathered that school was a trial, day upon day of skulking in the back row for fear of being called on. Possibly he stood alone at recess. Her own boys had been so easy with their friends, Frankie especially, so sunny and well liked. This boy, with his measured voice and forbearing demeanor, seemed more like someone she could actually be related to.

"I knew a man who juggled mice," she told him.

His eyes popped open, so she hauled out her midway story.

"You ran away?" the boy said. She could feel herself being deliciously reassessed. "You left your *mother?*"

"Times were funny, war in the air. I hemmed every skirt I owned that year, all the girls in Kimball suddenly flashing their calves." Felled by the child's listening gray eyes, she went on: "Mr. Holmes was the show's owner, a huckster if ever I knew one. His show wasn't very good, as midway shows went, more like a carnival you might see now at a shopping mall."

"Oh," the boy said. "I went to one."

"How was it?"

"The rides were very fast."

"Well, we had an old carousel Mr. Holmes won in a poker game — a bona fide Armitage Herschell two-row portable — put-upable and take-downable. Ever seen one?"

"No," the boy said, goggle-eyed. "I want to."

Ona had her cards out now and began shuffling. "We did the best we could with the carousel, some third-rate midway games, and a parrot who sang the Sophie Tucker version of 'Some of These Days.' Ever heard it?"

"Can I?"

"My Victrola's long gone," she said. "I went to the midway every night for seven nights running. And on the seventh night, I fell in love right there in front of the carousel."

How could it have been otherwise? The sultry evening, the smell of peanuts and drying mud, the steam carousel with painted horses posed for all eternity in an attitude of escape. "I can still see the wild white eyes on those horses," she told the boy. "You can't imagine the colors, nothing like the dullards you see nowadays. Pick a card."

The boy looked startled. "Now?"

"Whenever you're ready. In the meantime, I shall regale you." She had learned the word *regale* from Maud-Lucy Stokes, her childhood tutor, who had employed a flawless grammar that inspired little Ona's initial, inaccurate, and ultimately disappointing impression of America as a land of precision. Ona loved English from the get-go and paid strict attention, noting the cause-effect of language: her parents' syntactical shipwrecks, the tin peddler's casual profanity, Maud-Lucy's pristine enunciations. Style could move listeners to pity, to reverence, to the purchase of a stewpot they didn't need. Maud-Lucy taught Ona to compose a sentence with intention, and eventually she chose for herself a high-low hybrid that matched her ambivalence toward humankind.

"There I was," she told the boy, "standing in a huddle with some girls from my neighborhood, watching the handsome horses go round and round, when Viktor, the tattoo man's apprentice, sauntered over as if we'd already met in a dream. Beautiful, blond, Russian Viktor." He stole first her heart, then her virtue, and finally her money. "I'd never even held a boy's hand. I wasn't that type of girl."

"What type of girl were you?"

"Oh," she said. "Well. Innocent. Like you. Now, why on earth would I tell you all that?"

"I don't know." The boy's gaze fell on her like a strong slat of sunlight. She felt, briefly, unclothed. It was the mention of Viktor that put her in this state. Viktor, who would be one hundred nine. Dead and buried and flirting with her from the grave.

At last, the boy picked a card. He studied it for a full thirty seconds, then gave it back. She pretended to shuffle it into the deck. "Presto," she said, then flipped his card right side up onto the table.

The boy's mouth dropped open.

"For crumbsake, haven't you ever seen a card trick?"

"Not a good one. There's a kid in my class who does bad ones." He frowned. "Everybody thinks Troy Packard is so great."

A bully, Ona surmised. "Well, then," she said, spreading out the cards. "Look here."

She laid out the cards for a simple Bottoms Up, as she had for a generation of jittery schoolboys at Lester Academy in her capacity as the headmaster's secretary. To the youngest ones, the smallest and most scared, she taught the very trick she was teaching now to the boy.

He had remarkable fingers, was willing and avid, but possessed no knack whatsoever for misdirection. "You have zero wiles," she said. "Don't try this at school."

"The world record for a house of cards is one hundred thirty-one stories."

"Maybe you can go for that. Set a new one."

"I tried to set a new one."

"How many did you get?"

"I got eleven."

"That's one story per year."

He looked pleased and said, "Miss Vitkus, you have very beautiful hands."

On the third Saturday, in return for her first compliment in decades, Ona unveiled her entire arsenal of card tricks—the whole shebang, for free. But the boy proved too gullible to appreciate the difference between the obvious step-by-step of a We Three Kings and the multi-layered staginess of a Morning Mail. Though the diversionary tactic of telling stories during each slip and shift proved entirely pointless, she answered his questions anyway. It had been a long time, if ever, since another human being betrayed so intense an interest in the ordinary facts of her life.

The boy listened in a fashion she had not heretofore encountered: nothing moved. Not his eyes, not his shoulders, not his legs or feet. Just his fingers—a restrained but detectable ritual that looked like counting. From his lightly closed fist, one finger flicked open, then a second, a third, a fourth, and a thumb; then the other hand: one, two, three, four, thumb. Then the fists closed again, and the fingers jutted again, predictable, systematic. He appeared to be slicing her stories into items on a list, a form of prestidigitation that turned commonplace information into incantation.

1. Miss Vitkus came to America as a four-year-old child.
2. With her parents, Jurgis and Aldona.
3. From the country of Lithuania.
4. Which was run by the Russians.
5. Who tried to take all the Lithuanian men and put them in the army.
6. So Jurgis and Aldona moved to Kimball, Maine, where there were seven mills.
7. Jurgis got a job as an acid cooker and Aldona got a job as a rag sorter.
8. And they decided to make their little girl an American.
9. So they didn't talk to her in Lithuanian.
10. And they couldn't talk to her in English.

"Did you get lonely?" the boy asked. "If my mom didn't talk to me, who else would talk to me?" He curled his fingers and waited for another one-to-ten. She felt compelled to oblige.

"My parents did talk to me," she said.

One.

"It's just that their vocabulary was limited."

Two.

From the veiled years came the sound of her name: *Ona, what you got, Ona? Ona, smile nice, Ona. Ona, pretty dress, Ona. Ona:* their sole allowable native word, a meek comfort, a bubble of remembrance. An early memory floated in, Ona pressed against the door of her parents' bedroom, listening in panic and longing as they whispered in their mother tongue: *pushka-pushka-pushka,* mysterious susurrations that sounded like quavering trees.

Outside that room it was English, English, English. Aldona worked all day at the bag mill, Jurgis all night at the pulp mill, ferrying fresh words and phrases across the footbridge at shift change. When Ona was six they built their own apartment building, a wooden triple-decker with open porches. On an eighth-acre at the corner of Wald and Chandler, the Vitkus block rose up board by board, a testimony to foresight and grit. In the tiny backyard they revived a swatch of their beloved *Lietuva* in a garden so shrewdly planned that vegetables flourished through three seasons.

"What kind of vegetables?" the boy asked.

"I remember a lot of cabbage."

"Cabbage!" the boy said. Apparently it took nothing to astonish him.

1. Jurgis and Aldona saved up money to build a house in Kimball.
2. Which had three floors.
3. And was called a block.
4. Cabbages grew in the backyard of the Vitkus block.
5. Also parsnips.
6. Little Ona Vitkus and her parents lived on the first floor.
7. Some other people lived on the second floor.
8. And on the third floor lived a young lady from Granyard, Vermont.
9. Her name was Maud-Lucy Stokes.
10. She taught piano and tutored immigrant children in English.

Good talking, Jurgis said, bringing his little daughter to the third floor, to Maud-Lucy. Brilliant, sophisticated Maud-Lucy Stokes. Jurgis meant to say, *Teach her something! Our tongues are tied.*

"My own English was atrocious," she told the boy.

"Your grammar is excellent," he said.

"Not back then. My English was a chewed-up mouthful of American slang, salted with Italian and Franco specks I picked up from the street. My parents knew I'd get nowhere talking like a melting pot."

"But your parents didn't speak English. How did they know yours was bad?"

"They were foreign, not deaf," Ona said. "Maud-Lucy tutored me for free, merely because she wanted to. She tutored me every day."

"*Plus* school?" the boy asked, rearing back, horrified, the list forgotten.

"*In place* of school. School smelled like unwashed boys and wood smoke. The schoolmistress despised girls." Instead, Ona had climbed the stairs to the third floor every day to Maud-Lucy. Self-possessed, heavy-bodied Maud-Lucy, who cut her hair insolently short, loathed the passive voice, and kept a piano and a cat and a library of books with dark and stalwart bindings. Maud-Lucy, whose rooms smelled of ink and lavender. Who claimed to have no use for a man. Who longed for children and took Ona as a surrogate. Who fed adjectives to Ona like drops of chocolate.

"My goodness," Ona said, looking at her fingers. "Now you've got me doing it."

The boy abruptly hid his hands. After a moment, he said, "Did you miss your mom and dad? When you ran away to the circus?"

"Not a circus," she said. "Don't get the idea I was prancing around on an elephant."

"I won't."

"You're picturing me prancing around on an elephant, aren't you?"

He laughed then, a yip of pleasure. So far he'd exhibited little capacity for humor, only varying degrees of earnestness. "It was easier than you might think to leave them," she said. "I felt like Maud-Lucy's child by then. But she had to take care of her auntie that summer, back in Granyard, Vermont. At the time, I thought my parents were plotting a return to the motherland. So it wasn't that hard to run. I was fourteen, old enough. Maud-Lucy's the one I missed."

The boy was quiet for a moment. "There's someone who I think likes my mom. It's a secret." He looked away. "He might be my dad someday."

"Oh. Well, this was different."

"Sometimes I feel like this other person is really my dad. Same way you felt like Maud-Lucy was really your mom."

"I see your point."

"My real dad is excellent at music." He pointed out the window. "What's that one?"

"House finch," she informed him. The boy rushed to his backpack, extracted a pristine notebook, and added "house finch" to his list. "That's eight," he said. "Twelve to go." He peered out at Ona's spirea bushes, which were greening already, spring finally on the way.

"I miss the morning chorus," Ona told him. "The birds are all pitched too high."

"I have to remember five songs."

"Well, I can't help you there."

"If birds sang lower, you could hear them."

"You'll have to take that up with God."

The boy thought this over. "Are your mom and dad still alive?"

"For crumbsake! Add it up."

He paused a moment, calculating. "What happened to them?"

Few creatures on earth had ever asked her such a thing. "Their English improved," she said. "They got out of the mills and opened a grocery store. They worked till they retired, lived a little longer, then died. Same thing that happens to everybody."

"Not everybody," he said. "Look at you." His calculations took on a sudden, heated clarity that showed in his body. "Hey," he said, standing up. "I just thought of something." His eyelashes quivered.

His narrow hands went to his head as if trying to keep it on his shoulders. "What if—Miss Vitkus, what if you're—the oldest person *in the world?*"

Ona could think of two or three ways to take this news. "Goodness," she said. "I hope not."

He was hopping around her kitchen now, still holding his head, trying to contain his runaway glee. "*Hey,* Miss *Vitkus,* you could be a *Guinness . . . world . . . record . . . holder!*"

"Do I get a cash prize?"

"One, you get a *certificate,*" he said, his voice sailing. "Two, you get *respect.* Three, you get *immortality!*"

"Well," she said, "I suppose you can't put a price on that."

Then that pestering scoutmaster appeared at the door, and it was time once again for the boy to go home.

Chapter 4

Jailbreak Brew Pub smelled beery and old, though its patrons blazed with vitality: a thirtyish crowd, women with streaked hair and skimpy blouses, guys with gym-muscled forearms and fake tans. They liked to dance, these guys, hands gripped on the swiveling hips of some girl they appeared to be driving. They liked old rock-and-roll, the music of their parents.

Quinn was here for his weekly gig with his oldest friends, who composed a band called the Benders. In their heedless youth they'd penned a few middling tunes but over the years had morphed into a middle-aged cover band.

"Maybe you're working too much," Rennie said to him now. The Benders were on their second break of the night, Quinn at the bar sipping a heavily iced Sprite—his drink of choice since his cold-turkey promise to Belle eleven years back, on the night the boy was born.

"I'm not working too much, Ren." He'd missed a cue and mangled an intro, which never happened. He wasn't sleeping, that was all; but he kept this to himself.

The last thing he wanted was sympathy.

"When did you last have a night off?" Rennie persisted.

"I don't need less work, Ren, I need more. I've got—a debt."

"A debt? You own nothing." He made this sound like a compliment.

"Things have changed."

"I can get you a couple of shifts," Rennie said. He owned a direct-mail business that had seen Quinn through more than one dry spell. The musician's living was something he'd learned to manage over the years, imagining it as a streambed that flooded in one season, vanished in another. The trick was to keep standing in that fickle, vitalizing water as it rose and fell. He'd managed better than most. *You're not afraid of work, honey,* his young mother had told him before she died. *It'll be the best thing about you.*

"It's not that kind of debt, Ren." He could hear Gary and Alex chatting up a table of young teachers celebrating a birthday. His bandmates had grown up with him in a neighborhood of triple-deckers on Munjoy Hill. Now Rennie had his mailing empire, Alex his law firm, Gary his chiropractic office. Jailbreak was the highlight of their week. They were the fathers of bloomy and vibrant children, caretakers of lawns and tax returns and long-division homework, but in their hours of ordinary despair they believed they wanted the life Quinn had made for himself: a working musician.

"I'll, okay, I'll leave you alone," Rennie said, and withdrew into the burbling room.

Quinn hadn't craved a drink this badly since the night after the funeral, when he'd retreated deep into his Monday-night routine: tallying the week's projected income and expenses. He'd stopped in mid-stroke, a revelation arriving like a telegram from hell: his biggest expense, a boy who needed health insurance and school supplies and lunch money and haircuts and shoes and a college fund, was now moot. He took a breath and calculated the balance of what he would have owed Belle had the boy made it to age eighteen. The number was staggering, but he resolved to pay it, as soon as possible, like a penance. A tithe. He did not want his life to be easier now that the boy was gone.

That had been his last night off.

Now his phone vibrated in his back pocket. Quinn thought twice about answering—he'd been waiting for this—and his stomach pitched when he heard her. He took in her raging voice and pictured the phone connection as a purple thread, wet and umbilical, which bound them.

"I was going to put it back," he said. "Yesterday, in fact. But you wouldn't let me in his room." He tried closing his eyes slowly, to be with her, even like this. But now she bleated the boy's name, one time, two times, three. Quinn's eyes snapped open with each pitiful bark, *snap-snap-snap*, as if she were shaking him out of a coma.

"Belle," he said gently. "Calm down."

"I will not calm down! I will not! Unless you'd like to give me lessons, Quinn? Would you like to give me a lesson, you're such an expert on calming down? Can you do that, please? That would be a great boon to me in my hour of need, a lesson from a fucking *robot,* a lesson in calming down!"

"Belle. Jesus." He eyed the bartender.

"You could have told me you took it. But you were afraid, you've always been afraid." She was bawling now, sodden, phlegmy dollops of despair shuddering through the line.

"I'll bring it back, Belle," he said now. "Tonight, I'll bring it back, I promise. I don't know why I took it." Which was true. But now that he had the boy's diary, he wanted it to be his.

In his peripheral vision he caught Gary waving his sticks, calling Quinn back to the stage. Belle was crying at normal decibels now. "That was his private stuff," she said huskily. "You had no business taking it. You never earned the right."

"I know, I know," he said, frantic to soothe her. However meager his capacity for love—he'd been told by the woman after Belle that the dial barely moved in the gauge—he had splurged it all on her. "I went to Miss Vitkus's house, Belle," he said, feeling exactly as desperate as he sounded. "Like you asked. You asked me to go, and I went."

"That was your obligation. Like visiting your son was your obligation. It's something people do."

At least she was speaking to him. How many times had they talked at this hour of the night, Quinn wide awake, Belle fighting off sleep in order to find her way to him? He wanted to speak to her now, in their old way, late-night confiding, voices hushed lest they wake their wakeful son.

"Belle, I'll bring it back." Fifteen feet away were exemplary fathers and husbands who would know exactly what to say. Their wives considered them sensitive. Their children brightened their every hour. They believed in love, and God; they believed animals had souls; they believed their dead grandmothers watched over them.

"Those years you were gone?" she said. "Those years chasing your big fat break?" Her voice was quiet now. "I expected so much more of you."

"Belle, please."

"I wanted you to send us more than just money. To care more. We missed you—well, *he* missed the idea of you. I missed the actual you."

"I felt his presence," Quinn said. This dropped out of his mouth like a broken tooth—where had it come from?

"What?"

Her full attention graced through him. "In the old lady's house. It was just like he wrote in his diary. There was, quote, magic afoot."

Belle managed something like a laugh despite her sorrow, for the boy's syntactical oddities had always pleased her. He'd read obsessively—instruction manuals, record books, novels far too old for him—picking up linguistic baubles like a crow mining a roadside.

"Tell me," she said.

He wanted to ease her, mend her, pull her back from the lightless place into which she'd fallen. Knowing he was uniquely unqualified for this job only fortified his resolve. "It was like he was there in her house," he said. His breathing felt off. He was improvising wildly now, a mixture of what he'd actually felt and what he wanted to feel and what he imagined Rennie might feel, or Alex, or Gary. "For a second there, it was like he came back from"—he groped for words—"his disappearance."

After a long, coiled pause, Belle said, "Our son didn't disappear." She was all cried out. "What 'the boy' did, Quinn, is die. He got up on an exquisite May morning, rode out on his bike for no perceptible reason, and dropped dead before the sun fully made it over the horizon."

Why did she keep doing this? Over and over. Why? How he wanted to take that first warm swallow, that matchless comfort.

"Maybe if you came over there with me," he said. "Maybe you

could feel him there, in her house." This was the kind of thing that sounded right in his head, but spoken words came out so different. His effort missed the mark so spectacularly that it almost counted as a bull's-eye on some other target.

"I feel him *here*," she said. "In *his* house. The very house you yourself lived inside, twice, as a husband and father. You didn't feel him here, in his own house? You don't find that strange? To be so detached from your son's existence that you found his so-called presence in the house of a stranger?"

Her voice contained something new to her, an icy disconnection that he associated with a different type of woman. Three years ago, on the bus ride back from Chicago, passing sepia-colored depots and engulfed by regret, he'd embraced the naive hope of a soul in midlife: he resolved to become a better man. Belle and the boy had picked him up at the station, the boy motionless with misgiving. But Belle did not understand misgiving; she never had. *Come back to me,* she'd whispered to him in the dripping fog. *Be his dad.* They'd married again within weeks.

"Of all the things to take from me," she said now, her voice husking through the phone, "you take his last words."

"I'm sorry, Belle." He could hear the guys tuning up. His phone beeped. "Belle, wait, I'm about to run out of juice."

"What a surprise," she said, and hung up.

He faltered back to the stage, where the guys avoided eye contact. The bartender turned off the house music and Gary settled behind his drums. As Quinn strapped on his guitar, he said to Rennie, "I'll take a couple of shifts," to which Rennie replied, "You got it."

Quinn faced the sheening crowd and played by rote an opening lick he'd been playing since he was seventeen years old. He took the mic and howled.

Chapter 5

On the fourth Saturday, before attempting his chores, the boy presented Ona with a printout of the vital statistics of a Madame Jeanne Louise Calment of Arles, France, who died in 1997 with the apparently unbeatable title of Longest-Lived Person.

Ever.

"'One hundred twenty-two years,'" read the boy in a voice better reserved for sixteenth-century proclamations, "'and one hundred sixty-four days.'"

"That's ridiculous," Ona said. "Let me see that." There wasn't much, really; Madame Calment's life, like most lives, comprised a pileup of ordinary days, but that didn't prevent her, like most people, from bestowing advice. "Daily chocolate?" Ona said. "That's her recipe for a long life?"

Checking these immortal pronouncements, the boy asked, "What's port?"

"Wine. The French do like their wine." She looked up. "Where on earth did you get this?"

"Have you ever heard of the Internet?"

"Of course I've heard of the Internet. I went through the orientation at the public library in the spring of 2000. Big to-do about nothing. Worse than watching TV." She looked him over: beneath the misdirection of his genteel conduct and crisp uniform, he was a boy of the twenty-first century after all. Since her birth she'd witnessed the advent of automobiles, airplanes, automatic washing machines, atomic bombs, space shuttles, disposable diapers, and Touch-Tone, had received them all as a matter of course, her capacity for wonder peaking around 1969 with the moon landing; but this old-timey boy who carried a phone the size of a baby's rattle and plucked information from France out of a machine in his bedroom presented quite the conundrum. She smoothed her hands over her head, as if to tidy up the technology it had already absorbed.

He produced several more sheets—more interviews with Madame Calment, which Ona read start to finish, the boy looking over her shoulder. His breath was warm and on the sweet side. "Your Madame Calment is quite the little cock-a-hoop, I'd say."

"Read this one," the boy said, pointing.

Ona read, "'I have only one wrinkle, and I'm sitting on it'? That's what your famous record breaker chose to say? For all posterity? Or should I say for all posterior?"

The boy laughed out loud—that unnerving yip of his. It started and stopped as if on timers.

Ona merely *tsk*ed. "To think an honor such as this was wasted on a person of so little class." She looked at the woman's picture again—taken on the poor thing's one-hundred-twentieth birthday. "That face could halt an anvil in mid-drop," she muttered. She tried to compare Madame Calment's squashy visage with others she'd seen but couldn't think of a single soul within the squintiest vicinity of her own age, let alone Madame Calment's. She hoped her hair didn't look this bad. "How did the old crock manage it?"

The boy pointed once again to Madame Calment's page of pronouncements.

Ona said, "*Šokoladas ir vynas.*" Chocolate and wine. The words rattled out, and the boy cocked his head like a listening bird.

"There you go again," he said.

"I know." She tapped her skull, hard.

"When's your birthday?" he asked, slipping a notebook out of his pack.

"January twentieth."

He jotted down some numbers and slowly computed them. "That makes eighteen years and ninety-nine days to beat the record."

"I can't last that long," Ona said. "This woman is some kind of freak." But even as she spoke these words, the time between now and then seemed bridgeable. Since the age of ninety she'd awoken each morning with the thought, *This could be the day.* Now here was this French flapjaws redefining the rules of the race. Who could fathom God's calendar? "However," she told the boy, "I wouldn't mind giving Madame Parlez-Vous a run for her money."

The boy all but caught fire with glee. "One," he said, "competitors must set clear goals. Two, competitors must understand the competition." He returned to his backpack, unzipped one of its myriad pouches, and removed another sheet. "The oldest currently living female is Mrs. Ramona Trinidad Iglesias-Jordan. Age one hundred fourteen. Country of Puerto Rico. Mrs. Ramona Trinidad Iglesias-Jordan is also the oldest currently living person." He stumbled over the pronunciations. "The oldest currently living male is Mr. Fred Hale. Age one hundred thirteen. Country of USA." He looked up to see how this news was landing.

"Is there a record for oldest old crab?"

The boy took this question, like all questions, without irony. "One, a record attempt has to be sanctioned. Two, a record attempt has to be witnessed. Three, a record attempt has to fall within the bonderies of the law."

"One, you mean *boundaries*. Two, Puerto Rico isn't a country. It's a territory of the United States."

"Thank you." He flipped the pages of his notebook and made a brief entry on one list, then another.

Ona read over the sheet of brief but vital statistics, trying not to care and failing utterly. Madame Calment's record was ludicrous, certainly; but the others might be beatable. "Mrs. Puerto Rico might put up a fight," she said, "but how many people could possibly stand between me and Mr. Hale? Men have the life expectancy of gerbils. I might be third or fourth in line."

"I'll find out!" he fairly shouted, making another notation. He looked—full, is how she remembered it later. He bared all his short, bright teeth.

"Oldest currently living person," Ona said. "The 'living' part has a reassuring ring."

"You want the all-time record, though. For all posterity."

"Let's not get ahead of ourselves. We've got a couple of other players to pick off first."

Shutting his eyes, the boy recited: "'Competitors must *fully and completely* fulfill the requirements stated in the Guinness World Records record-breaker pack.'"

"What's in the—?"

"One, you get official Guinness World Records instructions. Two, you get official Guinness World Records witness forms. Three, you get—" He shook his head, mentally backtracking. "One, you get an official *claim* form. Normal track or fast track." He glanced at his notebook. "We'll do fast track."

"How many times have you done this?"

"Eight. But people take my ideas before I think them up."

As the boy wrote furiously—a "to do" list that reminded Ona what urgency had once felt like—she sat in a pleasing, lighthearted haze, observing the feeders through the window, imagining her name in a record book. All those demure round letters in the first name, followed by the stalky surprise of the surname. Ona Vitkus. She thanked herself for having the foresight to snatch back her maiden name, which in 1948 had been no small matter. She felt suddenly fond of her unremarkable life, that humdrum necklace of imitation pearls with the occasional glint of the real thing. The boy kept glancing at her as he would at a prize heifer, and she felt like one: round and healthy, clean and well brushed, a surefire winner.

The day's chores finished, she poured his milk and offered him cookies. "The Meals on Wheels pulled a fast one," she said. "I was just getting used to the animal crackers and they come up with these phony macaroons."

The boy chewed one up and made a face.

"I know," Ona said. "But I'm supposed to purr my head off never-theless, like a tabby cat grabbing up table scraps." It was the thing she liked least, so far, about her second century on earth—the presumption of neediness, the expectation of gratitude, the general public's disappointment at her refusal to be fulsome. Since when was a simple thank-you not enough? She'd had every species of do-gooder in and out of here for the past twenty-five years, from the Daughters of Isabella to the county social services, and every one of them, excepting this little boy, had found her wanting in the appreciation department.

It wasn't until later, after he'd finished his milk and double-checked his stalled list of birds, that the boy revealed the expanded nature of his mission. His every action was governed by an internal logic that she never did get the lay of. It was nearly time to go when he slipped a little machine from a secret pocket in his backpack.

The tape recorder was the size of a half-eaten chocolate bar, a present from his aunt, who worked for a newspaper in California. "We're supposed to tell an old person's life story," he said. "Mr. Linkman said old people love to talk."

"Oh, he did, did he?"

"Mr. Linkman said to interview our grandparents but I picked you."

Ona took in the diminutive machine, which the boy slid exactly halfway between them. She shook her head.

"You already told me ten stories," he reminded her.

"This is different."

"I won't play it back," he promised. "You don't have to listen." He looked at her beseechingly as he clicked a button.

"I don't know."

"What if you turn out to be a Guinness world record holder?" he said. "Everybody will want to interview you and your voice will get very tired." He passed his hand over the machine. "All you have to do is press this button. Presto, you can tell your life story and eat a pretzel at the same time."

Finally she consented, if only to prevent him from getting carried away again; his hopping around the kitchen last week had rattled her. He didn't move the way other children moved—he carried a marionette-ish precision in his wrists and shoulders—and it had made her feel sorry for him.

The boy rewound the tape and clicked it on again. "This is Miss Ona Vitkus," he said hopefully. "This is her life story on tape. This is Part One."

Ona inspected the tiny whirling wheels. Part One? Instantly, she began to divide up her years.

"Is it on?" she asked.

The boy put his finger to his lips, nodding. Apparently he planned to remain invisible. He slipped her a sheet of preprinted questions—prepared, presumably, by Mr. Linkman—and pointed to number one. *Where were you born?* There were forty-nine subsequent questions.

"I can't answer all these," she said. "We'll be here till doomsday."

The boy said nothing, staring down the machine as if it might speak in her stead.

"What do you expect me to do?" she asked.

The boy looked up. He mouthed the answer: *Regale me.*

Ona felt this turn of events a bit presumptuous—it was one thing to chitchat at the kitchen table, but quite another to compose your thoughts in a manner that might be graded by Mr. Linkman. But at this point in their friendship she found it impossible to refuse him. She had believed herself through with friendship.

"I'll answer the first one," she said. "But that's it."

Which it wasn't.

She blundered through some preliminaries, made inarticulate by stage fright. Finally, mercifully, he clicked off the machine. He smiled, showing his trimmed teeth. "That was very excellent." He clicked the machine back on. "This is Miss Ona Vitkus," he said. "This is her life story on tape. This is also Part One."

Chapter 6

Quinn took an early bus to Rennie's plant behind the mall, a sleek, hangar-size warehouse in which thrived Great Universal Mail Systems, the third-largest bulk-mail service in New England. The warehouse sat on a green picnic blanket of lawn. The entryway, constructed of glass panels secured by a floridly patterned girding, lent the place an air of domestic muscle, as if it housed the headquarters of a home-decoration concern. On sunny days the glass winked all day.

A young receptionist greeted him with a buoyancy born of an excellent benefits package. On her desk sat a vase of irises. "You're here to see—?" she asked. Her hair lay close to her head, a sexy, flapper-girl haircut. A befuddling image of Miss Vitkus as she might have appeared in the twenties visited him unannounced: she was dancing the Charleston in one of those skinny dresses, a reckless girl with shining cheeks.

Quinn introduced himself, wishing he'd shaved a little closer. "Rennie said he might have some shifts open."

"Oh, I'm *sorry*," she bubbled, getting up. "You came in the wrong way."

She eased him back toward the door and tapped a crimson fingernail against the glass. "See where the building turns? Like an L? There's what you want."

"Rennie's a friend," Quinn said. "I thought I might—"

"Oh, wow, he's in meetings all day today," she chirped. "Off-the-charts busy."

"We met in junior high."

The receptionist nodded, happy-happy. "Wow, that's great."

Quinn lingered a moment. Behind the smiling girl was a pastel screen, and behind that emanated a soothing white-collar air rush of business being transacted: doors quietly opening and closing, high heels drumming on carpet, a muffle of polite laughter. Rennie was back there someplace, and Quinn wished, not for the first time, that he'd been born with his friend's knack for contentment.

"Right down there, big black doors," the girl said, tapping. "You have to move your car if you parked out front. The line workers' lot is over there, see the pole lights?" She flitted back to her post and tried to smile him out the door.

"I know that," he said. "Tell Rennie I was here."

"Will do! Don't forget to move your car."

In the ell, Quinn encountered another receptionist, this one in jeans and a red T-shirt that read GUMS: WE MEAN BUSINESS. "I'm already on file," he told her.

"It's been over a year." She handed him a clipboard. "You have to do this again."

At the end of the new-employee orientation, a numbing routine that concluded with an assigned locker and a complimentary cafeteria ticket, Quinn followed a section leader into the plant, an open floor with exceptional light and the kind of ubiquitous machine noise that could either inure you to all sound or drive you slowly insane. He was assigned to a chicken-faced woman named Dawna whose clucking voice carried. Because Quinn had performed many of these tasks before—after the boy was born, after the first divorce, after his big return and hasty remarriage, and again after the second divorce—Dawna deemed him a genius quick study. They were buddied up in the Rennie system, composing a fabulous duo entrusted to a complicated station that sorted and labeled and routed mail by the literal bagful. The place vibrated with the sound of gears and ignition and conveyance and old-fashioned human exertion.

For the first fifty minutes he tagged mailbags; for the second fifty minutes he stacked the labeler. For the third fifty minutes he snatched

Zip Code–matched brochures from the conveyor and fastened them with rubber bands. Then it was time for lunch, which he got with his free ticket, and in the time left over he strolled the herringboned pathways of a sunny acreage called the "campus." Rennie's people got regular breaks, footrests, English lessons, and nine bucks an hour to start. There was almost no turnover. Quinn recognized a group of Somali women from his last go-round.

By two o'clock Dawna had graduated him to a station set up for a massive run of an office-furniture catalog. The machine performed separate tasks at complementary intervals, which had an almost lulling effect on his spirit until the sorter underwent a paper jam that required outside intervention.

The place spit him out at three. He sat in the back of the bus, nothing awaiting him but a long, empty, gigless evening. Normally he'd call one of the guys, get a burger someplace or sit in for supper with one of their burbling families, but he suddenly felt like a man in see-through skin. He recoiled from being looked at—looked into—by people who knew him.

At the first transfer, he impulsively caught the number 4 going west past Sibley Street. He pulled the cord, got off, and walked beneath a cool sun to Miss Vitkus's house. Affixed to the phone poles along the street were lime-green flyers that hollered NEIGHBORHOOD MEETING. They flapped like caught bugs.

Her house looked tidy. The grass was trimmed and the feeders blinked with birds. The place seemed freshly rinsed, and he felt a stab of pride to have had a hand in it.

"You," she said when she found him on her doorstep. She looked up the street. "How is it you don't own a car?"

"I sold it," he said. "I needed the cash." He didn't care how this sounded; at her age she'd probably heard everything.

"For what? Alcohol?"

"A conscience debt." Why was he telling her this? "It didn't work. Isn't working."

"Money rarely does." She said nothing more.

He handed her a five. "You owe me some magic."

She took the money, giving him a meticulous once-over, and let him into the kitchen.

Quinn sat down, his feet throbbing from Rennie's concrete floors. Her cards were stacked just where she'd left them, though the quarters were gone, and the newspapers had vanished from the counter except for a single clipping, neatly folded.

"My son says you inspire him."

She looked him over, unreadable. "Have you been drinking?"

"Not for eleven years."

"I have a whistle here," she announced, rattling a thin chain that hung around her neck. "They had a break-in down the street." From the depths of her rumpled sweater she extracted a plastic contraption, one of those summons buttons worn by old people who fear a solitary death.

"I press the button and bingo," she said, pointing to a box that looked like a piece of studio equipment from the forties. "Some Johnny-on-the-spot saves my bacon."

Did he look as untethered as he felt? He nudged the cards. "Do something." He didn't know what he wanted from her. She was the oldest person he'd ever met—shouldn't she know some things?

She hesitated, then moved creakily to the counter to snatch up the clipping. "You tricked me," she said. "You're the trickster, not me." She shook the clipping, her eyes big and angry.

He knew what it was.

"I had boys in here before him," she said, "and not a one of them cared to work. It's the fathers who end up here, but they come with a thousand excuses. The boy has too much homework, the boy joined a baseball team." She lifted her bunched chin. "You made me believe your boy was one of those."

Quinn stared at Miss Vitkus's neck, skin like crushed satin.

"Then I got an intuition. Something I'd half read, or half heard. I listen to the news. I read my papers, but not the obits. Not religiously, like I used to. Almost everyone I ever knew is dead." She picked up her glasses and wrestled them onto her face. "Unexpectedly, it says here." She looked up. "I should say so."

Quinn could barely meet her eyes, which blazed with grievance. "It's called Long QT Syndrome," he told her. "Something electrical goes wrong in the heart."

"A blinky electrical system?"

"Of the heart, yeah," Quinn said. "The first symptom is usually death."

Her voice softened. "How does a little boy get it?"

"You either acquire it through a drug reaction, or else you inherit it through a parent. He must have inherited it. It's rare. Obviously."

"Through a parent?" She frowned. "Are you next?"

"If you make it to middle age the risk goes away. What I didn't know didn't hurt me."

"If it *was* you," she said. "It might have been his mother."

"Let's assume it's me. His mother has enough weight on her heart." He tapped the cards, an old hand at misdirection himself. "I paid you the full amount."

"So you did." She took up the cards and began to work them, rocking the deck from one hand to the other. Her fingers, despite their aged knots, managed the rhythm. She'd been practicing.

"He's your only one?" she asked. Quinn caught her look: apparently they would be using the present tense.

"Just him," Quinn said, eyeing the cards' undulations. The boy had sat here, watching these same preparations. His son, expecting magic.

She fanned the deck. "Pick one."

He took the queen of clubs, slipped it back into the deck, and waited as she worked the cards. She turned over his card. "That it?"

Quinn nodded, surprised.

"I got a little flubby there for a second. I'm not myself today."

"Make something disappear," Quinn told her, wringing another five from his wallet.

Her eyebrows—or the creases where her eyebrows had once resided—rose. "The mark doesn't get to choose." She pocketed the money and waited. The air between them went still with possibility. All at once, so quickly that Quinn wasn't sure he'd actually seen it, she plucked the news clipping from the table, closed it into her freckled fist, then opened her hand again, revealing nothing but her own naked palm engraved with a century's worth of lifelines.

"Where is it?" Quinn asked.

"You paid for magic. I gave you magic." That she refused to pity him—that she was, in fact, furious—made him feel a little less bereft.

He gave her yet another five. "What else you got?"

"Children take what they get. But adults, nothing's ever enough." She added, "Your boy and I were friends."

"I should have told you," Quinn said.

She sat back and folded her big hands. "And here I was thinking he turned out like all those other boys, a layabout with no follow-through." Her mouth appeared to tremble, but it was hard to discern her meaning through the hatch pattern of wrinkles. "His sterling reputation in this house was being tarnished through absolutely no fault of his. I feel very bad about that. Why didn't that scoutmaster inform me? I have a working phone. Your boy and I had plans."

Quinn felt strangely heated, as if he'd been caught under a police lamp. He looked around the house for signs of unfinished projects. "What kind of plans?"

"It hardly matters now." Then he saw her expression change, as if second-guessing herself, or giving Quinn the benefit of the doubt. "He was a good boy and I'm terribly sorry," she said to him. "It's a pitiful thing to outlive your children."

"Is that what you did?"

"Frankie perished in the war," she said. "Randall died of cancer. He never did settle down—lots of ladies but no wife—though he was an excellent attorney-at-law. People said lovely things at his funeral."

"I'm sorry."

"This house was Randall's, in fact." She blinked at him. "Is there a worse indignity, do you think, than inheriting your children's money?"

"Probably. But I see what you mean."

"At the time I was low on funds and heading into the mixed blessing of a long life." She leaned across the table to say this.

"You don't have to explain."

"Randall was sixty-one. Not a long life. But not a short one, either." She paused. "Frankie's the one I miss."

A moment passed.

"His mother had to remind me before every custody visit," Quinn said. "Even then I didn't keep up. I barely knew him. That's the truth."

Miss Vitkus reached into the warm cavern of Quinn's jacket. He felt her hand on his chest, brief as an alighting bird, before she withdrew it, the folded obituary materializing on her palm, and inside that, his five-dollar bill. She gave them over without a word. From someplace far outside himself, he accepted a knifing pity for the boy, who was missing this. That he could muster a feeling beyond disgrace felt like magic enough.

"Why didn't you keep up?" she asked. She sounded merely curious. He surrendered then, yielding to her age, her lively face, her general mien of urgency.

"I didn't understand the way his mind worked," he confessed. An upwelling of sorrow befell him. Her eyes were still young. "I never figured out how to—how to be with him."

She took this in—without judgment, it seemed to Quinn—then said, "Randall and I never quite found our feet together. He was a good boy, but we had nothing in common. So independent, ambitious, even as a child. I never felt as if he actually needed me."

Quinn got up, pocketing the obit and leaving the money alone. "You want anything done? As long as I'm here?"

"I blew a light bulb in the parlor. I hate to get up on a chair."

He began with the light bulb, which required a stepstool. Which also needed repair.

He returned on Saturday, the appointed day, and the Saturday after that.

As May gave over to June, Quinn arrived in the boy's place, on time and carrying tools, fulfilling what he surmised to be the full breadth of the boy's commitment.

"I've got a cake here," she said. "You'll like it. It has a secret ingredient."

"Who doesn't like a secret ingredient?"

"I suppose you could call me Ona."

"You've been calling me Quinn."

"So I have. But you're a younger gentleman. I'm an older lady. It's up to me to give permission."

He was smiling now. "May I call you Ona?"

"Permission granted. My gutters are a mess, by the way."

So he cleaned out her gutters, rehung a door, replaced the stair treads on the porch, watched the slow arrival of summer. Each Saturday he stayed for animal crackers or cake, an exchange of five dollars, a doggedly rendered Double Detection or 7-Up or Queen of the Air. Sometimes, she made things disappear: cards or coins or hankies with hand-tatted hems. These came to be his favorites, these sly deflections, the clever here-and-gone, simple tricks that required little more than a middling prestidigitator and an observer desperate to be amazed.

Chapter 7

On the fifth Saturday, the boy arrived with bad news: Ona was a spring chicken.

She had three-digit rivals everywhere, from Saskatchewan to Siberia. This oversight—that he'd traced the "oldest man" and "oldest woman" titleholders but neglected to check for understudies—appeared to cause the boy a deep-churning chagrin.

He unzipped his backpack in slow motion. It always looked store-new, the shiny red of supermarket cherries. He read from yet another printout, his hard-packed expression at odds with his delicate features. "After Mrs. Ramona Trinidad Iglesias-Jordan, United States Territory of Puerto Rico," he read, "the second-oldest person in the world is a lady, country of Romania, also age one hundred thirteen. The third-oldest person in the world is a lady, country of Japan, also age one hundred thirteen. The fourth-oldest person in the world is Mr. Fred Hale. We know him already."

Finally he handed her the sheet. "If Mrs. Ramona Trinidad Iglesias-Jordan and the lady from the country of Romania and the lady from the country of Japan and Mr. Fred Hale die, then the oldest person in the world will be another lady, Mrs. Flossie Page, age one hundred eleven, country of USA."

"Hmm." Ona leafed through the shortlist—eighty-two official contenders, mostly women. Mrs. Japan and Mrs. Romania had unpronounceable names, the former free-floating with vowels, the latter fortressed by consonants. They had been listed by a research outfit committed to tracking the world's oldest citizens. All these rivals of intemperate age, the youngest of them a good eight years older than Ona, the oldest of them shy of the all-time record by nearly a decade.

Ona conjured a vision of Madame Calment snickering in her celestial rocking chair. "This print's too small," Ona said, getting up. "I need my glasses. Come in here."

The boy halted at the door of her parlor. She realized she'd never invited him past the kitchen. He laid the papers on her lap, then lighted on the arm of one of the matching wingbacks that had come with the house.

"Look at all these codgers," she said. "What the heck are they putting in their oatmeal?"

"You can't get in the running until you're a supercentenarian." The word galloped off his tongue as if he'd rehearsed it. "That means one hundred ten and plus. They think there's around four hundred in all. It's hard to track them all down." He hopped off the chair and ran a fidgety finger down the side of the page. "See, it shows their birthday next to their name. Years plus days."

Ona noted a woman from Oslo, another from Thailand, several from the American South, Annabelles and Elviras and Lavinias. A few men, mostly from Japan. "Who finds these people?"

"Researchers. Of gerontology."

She narrowed her eyes at him. "Is your mother a schoolteacher?"

"My mother is a librarian."

"You talk like a librarian."

"I don't have any friends."

"I don't either, really. I take tea with the ladies from church, but their health complaints can wear a body out. You're a nice boy. Why don't you have friends?"

"People don't like you unless you do sports. The card tricks didn't work out."

"I warned you," she said.

"One, I hate sports. Two, I hate band. Three, I hate lunch."

"I told you not to try those tricks at school."

"I'd rather do activities like this," he said. "I love doing activities like this." She wasn't quite sure what he meant. Visiting old ladies? Looking things up on his Internet? Convincing people to chase world records for something that took not one iota of talent?

"So," Ona said, "nobody's keeping track of the hundred-to-hundred-ten crowd?"

"There's too many. Almost one-third of one million if you count the whole world. Which I do."

"Where in blazes are they hiding?"

"I don't know," the boy said gloomily.

"And here I thought I was two or three pneumonias away from a record. We got all hepped up over nothing."

He shook his head sadly.

"It's all right," she said. "We'll wait them out."

She took out her cards to distract them both from disappointment and within a few minutes had him inside-out over a Hide the Jack that a below-average Border collie could have figured out in half a minute. He wasn't stupid—far from it—just overly agreeable.

"What happened to Viktor the beautiful blond Russian boy?" he asked.

Ona blushed. The Frenchwoman's ghastly photograph had been stuck in her head since she first saw it. Did she look like that, like a decomposing fig? Was it too much to ask this boy to mentally strip away her own cratered hollows, the baggy skin through which her bones showed like the hanger beneath the clothes? She had been lovely once. Could this twenty-first-century boy muster the drowse of imagination required to reconstruct her youthful body, her slender ankles and glossy shoulders, the oak-colored hair she'd crimped into Marcel waves with a potion of stiffened egg whites? Could he see beyond her overlaundered blouse and slacks to envision the bright poplin shirtwaist bought at McKay's Fancy Goods in June of 1916? She thought he could.

"You can't let a thing go," Ona said. "Have you ever noticed that?"

"I have deficiencies," he said ruefully, eyeing the cards. "What happened to Viktor the beautiful blond Russian boy?"

"Oldest story in the book," she said. "What a goosy girl I was."

He waited. With the unruffled patience of a cat. This did not seem like a deficiency.

"*Kūdikis*," Ona said, then put her hand to her mouth.

"What's *kūdikis*?"

She regarded him carefully; maybe it was the uniform, which could have been fifty years old; maybe it was his throwback manners; or the sea gray of his irises, which suggested an age and wisdom he could not possibly possess. "'Baby,'" she confessed. Her stomach knotted. "I never told a living soul."

His fingers began to flutter. "You had a baby? In the circus?"

Gently, she took his hands and closed his fingers. He tucked his hands beneath him. And waited.

"I came home from the midway," she said quietly. "In disgrace."

He waited some more. Her head felt composed. The kitchen went quiet. The yard went quiet. The air, the light, the dust on the sills, the names and names on the list.

"Do you know where babies come from?" she asked him.

"Babies come from a sperm and an egg."

The boy did not move.

"Well," she went on, hardly meaning to, "this baby was born and I gave him away."

The boy's fingers started in again. "Where's your baby now?"

"He's a doctor."

One.

"What kind of doctor?"

"Surgeon."

Two.

"Surgeon of what?"

"Hearts, if I recall."

Three.

"What's his name?"

"Laurentas."

Four.

"Laurentas what?"

"Laurentas Stokes."

"That's the same as your tutor lady. Maud-Lucy Stokes was your tutor lady that you loved more than your mother."

She tapped his guiltless forehead. "You don't need a tape recorder. You've got the recall of an elephant."

"Your baby is eighty-nine years old." His fingers stopped moving. Maybe he was out of categories.

"Eighty-nine?" Ona said, shocked. But of course the boy was right. She'd met Laurentas once—not counting his birth—in 1963 and had frozen him there in middle age, a hardy, nice-looking man with Viktor's coloring. For a time, they'd kept in touch—tellingly brief letters signed with their full names—and eventually their exchanges dwindled to the occasional Christmas card.

Ona got up, aware of the boy's eyes on her. She took a packet from her cupboard. "Here's the last one I have." The postmark was five years old; the one before that, eight. "We never got the hang of correspondence."

The boy examined the return address: Bridle Path Lane. "Does your son have a horse?"

"He's in a condo, for crumbsake," she said. "Since about ten years ago." *Retired at last, new condo very nice, happy new year. Yours, Laurentas Stokes.* She felt suddenly depleted. "You don't think so much of me now."

He blinked at her. "Why?"

"I told you my secret."

"What secret?"

She rattled the envelope.

"About your baby?"

"Yes!"

"That's a secret?"

Ona had not felt so powerless against her own fortress in decades.

"Of *course* it's a secret," she said. "My own husband never knew." Howard, so uninspired in the boudoir that he never discovered her scar. "And I'll have you know I did not foresee spilling my secret in the winter of my life."

But now that she had, a room opened up in her body, an empty chamber that called for filling up.

"Why did you name your baby Laurentas Stokes?"

"Maud-Lucy named him. I wanted to name him Joseph, after the husband of Mary, the unsuspecting virgin. Maud-Lucy took him back to Granyard and raised him among her own people."

"Did you marry Viktor?" the boy asked.

"You can't pin down heedless men." She smoothed the envelope. "After Maud-Lucy whisked Laurentas off to his beautiful life in apple country, I sorted rags in the pulp mill for two years, then my mother sent me to Portland for a secretarial course at Brooks School for Secretarial Studies, and after that I married Howard Stanhope, an old-man widower of thirty-nine."

The boy kept his kindly gaze upon her and said nothing.

"Life with Howard was mostly a misery," she told him. "That's a secret, too, I guess."

"I'm good at secrets," the boy said, studying her so intently now that she began to feel stripped after all—in a good way, stripped of decrepitude and shame.

"Enough," she said, returning to the boy's lists. "Look at all these names. I don't believe I've ever been in the running for something. Not in all my life."

"You can win," he said. "All you have to do is not die."

"That, my young fellow, might be easier said than done."

The boy set the recorder between them. "This is Miss Ona Vitkus," he said. "This is her life story on tape. This is Part Two."

"Do you think you could say something other than 'life story'? In a less portentous manner?"

What should I say? he mouthed. Though he made his initial announcements with pomp, he otherwise maintained his habit of silence by mouthing his interjections, pointing to Mr. Linkman's questions (*What are your strongest memories of World War II? In your opinion, what was the greatest invention of the twentieth century?*), or writing new ones on the fly, impeccably spelled and divided into parts and handed over cautiously, lest the rustling be picked up on tape.

Sometimes he turned off the machine to ask a left-field question — *What did your baby look like?* — that left her flummoxed and strangely willing as he flicked the machine back on to immortalize her response. His motionless attention had the serumlike effect of loosening both her tongue and her memory. Sometimes he forgot what was secret and what wasn't. Eventually, so did she.

* * *

This is Miss Ona Vitkus. This is her life story on tape. This is Part Two.

Do you think you could say something other than "life story"? In a less portentous manner?

. . .

I don't know. Memories. Shards. Little—little nothings that add up to—something, I guess. I hope.

. . .

All right. Fire away.

. . .

What difference does it make what he looked like? Skinny, jaundiced little thing. Bald as a boiled egg. Poor soul had a devil of a time getting born. I was a big-boned girl and he had no more heft than an August potato, but still he had to be cut out of me. Do you know about that? Cesarean?

. . .

Well, you're a reader. I guess you know all kinds of things.

. . .

Were you, now? Well, Laurentas wasn't premature, he was late. Thank God I was young. Hard to believe now, but I was. Young and hardy.

. . .

That's very kind. Thank you. Where was I? One little compliment and I'm all balled up.

. . .

The baby, yes. Papa cut the baby out, a neat trick that rivaled anything I'd seen on the midway. My own father, with his farmer's face. If not for Papa, I'd have died. I'm not upsetting you, I hope?

. . .

Good.

. . .

Oh. All right. For posterity, yes: Jurgis Vitkus. My good father. He gushed tears beforehand. And afterward. But not during. During, he was steady as a post. You saw no blubbering from me, either. I'd dragged home enough shame as it was. So I stood the pain for two and a half days, until finally my father—who as far as I knew was a cherry farmer turned acid cooker—unearthed a leather bag from someplace in their bedroom and produced a scalpel so shiny it hurt my eyes. I didn't know what to make of it. "Papa," I cried to him, "Papa, what are you doing!"

. . .

Well, I thought—for a minute there, I thought he intended to murder me in my bed for canoodling with a Russian.

. . .

. . .

I'm sorry. I forgot you for a second.

. . .

The beginning? Well, I was glad to be back home from the midway, despite everything. I was obviously with child. Maud-Lucy came back from Granyard to take care of me.

. . .

Oh, but she *jilted* her ailing auntie. For *me*. Papa's English had improved somewhat over the years, but his written communication was a fright. Mama's even worse. Such spelling you simply would not believe. I never saw the letter, but Maud-Lucy got the idea I was half dead from consumption. Imagine her shock to find me perfectly hale and big as a pumpkin.

. . .

Oh, but I was! It takes a little imagination, but I was a round and vigorous girl.

. . .

You certainly *do* have a good imagination. Who's the one who imagined my decrepit old self as a record breaker?

. . .

There you go. Anyway. Maud-Lucy took immediate charge of my confinement, reading to me in her third-floor parlor while I ate tinned marshmallows and kept my feet up. She played piano and sang to me and read out loud a very long novel by Mr. Charles Dickens.

. . .

Bleak House. It took her days to read that book. I was so happy. It's possible that my circumstances—being coddled by the woman I loved most in the world—misled me into believing that time could be peeled back. You're too young to know how alluring a notion that might be. I kept forgetting that a baby was en route. But when my time came, oh, what a string of surprises.

. . .

One, Maud-Lucy Stokes was bone useless: boo-hooing start to finish, her hands rubbed raw from wringing. Mama fed me whiskey in a porcelain egg cup bordered with hand-painted ivy leaves. Something else from the motherland that I'd never seen. "*Sha, sha, sha*," she kept saying. "*Sha, sha, sha*."

. . .

I have no idea, though I took it for comfort. Maud-Lucy was just a flitter-flutter at the periphery, bawling and yelling at Papa. Quite rudely, I might add.

. . .

"For the love of God, Jurgis, get her to the hospital!" Surprise number two—that's right, count 'em up—Papa and Mama defied her. "No," they said. "No no no."

. . .

Because the Kimball hospital was a grim and perilous place. Mama heard stories of this one or that one, and it always ended the same: *Go inside, not come out.*

. . .

Surprise number three, oh, that was the doozy: Papa with a scalpel. He gave me something from his satchel, a powder that Mama mixed with the whiskey, and I fell calm. "Ona-my-love," he whispered. His eyes were so blue and fond. "Don't scare, don't scare," he said. So I didn't. I didn't "scare." I did go a little hazy, though, as you might imagine, floating there, connected to the shushing of my parents, about whom I knew so little. I longed to speak to Papa in the language they'd denied me. But it was too late; I was Maud-Lucy's American girl. I couldn't summon a single word. "I thought you were a cherry farmer," I said to Papa. "Also doctor," he said, and the next thing I knew Laurentas was screaming his head off. An August potato with good lungs.

. . .

Never. Maybe they didn't have the vocabulary. How do you come up with the American words for scalpel? For whiskey in an egg cup? For country doctor and cherry farmer who packed up his family to take a job in a mill five thousand miles from home? It must have been a complicated story.

. . .

Maud-Lucy, well. It hadn't yet occurred to me that she planned to raise the baby in Vermont, among her own people. How could a woman like that return to those boring apple trees? Those big, square uncles and sickly aunts?

. . .

Well, she could. She did. Maud-Lucy herself was a big, square woman. It took me a time to sort out that she wasn't beautiful. Too plain for a rich man, too bright for a poor one. Unmarried ladies took the bottom rung of the ladder then. Maud-Lucy had stopped off in Kimball in 1905 on her way back from a trip to the Rangeley Lakes to paint the landscape, a trip she'd made to defy her father, who was trying to marry her off to a dullard who sold trees. Her father's mistake was in educating her beforehand.

. . .

There was an upset on the tracks, so the passengers spilled out to find rooms in town for the night, and Maud-Lucy ran into my mother coming out of the *Kimball Times* where she'd just placed an ad for tenants. Their building wasn't three days finished.

. . .

We did. We thought it was God himself running the show. My mother had me by the hand, a little girl with plaited hair and a dress hand-stitched from flour sacks. Maud-Lucy always said I looked bathed in light.

. . .

I know, isn't that grand? That was our beautiful story: love at first sight. She stayed with us that night and couldn't leave me.

. . .

True, there was the tree-selling dullard waiting back home. But you make your stories, and that was ours. It was true enough. In the end, she went home anyway, with a baby in her arms.

. . .

Mama and I walked her to the station. Maud-Lucy looked the same as always—no hat, no gloves, an overdone coat from the 1890s. You know, I can still feel the cold if I try hard enough. It was one of those blue and blustery days. Maud-Lucy took her ticket, then opened the blanket to show the baby's face. I hadn't seen him since the first day. I didn't want to kiss him, but Maud-Lucy insisted. He smelled like a ripe peach.

. . .

Mama was crying, to be honest. "Is good life for boy," she said. Then Maud-Lucy stepped onto the car. All I could think of was crows.

. . .

You know the way they hop, all black and flapping? Then the train whistle started up. I can still hear it.

. . .

Whooo, it went. Like that: *whooo*. In my head I was shouting over the noise: *Is good life for* girl. *Is good life for* girl, *too*.

. . .

Well, I watched her go, what else? I was just a baby myself. The train vanished down the tracks, speeding Laurentas to a future filled with science and literature and sizzling conversations that led to a thing being looked up or written down or sent away for. I was the only creature on earth who understood how happy he'd be. Away he went, taking her wit, her zeal, her notorious independence. Her love for me.

. . .

. . .

Sorry. What?

. . .

No. She never even came back for her piano.

Chapter 8

The boy had decided to take no chances. On the sixth Saturday he brought her a list of the most statistically dangerous pursuits, ranging from death by cave diving (*getting lost while; running out of air while; being eaten by sea creature while*) to death by door (*walking into; burning alive while searching for key to; discovering stairs removed from other side of*). There were fifty-two items on the list.

"Read this just in case," he cautioned. "You don't want to get all the way to one hundred twenty-two years, one hundred sixty-four days, and then accidentally die because you"—here he reconsulted his list—"cut off your thumb while slicing a bagel."

"I wouldn't want to go like that at any age."

After they'd perused the List of Death and Dismemberment, he produced an addendum: home exercise routines for the elderly, plus an updated inventory of supercentenarians (the woman from Japan had died, along with a sketchy contender from Guam), plus ten supercentenarian profiles he'd procured from God knows where. She envisioned the boy's Internet as a magic cube that crackled with news.

"Look here," Ona said. "The Hartley woman still reads without her glasses." She squinted through her own glasses, shuffling the sheets. Some of the profilees were half blind or deaf or off their rockers—these she skipped over with a shudder—but most of them weren't. "This Wong fellow mows his own lawn. He could be a problem."

The boy said, "Maybe we can think up a record to hold your place till you get older."

"You mean in case I don't make it."

His eyes flew open. "No! That's not what I meant!"

She believed him.

"Oldest sky diver is taken. Plus oldest pilot. Plus oldest showgirl."
He frowned. "But the record holders are way younger than you. Are
you interested in breaking a record that has already been set?"

"Not without a bone transplant."

He ticked off a preposterous list of possibilities—wing walking,
pogo-sticking—and at the end Ona could think of no plausible record for herself except Oldest Woman to Have Sat Around Wasting
What Turned Out to Be Seventeen Years After Louise Died.

"You're thirty-six days older than when I first met you," the boy
said, setting up the recorder.

"Ditto."

He peered out the window. "Can you hear those?"

"No," she said ruefully. She could see them—goldfinches quarrel-
ing—but their music was beyond her hearing.

His face filled with sympathy. Then he said, "I need six more birds
for my badge."

"Spring is nigh. You wait." She smiled at him, lightheaded with
sudden affection. He was so young, and for that alone she liked him.

"Is that your car out there?" he asked.

"Of course that's my car." Randall's old Reliant. "Who else's would
it be?"

His eyes moved to her, pinning her in place. He had something.

"Does it work?"

"It most certainly does. I have it inspected and registered once a
year. A man from the Knights of Columbus takes it to the service station for me, since I was unable to renew my license last time I tried
and I can't sashay into a car-inspection establishment with an expired
license in my wallet."

"Oh," he said. "Darn."

"That's not the word I used."

"I thought you might be a driver. A car driver."

"I didn't say I wasn't a driver. I said I didn't have a license." She leaned in. "Because of my age I was required to take a road test, and the sixteen-year-old tester flunked me."

"Maybe he made a mistake."

"I told the church ladies I passed." She hoped he wouldn't mind. "I told a fib."

"I told a fib, too," he said. "I told my dad I like music. But I don't. There's too many chords, and it's hard to keep your fingers in the right place."

"Now listen," she said. She straightened up and sang a few bars of "Beautiful Dreamer."

"That was excellent, Miss Vitkus."

"See there, you do like music. It's musical instruction you dislike, and I can't say I blame you." She tapped his ghostly hands. "In any case, I drive my car one and a half miles to the supermarket and back once a week, same route every time."

"That sounds very safe." His sweet mouth softened.

"Tell it to the nosey parker down the street. You know what a Realtor is?"

"A Realtor is a person who sells houses."

"Well, this Realtor is a person who *snatches* houses. You see her picture on lawn signs all over town. Lime-green blazer, high red hair. She's dying to sell this place out from under my creaky old feet and watches my every move like a cat watching a mouse."

"Does she have a pink face?"

"That's the one."

"Don't let her sell your house out from under your creaky old feet."

"Don't you worry."

The color of his eyes did its odd shifting, gray to blue-gray; it was one of the first things she'd noticed about him. "Mr. Fred Hale, age one hundred eight, country of USA, holds the record for oldest licensed driver."

"Wait a sec. Isn't Mr. Fred Hale one of my chief rivals? Age one hundred thirteen. Am I recalling correctly?"

"Mr. Fred Hale, age one hundred thirteen, holds the record for oldest living male. But he also holds the record for oldest licensed driver. But his age for oldest licensed driver is one hundred eight. Not one hundred thirteen."

"Somebody probably grabbed it away the second he passed the test."

"I never thought of that."

"Maybe it was a ceremonial record. Maybe he never intended to use his shiny new license."

"I never thought of that, either."

"Well, I don't want a ceremonial license. In fact," she said, "I would love nothing better than to once again become a legitimate driver. I could roar right past Mrs. Pinkface Billboard and she wouldn't have a thing to say about it."

He stood up. "Can you get your license back after they take it away?"

"I'd have to pass a written test. A baby monkey could do that. And an eye test. My eyes are good. It's the road test that jumbles me up."

His hands flew to his head. "Miss Vitkus, if you pass the written test, and if you pass the eye test, and if you pass the road test—"

"Keep your shirt on. I'm going to have to practice. I've been driving right along—that's a secret—but not with any plan to pass a test. I'm going to have to brush up."

"You need a book."

"What kind of book?"

"The kind that teaches you how to drive," he said. "Then you can have your license back, and then in four years plus one more day than the record-breaker age of Mr. Fred Hale you'll be an official Guinness world record holder."

"But in four years I'll have to renew my license yet again. It's every four—"

"Which you will, right? You'll go to the driving place and ask for another road test so you can renew your license for another four years, right?"

"I'll be one hundred eight years old, for crumbsake! And anyway, you'll be fifteen. You'll have moved on to other things."

"Oh, no," he assured her. "Every Guinness world record holder has a support team." He paused. "I'm your support team." He paused again. "You can do it."

"Oldest licensed driver. Age one hundred eight. Imagine."

"But you're going for longest-lived person, too. The all-time record. Don't forget."

"Rest assured, I shall keep the ultimate goal in mind," she said. "In the meantime, we've got ourselves a dandy placeholder to shoot for."

"You might end up with two records!" He grabbed his hair with both hands. "Two times in the book! Two times immortal!" Once again she had this strange, lovely boy hopping in glee. Right in her kitchen. Where glee had not been in residence since Louise's passing. Glee, in the form of this boy who might single-handedly will her to live another two decades.

"Let's call the Department of Motor Vehicles right now. Hand me that phone book."

He grinned. She loved his short teeth.

Which is how she wound up on the following Saturday, driving the Reliant past the supermarket and back, being coached by an eleven-year-old child. She'd had to talk him into skipping his chores. She felt foolish, but he was a good coach. Calm and methodical.

"How many seconds of following distance are required on slippery roads?" he asked as she edged into the light weekend traffic of Brighton Avenue. He'd been quizzing her from a booklet authorized by the DMV.

"What difference does it make? I never drive in the rain." But she slowed automatically, for indeed she'd been following a tad close.

"You might get this question on the real test."

"Fine." She glanced at him. "Five seconds?"

"I'm sorry, that answer is not correct. The correct answer is three to four seconds."

"Ask me another."

"In city traffic, the driver should try to look how many blocks ahead? One, two, or three?"

She was following too closely again. His questions were serving as a guide, she realized. He had her preparing for the road test and written test simultaneously.

"Do your teachers tell you you're smart?"

"Mr. Linkman tells me not to count things." He was still focused on the booklet, not letting her slide past the question. "Mr. Linkman was my teacher in the fourth grade, also. He told me not to count things then, also."

"Two?" she said. "Two blocks ahead?"

"I'm sorry," he said. "That answer is also incorrect. The correct answer is one block ahead."

"For crumbsake," she muttered. "Is there a record for oldest unlicensed driver?"

"No," he said. "They discourage criminals."

"It's a crime for an old lady to drive herself to the supermarket?"

"You have to have a license. That's why they have practice tests. So you can improve." He turned a page. "This is practice test one. There's six in all." He looked up. "Make sure you click the turn signal in time to—"

"I've got it," she said, turning into an empty neighborhood street. "How is anybody supposed to pass this stupid test? It's full of useless information."

"You said a baby monkey could pass the written test," he reminded her. "It's the road test you worried about."

She pulled over. "My head's all woolly," she told him. "This is harder than I thought."

"But you said this was the easy part. What about the eye test? Is the eye test going to be harder than you thought?"

"Now, don't start fretting."

He looked around. "When you park near a curb—"

"I know this one!" she said. "Park as close as you can to the curb, but no farther than eighteen inches."

"That's correct!" he crowed. "That's the correct answer!"

"Try me again."

"When parking in the vicinity of a fire hydrant—"

"Ten feet!"

"That's also correct!"

"Don't act so surprised." She put the car back in gear. "Okay, I've got my wits back. Let's swing toward my house, and you can quiz me on the way."

"Miss Vitkus?"

"Wait, I'm concentrating."

After she crept back out to Brighton Avenue, just a few blocks now from home, he said, "You did very excellent, Miss Vitkus, but you might have to study a little harder."

"Yes, I know." She sighed. "Because we're on a mission."

"That's the correct answer!" She glanced at him and saw he was smiling. He'd made a joke, a pretty good one at that.

When they got back to the house, he insisted on completing his chores—was in fact verging on panic that he'd be doing them out of order—so she called the scoutmaster and asked for a later pickup. She arranged his cookies on a plate, poured some milk, and flipped through the practice manual as she waited. She would study harder; she did not want to disappoint him.

"Take a load off," she said when he came in at last, and for the first time since they'd met she found herself eager for the recording session.

"This is Miss Ona Vitkus," he said. They were up to Part Five. She had a pretty good idea how many parts he had in mind.

He began with a question of his own, passed across the table in immaculate penmanship. His handmade questions, the product of silent forethought, invariably unhooked a shut gate, leaving her to brace against an onrush of memory. The surprise was how little she minded. He turned off the recorder when she asked him to, or when she got to a stopping place that satisfied his Byzantine logic, or when the scoutmaster rang the bell. Only then, the tape gone mute between them, did she understand how far she—she, who never went anywhere—had been willing to travel.

Over the following Saturdays, they fell into a pleasant routine that included chores, stories, and driving instruction. They also pored over their ever-changing list of rivals, a gerontological game of musical chairs that was more entertaining than cards.

"Mrs. Difilippo died," the boy said.

"So I see," Ona said. She'd been rooting for Mrs. Difilippo, age one hundred eleven, because she'd divorced three husbands and still lived alone.

"What are the two most common types of interchanges?" he asked. He'd taken to giving her pop quizzes, apparently a specialty of Mr. Linkman.

"Diamond and cloverleaf."

"That's the correct answer. When is it legal to pass a vehicle on the shoulder?"

"Trick question. Never."

He grinned.

"That's right," she said. "I studied."

As her rivals dropped—not like flies, like petals, bright and melting—she felt regret, along with a fragile thrill over her own accumulating days. The names seemed borrowed from a ship's manifest, a list of refugees from a war no one knew was raging until they discovered themselves the last ones standing. Rosalie; Vittorio; Yasu; Clementine. She thought of them as family, as familiar and mysterious as the boy who had introduced them.

AMAZING FEATS

1. Oldest chart-topping female singer. Cher. Age 52. Country of USA.
2. Oldest Olympic medalist. Oscar Swahn. Age 72. Running Deer shooting team in 1920 Olympics. Country of Sweden.
3. Oldest female marathon finisher. Jennie Wood-Allen. Age 90 years and 145 days. Country of Scotland.
4. Oldest bridesmaid. Flossie Bennett. Age 97. Country of East Anglia.
5. Oldest pilot. Colonel Clarence Cornish. Age 97. Country of USA.
6. Oldest parachutist. Hildegarde Ferrara. Age 99. Country of USA.
7. Oldest practicing doctor. Leila Denmark. Age 103. Country of USA.
8. Oldest bell ringer. Reginald Bray. 100 years and 133 days. Country of UK.
9. Oldest serving parish priest. Father Alvaro Fernandez. Age 107. Country of Spain.
10. Not oldest but most working guitar player. MY OWN RESEARCH!!! Quinn Porter. Age 42. Country of USA.

Chapter 9

By the time the boy arrived on the ninth Saturday, Ona realized she'd been looking for him long before his appointed hour. To hurry the time, she opened the window and listened for birdsong. She caught snippets of robin, the scolding of a crow, a single syllable from a white-throated sparrow's eleven-note call. She thought she heard the distinctive voice of a grackle: like a rusty gate. But everything else was gone and she wished it back.

At last he arrived and after his chores announced that he had news.

"I'm going to be a gerontology researcher," he told her. He had three voices: monotonic, tremulous, and proclamatory. This was proclamatory.

She put out a cake that had taken her two engaged and fragrant hours to make. "You'll be a jim-dandy gerontology researcher," she told him.

"One, they need help. Two, there's a lot of imposters trying to get on the list."

From his bottomless pack he extracted a list of frauds. Buster Balen from Phoenix (claimed age, 105; actual age, 91); Floria Perez from Baja California (claimed age, 114; actual age, 101). The list was long.

"I never thought of imposters," Ona said, a dismaying oversight beginning to dawn. "How do they—how do they wangle onto the list?"

"They cheat," the boy said. He showed her: Mr. Balen had been caught passing off his father's papers as his own; Mrs. Perez had been exposed by her daughter, whose proven age put her mother in labor at age fifty-six. "You need three docs," the boy said. "But they have to be authenticated."

"Three?" She stared at him, disbelieving. "*Now* you tell me?"

He opened his mouth, equally stunned. "You don't—have docs?"

"I thought you called these people up on your one-hundred-tenth birthday and bingo, you're official."

The boy shook his head fearfully. "They don't ever believe you! They check your docs! That's what gerontology researchers do!"

Later, Ona would attribute the full flowering of her—desire? competitive spirit?—to the confluence of the bright day, the memory of birdsong, the ongoing recording project, and the boy's sky-pink cheeks; but at the time it seemed an imperative sent directly from the Other Side by Lucy Hannah or Margaret Skeete or even the great Madame Jeanne Louise Calment herself. She snatched her grocery list from the fridge, flipped it over, and started writing.

"I'd like to enjoy my fame *before* I'm dead, thank you very much," she told the boy, who kept a hawkish eye on her pen. "Let's see. Docs." She thought a minute. "I've got a current Visa card. And Social Security. My library membership's all kept up."

He said, "Do those—do those things prove your age?"

Ona stopped writing. "It's ID," she said. "Proof that I'm who I say I am."

"ID is one category," he told her, his body seeming to melt with apology. "Docs is a different category." He switched to the tremulous voice: "You need *docs*."

"Such as?"

"One, birth certificate."

"I'm not sure I have one."

"Oh, no." He hesitated, stricken. "I made a big mistake," he said, collapsing against the chair back. "I thought all Americans had docs."

"Now, listen," she said. "You're forgetting my driver's license. If all goes as planned I'll have that shined up in no time, not to mention a head start on my placeholder record, and my birth date will be right there, along with my height and weight. Problem solved."

"They won't count your driver's license." He began to quote: "'We prefer documents obtained in childhood.'"

"We do, do we? Why?"

"Because adults lie about their age." He glanced at the imposter list, then back at Ona.

"Well, I'm not lying. I know how old I am."

"But they're a big company!" he said, nearly coming out of his chair. "They have big rules!"

She put her hands on his narrow shoulders. "Let's be calm about this."

"All right," he said. But his eyes went huge with alarm.

"We'll need a little more information, that's all," she told him.

"I can do that. I'm good at information."

"You are indeed." She tapped her pen. "Now, it could turn out they need things like fingerprints. Or a baptismal record. I was baptized in a Lithuanian country church that's probably a Burger King by now. I don't know the village, let alone the church, and there isn't a soul left on earth who could tell me." She laid down her pen, astonished. "I don't know where I come from."

A rainfall of words pittered down: *Pasienis. Laivas. Kelione.* Border. Ship. Journey.

The boy looked near tears. "What do we do?"

She patted his shoulder. "Start counting."

"One," the boy said softly, "birth certificate." He tore a page from his own pristine notebook—she couldn't begin to know what this cost him—and wrote at the top, PROOF. Then he recorded the first item in a careful, kindly hand that seemed to soothe him. He looked up again and handed her the page with solemnity, as if he were the parish priest from that long-vanished church, confirming her existence.

He assured her he'd return with a list of exactly what docs she would need. When the time came to record her, she felt jittery and short of days. The tape was running out; a sliver remained on one side, a fat coil—her life!—on the other. "Part Eight?" she said. "Are you sure?"

They recorded Part Eight.

"You won't give this part to your teacher," Ona said. "Or that other part."

"I won't," he said. He knew. Possibly he had always known.

When the scoutmaster arrived she asked him to wait outside. They recorded Part Nine. The scoutmaster ran an errand, then returned. But she had to finish. She asked him to wait some more. They ended up with ten parts because the boy was the one running the machine.

Which was just as well. Ona had no more. The boy had taken it all. Or, she had given it.

She spent the remains of that day scouring the house for her birth certificate until she remembered what had happened to it. She intended to tell the boy, but on the tenth Saturday he did not appear. Nor did he appear on the Saturday following, when her bushes suddenly quavered with a mixed flock of jewel-colored birds that Ona could not hear.

On the Saturday after that, his father came.

PART TWO

Sūnus (Sons)

Chapter 10

Quinn's days jammed up with work. Out of each week, after completing his chores for Ona, he isolated a few hours to go to the bank, deposit his cash, and write out a check for twice what he'd been paying before. Then he took a bus to Belle's house to lay the money down. This ritual gave him too much time to think, but he believed it necessary to pay in person.

Visiting her was no longer easy—that, too, seemed necessary—for it meant facing the gauntlet of Belle's formidable sister, Amy; or one of their blowsy aunts; or sometimes their jittery mother; or, worse, their father; or, worse still, Ted Ledbetter. Quinn went anyway, because it was the least he could do. Also the most. She'd forgiven him the theft of the diary—he'd unhanded it, and she'd accepted it, in silence.

As the bus let him off near Belle's neighborhood, his phone rang. "Hey, Pops," came a voice he knew. "We need you."

"Let me guess," Quinn said, walking against a stiff breeze and slashing sunlight. "Cousin Zack ditched you last-minute for another spin in rehab?"

"It's a *disease*," Brandon said. He was twenty-one and had a friend in Jesus. They all did, and why not? Young and lucky, inheritors of dimpled chins and great teeth. They called themselves Resurrection Lane.

Quinn jimmied his calendar out of his pocket. "When?"

"Tomorrow. Eight cities, seven days. We're back late Saturday."

"Things looking up in the praise trade?"

Brandon laughed his clean, tenor laugh. "We're on *fire*, Pops."

"I'll ink you in." Resurrection Lane paid well and promptly, thanks to Sylvie, Brandon's fast-talking, deal-making supermom. Quinn had never met cousin Zack, the bad-seed guitarist whom Quinn was being hired once again to replace.

"Awesome, he's inked in!" That was Tyler, Brandon's brother, crowing in the background. Their cousins, Jason and Jeff, collectively known as the Jays, rounded out the prayer circle.

"Oh, wait, hold on," Quinn said. "Wait a sec." He had Saturday-morning chores: yet another week as Ona's Boy Scout, and he hadn't disappointed her yet.

"Pops—?"

"No worries," Quinn said. "I'll work it out."

"Awesome, he'll work it out!" One of the Jays. Quinn felt a flush of pride, disquietingly paternal. Despite the group grace every time you so much as reached into a bag of Cheetos, Quinn liked them. They wrote hummable songs and acted like pros, though their puppyish affection sometimes made him think of Jesus herding apostles from town to town. He'd taught them famous licks from Hendrix and Clapton, advising them to hold their guitars low on their bodies. *Untuck your shirts, for crying out loud. You look like the Dave Clark Five.* They'd called him "Mr. Porter" until he told them to knock it off, then started calling him "Pops," which stuck.

"Remember last March in Worcester?" one of the Jays broke in. "That song we tried out? We changed the intro and added a bridge, just like you said, and they're playing it on the *radio*, no lie!"

He meant Christian radio. But still. Sylvie had muscled the song into the hands of a friend-of-a-friend deejay in Omaha, who played it more or less continuously for three weeks, whereupon the name Resurrection Lane miraculously washed over both coasts like parted halves of the Red Sea.

"It's happening, Pops!" Tyler again, or maybe Brandon; they talked the way they sang: a blend. "We did you proud."

"Hear it, hear it," Quinn said as he signed off. The boys laughed, because that was the name of the song.

He made his way to Belle's door, pausing a moment to steel himself, but the door flew open and there was Amy.

"She's sleeping," she informed him. "She's got day and night reversed."

The irony of this revelation landed hard—their biorhythms had never matched up, and now, it seemed, they did.

"I'll wait," he said.

Amy's face closed up. She was more striking than Belle, darker and smokier and possibly even beautiful, but she carried their father's pugilistic air, leading with her chin even when she didn't have to. She glanced at the check in his fist. "Quinn," she murmured, "what exactly do you think you're buying?"

He said nothing, followed her into the kitchen, where she resumed scrubbing Belle's sink as if intending to make it disappear. Sunlight flinted through the windows. The whole place clanged with an empty, metallic gleam, whether from Amy's brutal applications or Belle's shedding of material goods, hard to say. The toaster appeared to be missing.

"Uh, Amy?"

He waited until she looked up—at him—but she gave away nothing beyond the haggard nakedness of her face. Instead, she wiped her hands, opened the fridge, and poured out some lemonade with a great clattering of ice.

Amy stood at the counter, sipping mutely. "What can I do for you?"

"She wants me here," he insisted, because he'd begun to believe it.

"Be that as it may, the time when your presence in this house would have done her any good is long past. She has a perfectly nice man in her life."

He glanced around. "I don't see him anywhere."

"He has kids," she said. "Whom he spends rather a lot of time with."

The words stung, but he wasn't sure whether she'd aimed them directly at him. In times of pain or rage, the Cosgroves resorted to the vaguely British terminology of the once-removed. *Rather. Not quite. Be that as it may.*

"I'll wait," he said again. "She was never any good at napping."

"She's good at it now."

He did wait, observing in silence as Amy padded back and forth with an array of cleaning supplies. From their mother, the Cosgrove girls had learned to scrub their way out of despair. There was no detergent in existence for what ailed them now, but Amy heaved into the old standby nonetheless, with an alacrity bordering on violence, much sloshing and clanging coming from the adjoining rooms. He listened to these sounds—like an animal crying hard, he thought—until she appeared again, hands red and raw.

"Are you staying all summer?" he asked her.

She opened a little closet—he'd once kept his gig bag in there—and took out a dust cloth. Back in LA she wrote a syndicated financial column, but she'd moved her headquarters to the guest room across the hall from the boy's shut door. "I'm waiting for the legalities to settle."

He watched her unfold the cloth, then fold it again, into perfect quarters.

"What legalities?"

"If you must know," she said, "we're looking into wrongful death."

"We—?"

"Well," she said. "Not you."

"Who are you suing?" he asked, genuinely bewildered. "God?"

"Don't be absurd." Her eyes, a dark gold-brown, recalled the doomy hue of dying leaves.

"Who, then? His doctor?"

She said nothing.

He recalled the pediatrician as an old-school type who believed children outgrew everything. He'd never met the woman himself, but Belle had her on speed dial. The name came to him: "You're suing Dr. McNeil? You're kidding me."

"Dr. McNeil retired. Belle switched to CenterMed."

"CenterMed, then," Quinn said. He knew the place: huge practice, you never saw the same person twice, but you could get in on short notice. "You're suing them? For what?"

"Not them, a PA who works there. Physician's *assistant*. They're supposed to *assist*. Anyway, the less you know about this, the better."

Leave it to the Cosgroves, who would indeed sue God if such a thing were possible. He imagined them dragging Belle through airless hearings as her pallor turned to ash. Now he was angry. "You're suing a PA for not detecting a condition that's undetectable? Look it up, Amy."

"*You* look it up," she snapped. "If you're dispensing drugs to children you're supposed to comprehend the fine print, which is there for any competent medical professional to take under advisement."

Quinn's understanding went tight and wiry, like a guitar string about to break. "What are you talking about?"

She folded her arms. "Long QT is either inherited—"

"I know that," he said. "I know all that."

"—or acquired. There's no way to tell after the fact. If he inherited it"—here she glanced at him with suspicion—"he'd likely have lived a long life in blissful ignorance, but the drugs tipped the scale. If he *didn't* inherit it, then the prescription did the job all by itself."

Amy's information was coming in as if on tape delay, the import of the words arriving a beat or two behind the actual words. "Make *sense*," he said. "What drugs?"

She hesitated. "Antidepressants," she said. "For chronic anxiety. Why don't you know this? The pills weren't doing squat, so the PA added a titch of antipsychotic about two months before he died."

"Anti-what? Jesus Christ."

"They're supposed to help with night terrors." A tear dropped down her cheek and off the tip of her chin and into the hollow of her throat. "But the PA was too rushed, too busy, over his head—something."

Quinn just stood there in the tin-bright room, weak and clueless, wondering what the hell were night terrors, unless she meant that eerie, soft, wee-hour keening, the boy sitting up, eyes translucent and pinned open and unconvincingly awake.

His head ached. Didn't Rennie's daughter take medication? And one of Gary's perfect little sons, come to think. The guys talked about these things all the time and now he wished he'd paid more attention. Every kid in America had prescriptions these days, he knew that much. "What were the chances?" he asked at last. "Are we talking, like, one in a million?"

"He should have ordered an EKG first. He should have done the research. He should have *looked* it *up*."

They stared each other down for a few moments, the air between them charged with old rivalry.

"When is she going back to work?" he asked.

"She tried," Amy said. Belle worked at the state archives, where she often aided ordinary people in their quest to nail down their ancestral trail. *What's the point?* he'd asked her once—he who had never known a grandparent, whose mother had died young, whose father and brother were as distant as ideas. The question was a throwaway, a verbal shrug; but Belle responded with her usual thoughtfulness: *They hope their descendants will do the same for them.*

"She tried twice, actually," Amy said, "but she can't bear the names of the dead." She turned on him then, her face soft from weeks of crying. "How is it that you're working so much, Quinn?"

"I—it's what I do."

"Why aren't you prostrate with sorrow? Why aren't you home right now, writhing in your bed of pain?"

Because, he believed, he had not earned the release of grief.

"Maybe if you'd been a different sort of father he would have been a different sort of kid," she went on, her breath coming hard and uneven. "A kid who wasn't so afraid, who felt safe in his bones, who didn't need two prescriptions to face the wall of the world, who didn't have to number every goddamn item in his universe, who didn't have to ride his bike through the neighborhood at five in the morning for whatever incomprehensible reason and be killed by his own heart and found on the sidewalk with a gash in his cheek." She covered her face.

"Oh, God," she breathed. "Oh, my God, I'm disgusting." She looked up blearily. "This isn't me, Jesus, please, this isn't me."

Quinn gaped at her. Despite everything, he still thought of her as family. He suffered her anger now—desperation, misery, whatever it was—even welcomed it as his due, because the thing he'd felt since the boy's death did not count as suffering. His heart hurt for her, for Belle, for all of them. And for the boy, especially the boy, vanquished by a deranged God before getting a decent toehold on his full three-score and ten.

"You liked me once, Amy."

"I did." She wiped her eyes with one bunched fist. "But not as a husband for my sister." He could barely hear her. "I admired you. The artistic life always appealed to me, but I didn't have the guts to go for it."

"Going for it is easy," he said. He'd always liked her throaty singing voice; she'd sat in with the Benders a few times in their loose and headlong youth. "Sticking with it . . ."

"High price."

"I guess."

She crossed her arms and held herself. "I was counting up the number of days I spent with him," she murmured. "What does that say about me as an aunt, that I can count the number of days I spent with a child who was on earth for eleven years?"

Quinn was beginning to see that Amy was here not because her sister needed her, but quite the opposite. It was Amy who'd bought the red bike he'd been riding on the clear, sweet morning of his death.

"How many?" he asked.

"What?"

"How many days?"

"Sixty-one," she said, then her voice dropped as if from a great height. "Sixty-two if you count the funeral." She was forty years old, with a married boyfriend and a craving for children. It struck him then that she was vying with him not for Belle, but for the boy.

"You live in LA," he said. "Sixty-one days is a hell of a lot of days, considering." She was weeping now. "Amy. Remember that mini tape recorder you sent to him a couple of years ago?"

She mopped her eyes with her sleeve. "Uh-huh."

"He carried it around like a pet."

"He did, I know."

"It's the only material object that he didn't own ten of. He adored you, Amy. You have nothing to regret."

"I—" she began, then he followed her gaze through the knife-clean windows. The breezy day had died, in its place a paralyzing sunlight, beneath which he received the numbing sight of a pajama-clad Belle moving methodically along the edge of the backyard with a pair of clippers, snapping fully bloomed heads from a vibrant bed of flowers.

"What is she doing?" he asked.

"I thought she was in bed."

"I'll go," he said.

"Quinn?"

He turned. She was still crying a little.

"Thank you," she said, then resumed her drubbing, leaving him to head outside, slightly disoriented, thankful that Amy hadn't asked him for his own shameful number of days.

He trudged down the long slope of the backyard, which was famously difficult to mow. The boy had been too scrawny to control the electric mower, though he'd mastered the push mower, a relic from Eric Chapman, Belle's besotted neighbor. Today the lawn looked pool-table smooth, the work of an adult—Ted Ledbetter, no doubt—with impeccable organizational skills.

Belle had moved to a stand of daisies that hemmed the prefab toolshed—a father-son project that had languished for months until Quinn arrived for a custody visit and found it fully assembled, painted a stolid shade of green. Ted and his sons had turned the thing into a Scouting project, a happy endeavor that earned all the boys a dual badge in something like woodworking and teamwork. She clipped a blossom and watched it float to the ground.

"That one looked okay," he said.

"I find their sunshiny faces unendurable." She offed its neighbor.

"You, uh, probably don't want to decapitate all of them."

"How would you know what I want?" she said, but allowed him to take the clippers and lay them on the grass.

"Is the lawsuit your father's idea?"

"People have to fill their lives with something. I told him I'd sign the complaint if it'd make everybody happy."

"You don't have to do what your father says." Mac Cosgrove was an ex-titan of industry who wore wingtips on weekends, a hard guy to say no to, especially if you were a Cosgrove girl. "These things can take years, Belle."

"I don't care who gets sued, or how long it takes. I just want to be left alone." She looked up. "How's the Scouting?"

She always began here, wanting to know everything: how many scoops the feeders had required; which of the porch steps—which one exactly—he'd repaired.

"She gave me cake."

"What kind?"

"It tasted like chocolate but she made it with tomato soup."

"Your hearing must be getting worse."

"No, really. Secret ingredient. She wouldn't give it up the first time she made it, but today I shook her down." He paused. "I've got only a couple more weeks."

"Then your fatherly duties will officially be over." She didn't look to see how her words had landed. Instead, she squinted at the sky, asking, "What else have you got?"

"Did I tell you she gets three papers?"

"Which ones?"

"You mean which actual papers?"

"Yes. Which actual papers?"

"*Press Herald. Times. Globe.*"

She nodded, three quick snaps of the head. Counting, he realized. She looked alarmingly unhinged: much-sweated-in pajamas, sleep-slitted eyes, hair mashed on one side.

"She keeps up, is what I'm saying. She's in ridiculous shape, considering."

A trace of her old smile. "Better than you, I bet."

"*Touché.*"

Belle ran her fingers over the remaining blooms, ruffling the petals as if in apology. He waited until she finally looked at him.

"I didn't know about the drugs," Quinn said, ashamed.

"Don't second-guess me," she said. "I can do that perfectly well myself."

"I'd never second-guess you." He gazed at her helplessly. "Belle, you were a beautiful mother."

"He thought so. He wrote it down." She closed her eyes. "Quinn, just tell me. Did you get yourself tested for Long QT?"

"No."

"Because if you did—"

"I didn't."

"Were you afraid to find out you have it?"

He hesitated, then told her: "I was afraid to find out I don't have it."

He watched her as it sank in. "Remember the time I borrowed my father's car," she said, "and then rear-ended the house with it? He still thinks it was you."

He laughed, in spite of everything. "That's okay. He never liked me to begin with."

"You took one for the team is what I mean," she said. She sat down on the grass and he knelt beside her. She asked, "How are you, Quinn?"

His eyes stung: that she asked; that she meant it.

"I'm going on the road with the God Squad."

"I always liked those kids. Cousin Zack back in rehab?"

"Bingo."

She picked at the grass. "The thing is, Quinn, even if we both have Long QT, let's say we both have it, there's no point in knowing. We're home free, our chance to die young long past." She shook her head. "His chance, too, would have passed him by, except for the pills I gave him. I've read all the literature, Quinn. It's the pill that did the job, either all by itself or as an 'enhancer' to his preexisting condition." She laughed a low, sad not-laugh. "What a word, *enhancer*. That extra pill, that harmless-looking salmon-pink pill I gave him every day for two months with a chaser of apple juice."

"Belle, why are you doing this?"

"I wish I'd died young." Her face looked whipped by branches. "But then I never could have brought that lovely child into this world."

"Belle. Sweetheart."

"Thing is?" she said. "The damn things *worked*." Her mouth quivered. "He wouldn't come out of his room without counting everything in it. I mean everything. He was sleeping *under* his bed."

"You could have told me."

"Oh, Quinn," she said. "When would the subject have come up?"

"I guess it wouldn't have." His custody visits had dwindled to pitiful, twice-monthly suppers in theme restaurants, the boy answering Quinn's predictable questions in complete, often numbered sentences—the verbal equivalent of a chain-link fence. *Does he bore you?* Belle had asked him, incredulous, after that final canceled visit.

"He was better," she said now. "Couldn't you see it? Wasn't he better?"

"It's not your fault, Belle. It's nobody's fault. The odds were astronomical."

She closed her eyes. "Our one-in-a-million boy."

"Who had a beautiful mother." Beneath her horrible pajamas her shoulders were oddly canted, as if her body had decided to collapse without her full permission. Such immense effort, it seemed, just to hold yourself upright.

"There's something you should know," she said. "I didn't tell you before because my father thought you might interfere." Quinn waited uneasily; any mention of the old man usually heralded bad news.

"You probably know the PA," Belle said finally. "He introduced himself to me as Richard, but it turns out everybody calls him Juke."

"Juke Blakely? He's a PA? The one you're suing?"

"He was new to the practice. I should have known. If only I'd asked more questions. If he'd introduced himself as Juke, I might have. I might've shown more prudence when it came to my son. My own unforgettable child."

Quinn, whose own acquaintance with prudence hardly warranted a mention, experienced an acute, electrical dread on behalf of Juke Blakely, who had stood next to Quinn at the rail of a ferry to Ransom Island on the day before the boy was born. They'd been met at the dock by three guys driving candy-red pickups, who loaded their gear and took them to a summer house perched atop a grassy cliff. The island's owner had instructed the band—a party band called Fly by Night—to wear white shirts and black jeans, an expenditure Quinn intended to recoup at the end of the night in the form of quality alcohol from the outdoor bar. The gig coincided with his final tumble off the wagon before sobering up for good.

Juke Blakely had a good ear and quick fingers, and Quinn sought out his company during the first break. They sat on a flattened boulder and watched the sea and shared their envy for the tiered house with its tennis courts and bandstand and ludicrous view. They were both thirty-one, both married, both liberal-arts dropouts with a two-year tech certificate in electronics repair. Juke had savings, though, and a five-year-old kid. He was looking to go back to school for something practical, possibly in the medical field.

The status quo reigned until sundown—set lists heavy on Van Morrison, lame jokes from Freddy the bandleader, endless introductions of people in remarkable clothes, several rounds of "Happy Birthday" for the half-drunk birthday girl. Quinn went a little tipsy himself on the sea air, the smiling guests connected vaguely to the movie biz, the sensation that he himself was part of a movie. Around nine thirty, the birthday girl's stepdad presented—*ta-da!*—the surprise guest, his old family friend, David Crosby.

David freakin' Crosby, of Crosby, Stills, and Nash. Quinn went light in the head, sensing everything around him as suddenly hand-colored and fattened up and deep and rich and ownable. Even the quality of dark began to change as stars emerged from the blue-black sky, first faint and slow, then bright and fast. David Crosby strapped on a borrowed guitar and asked, "What'll it be?" They played the ones they knew, the ones everyone knew, Quinn and Juke and David Crosby—*Dave,* he called him, *Dave*—trading lead lines for a while, then Juke seemed to understand Quinn's urgency and backed into the rhythm role. For this one favor, Quinn never forgot him.

A brotherly cohesion overspread the bandstand that night, subtle as the progress of the moon. Quinn and Juke exchanged looks of awe, fully receiving this memory in the making that ended softly, so softly and sweetly, with "Teach Your Children," the throwback song Quinn had listened to a thousand times as a lonely teenager in his room at home, bent over his guitar, eyes half-masted, shutting out his father's anger and his brother's obsessive goal setting, pretending his mother was still alive and humming along and tapping her hip in that way she had. *Dave* took the melody, Juke the harmony, and Quinn simulated Jerry Garcia's steel guitar by treadling his volume pedal exactly the way he had in high school. Threaded voices lifted and flew, shawling over the guests who drew nearer and linked arms out of nostalgia or maybe even love, a gathering of woven souls marooned high above a green and thrashing sea.

As the song rolled out to the stars, Quinn could hear his friend Dave laughing between lyrics, drunk on the exquisite setting, the music, the adoring crowd in their swaying bliss. *Look at this guy!* he chortled into the mic. *This guy's amazing!* Quinn laughed, too, acknowledging the shout-out as his fingers moved between frets, and the song went on, and wound down, and faded beautifully away, and then it was gone forever. Applause, applause, then the juiced-up birthday girl climbed the bandstand steps in her rackety heels, commanded the guest of honor to say something more, so he said, *I love this beautiful place!* Quinn heard "place" as "place in time," and he loved it too. He loved this beautiful place.

Sometime during that long, enchanted night, Quinn bade farewell to ol' Dave; he recollected a sturdy handshake, an insider's chuckle. At dawn Quinn turned up at the ferry landing, squinting into a crimson sky and suffused with the ardent, mistaken, hungover belief that David Crosby wanted to play with him again sometime, maybe take him on the road. Deeper down in his consciousness swam a watery recollection of phone numbers being exchanged, though he could not find such evidence on his person after rampaging the same six pockets for days.

He'd been telling the shined-up version of this story for eleven years, leaving out the ending. After he burst through the door with his new and shapeless plans, he found on the table a note from Amy: *Get your ass to the hospital. You're a dad*. It was Juke Blakely, helping to unload gear, who'd offered to drive him there.

Now the story—his wonderful story—felt like poison. He stood in the mowed backyard among the bright corpses of flowers. He said, "Does Juke know what's coming?"

"I don't know."

"He wasn't a PA when I knew him," Quinn said. "He had a kid, though. And a wife. A good egg, I always thought. Good player, too."

"I can't listen. I can't listen to this."

"All right," he said. Maybe he was wrong; maybe revenge—a long, protracted lawsuit—would get her over the hump. "Belle?"

She scrambled to her feet.

"I'm not second-guessing, Belle," he said, following her up the slope to the house. "I'm not. I'm just asking. Amy said chronic anxiety. Is that what he had?"

"I don't know what he had." She turned. "What he had was *us*. My body plus your body, and it made him who he was."

Belle looked at him, distractedly at first, then intently. "This is none of your business anyway," she said, very quietly. "It's not your business now." Her armored expression faded then, in stages, until the old Belle, the real Belle, the Belle who liked children and old ladies and him, appeared as a rush of blood in her cheeks. Her arms dropped to her sides. "I don't cry," she quavered. "I don't cry because I can't stand to wound them with my pain."

"Wound me," he said, and this she was willing to do. She pitched herself into his arms, her cries soft and sloppy and heart-crushing. Her anguish left him feeling justly pummeled and rendered his own afflictions hardly worth mentioning. His own misery—or whatever you called it—existed as a mounting pressure, like breath held too long underwater. She cried and cried and he took it standing up.

"Ted's been a rock," she said at last, swabbing her face with her sleeve. "Just an absolute rock. But he went through so much when his wife died. And he—he has his sons. I keep resenting him for it. I'm sick with envy." She lifted her bloodshot eyes. "I'm telling you this because you won't judge me."

"It's all right. You're entitled."

"No. I'm really not entitled. They're beautiful boys. They've been so kind. Even the youngest, Evan, he's only nine, he's been so kind. But it's there anyway. The envy. I'm aching with it." She waved him away. "And Amy, my God. I feel like a specimen under glass."

It was time to go, he could see that, so he walked her back up the slope to the breezeway. He slipped the check from his pocket. He'd kept back just enough to keep his landlord paid and had taken to turning off lights behind him, making his morning coffee at home, switching to black to save money on cream. He'd disconnected his landline and bought a cell phone package even cheaper than the one he'd been using before.

"I wasn't bored," he whispered to her. "It was never that." He laid the check on a small table that had once held their joint mail.

"You have to stop, Quinn. Money is—irrelevant."

"It's what I have."

"What you owe him," she said quietly, "you can never pay."

She let the check lie there. She didn't pick it up or give it back. She just let it lie. Her anger toward him was gone, he realized; in its place, pity.

"Ask the God Squad to pray for me," she said, then went into the kitchen without him.

Eventually, he left. Giving her money only made him feel worse. He supposed that was the point.

After the bus dropped him off downtown, Quinn walked home by way of the art museum, where he peered through the fence, looking for the sculpture he always looked for: a massive human figure made from a net of steel wire, its insides packed with stones. A human figure literally weighted down, one colossal knee resting on the ground, torso bent nearly in half, head bowed but not bent. A man, Quinn thought, suffering in private. The man was mute. Sheltered by small sweet trees. To find him you had to already know he was there.

Quinn took out his phone, which had a 104-year-old woman on its call log; how had this happened?

"Oh," she said, recognizing his voice. "I thought you were going to be a man from Pakistan trying to sell me a credit card."

"I can't make it next week," he said, and could have left it there, but she'd tripped him up by knowing him at hello. He added, "How's Sunday?"

"Do you assume," she asked him, "that one day is the same as another to me? Because I'm old?"

"I've got a gig I can't pass up."

"I make my biscuits on Sunday morning."

"Make them on Saturday."

"After that, one of the ladies picks me up for the ten-thirty Mass."

"Then I'll come early."

"You never come early."

"I'll come early, Ona."

If you stared long enough, the sculpture appeared to quaver, as if the rocks themselves were breathing, giving breath to the man. "There's these—kids. Their lead guitarist's gone again, and I'm in, and it looks like they're on the brink of something."

"Uh-oh."

"Something *good*," he amended. "A *good* brink."

"Oh. I thought they were planning to jump off a cliff." She paused. "Are these boys—do they play rock-and-roll music?"

He smiled to hear her say it. "Gospel rock," he said. "Nothing in it to worry your grandma."

"My grandma's far beyond the reach of worry."

"They're gallingly talented. And their mother's a walking bank."

"Aha. Opportunity knocks."

"Let's hope."

"Hope is a perilous thing, Quinn."

"So I hear." He'd thought himself finished with hope, but here it was again, that urgent, nearly spiritual ache, an open wound looking for a balm. How did Ona know this?

"Sunday's good anyway," she said. "I like the Saturday Mass." She sounded chirpy. "Even if one day *is* the same as another around here, it's not polite to make a lady admit it."

"I'll make a note."

"You do that."

"Biscuits sound good," he said.

"I'll make a note."

The sculpture was still breathing, or appearing to. Quinn felt suddenly stone-heavy himself, a caged body packed with rocks, a stone man hiding under the trees. *Get up*, he whispered, but the stone man remained where he was, suspended, poised to rise up despite his burden, or to give in at last to the force of its staggering weight.

HEAVY

1. Heaviest butterfly. Over 25 grams. Queen Alexandra's birdwing. Country of Papua New Guinea.
2. Heaviest baby born to healthy mother. 22 pounds and 8 ounces. Country of Italy.
3. Heaviest bus pulled by hair. 17,359 pounds. Pulled by Letchemanah Ramasamy. Country of Malaysia.
4. Heaviest annual rainfall. 38.94 feet per year. Mawsynram. Country of India.
5. Heaviest object removed from stomach. 5 pounds and 3 ounces. Ball of hair. Country of UK.
6. Heaviest flying bird. Great bustard. 46.3 pounds. Country of Hungary.
7. Heaviest heart. Up to 1,500 pounds. Blue whale. Country of the oceans.
8. Heaviest cat. Himmy. 46.8 pounds. Country of Australia.
9. Heaviest dog. Kell. 286 pounds. Country of England.
10. Heaviest man. John Minnoch. 1,400 pounds. Country of USA.

* * *

This is Miss Ona Vitkus. This is her life shards on tape. This is Part Three.

I don't know about *shards*.

. . .

Because it makes me sound like something broken and un-put-back-togetherable.

. . .

Memories, then. But they're not, really. They feel like something else.

. . .

Never mind. *Shards* is fine. Go.

. . .

I'll tell you where I was: waiting. Same as the mothers now. Same as the mothers from the beginning of time. Randall was in law school, padding off to his tax-code classes on two flat feet; but Frankie, he joined the navy. Over my nearly dead body.

. . .

"Think of all those shocked-up boys who came back from the first one," I told him. "Take a look at your own half-buttoned father." But Frankie wasn't a listener, like you. Frankie was a talker. He wrote the most beautiful letters, from his LCT in the northern Marianas.

. . .

It's a large vessel that carries things. Tanks and men, mostly. It carries them across God's great green sea and then dumps them spank into harm's way. You should have seen his letters. Howard kept them from me when I left.

. . .

"I saw a bird with ten-foot wings, Mama." "I like my shipmates real well, Mama." That kind of thing. "The skies here turn such colors, Mama, like a fighter's bad-punched eye." My Frankie had a way with words.

. . .

Well. Six months later, after the Battle of Saipan, a sniper got him on one of the boys' rare evenings ashore. The rest of the fellows were on the beach watching a movie, but not Frankie. Frankie pilfered a jeep and off he went, unauthorized as usual, a joy ride down a secured road. Which was not as secure as he thought. There was liquor involved, no doubt. And a girl. Even out there in the middle of God's empty palm, Frankie would have figured a way to work in a girl.

. . .

You know, I wondered the same thing? The exact same thing. But nobody could tell me. They didn't think it was important. I figured something with Bob Hope in it.

. . .

Oh, Bob Hope was wonderful. Very funny man. So that would be my guess. Bob Hope and Bing Crosby, probably one of those dopey road movies with Dorothy Lamour prancing around in her white sarong. All those well-behaved boys with better mothers, doing what they're told, watching pretty Dorothy Lamour. And then there's Frankie in his jeep speeding past a field of sugar cane.

. . .

Possibly. I never thought of that. Hmm. The sky out there is so famously open. But jeeps make such a commotion. And the sound system would have been a little on the mushy side. I don't imagine he could make out actual words. But maybe he fiddled out the funny parts just from the rise and fall, the timing. Bing and Bob were famous for their timing.

. . .

Me, too. I hope the sound carried. I hope he died laughing.

Chapter 11

Quinn hadn't entirely believed the Omaha-deejay coast-to-coast story until he got on the road and discovered shiny throngs of boys and girls wearing Resurrection Lane T-shirts and singing all the words. They bought the boys' CD in multiples, the shows went long, and Quinn winged through the prodigal cousin's smeared charts, improvising his own sluicing guitar hooks in a state of dislocation and glee.

It was just a job—with a fangless pack of absurdly talented Jesus lovers who called him Pops—but the same thing happened every time: he cared. They pestered him for advice and he gave it out like money he didn't need, feeling expansive and necessary. He shuffled the set list in Providence, tweaked a muddy house system in Springfield, finagled the primo spot in a Worcester triple bill. He cared about their quadrupling crowds and T-shirt sales. He cared about their music—straight-arrow constructions aquiver with chordal surprises—and he cared about what their music did to all those upturned faces. At the end of each night his jaw ached from smiling.

As usual, Sylvie kept showing up to keep an eye on things, though with Quinn aboard the usual glitches didn't much signify. He'd rewired a faulty connection during the sound check, which to Sylvie was the equivalent of building a microwave oven out of paper clips and a Zippo. "How do you *know* everything?" she asked.

The answer: twenty-five years futzing with hard-used equipment, coaxing balance and tone out of barrooms with ass-crap acoustics.

"My boys can barely manage a wall plug," she said. "Doug's even worse. I married a *brain surgeon* who can't reset our house alarm." This was their last night, intermission, and they were hanging out at the swag table, where Sylvie guarded a trove of T-shirts emblazoned with the band's motto, WALK THE LANE, in crucifixion red. She turned to her helper, a volunteer from campus ministry, a florid man in a gingham cowboy shirt. "Did anybody do a headcount?" she asked.

The man said, "Six hundred, easy."

Quinn let the number settle.

"It's that song," the man said. "The local guy's been playing it."

"Quinn told them to save it for the encore," Sylvie said. She kissed her fingers and swatted Quinn's chin. "Make 'em wait, says the expert." She was fifty-five and looked younger than Quinn, her skin lasered smooth as a nectarine, her hair expensively sun-kissed. As she scanned the room, her shrewd eyes narrowed behind her sleek, urban eyeglasses. "Last time we were in Boston, forty-seven people showed up." She had to yell a bit over the milling crowd.

"Sometimes you get lucky," Quinn said.

"Fifty weeks on the road isn't luck," Sylvie said. "Here you go, sweetie." She handed a shirt to a girl who gave Quinn the eye through the purplish slats of her bangs. The Christian circuit wasn't always as vanilla-pudding as people thought.

"If fifty weeks on the road were luck," Quinn said, "I'd be living pretty large by now."

Sylvie regarded him thoughtfully. Over the past three years they'd spent enough time in each other's company to become friends, after a fashion. "I suppose this must be galling," she said, "to someone who's kicked around as long as you have."

Onstage the boys were orchestrating the altar call, exhorting the unsaved to make themselves known to Jesus. Nothing too fire-and-brimstone; it sounded more like an invitation to a backstage party. Sweat-beaded fans swirled stageward to be prayed over by faith coun-

selors who led them to rooms and corners for a teaching moment
and complimentary Bible. The idea was to get right with Jesus, then
fill out a decision card, which came in cartons of two hundred and
included checkoff boxes: *I commit,* et cetera; *I recommit,* et cetera;
I want more information on, et cetera; *I wish to receive Resurrection
Lane's weekly e-mail meditation.* This was the ministry portion of the
show, scheduled for certain preselected venues, the details of which
the boys spent many long hours finessing.

It was understood that Quinn skipped this part.

"Sometimes," Sylvie was saying, "I wonder if Doug and I got carried away bestowing the ol' work ethic. They do nothing but rehearse
and perform. And pray, of course. Pray pray pray."

"You make it sound like a *bad* thing."

"For your information," Sylvie snapped, "Doug and I are Unitar-
ians."

Quinn laughed. "You're kidding."

"They think cousin Zack walks on water. He came out of his first
rehab all Rock-of-Ages and they swallowed the whole enchilada." She
made change for a teenager wearing a JC ball cap. "I guess I should
be thankful they didn't stuff coke up their noses. Instead, they took
a big soft Jesus pill." She looked at him. "They tend to relax when
you're here, Quinn. *I* tend to relax when you're here. That's what I
really meant."

To the cowboy-shirt man, Sylvie said, "Can you hold the fort?"
as she urged Quinn into a nearby alcove. "My kids think everybody
means well," she said to him, her voice rising again over the gabbling
crowd. "They think nothing bad can happen, despite their cousin's
upstanding example. You've got kids, right?"

He didn't say yes, but he didn't say no, either. The band hadn't
heard about the boy's death—or, if they had, they hadn't connected
it to Quinn. He preferred things this way, though he experienced a
muted twinge, too distant to matter, wondering how he could have
known these boys and their mother this long and let so little of himself

escape. They regarded him much the way he'd regarded his teachers in grade school, who ceased to exist once they left the brightly lighted classroom.

"Even Brandon," she went on, "who should know better—twenty-one, *married,* an actual *grownup*—he's such a pie-in-the-sky little wisher. And why not? Everything's gone splendidly, thanks to good old Mom. But I'm afraid they might be under a false impression—a *completely* false impression—of the music business. Do you think they're under a false impression of the music business?"

"Brand-new Winnebago," Quinn said. "That's kind of a false impression."

Sylvie, who could be snappish about her money, said, "That's not what I meant."

"If you mean the guys who showed up in Providence," Quinn ventured, "the ones in the really obvious sunglasses? Then that's a different story." He slid her a look. "What are they offering?"

"Nothing interesting," Sylvie said. "Yet."

The main floor teemed with fans, some in tears, Bibles clutched to their chests. The place smelled, strangely, suddenly, of lilac. "Doug thinks I'm way over my head," Sylvie confessed. Her industrial-looking earrings winked as she moved. "My kids are jugheads when it comes to the business end. Zack's the only one who ever had an actual *job.* The drug addict who brought them to Jesus. How ironic is that?"

"Off the scale, I'd say, if you're really asking."

"I mean, how convenient is it to spread the One True Whatever when Momma's covering overhead?"

"Be my momma," Quinn said. "I could use the overhead."

He could always get her to laugh. "Oh, I'm just venting," she said. The house lights flashed. "Can I just say? These people"—she waved her hands in vague directions, indicating who-knew-what—"they *annoy* me. I miss decorating. This isn't my true milieu."

Sylvie's true milieu, Quinn gathered, was showing carpet samples to handsome women with frozen foreheads. Quinn's true milieu was his guitar, and it had never mattered much where or when he played it. But now—shepherding these shiny boys from town to town, these boys standing at the threshold of luck and fortune—an old, thin, discomfiting hope began vining through him, a hope that twenty-five years might be dropped into a slot called "Before." He'd thought himself done with all that hope.

"Everything is"—Sylvie's fingers fluttered—"*poised*. They're poised for something."

"I don't hold it against them."

"I didn't think you did. Why would I think that?" She adjusted her power-lunch eyeglasses. "This was a lark that got away from me, is what I'm saying. If I want to get off the train it's too late."

He saw now: she was scared. She charged back to the table and knocked a tower of fridge magnets into a box. "Five minutes, people!" She turned to Quinn and faced him squarely. "I didn't mean to imply that I can't handle myself. I can handle myself just fine."

Her mouth softened; she looked—briefly—her age, and Quinn realized why she confided in him. Astonishingly enough, if you were somebody like Sylvie—a human lightning bolt—then somebody like Quinn looked right in his skin.

The house lights flashed again, and Quinn worked his way back to the stage, accosted en route by the girl with purple bangs, who asked him to sign her CD, which Sylvie had packaged with a soft-focus photo of the boys at sunrise. Even Zack—older, thicker, with his beetled forehead and coke-pinked nose—looked freshly released from church. "I'm not in the band," Quinn told the girl, shouting to be heard. "I'm subbing for Zack."

"Oh," she said. "Now I get it."

Get what? His age-wrecked face? Up went the stage lights, the crowd noise, the amplified opening notes of the final set. With the crowd singing along, he tried not to care that he was only the sub, that the night's doting audience was not his. He absorbed the upswell of affection, the *whoop-whoop-whoop*s, the indecipherable chants, the baffling gestures of Christian approbation. He didn't mind the decision cards flaring from their waving hands. He didn't even mind their sweet, saved faces, as long as they asked him to play.

By two o'clock they were homeward bound, Brandon at the wheel, the interstate flickering with moonlight. In the cushy cabin, tiny lights revealed earnest puddles of activity: the Jays played a sluggish round of Hearts, and Tyler, parked in a bolted-down armchair, had been thoroughly hijacked by a moldering copy of *Carrie*.

As they passed the Wells exit, Quinn realized he'd missed his Friday shift without alerting Dawna, his sprightly team captain. "Shit," he muttered. "God*damn* it."

"Language," said one of the Jays. He laid down his cards. "Something wrong, Pops?"

"I disappointed someone."

"Not us," he said. "You rocked the house."

Quinn hoped this was the beginning of a larger, more fruitful conversation about how, exactly, he'd rocked the house in a manner heretofore untried by Cousin Cokehead. He'd been waiting for just such an opening—had planned to make his case, plain and simple—but the boys fell silent, except for Brandon, who was rehearsing his part in one of their new songs, his crystalline tenor burning with conviction. These kids did not consort with irony; even so, Quinn couldn't help imagining himself as a fixture here: resident heathen.

The boys were out past their bedtime, having finished loading up around one. No one had mentioned Zack since Tuesday, though there had been a few furtive phone calls after Sylvie took off in her Miata and left Quinn in charge of packing up. If he was reading between the lines correctly, Resurrection Lane was about to become one man short. Permanently. "What're you laughing at?" asked Tyler, looking up from his book.

"The spin of the wheel," Quinn said enigmatically.

"There's no spin of the wheel," Tyler said. "There's only the unfathomable intentions of the Lord." He grinned; they knew what they sounded like but couldn't help it.

A giddy chorus of amens followed. The boys were sleepless and junk-food punchy; yet, being young and resilient, they gave off the sheen of freshly washed apples.

"Does the Lord unfathomably intend for you to sign a contract with the dudes from the other night?" Quinn asked.

The boys went silent; clearly Sylvie had ordered them to keep their mouths shut.

"We're praying about it," Brandon let slip.

How had these boys, these *children,* cracked open a door that Quinn had body-slammed so often, so uselessly? All those years, all those bands, all those almosts, all that old, unslaked thirst.

He let a few miles intervene, then got up and made his way to the front, where Brandon kept his hands on the wheel at a precise ten o'clock/two o'clock position. He had the face of an archangel and a wife who taught second grade.

"So. Okay," Quinn said, buckling up. "I had a great time."

"Have guitar will travel," Brandon said.

"Right," Quinn said. "But what I'm saying. If your man doesn't come back."

"He'll be back," Brandon said. "He always comes back."

"Right. But if he doesn't." Quinn turned to address everyone, feeling the hot possibility of a burning bridge at his back. "I'm just saying. I've never missed a gig." He'd gigged with the flu, with a broken ankle, with an eye-gouging hangover, with a new baby at home who cried for seven hours at a crack. He'd never even shown up late.

They had calm eyes, these boys; calm blue eyes full of sincerity, a compassion born of material ease. They'd grown up in sunny houses brimming with toys and now they had a minor hit being played on the radio, industry types nosing around, family money older than Moses. He was thinking: managed tours, main-stage concerts, civic centers, and symphony halls. He was thinking: *Belle, I made it. Here's your half.*

Quinn's head pounded with panic. "You guys don't think that maybe your man isn't totally committed to, uh, walking the lane?" He could feel all those calm eyes and felt clumsily exposed.

"He's family," Brandon said. That was that.

When they pulled up in front of Quinn's building the night was late and still. Brandon hopped out to set Quinn's amp on the sidewalk, and for a stinging second Quinn felt like a veiny old man. The neighborhood looked bereft at this hour: apartment buildings dark and silent, cars bumpered along the street and abandoned till morning. You could see the bridge from here, and a sliver of the bay, but nobody ever thought to call this a view.

"You know you're our man, Pops," Brandon said. His summery eyes didn't waver. "The man we count on." It was then Quinn noticed the others watching him from the rig, and he wondered if his son would in time have looked at him this way.

He waited for them to drive off, then hauled his stuff upstairs. Certain women found the place charming, though he'd suspended his desires in the wake of Belle's bereavement and his own confused misery. In the bedroom he had a double bed, monkishly made up, and wooden shelves burdened with books and music. On the eye-level shelf he'd placed the photograph of the boy.

A memory came winding back, Quinn returning home to find the baby lying awake and staring through the moonlit bars of his crib. He recalled the shimmering nighttime room, the baby lying silent, and his own sudden need to play his childhood guitar, a gift from his own mother, which he'd stored as a slender hope beneath the baby's crib. He sat close and played as softly as he was able, singing a lullaby his mother had sung to him, aware of the baby's lunar gaze, fixed first on the shiny guitar, then on Quinn, as if he understood where music really came from. Quinn felt touched by birds as the baby fell finally asleep, but whenever again he tried to play for his son, the baby flinched and clenched and whimpered, until their midnight moment came to feel like something he'd dreamed.

Propped in a corner of his bedroom now stood the same guitar, the soundboard scarred from hard use. He kept it the way you keep an ailing dog, out of sentiment and gratitude. He brought it to his bed and tuned it to an open G, breathing easier, trying to shed his awful thirst. In the morning he would fill Ona's bird feeders and mow her lawn; later, he would bring half his week's take to Belle. He closed his eyes in gratitude for these obligations, however small.

The night drained away. Quinn played softly, head bent close to the soundboard, and entered a state of grace that could be called—loosely, generously—prayer. At dawn he lay back against his pillow and fell asleep with the guitar in his arms.

* * *

This is Miss Ona Vitkus. This is her life memories and shards on tape. This is Part Four.

. . .

War? Again?

. . .

That's true. Those other children in your class, they'll be interviewing grannies who recall only the second one. Maybe not even that one. You'll have the oldest interviewee by a good forty years.

. . .

I wouldn't be the *least* surprised if Mr. Linkman awarded extra credit.

. . .

We didn't call it World War I. How could we imagine there'd be a second?

. . .

Well, I was here.

. . .

What, did you think I went overseas in a helmet? I was right here in Portland, Maine, working ten hours a day in a typing pool and living with three ninnies in a freezing apartment.

. . .

Elm Street. Which actually had an elm, a real beaut, right in front of my building. Six months after the Armistice, Howard spotted me on my way back home from my neighbor's sister's house near the park. I'd gone over there to hear a record on their new gramophone.

. . .

Oh, but the elms were still alive back then. Portland was loaded with elms. You never saw such trees. It was springtime. May. The war was over and the Spanish flu, too, which took five girls at the insurance company where I worked. They shut us down for two weeks in November, and it was hard to get warm because the movie houses closed, too. Dance halls, churches, everything shut up tight. And in the meantime all those shocked-up boys coming back by the busload, some of them missing arms and legs. By May, the entire city was ready to wake up after a frightful dream. And here was Howard Stanhope, the courtly widower I'd known as a child, calling my name through the springtime.

. . .

It's an old-fashioned phonograph. A record player. The first song I ever heard was "The Star-Spangled Banner" sung by Margaret Woodrow Wilson, the president's daughter.

. . .

Good Lord, no, it was terrible. That poor girl sang like a strangulated mosquito.

. . .

I couldn't. I'm not good at this kind of thing.

. . .

Oh, I don't know: *meeeem meeeem meeeem,* like that. Kind of like that.

. . .

Don't laugh, she couldn't help it. Oh, now you've got me doing it!

. . .

Yes, so there was Howard on the corner of Elm and Congress, flagging me down in his gentleman's voice. "Miss Vitkus, is it not?" he calls to me. You know the type? Mr. Charming?

. . .

Well, I *was.* I was *delighted* to be recognized. By someone from home, especially. Last I knew he was running a music store on Mercantile Street in Kimball. Oh, the times were so bad. I was nineteen years old, a grown woman, but I think I was still waiting for Maud-Lucy to come back for me. And now here was this hat tipper who remembered my name. I was a dunderhead who mistook my own delight for love.

. . .

Here's the World War I part: Howard exceeded the draft age by a considerable amount — closing in on thirty-nine years old — but he'd signed on as an ambulance driver when everybody else was applying for deferments. I'll give him that. He came back ruined, but his particular ruin didn't show in the usual ways.

. . .

For starters, his hearing was conked out on one side and he had to listen close, so people mistakenly thought he'd come back from France just dying to reconnect with his fellow man. He looked and acted perfectly normal, a salesman with immaculate manners.

. . .

Stanhope Music Company. He'd sold his Kimball store to go to war and after that moved to Portland to take over his father's store of the same name. It was over on Forest Avenue. I went to work for him, just as the first Mrs. Stanhope did back in Kimball. Eight months later, in an unforgivable failure of imagination, I married him.

. . .

Because I was lonely, I suppose.

. . .

Well, thank you. It did seem like a perfectly good reason at the time. Our house on Woodford is still there. Somebody turned it into a place where they lard you with seaweed to make your skin look young.

. . .

Of course it doesn't work. Nothing works. There isn't a magic trick on earth that could restore my youth and beauty.

. . .

How kind. You tell your parents they raised a polite young fellow.

. . .

Your mother, then. Where was I? Howard. I didn't know how war-wrecked he was until it was too late. You should tell your Mr. Linkman that the women got shocked up, too. You should ask some of these young wives right now, in this idiotic war going on right this minute in a country most of us can't find on a map, all these poor men—and women, too, imagine that, women with babies at home!—dragging back to America all wrecked up with the things they've seen and done.

. . .

I didn't mean you. I've no doubt you can point out Iraq on a map. Oh, let's not talk about war. For a lot of people war isn't a topic, it's a stone on their heart. Did you know I cast my first vote in 1920?

. . .

Exactly, the first year women were allowed. You certainly know your historical dates. Oh, I told you another fib. I did cast a vote, but it wasn't official.

. . .

Because I was two months shy of twenty-one on voting day. That whole fall, Howard was getting recordings into the store—two a month, one from the Democrat and one from the Republican. Two dollars each, for a three-minute speech. Howard made his Republican customers buy theirs, but you could hear the Democrat for free. People came in by the dozens to listen to Governor Cox. On purpose.

. . .

Same gobble-gobble as nowadays, about President Wilson's war saving civilization. I don't mean to make more of it than there was, but as Election Day got closer you could hardly get through the door.

. . .

Of course not! Howard wouldn't let me near that gramophone! My job was to provide cider and cookies, but secretly I was planning my vote.

. . .

Because it happened that one of our customers was in the same boat as me, another January birthday. Jane, her name was. Jane Baxter. The Baxters lived in a handsome house in the West End; this was way before landlords began chopping those beauties up. Mrs. Baxter came to the store once a week for her sheet music—she played the viola—and if I was tending the counter we'd chat.

. . .

Heavens, no, Jane was far too rich to be my friend. A different class of woman altogether. She wore diamond studs, a gift from her handsome husband. She was planning a practice election in her house for twenty-year-old women too young to make the vote. Twelve noon until one o'clock, results revealed at the stroke of one fifteen. She invited me.

. . .

You bet I did! I got to Neal Street at twelve sharp on voting day and the place was brimming with women. All those fresh, polished rooms, with feathery masks from Africa hanging all over the walls. We had punch and cream puffs, and Jane's sister played a shined-up harp. The voting booth was at the back of the parlor, where we marked our sample ballots.

. . .

I don't recall. It didn't matter, not to me, whether they resembled real ballots or not. I filled one up and put it into a decorated box. Jane's sister tallied the votes and recorded them in the exact kind of ledger we used at the store. The suspense was delicious. There were a lot of suffragette types, as you might imagine. Mr. Baxter was no-where to be seen.

. . .

A lady who agitates to get the vote. They went around the country making speeches. Some were a bit on the mannish side, to be honest. Sometimes people threw things at them.

. . .

Oh, yes, and some got hauled off to jail just for speaking their mind. But there were plenty of other types there, too, mousy little ladies like me with babies on the way.

. . .

Twenty-seven women in all. I didn't know a single one of them save for Jane. We sipped our punch, we predicted which man would win, we joked about putting Jane's sister on the ballot. There was so much laughter, so refreshing. Jane's other sister, who was thirty, came over before the final tally and spoke for fifteen minutes on what it was like to vote for real.

. . .

Oh, it was thrilling. But by the time I got back home I'd fallen into a gloom.

. . .

Well, I'll just tell you: I had no friends. Not Jane Baxter, not anybody.

. . .

Now, that's a shame. A boy your age shouldn't know how that feels. I had it easier than you, because Randall was born a month later, and you forget about friendship when you're raising babies and running a store and keeping your husband from stabbing the furniture with a carving knife over his failure to publish his lamentable songs.

. . .

Howard asked me the same thing, so I told him: Eugene Debs. "A Socialist?" he said. He couldn't believe it. Like this, all pop-eyed: "My wife voted for a *Socialist?*"

. . .

I know. My vote didn't count. That's how Howard looked at it. But secretly, I fancied that Mr. Debs might find out, through friends and associates of the Baxters, that an underage lady voter on Woodford Street wanted him to be president.

. . .

The next time? I had two babies by then and voted for Mr. Robert La Follette, and this time it counted.

. . .

Oh, goodness, Howard was beside himself. "Another Socialist?" he said. "He's not a Socialist," I told him right back, "he's a Progressive." Poor Howard was spitting out his oatmeal. "Why, Ona? For God's sake, why?"

. . .

Because I could. That's why. I was a married woman who owned nothing. Not even my clothes. But I owned my vote, didn't I? Why wouldn't I vote for the Socialist? Sometimes I can't believe how long I lived with that stingy, suspicious, sad, sad man.

. . .

Twenty-eight years. A blot of time, really. I got another twenty years after that at Lester Academy, sitting at my rolltop desk outside Dr. Valentine's office, feeling every minute as if something pizzazzy was just about to happen.

. . .

No, not really. I typed and filed all day long. But it's the *feeling* I loved—that feeling of expectation.

. . .

I suppose it was, a little. A little like going for a record. And after that, *zing bang*, another twenty years as a retiree. They zipped right by, too. Then twenty more, as the old crab. And now—

. . .

Oh. Well, thank you. But my point: I might have another twenty in me. And here I thought I'd lost all my fight.

. . .

You betcha, my steadfast little fellow. We'll get that Frenchwoman's goat yet.

. . .

Oh, all right: *meeeem meeeem meeeem*.

Chapter 12

Ona watched from the window as Quinn dispatched his duties, ending with a hose-down of the front walk, his T-shirt puckering with sweat. He had excellent forearms and muscular hands, probably a side effect of playing guitar all his life. When he sauntered into the house and took a brownie without asking, she realized how long it had been since someone paid her the compliment of presumption.

Another word dropped from the ether: *sūnus*. Meeting the father had put her in mind of sons.

She gave him some milk and looked him over. "Your hair wants cutting," she said, intending to sound affectionate, but her voice contained the static of old age and blandishments came out like everything else: inverted. She was a walking opposite.

He laughed. "Haircuts cost money, Ona, and you've been fleecing me blind for weeks."

Had it been weeks? Really? He'd put up her screen doors, taken down her storm windows, reseeded the dregs of a lawn that had once filled her with pride. She'd been out there herself in these suddenly bright days, weeding around the rhodies and reviving a dormant yen for physical exertion, resuming her daily, now halting, walk down the street. The neighborhood looked verdant, changed, almost foreign, as if she—or it—were returning from a very long trip.

"Wow, have you ever been holding out," he said, popping the rest of a second brownie into his mouth. He ate like Frankie, as if he'd never had a meal. And he had Frankie's eyelashes, long and wet-looking.

"The secret ingredient is crushed walnuts," she informed him. "I'll make another batch for you next Saturday."

He halted mid-bite. "Ona. Today's my last day."

"Oh." Everything stopped. "I'll be darned. Are you sure?"

"Seven weeks. This is week seven."

"I must have lost track," Ona said. The fact of his leaving began to thud painfully, like a heartbeat, a tender spot heretofore unrevealed. "I suppose I should have been counting."

He picked up her playing cards, which was not allowed. "How about one for the road?" he asked.

She snatched them away lest he discover the stacked aces for Invisible Vision, a trick that depended on a digital dexterity he could only dream of, he of the long, lovely, guitar-playing fingers. The trick had returned to her during the news one night, a keenly recalled set of instructions. It was worth something, this trick. Five dollars was a bargain.

He waited her out. Presuming. Expecting a trick for free. Then he smiled again, a shock of a smile that made her wonder about the ninety-nine-point-nine-nine-nine-nine percent of his life that did not take place here on Saturday mornings. Asking for a trick today was a kindness, she realized; a kindness to a creaky old woman who would miss him. He had never insulted her with pity; not once, until now.

"Five bucks," she said.

"No can do."

"Were you dissatisfied with the previous tricks?" she asked. "Did I not provide the suspense and satisfaction for which you willingly paid?"

"Seriously, Ona. I'm out of fives."

"Maybe if you didn't drink so much you'd have enough left over for entertainment."

He laughed out loud, and she had to laugh, too, because she knew he didn't drink, and that once he had. Her rejoinder recalled an earlier stage of their friendship; it acknowledged the subtle trajectory of their brief acquaintance; it implied a road that had rippled and dipped and wound up here, now. She had not trusted him; now she did.

"Are you actually going to refuse me a trick?" he asked.

And Louise: she'd done hundreds of tricks for Louise, especially in her last lucid days. Beautiful, dying Louise. From the cloudless anywhere dropped another word: *draugas*.

Friend. She might as well admit it: her heart was breaking.

"What?" Quinn said.

Her body went hot—like a hot flash, really. She felt fifty again. "Pick a card," she said. She snatched the ace of spades from his hands, jammed it back into the deck, then reached behind him to pluck a card from his collar. "Is this your card?"

"You know it is."

"If you're going to go, Quinn, you might as well go." She crossed her arms. "*Iki*," she said.

"Is that goodbye?"

She nodded, her eyes stinging. "Don't ask me how I know. Because I don't."

How could she blame him for leaving? The difficulty of the parent completing tasks begun by the child was not lost on her. When Frankie was killed she'd been the one to close his modest bank account, to give away his books and guitar, to inform the college in which he had been enrolled that he would now be deferred for all eternity.

Parents outlived their children sometimes; this was a fact. But the boy hadn't been at war, like Frankie; or, like Randall, a cancer victim in late middle age; he was just a Boy Scout doing who-knows-what at five o'clock in the morning. Why had she allowed herself the modest pleasure of falling for him, even a little? She'd entered her second century believing she was through with death, not counting her own.

And why not? What, really, were the chances? The boy was *eleven*. She had ninety-three years on him. But the boy was gone for good, and so, now, would the father be. The father, in whose company she had come to feel the living presence of sons. His son, and hers.

Quinn rose to leave. "I'll call you sometime, Ona," he said. "See what you're up to."

"Nothing too interesting, but I appreciate the gesture."

"You knew it was seven weeks, right? That was the commitment?"

"I did indeed," she said. "I lost count, is all."

"I work weekends, Ona. I go to bed at three." He looked suddenly stricken, like a man who'd left a kitten by the roadside. "I mean, I couldn't keep this up indefinitely."

"You did fine." She patted his hand. "Could you get that saucepan down for me, as long as you're here?" She pointed to the top cupboard. She would make a soup today; she would drive herself to the supermarket with her fraudulent license and buy some vegetables and chicken thighs and make a soup to fill the afternoon hours and after three or four days throw half of it out.

"Your wish is my command," he said.

My wish, she thought. *What is my wish?*

He set the pot on the counter. Then his face went still, focused on something behind her. She turned to find a slight and spiritless woman standing on her porch. Even through the mist of the screen Ona knew exactly who she was. In an unexpected burst of solidarity, Ona hurried to the door.

"Up with the birds, I see," the mother said to Quinn.

"I was," Quinn said, "if owls count."

In the mother, the trace of a smile: her expression held so many competing emotions that Ona had to avert her eyes. For Quinn's part, he regarded his ex-wife with a tenderness that gave Ona to believe all would be put to rights.

Ona said, "How do you do?"

"How do I—?" Her hair wanted washing. "Oh. Awful. But thanks."

"I'm so sorry for your loss," Ona said. The door was open, but the mother—Belle, that was her name, Belle—stayed put. She appeared to have forgotten where she was.

"Your boy was my best one," Ona offered. "So punctual. I enjoyed his company very much."

"He was wonderful company," she agreed. She had the boy's wide, oceanic eyes. "A lot of people didn't understand that."

Ona checked the driveway and wondered how the poor thing had managed to operate her vehicle, a jeeplike affair too big for her. She walked straight into the house and stood there—facing Ona as the boy had, awaiting instructions. Quinn she ignored.

Ona didn't like being stared at and couldn't think of a polite way to say so. "I'd have attended the service," she said, "but I didn't find out until after." She flicked a look at Quinn, who'd gone mute. "I felt very bad about that. Very bad indeed."

"It's all right. I don't know who was there and who wasn't." Belle plundered the deep purse and dug up an oversize manila envelope. "This came to my house. I assume it's for you."

It looked official. Ona took it with trepidation, for she'd learned from her parents to distrust official-looking things. But the envelope contained nothing more concerning than a record-breaker pack from the London headquarters of Guinness World Records. It had been opened already and appeared well thumbed.

"These people write to him all the time," Belle said. "I almost tossed it, but then I realized I was holding his final thoughts, in a way. His last preoccupation."

The mother moved on to the parlor, glancing around. "Quinn felt his presence here, did you know that?"

"I did not," Ona said, again glancing at Quinn, who was watching his ex-wife as if she were a maimed animal: heart-rending and dangerous.

"It was an amazingly un-Quinn thing to say. Blowing smoke, probably, trying to free himself from an interpersonal spider web. If there's one thing Quinn Porter hates, it's interpersonal spider webs."

"I'm standing right here, Belle," Quinn said.

Belle monitored the ceiling, as if expecting the boy to materialize out of a light fixture. "He's been giving me money. From anyone else, it would be insulting, but I know why he's doing it." She paused. "Quinn's a decent man with some broken parts."

Quinn said nothing. He was patient, it seemed; forbearing. She had never noticed this.

"He's been most helpful to me," Ona said.

Belle waited—a long while, it seemed. So Ona leafed through the Guinness forms just to hear a rustle of sound. Still, Belle waited, and Quinn watched her waiting.

Not knowing what else to do, Ona read the cover letter aloud, a handwritten missive from a "recorder" with the un-British name of Florence Wu. She'd taken a shine to the boy and troubled herself to explain to him exactly what his "elderly friend" had to do in order to make a run for the record of (a) Oldest Living Person, (b) Oldest Living Female, (c) Longest-Lived Person, or (d) Oldest Licensed Driver. Same in all cases: amass documents. *The docs,* she, too, called them, with the usual warnings and caveats about authentication and fakery.

Finishing, she blushed hotly. "This was just a bit of foolishness on my part," she said.

"He entered you in four categories," Belle said. "What are your chances?"

"I'm far too young for a, b, and c. As for my license, your boy prepared me quite well for the written test, but I have remaining concerns about the road test."

"Maybe you just need a refresher," Belle said.

"I don't have the proper docs. It was all pretend."

Her guests went quiet, so Ona again filled the breach by laying out the p's and q's of record making. She related the probable number versus the official number of supercentenarians worldwide; provided an oral précis of recent record holders; added all she knew about the obscenely long life of Madame Jeanne Louise Calment. Her voice took on an authority borrowed, to the subtlest inflection, from the boy. Her recitation seemed to calm the boy's mother—Belle, this strange animal in her house—and she herself felt calmer. How tranquilizing it was to arm yourself with information, how consoling to unpack the facts and then plant them like fence pickets, building a sturdy pen in which you stood alone, cosseted against human fallibility.

She missed him awfully.

"So," Belle said, "you're—what? Just floating in space? Nothing to prove you actually exist?" She made this sound magnificent.

"I have ample proof of my existence," Ona said. "Proving the duration of that existence is another matter." A whiffling drop in blood pressure went straight to her head; she preempted a dizzy spell by sitting down.

"Belle," Quinn said—certainly it was about time—"let me take you home."

"In what? A pony cart?"

"In your car. Then I'll take the bus back into town."

Belle either didn't hear him or chose to ignore him. "I guess you two were in cahoots," she said to Ona. Again, a trace of a smile. "He had your age calculated to the day—he talked about you incessantly—but I didn't realize what he was up to. I'd been trying to ease him away from world records and onto something a little more productive." She glanced at Quinn. "Scouts. Music."

Quinn kept still. Biding, Ona thought. Biding struck her as a handsome quality in a man.

"I may have instructed him to keep it under his hat," Ona admitted. "And I don't relish being found out now."

She wondered, not for the first time, what had happened to the tape recorder. She'd confided such private things, and now they existed someplace, possibly in a secret sleeve of the boy's backpack, undiscovered. Perhaps undiscoverable, that earthly link between herself and the boy. She didn't know how to ask without exposing herself. She stood up slowly, blood tossing in her head.

"My son loved secrets," Belle said. "Surprise-party-type secrets, not deep dark ones." Quinn had slid his arm lightly across Belle's shoulders, but she seemed unaware of him.

"This was the surprise-party type," Ona told her. "Of interest to no one but a blundery old hen." She stuffed the record-breaker kit back into its envelope.

"Belle," Quinn said, "why don't I—"

"Surely you have a birth certificate," Belle said.

"Not at hand."

"What does that mean?"

"My birth certificate," Ona said, "is in the possession of somebody I haven't seen in a very long time. That's all I care to reveal about the matter."

Belle tapped the envelope, which Ona held crushed to her chest, as if the envelope were the boy, whom she had never hugged in real life. "I'd like to see you get in the record book," Belle said. She turned to Quinn. "I'd really, really like to see that happen."

Ona felt caught, thoroughly discombobulated: exposed as a goosy girl in her own house!

"Can't you ask the person who has your birth certificate—?"

"Belle," Quinn said quietly, "I think she prefers not to say."

Belle seemed to come to herself then—or whatever facsimile of herself she could muster. "I'm sorry. I'm just—I'm just dreaming. I don't know what I'm doing." She took Ona's hand and squeezed. "My son liked you, Miss Vitkus. He liked people who paid good attention. Thank you for your good attention. That's really all I came to say."

And then she was gone, Quinn walking her to her too-high vehicle, where they exchanged some tender, indecipherable words. Then she got into her car and drove away.

"My goodness," Ona said when Quinn returned. "I don't believe that poor thing is fully buttoned."

"That's not her. She's still in shock."

"Someone should be watching her."

"Someone is." His face—like Frankie's, easy to read—showed a flood of love and shame.

Quinn looked around. "Anything else? As long as I'm here?" He was in a hurry now. She felt like her little-girl self waving to Maud-Lucy Stokes from a train platform.

"I have something for you, Quinn," she said. "I was saving it for your last day, which I didn't realize was so hard upon us." She opened a drawer and handed him a small, well-preserved phonograph cylinder she'd found in a box of oddments during the fruitless hunt for her birth certificate.

"'Some of These Days' by Sophie Tucker," Quinn read from the label. "'Nineteen eleven.' What is this, a recording?"

"I suppose you'd need an Edison machine to play it." She saw her mistake: she'd given a musician music that couldn't be heard.

But he was smiling, lifting the cylinder from its case. The cloudy trail left by the boy's grief-shocked mother lifted a bit as he admired the strange old thing. Even to Ona it looked strange, and she had a vivid, momentary sensation of being back in Maud-Lucy Stokes's third-floor apartment: whatever Quinn washed his hair with smelled like Maud-Lucy's starched doilies.

"This is great, Ona. And what's this, the sheet music?" he asked, removing a discolored paper sleeve that had been curled inside the case. "'Hiding Place' by Howard J. Stanhope?"

"What," Ona said, "let me see," but he was right, it was one of Howard's seventy-five-year-old song sheets. How it had wound up in her things she couldn't guess; maybe Howard had stashed it there in the hope she'd come across it one day and miss him. She did miss him, oddly enough, in the generalized way she missed her whole life.

"Howard's flaming ambition was to get into Tin Pan Alley," she told him. "But he was a dreadful songwriter."

"Ambition like that can kill a man," Quinn said, then hummed the opening bars, puzzling out the melody.

"You can read off a sheet?"

"A little credit, please."

Maud-Lucy had been a marvelous sight reader, and Howard, too; but she had never met another one. She'd enjoyed Quinn's stories of the road. He'd spent the week with the religious fellows, which had struck her as an odd match until he admitted what they paid; this week he was going off with them again. His stories reminded her of trailing Maud-Lucy to the Kimball Opera House to hear tales of the Congolese jungle or the Wild West, a world apart.

"You can't imagine how much money Howard burned through," she said, "on all manner of scalawags who promised to make him rich."

"I guess some things don't change." He flashed her a self-deprecating grin. This was how their friendship had progressed, in increments measured in twitches.

He faltered his way through the song, which Ona remembered as a silly thing about making up with the Lord over a bottle of whiskey—a product of Howard's religious phase, after Frankie died and before she left. How many times had she sat in that ruffled green chair on Woodford Street, listening to Howard's flat, Protestant voice, all the while dying to tune in Jimmy Durante on their tabletop Crosley?

"Howard was a teetotaler," she told Quinn. "Prohibition had absolutely no effect on us."

Quinn was still humming. "Honestly, Ona, it's not bad."

"Those religious fellows of yours might like it," she said. "Those boys on the brink."

"Maybe," he said. He hummed a few more bars. "I'm hearing it with a music-hall vibe."

Ona didn't know what a *vibe* was, exactly, but the word recalled the quivering boxes of unsold song sheets delivered by truck to the Woodford Street house. Poor Howard, with his grand delusions. Then it struck her: she'd given Quinn the cylinder to make herself appear musical.

"I hope you're not planning to let those boys save you," she said.

He looked up slyly. "Not in the way they think."

"Oho," she said. "Something up your sleeve."

He shrugged. "You get a big enough audience, it doesn't matter if you're praising God or the devil."

"The Lord and I worked out our differences over time. But I think I like you better in league with the devil."

"I'm about as devilish as an actuary, Ona," he said. "It's work, that's all. Work I love."

"That's a handsome thing indeed," she assured him.

He added quietly, "You want to think your choices were worth something." He resleeved the music sheet and put out his hand. "I've enjoyed knowing you, Ona."

"You know nothing about me," she informed him. "I told you nothing."

"You'd be surprised how well I read between the lines."

All at once, she felt seen, and she forgave him for leaving.

Then, a cheerful rooty-toot from the driveway, where the scoutmaster was pulling up in his gray van. "Hello, Mrs. Vitkus!" he called, getting out. "Sorry we're late!"

Handsome, hale, well intended, he strode up the walk, towing a boy—a boy of the same age as the previous one—who wore an ill-fitted outfit with a single badge. This boy did not have round, serious, dove-gray eyes. This boy did not have wrists the size of stripped twigs. This boy did not say, "It's a pleasure to meet you," like the romantic lead in a movie from the forties.

This boy, in fact, remained mute—as did Ona—as the two men eyed each other.

"Just finishing the job, Ted," Quinn said. "To the letter."

"That's what I heard."

The young Scout swiveled his head from one man to the other.

"I wasn't expecting a new boy," Ona said.

"We didn't want to leave you in the lurch, Mrs. Vitkus," said the scoutmaster. His uniform was cleanly pressed despite the wilting heat. "This is Noah."

The new boy mumbled something unintelligible. Oh, he would not do. He'd prove dull, or sullen, or allergic to work. In any case, she wanted them both gone, these twin pillars of the community in their tan shirts. Besides, if she were to get another boy, she'd want a Sunday boy. Or a Tuesday boy. She did not want another Saturday boy.

"You're a week early, Ted," Quinn said.

The scoutmaster dug for the same gizmo he'd used last time. "Let's see," he said, stabbing a tiny screen. "Nope. Here it is. Right here." He had a nice-looking, earnest, trustworthy face.

"There were seven weeks left to go," Quinn said, "and this is week seven."

So many, many weeks now gone: the son's winter-spring Saturdays, the father's spring-summer ones. All of a piece, an ongoing beginning, until today: the end.

The mention of the boy, however oblique, deepened the pall over the little crowd on the porch. The new Scout withdrew into the scoutmaster's treelike shadow, betraying a vacant discomfort. Oh, he wouldn't do at all.

"Next week it is, then," the scoutmaster said, snapping shut his calendar. "This is Noah, by the way. I guess I already said that."

As the visitors hupped back to the van, a whining note emanated from the smaller one, who clearly found his charity assignment unequal to his expectations. Did he think she'd killed the boy herself? She felt once again like the crone in the dead-end house.

"Apparently the sainted scoutmaster can't tell time," Quinn said. "Did I mention he's got a thing for my ex-wife?"

"You most certainly did not."

"She's probably in love with him."

"Oh, my."

"Devoted single father. Wife died. A hard guy to hate, in other words, but I seem to be able to manage it."

"Well, he's prepared," Ona said. "And kind and obedient, if you like that sort of thing."

Quinn laughed, the spell broke, and their goodbye arrived at last. He gathered up the cylinder, his musical gift, and put out his hand. She accepted it, hanging on, then letting go.

"The place has never looked better, Quinn," she told him. "Thanks for your—for your good attention."

"My pleasure." He trotted down the steps.

"*Ir man malonu,*" she said.

He turned abruptly. "What was that?"

"I think it means 'My pleasure.'"

Poised on the bottom step, his present tucked under his arm, his cheeks suddenly pinked up like a girl's—like the boy's, come to think. Was it too much to hope that he was sorry to quit her? Behind him, the hosed-down walk still glittered with spray, reflecting dime-size bits of sky. Before she could stop herself, she blurted, "I need a ride to Vermont, Quinn. To Granyard, Vermont."

He regarded her for a long moment. "Who's in Vermont?"

"My son," she said. She waved away his next question. "My first son. I was practically a baby myself." She hesitated. "I told your boy. I suppose it's not a secret anymore."

And so she told the father what she had told the son. Not all of it. Most of it. The father took it in, his eyes dark and warm, with those Frankie lashes.

"You'll have to wait a week," he said. "I'm booked with the God Squad." He fiddled his calendar out of his pocket and she felt a little wing lift of delight.

"A week will be fine."

"And we'll have to take your car."

"It's a good car, Quinn. Not a speck of rust. Twenty-five thousand miles on the odometer."

"Maybe I can give you a driving refresher en route," he said. "As long as you're going for it."

"I'm a menace on the highway. With an expired license to boot."

"That never stopped me," he said, and as she watched the father smile, she caught another bewitching way in which the son might have come to resemble him.

TRAVEL

1. Longest backward walk. 8,000 miles. Plennie Wingo. Country of USA.
2. Largest pedal-powered vehicle. 82 riders. Country of Sweden.
3. Longest car trip. 383,609 miles. Emil and Liliana Schmid. Country of Switzerland.
4. Fastest bathtub racer. Greg Mutton. 36 miles in 1 hour and 22 minutes and 27 seconds. Country of Australia.
5. Largest parade of BMW cars. 107. Country of Netherlands.
6. Fastest time nonelectric window opened by dog. 11.34 seconds. Striker. Country of USA.
7. Highest limousine. 10 feet and 11 inches. Country of USA.
8. Greatest speed achieved on motorized sofa. 87 miles per hour. Edd China. Country of UK.
9. Heaviest car balanced on head. 352 pounds. John Evans. Country of UK.
10. Oldest licensed driver. Fred Hale. Age 108. Country of USA.

PART THREE

Kelione (Journey)

Chapter 13

Ona woke on departure day with a terrible word in her head: *mirtis*. What if Laurentas was dead?

She shook the word away. Surely Laurentas was alive and thriving, enjoying life at the address crumpled into her purse; he had to be. She envisioned the day ahead with a fervor borrowed from the boy, with whom she shared a stake in its outcome. This journey was for him, and so: Laurentas had to be alive.

In her hasty preparations for the trip, however, she kept forgetting its purpose. Travel became an end in itself: the novelty of it, the pleasure. She had her hair done for the first time in twenty-five years by a girl who stiffened Ona's white wisps into a lacquered helmet costing too much money that she didn't mind paying. All week she'd felt young and impulsive, telling Louise in her head: *I'm taking to the road with a slipshod musician*.

An odyssey, after all, composed her first conscious memories, recalled in bright, unrelated glints: An exhausted horse being shot for food. A Gypsy offering peaches from a sack. Clouds of dust the color of pulverized roses. She recalled mashing her face into her father's neck, her mother's tears dampening the pages of a contraband book written in the forbidden Latin alphabet. They walked and walked, missing their bloom-heavy dooryard, their chickens and cherry trees, their dearest farm that would be burned a decade later by the Germans, an outrage recorded in a letter from Uncle Bronys, the envelope marked with a black cross: death in the family.

Despite the dust and misgiving, there existed on that journey an air of moving *toward*. Toward what, it hardly mattered. Ona had been born on the twentieth day of the twentieth century, a good omen to her superstitious Catholic parents. They chose a country that embraced progress as a sacrament. Aldona bribed a border guard, claiming her sick child needed a special type of doctor, a story deliberately elaborate and confusing, Ona wailing on cue. The guard—a rangy teenager—waved them through, a seemingly desperate woman dragging a small girl and a few days' worth of supplies. Over the border they went, Jurgis secretly entombed beneath the planks of a donkey cart. They reached a city, finally, and a ship, and made the perilous crossing with the words *Kimball, Maine* pinned to their coats.

This was their story, pieced together from the tatters of their English, but only now did it feel to Ona like a lived experience. She recalled a lot of coughing, an uneven horizon, a piece of cheese with star prints of mold that her mother nibbled clean before offering little Ona the rest. And long, fretful conversations between her parents, who disdained their cohorts sardined into clammy, flea-ridden quarters. They murmured their dread of losing their papers, their hatred for the Russian army, their relief at having made it this far without detention.

In dropped another jewel, an uncut sentence: *Dievas davė dantis, Dievas duos duonos.* God gave us teeth, God will give us bread.

She must once have known her mother tongue, to recall these things with such urgency. Ona had no use for irony, but she nonetheless found it cruel that her parents fled in part because the Russians tried to take their ancestral voice. She wondered if their language bided somewhere secret in her body, not the chips and bits that had recently dropped from nowhere but a fully formed fluency that might yet erupt at a moment of willing surrender.

In her life so far, such a moment had not presented itself.

Quinn arrived exactly on time. "Rise and shine," he called, the screen door banging behind him.

"I rose four hours ago," she said. "The shining I shall leave to younger persons."

"Ona, you look shiny as a new tuning peg. Look at that hair."

"I could go to war with this hair," she said. "It cost me forty dollars."

His cheeks were all pinked up. Travel agreed with him, and she might have known: people like Quinn, always running from themselves, loved the road. He took her things and escorted her to the car. He'd made such a fuss about its vintage, its "legs," owing, she felt privately bigheaded to hear, to her habit of starting it up twice a week for grocery shopping. Quinn helped her into the passenger side, cupping her elbow with his long fingers, provoking in her a paradox of helplessness and vigor.

She smoothed her slacks across her thighs as Quinn jaunted to the other side and took the wheel. She expected a leadfoot type who'd make the drive in record time (she wondered what the record actually was), but he proceeded with stupendous caution, bypassing the most obvious highway entrance and making a sudden turn into a neighborhood of well-kept houses.

"Where the heck are we going?" Ona asked.

"On a rescue mission," Quinn said. "Damsel in distress." He pulled up to a white Cape two blocks off Washington Avenue. With a jolt of dismay, Ona realized where they were.

"We're taking an unbuttoned mother on a road trip?"

"She asked to come," Quinn said. "You have no idea what a relief it is to grant her a wish."

Belle came out of the house, carrying a stuffed satchel. Another woman bounded after her.

"Uh-oh," Quinn muttered.

Unlike Belle, the second woman was dark-haired and sturdily built. From a distance she bore the same untouched, untouchable quality Ona remembered in the girls from Henneford Academy, Lester's sister school, but closer up the façade melted off. She was grieving: taut and haunted.

"May I please speak to you, please?" the brunette asked Quinn.

As Quinn got out of the car, Belle slipped into the driver's seat.

"Belle—"

"I'm taking the wheel," she said to him. "You're a terrible driver." The skin beneath her eyes was purpled with fatigue; it had been nearly three months by Ona's count, too long to last without measurable sleep, though she herself had done the same after Frankie.

Quinn studied her for a moment as the brunette glowered at the lot of them. "All right," he said to Belle, then turned to the brunette, who began to berate him in a stage whisper.

Belle tossed her bag into the back seat, where it merged almost conjugally with Quinn's duffel. Ona patted her stiff, see-through hair. "May I ask?"

"I told Quinn he couldn't do this alone."

Ona bristled. "I don't require a nurse."

"I wasn't planning to nurse you," Belle said. "I was planning to get the hell out of town." Her eyes brimmed. "You don't know how badly I want to jump out of my skin."

But Ona did know. After Frankie, it would have been a balm of the first order to simply get into a car and *go*. She tried to swallow her consternation. She did not want to be one of those old people who detest change—Louise had warned her against this very thing. But she couldn't help reeling with disappointment. Last night she'd worked her balky faucets to fill the tub high and spritzed the water with almond oil. This morning she'd dabbed perfume behind her ears. She hadn't counted on being the third wheel. Already too hot in her long-sleeved blouse, she felt like a collapsed pudding, a leftover that someone had forgotten on the seat.

Belle flipped open the glove box. "No map?"

"I have a map," Ona said. "I'm not so feeble-minded as to embark on a road trip without a map."

"We'll make do." Belle tinkered with the rearview mirror; Ona caught a whiff of body odor. Just outside, Quinn and the brunette were engaged in what might generously be called a discussion.

"That's my sister, if you wondered."

"I didn't," Ona said.

Ona stared ahead, ashamed of herself. Who was she to begrudge the poor woman some breathing room?

"Quinn told me about your son," Belle said. "I hope you don't mind."

"I suppose it doesn't matter whether I do or I don't." To her surprise, though, she didn't mind. Her secret had been released into the air, harmless as a butterfly. She couldn't quite remember why she'd kept it so hard pressed to her chest. For ninety years.

"Being with you," Belle said, "helps me believe that my son is still in the world somewhere." She blinked hard. "Thank you for that."

"You're welcome," Ona said. But for Ona, it was the opposite. She'd tucked the boy safely offstage, in a species of Limbo. He was less than real but more, much more, than a memory: a voice speaking from the wings, an impression of living stillness. But with the tormented mother lurching into the floodlights it was impossible to forget he was dead.

Now Quinn was back. "Amy called your father," he said, getting into the back seat. "The great man's on his way."

The sister scurried to Belle's window, holding a tiny pink phone. "Sweetie, can you at least wait for Dad?"

"Tell him it's a little late to be playing Dear Old Daddy," Belle said. "Isn't there a company somewhere that needs plundering?"

"Call me when you get there," the sister said. "Can you please do that, please?" She folded the phone into Belle's hand, then kissed the tops of her sister's fingers. "Don't let him talk her into anything," she instructed Ona, to whom she had not been introduced.

Belle sighed loudly. "Tell Dad we're taking a mother to see her son. A very nice mother, his own grandson's community project."

Ona began, "Excuse me—"

"You're booked at the Apple Country Motor Court," Amy said to Quinn. "When you don't book ahead you end up sleeping in the car."

"That was fifteen years ago, Amy," Quinn said.

"Ted's furious about this, for the record."

"Then where is he?"

"With his children," Amy said. "Spending time with his children." She leaned far into the window. "This is on you," she added, pointing at Quinn. Then she gave Belle's hair a motherly swipe and turned back to the house.

"That was hardly necessary," Ona said.

"Actually," Quinn said from the back, "it was."

Belle snapped on her seat belt. "Amy has always been a bear."

Ona said, "That's one word for it."

"Be glad she didn't insist on driving us herself."

"Oh, I am. Your sister strikes me as the type of driver who raises the rates for everybody else."

"Good one, Ona," Quinn said, and Ona felt ridiculously pleased.

Belle started the car—the getaway car now, it seemed—and fiddled with the controls. "Where's the AC?"

"It's a car," Ona said, "not a berth on the *Queen Mary*." She was still chafing from being referred to as a community project.

Belle fanned her delicate clavicle with the collar of her blouse. "I myself am an excellent driver, Miss Vitkus. I'll get you there, safe and sound."

"Not if your father gets here first," Quinn said. "Step on it."

At last they pulled away, at a prudent and acceptable speed, and within minutes they were on the highway. As their distance from home increased, the travelers established a serviceable rapport. They talked awhile about the upcoming elections, and the war, and the Red Sox, before drifting into silence. Half asleep and peering down the years, Ona found her mother standing near a window, her hair tied back by a frayed length of ribbon. Branches scratched against a lintel. A white dog sighed. Where was this? Was it possible to remember a land she had left at the age of four? Was anything truly retrievable after a hundred years?

An hour later, as they crossed the New Hampshire border, Belle picked up a dropped stitch: "My father's a hard man," she said to Ona, "but he built himself up from nothing. He had goals. You have to admire that. Of course, he sacrificed his family." She shot Quinn a layered look through the rearview. "Some daughters are more forgiving than we are. Dad got stuck with unforgiving types."

"You're not the unforgiving type," Quinn said. Ona strained to hear him. "Amy, maybe. Not you."

They were speaking in code, Ona knew; perhaps this was the only way they could speak. She lapsed into silence, until it occurred to her that it was her very presence that made their communication, however painful, possible at all. She'd met the woman only once, but wasn't it likely that this version—this snappish code talker—was closer to the real Belle than the timorous little creature who'd haunted her house last week? Is this why Quinn seemed so content back there, so unworried?

"What's your father's trade?" Ona asked.

"Toys," Quinn said, "but don't let that fool you." He dangled his arms over the seat the way Randall and Frankie used to do in Howard's Model A.

"He started with a toy plane," Belle said, with some pride. "It came in this cute little airplane hangar."

"It made him a millionaire within seven months," Quinn said, "and after that he paid someone to trace the Cosgrove family tree all the way back to a crowd of minor dukes, and that's how Belle and Amy grew up thinking they were royalty."

Ona realized they were playing out an old script. Louise called this sort of thing "pair bonding," the equivalent of birds passing a berry beak to beak.

"It wasn't seven months," Belle said.

"That's how he tells it."

"It was seven years," Belle said. "Quinn's an exaggerator."

"Cosgrove?" Ona asked.

Belle nodded.

"Cosgrove Toys? That's your father?"

"In name only. He visited us from New York a few times a year." Belle passed a truck driven by an old man who looked terrified. "Once he spent three solid years in Taiwan while we stayed home. It's a miracle they're still together. He came back up here for good after he retired."

"I think they call it jail," Quinn said. "The great man did some short time for tax fraud."

"Tax *evasion*. It was almost legal."

Ona said, "I remember that toy airplane. The Future Flyer."

"That's right!" Belle said, brightening. "The Future Flyer."

"The boys at Lester used to smuggle them in," she said. "Lester Academy. Perhaps you've heard of it. I was a professional secretary to the headmaster."

Belle gave her a quick glance, then returned her eyes to the road. "I figured you must have worked."

Ona twittered inwardly to have been recognized as the employable type. "It's a condo development now," she said, "all those handsome buildings disfigured by the most repulsive grillwork. People ought to go to jail for *that*."

Belle smiled. Ona remembered this part, the effort of presenting an altered self to the world, the strain involved in a simple conversation.

"You live alone?" Belle asked.

"I had a friend, but she died."

"Pets?"

"Two cats, but they died, too."

"I can't hear you back here," Quinn said. He jutted forward again, emitting a whiff of hair product, the starched-doily scent that recalled Maud-Lucy's parlor.

"I was telling your lady about my cats," Ona said. Ginger, a marmalade tabby, had died first. When Kit's turn came, Ona did not replace her, unwilling to let a helpless cat outlive its mistress.

That was back when her hair was still growing. She could have gone through another cat and a half by now.

As the miles clipped along, Quinn gave up trying to hear them and nodded off in the back. Ona or Belle made occasional observations—hawk on a signpost, Harley going too fast—and watched the road together. "You know," Ona said, "I might just have one of those little planes in the house somewhere. If I find it, I'll be pleased to give it to you." But she hadn't run across one in her mad and fruitless search for her birth certificate.

Belle smiled for real then. "You're exactly the way he described you," she said, to which Ona made no response but to blush so hard that her eyelids heated up. Quinn was snoring lightly now, and she realized that she wasn't the third wheel after all; he was.

In Keene they stopped at a diner, where Ona offered to treat everyone to lunch with money from her long-dormant travel fund.

"No, no," Belle said.

"Let her," Quinn said. "She's not helpless." He rapped a knuckle on Ona's wrist—it actually made a sound, bone on bone. He was presenting her, she saw this now, as his prize, like a cat dragging a blood-sticky sparrow to the mistress of the manor. Normally these things infuriated her, but because he had no other prize to give—and because he knew she knew this—she felt useful, almost jubilant. She was having a bang-up time. Whether or not the visit with Laurentas turned out the way she hoped, the trip would be worth the trouble.

As she opened the menu, Ona felt momentarily unborn, as if her long life had been a warm-up for the real show, on which the curtain was about to rise. She ordered a grilled cheese and a strawberry short-cake, expecting to eat it all.

* * *

This is Miss Ona Vitkus. This is her life memories and shards on tape. This is Part Five.

. . .

As a matter of fact, I did see him again. Maud-Lucy made him promise. A deathbed promise, hard to refuse.

. . .

November of 1963. Same day the president was shot.

. . .

Not Lincoln. For crumbsake! *Kennedy.* Riding along bareheaded in Dallas and *boom,* the end of America. The news wasn't two hours old when Laurentas turned up at my door.

. . .

I don't recall exactly. "Hello," would be my guess. He might have called me Mother. Frankie used to call me that as a joke. "Yes, Mother, right away, Mother"—meaning he intended to do the opposite of what I asked.

. . .

I'd say it was—awkward, as you might imagine after so long. He was forty-eight years old. I asked him to sit. He took a chair at my kitchen table and cried for about five minutes.

. . .

It was. Oh, just dreadful.

. . .

To be honest, I never knew whether he was upset about the president, or about seeing me.

. . .

Well, now, that's true. She was his mother, after all, and she died hard. He'd been through a lot. There was a divorce in the works, too. His second wife, as I recall.

. . .

Yes, I suppose it was. Very hard. But sometimes divorce is a good thing.

. . .

No? Never?

. . .

All right. Divorce is never a good thing. But sometimes it has to be done. Certainly in my case. Howard was turning into a lunatic.

. . .

Let's agree that "sometimes" is the correct answer. But not everything has a correct answer. You're going to have to learn that someday. Can we—?

. . .

Yes, so, I left the TV on low all evening. People kept coming on to say what Jackie was doing.

. . .

That was the president's wife. She had blood on her suit. People couldn't get over that. I asked Laurentas about his upbringing among the apples and uncles and piano music, but eventually he ran out of things to say and turned to the screen. I made dinner, and then I sent Laurentas down the street for a bakery pie in honor of Maud-Lucy, who loved her sweets. He went, too, like a real son, buttoning his coat on his way out the door.

. . .

Pardon?

. . .

Oh. Yes. It was. It was awful to hear about Maud-Lucy. She'd been invisible to me for decades, but the news—well, it rang all these chimes. *Bing bong bang*, all these hurt places clanging to life. My good Lord, what a dreadful day that was.

. . .

Indeed he did. He asked about Viktor straight off. Why else do you think he came? He had Viktor's eyes, you know, with these peppery flecks in the irises. I couldn't find myself in there at all.

. . .

Well, Maud-Lucy had told him the story already, on her deathbed. All I could think to offer in the way of extras was that his father, at least as a boy of eighteen, had been a marvelous tattoo man. He was gentle, I told Laurentas, which was true if you came to him for a tattoo. His specialty was roses. Very meticulous and accurate.

. . .

Little furls, a thorn or two, discreetly placed.

. . .

That's none of your business, I'm afraid.

. . .

No, no, it's all right. You're a child. You don't know what's proper to ask a lady and what's not. And if you must know, I do have a tattoo, and it's in a place I can't show you.

. . .

Don't apologize. To be honest, I'm rather pleased you asked. And that you weren't surprised by the answer.

. . .

Because a lot of people think I'm a piece of statuary with no past, that's why. And here you are in my kitchen, reminding me that I'm me. Now, where—?

. . .

Right. I asked Laurentas, "Are you a doctor?" Maud-Lucy promised me he'd become a doctor. "I'm a surgeon," he said. "Your natural grandfather was a surgeon," I told him, "except in America, where he was an acid cooker. And your natural father was good with a needle. Excellent hands."

. . .

Why, thank you. It didn't occur to me at the time that Laurentas might have inherited his hands from me, because what he said next nearly set my hair on fire.

. . .

"If I'd known about you, Mother, I'd have visited sooner."

. . .

Exactly. She didn't tell him *word one*. All those letters she wrote, Dearest Girl this and Darling Girl that. When he turned two she asked for a photograph to keep next to his bed. Do you have any idea what it cost me to procure a photograph in 1917? Here I thought my countenance would remind her of that little girl she had taught and loved, and that she would make sure Laurentas thought well of me, and the whole time she was erasing me in the most calculating fashion imaginable.

. . .

Yes! The very same Maud-Lucy Stokes who landed in Kimball by accident and stayed because of me. Forty years later here was our son, standing in my apartment on the day of the president's regrettable death, a teary-eyed surgeon in a handsome suit, missing his mother.

. . .

Oh, I painted a pretty picture: Her cats on the piano. Her books in the parlor. Her houseplants and tablecloths. I told him how girls and boys lined up at her door for lessons, even the children of the town founder, who'd financed and stocked the Kimball schoolhouse himself.

. . .

Because it was the same as telling him about me. I was Maud-Lucy's girl. I gave Laurentas all the letters she'd written, all those beautifully inked missives on pastel paper, all her poetic thoughts on music, on the greening or waning of the apple orchards, all her motherly advice on how to wear a hat veil or keep gloves from yellowing. They weren't really mine anymore. "You'll find delightful accounts of your babyhood," I told him.

. . .

She stopped writing when he reached the age of eight.

. . .

Maybe she feared I'd take a notion to visit. He was at the age when a little explaining would be required. But I had children of my own by then and was in no position to travel.

. . .

Laurentas? He said he was sorry. I suppose he was.

. . .

I said, "I had two more sons. Maud-Lucy was your mother always." But I didn't feel as sanguine as I sounded. Inside I was swimming with rage. All this while I could hear Walter Cronkite, who was sounding more gut-punched by the second.

. . .

A newsman, back when newsmen had to know things. Laurentas took the letters. I had them wrapped in muslin.

. . .

He said, "Thank you for these. She was a wonderful mother."

. . .

I agreed, of course. Who would know better than I? "I'm sorry for your loss, Laurentas," I said to him, and then he got up to go. He headed down the stairs, and I stood on the porch, hugging myself against the cold, waiting for him to reappear on the street below. You could hear people's televisions all up and down the street, everybody gripped by the national tragedy, and there I was on the porch in my flimsy sweater with my own trivial tragedy unfolding on top of a real one, my silly story about a girl betrayed by a woman, but it fell on me all of a sudden, with such—force—so much harder than it might have, I suppose, on a day when poor Jackie wasn't wearing blood on her suit.

. . .

Nothing, really. What else was there to do? He came at Maud-Lucy's behest. He had a big, complicated family already and that was enough.

. . .

I watched his handsome Chrysler edge down the street. I wondered where he planned to stay the night. Perhaps I should have asked him to stay with me.

. . .

Then—? I suppose I went back inside. I turned out the hall light, returned to my parlor, sat down on my couch, and cried my eyes out for the president.

Chapter 14

By the time Quinn thought to ask Ona for her son's address, it was four in the afternoon and Belle was passing the WELCOME TO GRANYARD sign. The sky bore down on a puzzling stretch of village-style condo developments, a far cry from the apple-green raptures he'd been led to expect.

"Hey," Quinn said, catching sight of a granite pillar. "I played here once." He'd forgotten the name but now there it was: Hobson Christian College, a quintet of soulless buildings on twenty acres of desecrated farmland. A technical glitch during sound check had sent the boys into a tizzy of disbelief until Quinn told them, *Guys, it's a fuse, no prayer required*.

"Where to, Ona?" Belle asked, slowing down. They were on a first-name basis now, united in female solidarity after a twenty-minute conversation about cats. How women cemented alliances over less than nothing impressed him anew.

"How's that?" Ona said, cupping her ear. They'd rolled down all the windows, which in Quinn's opinion just spread the heat around. But at this point no one was listening to him.

"The *address*," Quinn said. "You—have it, right?" He and Belle had always traveled this way, back when they traveled: mapless, hurtling through space on instinct and whimsy. With Ona aboard, looking dangerously friable, this modus operandi lost a measure of its once-youthful verve.

"Of course I have it," Ona said. "Do you take me for a goose?" She delved into the murky pit of her big black purse. The things she excavated—Life Savers, crumpled tissues, grocery receipts—had fuzzed over with age. "I know it's in here," she fretted. "It's something to do with horses." Again she plumbed the tenebrous depths, quivering with effort, her newly coiffed hair now jutting from her head like feathers on a badly plucked chicken.

She looked up. Except for the bright, stabbing eyes and a slash of lipstick, she all but dissolved against the sun-white background of the windshield. "I put it in this handbag," she said. She glared at Quinn. "Did you take it?"

"Why would I take it?"

Ona puffed out her withered lips. "Maybe you took it to check the address?"

"I didn't."

"Quinn, you have the memory of a mayfly."

"I think I'd remember ransacking a lady's purse."

"There's always the phone book," Belle said. "Don't worry, Ona, we'll find him." She'd gone clammy in the melting heat, Quinn noted; he felt like a tour guide who'd led his party into a quaint town square only to discover a public hanging.

"I must have put it in my overnight case," Ona said, more fretful now.

"Let's check," Belle said. "We'll check." She pulled into a Citgo station and opened the door to a blast of thick, chewable air.

"Wait, wait," Ona said, producing a wrinkled envelope from the guts of her purse. "Here it is." She was aging by the minute. What in hell had he been thinking, taking a woman her age on a trip of this length in a car with no air conditioning? She'd gone since lunch—two and a half hours—without moving. Was that dangerous?

Quinn examined the envelope. "How old is this?"

"What difference does that make?"

"You called ahead, right?"

"It would have been awkward to call ahead. I did not call ahead."

"Fourteen-twenty Bridle Path Lane," Belle read. She looked calm, motherly. "I bet we're not far. I have a feeling."

Quinn felt like both the mark and the con. Ona had swindled him into this trip, but not before he'd misled her into believing he'd be thrilled to do her a favor. Which—when push came to shove—he was. Which was something. He hung onto that, hoping it would get him past the next twenty minutes, at which point they might discover that Ona's son's house had collapsed in a storm, or changed owners, or been converted into a Pottery Barn.

"Ask that girl for directions," Ona instructed him.

Despite his misgivings, he went through the motions, crossing the blistering macadam to consult with the gas attendant, a teenage redhead with cheeks the color of apricots. She reminded him of the young Belle, same ravenous expression. Belle had lost that expression over the years, becoming not so much sated-looking as merely no longer hungry; but since the boy's death that hungry look was back, in a way that did not, could not, arouse him as it once had. *Ravenous* was the wrong word now: *starved*, more likely. He bought three candy bars, then sprinted back to the car as if running from a mistake.

"It's up ahead," he announced. "Three or four miles." He handed out the melting candy.

"I had in mind a place where the river cuts the land into green slopes," Ona said, as Belle pulled back into traffic. "Maud-Lucy wrote the loveliest descriptions. They lived in the outskirts. Maybe it's prettier there."

Bridle Path Lane was a right-hand turn, a long, paved hill flanked by cakelike houses and ending at a compound of low brick buildings, four wings connected to a sparkling atrium, glossy as a butterfly's belly. Out front hung an artsy wooden sign: ORCHARD ACRES CONDO-MINIUMS. Swinging below that, on a ladder of panels of the sort used to advertise ice cream flavors, hung the caveats: INDEPENDENT LIV-ING; SEMI-INDEPENDENT LIVING; ASSISTED LIVING; EXTENDED CARE; MEMORY CARE. Below that, in irrefutable calligraphy: 1420 BRIDLE PATH LANE.

"This is a nursing home," Belle said. She snatched the envelope from the dashboard.

Ona frowned. "He said condo."

"This can't be right." Belle gaped at the tiered sign. "How old is your son?"

Ona got out stiffly, appearing to shrink in the white-bright air, her clothes fading with light as she picked her way around a rotund planter exploding with petunias.

"Ona, wait a sec," Quinn called, but she paid him no mind. The entrance was mercifully close, an automatic door that opened silently and swallowed her in.

Belle was breathing hard, sweating and open-mouthed. "Oh, God." She glanced around in desperation. "Oh, God. What if he's in a coma?" Her poise puddled away on the instant and her voice dropped to a whisper. "He must be—what? Seventy-five?"

"Eighty-nine."

"Oh, my *God*. I was thinking, you know, a *son*. He's *eighty-nine?*" She shook her head as if trying to dislodge information.

"Belle, she was a kid. I told you the story."

"I realize that," Belle snapped. "Don't you think I realize that? I didn't do the goddamn *math*." Her shirt, he noted for the first time, was stained. "You said she had a son she hadn't seen for a while. Of course I know—I know she couldn't possibly—I forgot. I didn't do the *math*."

Anticipating consequences had never been Quinn's strong suit, but as he shepherded Belle inside he considered possible outcomes—including but not limited to Ona's sudden death and Belle's emergency admittance to the nearest psych ward. He ranked these things, from most likely to least, in the panicky fashion that used to drive needles into his eyeballs when the boy did it.

The reception area resembled the lobby of Great Universal Mail Systems: patterned carpet, fake-crystal chandelier, a glass reception desk, and potted trees. Ona had vanished. From behind a set of double doors came the sound of the thing being hidden: the metal-on-tile scrape of walkers and four-prong canes, a start-and-stop that suggested thoughts lost in mid-stride. Quinn's mother, young and cancer-ridden, had died in a cut-rate model of a place like this. As a kid he'd managed to bear the humid odors of illness and age and the bus-station aesthetic of the day room; it was the off-key clanking of orthopedic hardware that stabbed him deepest, that arrhythmic, purposeless, ever-present percussion. *Clank . . . rest . . . clank-clank-rest . . .* He tried to assemble a tune out of the mess—a childhood habit—but no organizing principle unveiled itself.

The lobby was icily air-conditioned, and Belle was shivering, staring morosely at her shoes, which, now that he looked, weren't an exact match. One had a round toe and the other a slightly less round toe. "I don't know what I'm doing," she murmured. "Do you know what I'm doing?" She waited, as if Quinn, who could never answer easy questions— *What time are you coming home?*—could suddenly answer hard ones. "We'll go home tonight if you want," he said, soothingly. "I'll get a room for Ona and drive back for her tomorrow."

She was crying tearlessly, something he'd never once seen her do in the twenty years he'd known her. Was it true that a person could be all cried out? "I don't want to go home," she whispered. "I don't want to *be* home. I don't want to be anywhere." She hid her face for a minute, but when she dropped her hands her eyes came up dry.

A tall, slender woman appeared out of nowhere. "I had an aide show your mother to the restroom," she said. Quinn took in her long legs and painted toenails and strappy sandals. Low-cut blouse, smart little jacket—white but not nursey. Her earrings changed color as she moved her head.

Her name was Arianne. She offered them a corporate handshake and water from the cooler. "Are you thinking of a move for your mother?" she asked, collecting their drained cups.

"A move for my mother would be fabulous," Belle said listlessly, "but first you'd have to pry her out of her house."

Arianne gave Belle a whip-quick once-over, apparently rethinking the identity of the next Orchard Acres invitee.

"You'll have to pardon me," Belle said. "My son died."

"I'm sorry," Arianne said, abandoning her sales voice, not quite knowing where to look.

"She's not our mother," Quinn said. "She's a friend of ours looking for someone who, I guess, lives here." But he couldn't come up with a name. There were no Vitkuses on the premises.

At last Ona reappeared, looking heat-soaked, crushed, sat on. "I would like to see Laurentas Stokes, please," she said, all business, though her voice was fissured with fatigue. "Perhaps he's a doctor here."

"Oh, for goodness' sakes," Arianne said. Her laughter was filled with air. "You mean Larry." She leaned into Quinn, having pegged him as the responsible party. "He still lives in B wing but spends afternoons over here. This is extended care. Worry-free care for your loved ones." She glanced at Ona. "Are you a relative?"

"I gave birth to him," Ona said, "if that's what you mean."

Arianne's befuddled smile hung Cheshire-cat-like, unsupported by the rest of her face. Belle fidgeted on her feet as if the floor burned. "Follow me," said Arianne, so they did, making a silent parade through the double doors and into the fluorescent realm beyond. Quinn took Ona's arm, assaulted by doubt and worrying only at the point when to worry changed nothing—Belle's long-standing accusation made manifest.

The day room was studded with parked wheelchairs claimed by squashed, staring people. Though Ona undeniably blended in, Quinn saw that she was just as exactly a thing apart. He thought of the body-snatcher movies, how clever the aliens' disguises, but all the same you could just tell. "Which fellow is he?" she asked. She seemed greatly agitated, flinching in her skin.

"Right here," Arianne said, somewhat wary. She led them a few paces away, to a rangy man in a high-tech chair near a large window that looked out on a courtyard. Around his neck hung a stethoscope and a pair of binoculars.

"Larry," the woman said, touching his shoulder, "you have visitors."

Larry turned around with effort, a sweet, mellow smile lighting his features. He had Ona's wide forehead and charged eyes.

"What are you doing in here, Laurentas?" Ona demanded.

"Do I know you?"

She put her hands on her hips. "It's Ona Vitkus."

"Say again?"

"ONA VITKUS," she repeated. "YOUR MOTHER."

"Well, my gracious. So it is," he said. His words slurred faintly. "My gracious me, what a surprise."

"What are you doing in here?"

"I live here," he said. "My gracious me."

"He's having a wonderful day, aren't you, Larry?" Arianne said. "I'll leave you all to catch up." Her fading footfalls left Quinn bereft.

"I retired in '92," Larry was telling Ona. "My children all settled so far away." He pointed across the courtyard. "That's my place, the corner unit. Independent, you understand. They give me three squares a day in the dining room."

Quinn dragged a chair to Ona, and to his relief she took it, though she made a point of perching on its edge. Was she trying to look young in front of her ancient son? Whatever her motive, it prompted in Quinn a jolt of affection.

"This is no place for a healthy man," she said. "A doctor, up to his withers in sick people?"

Quinn sensed Belle at his back; her keen attention had a nearly musical quality, like a rest between measures.

"I had a little stroke last year," Larry said calmly. He fiddled with his stethoscope. "But I still manage rounds from this chair." He smiled around at his default patients, who exhibited varying levels of interest in the visitors. "They find me reassuring."

Ona said, "I thought you moved to a *condo,* Laurentas. I live in a house."

"It *is* a condo," Larry said, confused. He pointed again. "I've been watching for the yellow-breasted chat," he said then. "I had one yesterday. Unusual for here." The courtyard had little paths, a bird-feed-ing station, and a lush topography of flowering bushes. Quinn craned his neck to see, though what a chat might look like he had no idea. The boy would know. The boy had been listing birds along with ev-erything else. "The view's better from over here," Larry said.

Ona blinked at her son, looking miserable. An aide whisked in, carrying a tower of folded sheets, then disappeared behind another set of doors.

"I bet he was good-looking," Belle whispered. She was gazing at him, enraptured. Quinn didn't want to stay for this, whatever it was; everybody here at cross-purposes.

"I feed birds," Ona said.

"Pardon?"

"I feed birds. IN MY OWN HOUSE. This fellow here comes to help me, although he's finished now. Done with his duties. THIS FELLOW HERE." Now everybody was looking at Quinn as if they expected him to pass out pills or examine their feet. He'd put on a new T-shirt this morning, and a freshly washed pair of jeans, and was suddenly glad.

"I don't recall that," Larry said. "It must have slipped my mind. Things do, lately, I regret to admit." He patted the top of his head. "This fine old brain."

"I didn't feed birds back then," Ona said. "Back then I was busy. I WAS BUSY."

"Weren't we all, dear." He smiled, revealing the same large, square teeth as his mother. His curiosity about her seemed mild, considering. He was a man enviably at ease, accepting the pace and vagaries of age. Dr. Stokes must have been a bygone type who traveled from house to house, whistling "She'll Be Coming 'Round the Mountain." Quinn liked him; he chanced another peek at Belle, who had relaxed utterly. This mother-son reunion had to be far from her expectation—the son decades older than her fantasy, for starters—and yet she seemed transfixed. Satisfied.

"What happened to your things?" Ona asked.

Larry tapped his ear as if to jump-start a hearing aid, though he wore none.

"YOUR THINGS," Ona repeated. "Your furniture. Books. Important papers. WHERE ARE YOUR THINGS?"

"Oh, my gracious, my things," he said. "What an undertaking. The girls took the silver. The boys have the tools, I believe. The rest went in a house auction." He adjusted a switch on the arm of his chair and the back reclined. Nothing was happening at the bird feeders. Quinn began to wonder if a yellow-breasted chat might be something on the order of a dodo, some extinct species with no chance of showing up.

"It's awfully nice to meet you," Belle said.

Larry tipped an imaginary hat. "What have we here?"

"I'm Belle." Was she beaming? She was beaming.

Larry consulted Ona again. "Would you have wanted something, dear? I'd have saved something for you, had I known."

"Did you come across my birth certificate, by chance?"

Larry tapped his ear again.

"MY BIRTH CERTIFICATE."

"What in the world would I be doing with your birth certificate?"

"My parents gave my papers to Maud-Lucy for safekeeping. YOUR MOTHER TOOK IT."

Belle nudged Quinn, harder than she probably meant to; she was standing very close. "What is she talking about?" she whispered. But he didn't know. Ona hadn't given him the full story.

Ona put a gaunt hand on her son's gaunt arm and leaned into his ear. "She kept such things in a red enamel box." When he turned to face her, she straightened up. "My parents were GREATLY PARANOID OF CONFISCATION," she continued, "with good reason. And your mother was the ONE CREATURE IN THIS ENTIRE COUNTRY WHOM THEY TRUSTED WITHOUT RESERVATION."

One of the captives called out like a baby bird—"*Dawk*tor, *dawk-*tor, *dawk*tor."

"Excuse me a moment," Larry said. He motored to the west corner of the day room, where he indulged a hairless woman in a minute of conversation, listened to her heart, then returned.

"I do very little," he explained, "except relieve fear."

"I NEED MY BIRTH CERTIFICATE, LAURENTAS."

"I don't have your birth certificate." He resembled her eerily when he spoke, something in the shape of his lips, those square teeth. "Wouldn't it be more likely that you have mine?"

Ona said nothing for a beat or two, then charged ahead: "We're talking about people who kept their money in a FLOUR BIN," she said to her son. "They owned an apartment building and later a grocery store, but they were afraid of everything. They couldn't settle. That was their problem. They couldn't settle into their own skin." Her voice took on a different sheen, briefly. "Your mother was the opposite."

"I'm sorry. Come again?"

"YOUR MOTHER. WAS THE OPPOSITE. That woman could settle anywhere. Not like these people nowadays. THESE PEOPLE," she repeated, gesturing toward Quinn. "These people nowadays have no idea where they are. Wherever they are, it's the WRONG PLACE."

Belle laughed softly; Quinn felt her cross over to somewhere he couldn't grasp and the day went irreversibly awry. He was a team of one, facing three inscrutable people who appeared to have sudden, passionate, possibly conflicting blueprints for how the next few moments—or hours—would go.

"If my mother took something of yours," Larry said, "it would have gone up in the fire, along with everything else."

"What fire?" Ona asked. For the first time she turned to Quinn—*Can you get this fellow to talk sense?*—but he couldn't help her. He stood there, suddenly freezing in his newish T-shirt, trying to puzzle out her purpose. One thing was clear: she hadn't come for a tearful reunion with the fruit of her womb. She'd come for her birth certificate and that was it. If only he'd listened more literally. But he'd have taken her to Vermont anyway; he knew this about himself, all of a sudden, and it surprised him.

Ona repeated, "WHAT FIRE?"

"*The* fire," Larry said. "I was an infant, of course, but I think I remember it, she spoke of it so often. The family homestead, you see. Seven buildings and one of the orchards gone overnight."

Quinn looked from one to the other, then to the window, as if Larry's bird might appear like a carrier pigeon with a code wrapped around its ankle. "He, uh, doesn't have it, Ona."

"YOUR MOTHER WROTE TO ME FOR YEARS FROM THE SAME ADDRESS," Ona said. She was squinting hard at her son, perhaps double-checking his identity.

"Her father built a new house over the burned one. Two, actually. One for himself and one for us." Larry smiled dreamily. "Oh, my gracious me, I miss the place. We sold it, in the end, to an outfit that turned the whole works into a housing development. I'll answer to the Man Upstairs for that, but it pays for my upkeep."

"Well," Ona said, "isn't this a pickle."

Larry looked up. "I'm afraid I've forgotten your name."

The moment clanged. Quinn tried to catch eyes with Belle, but she was studying Larry, oblivious, someplace else entirely.

Ona leaned very near the furl of her son's ear. "Ona," she said. "Vitkus."

"What is that, Polish?"

"It's Lithuanian."

"No fooling?" he said. "My natural mother was a Lithuanian." He shook his head, looking pained. "How do I know you, dear?"

The arctic air conditioning had electrified Ona's ruined hair, which all but levitated from her skull. "Your mother and I were friends," she said, too softly, really, for him to hear. She got up and extended her hand. "We'll be going now. Goodbye, Laurentas."

Alerted by the motions of departure, Belle came to. "We're leaving?"

"Stay," Larry offered. "The ladies here make spanking good coffee."

Belle smiled. "That sounds wonderful."

"We'll do no such thing," Ona said. "I have urgent business elsewhere."

Quinn was only too happy to get the show back on the road, but Belle had other plans. "I wouldn't mind seeing that bird," she said to her new friend, meeting his eyes in a way that Quinn knew, from long experience, would melt the calcified cockles of the old geezer's heart. "That yellow-breasted whatsit."

"Chat," he said, offering his binoculars. It came to Quinn then that the man had lost the use of one arm.

"My son likes birds," Belle told him.

Larry, who appeared to have no trouble at all understanding her, said, "The more the merrier."

"We were leaving," Ona said.

Belle stared out the window. "I'll stay here with Larry."

"You look very fine, Laurentas. I'm glad to know you're well. Goodbye." At this, Ona made for the day room door.

"Uh . . . ." Quinn said.

Belle was already far away, in Ona's vacated chair, conversing with Ona's son about birds and children. Larry had four daughters and two sons and nine grandchildren and a platoon of greats and great-greats — Ona hadn't asked a single question on that score — but they were wanderers, it seemed, all his progeny had their eyes on the horizon. "My natural father was a circus man, you see," he told Belle with rueful pride, bathed in the light of her attentions.

She's working you, brother, Quinn thought. In an earlier time he'd have said this aloud, which would have amused Belle, made her laugh right out loud and confess to being an incurable flirt around old men and little children. This was different, he saw now, her raw, fractured self shining out at a moth-eaten old gaffer who connected her in some unknowable way to her lost child. How at home she seemed here. It was like seeing her from the inside out. Is this what she'd been asking of him all these years, to see her this way? Was he fulfilling her frankest desire, at last? With her profile blurred by the harsh light crashing through the window, her fair hair whitened by that same light, she might have been eighty-nine herself, sickly and shaking and stripped of her powers. He imagined himself husbanding an elderly wife into her twilight, and the tableau woke in him yet one more way he would have failed Belle in the end.

He turned away, walking straight through the lobby and into the waning afternoon, where he found Ona standing at the entrance, all but melted into the pavement. Rattling with alarm, he eased her to the car with as much care as she'd accept, unrolled all the windows, then moved the car to the far end of the lot, under a large and sheltering tree that probably graced the cover of the Orchard Acres brochure. He rustled a bottle of water from his duffel. The car smelled a little off, the effluvia of the day room apparently having clung to their clothes. His friend (this is how he thought of her, holding the water while she adjusted her sticky clothes) had fallen into a black mood.

"Ona . . ." he began. "Do you want to go back in?"

"Why would I go back in that place?"

Quinn took this in. "It was kind of a short visit. That's all I'm saying."

"The purpose of this trip was my business entirely. You offered to take me and I accepted."

"Because you said you were after a big reunion."

"If you'll review your own blinky memory, I told you I needed a ride to Vermont. You and your lady read the cards however you pleased. People usually do."

He wondered if all good-deed-doers felt this insulted when they didn't get to pick the exact specifications of their charity. "I canceled a gig for this," he said. He wished himself back in Maine, shielded by his guitar, giving chatty, dancing people exactly what they expected.

Her eyes filled. "I'm sorry to have inconvenienced you, Quinn."

"I just—Christ, Ona, it's just a stupid record book full of people who will literally stand on their heads for immortality."

"Eyeball poppers and chain-saw jugglers," she said. "Yes, I am well aware. But I wanted this. I didn't realize it at first, but now I do." Before she stopped speaking to him, she added, "You have your music to outlive you. You wouldn't understand."

By the time he absorbed Ona's spectacular misperception of Quinn Porter as the possessor of a musical legacy, she was beyond reach, peaked and mute and seemingly flattened by unmet expectation.

Belle, for her part, returned looking reborn. "I saw a chat," she said. "You really missed something." To Ona, she said, "You have a beautiful son." Then she ordered Quinn into the back seat and put the car in gear.

FAMILY

1. Biggest family reunion. 2,369 members of the Busse family. Country of USA.
2. Most children born to one woman. 69. Mrs. Feodor Vassilya. Country of Russia.
3. Hairiest family. Victor and Gabriel Ramos Gomez. 98 percent of bodies covered in hair. Country of Mexico.
4. Most albino siblings. 3. Unoarumhi family. Country of UK.
5. Most statistically dominant father-son duo in Major League Baseball. Bobby and Barry Bonds. Country of USA.
6. Most populous country. China. 1 billion plus. Country of China.
7. Biggest blood donation. 3,403 donors in 12 hours. Country of Colombia.
8. Largest turkey farm. 10 million turkeys. The Matthews family. Country of Great Britain.
9. Largest gathering of clowns. 850. Country of UK.
10. Longest human chain. 370 miles and 2 million people. Country of Estonia, Latvia, and Lithuania.

Chapter 15

Ona hoped they took her shameful emanations as the after-odors of the day room. Oh, that awful place, filled with old crocks who'd quit their lives with no more fight than a grasshopper gave a house cat. She'd stood in that day room for ten mortifying minutes, hollering like a fishwife into the tattered eardrums of her firstborn, all the while stewing in damp underpants and the dreadful knowledge that she wasn't the only one. For all her trouble, she'd gotten exactly nowhere.

"There it is," she said, spotting a sign: Apple Country Motor Court and Café.

"It's only five o'clock," Belle said. "We could do some sightseeing. Larry says there's some beautiful country here and we just happened to land in the ruined part."

"No," Ona pleaded. "I'm—ill."

Belle eased into the parking lot and Ona got out. "I need my bag right now," she said. "This *minute*."

Belle looked at her queerly and gave Quinn the keys. He opened the trunk, his free hand cupping her shoulder. She'd made it to the nursing-home restroom on time—a public-face restroom with gleaming tile and a dish of little pink soaps—but in her rush to lock the stall she'd snagged her blouse and her bladder leaked before she could fully sit down and here she was now, one hand fisted over the ripped-out button, her drawers pasted to her nether parts, staring into a dead-empty trunk. Her bag was gone: the beehive overnight case with which she'd left Howard in 1948.

"Oh," Ona gasped. "Oh, no."

Quinn said, "Damn. I must've left it in the house."

After that things went flooey: she lost some time, though not her feet, apparently, for when she came to, she found herself safely upright, her companions accepting keys from a skeletal boy—raised on apples, apparently—behind the motel's reception desk.

Belle steered her to a ground-floor room. Quinn had the room next door. It appeared the ladies were going to share. Had she agreed to this?

Belle sat on a bed as Ona made for the bathroom. She peeled off her slacks, damp in spots but not soaked, but her drawers were beyond redemption. Her shirttail (far too long; it had belonged to tall, long-waisted Louise) was dank and wrinkled where she'd shoved it down into her slacks. She stood there on the cold tile, entirely undone, feeling like a witless old bat in a ripped blouse and nothing else, surrounded by mirrors. Her wonderful trip had now been ruined twice over.

She sat on the toilet and bawled. It was Frankie she'd wanted to see: Frankie at eighty, looking old or looking young, stroke or no stroke. The second she'd laid eyes on Laurentas—Larry!—a picture of her darling, unreachable Frankie had exploded in her head, his countenance as merry and candid as ever.

"Are you okay in there?" The door creaked open and Belle peered through the crack. She looked almost healthy—the visit with Laurentas had restored her color—though Ona distrusted her boomeranging moods. She seemed harmless enough as she slipped into the bathroom, her face as open as a magnolia leaf. Out of options, Ona decided to submit.

"I've wet my drawers," she whispered. "Not clean through, you understand. But I don't fancy putting these clothes back on." She wiped her eyes. "My bag is gone and I've nothing else to wear."

Belle plucked a towel from the rack and offered it sympathetically. "The same thing happened to me once, when I was pregnant," she said. "I was with Quinn at a gig and had to ask the bartender for a towel." She filled the sink and drubbed Ona's slacks and drawers with bar soap. "Is your shirt all right?" she asked, twisting the bathtub faucets with no more effort than it took to snap a finger.

Ona let go of the rip. "Don't look at me, please."

Belle helped Ona off with her blouse—"This is our little secret," she assured her—and into the tub, which received Ona's disgraced and flapping carcass with a slosh of disapproval.

Time passed, some of it lost. When Ona got out of the tub—she insisted on doing this herself despite Belle's offers from the other side of the door—she found her things dripping on a towel rack and on the closed lid of the toilet some dry, youthful clothes that she, apparently, was expected to put on.

"What are these?"

"It's all I've got," Belle called in. "Your stuff won't be dry for a while."

"I should have worn polyester," Ona muttered, inspecting a folded pair of blue jeans, a sleeveless red blouse, an A-cup brassiere, and a pair of silk underpants with a pattern of butterflies freckling the seat. Everything freshly laundered and pressed—the overprotective work of the dark-haired sister.

She examined the underpants as if excavating her lost womanhood. It had been over fifty years since she last bled. She stepped into them and hiked them up, half expecting a genie to appear with an offer to restore her menses. The butterfly-patterned silk hung on her like another deflated muscle. How had this happened? She gazed down at the baggy casings that passed for breasts, the vertical pleats of her thighs, and yanked the panties off her body so hard she tore the band.

A butterfly had been Ona's first gift from a boy. Fourteen years old, waltzing home from a dance at the Mechanics Institute, comparing dance cards with the girls from Wald Street. Just then Mervin Fickett, a bucktoothed boy from the School Street livery, caught up with her in front of the Thibodeau block to thrust the iridescent treasure into her palm. Pinned to a stiff square of velvet, the murdered thing shone with reflected moonlight. Where Mervin had acquired such a jewel he would not tell, but he wanted her to have it because, he informed her, slurping the words through his crisscrossed teeth, the wings matched her eyes exactly.

The lovely creature left her woozy with desire—for what, she did not know. On this first summer night of 1914—the summer of no Maud-Lucy—silly, sweet Mervin Fickett laid the first innocent stone in a path that would track the rest of Ona's life. As Maud-Lucy nursed her auntie back in Vermont, Ona turned up at the midway, stunned once again by desire; in ten months' time she'd be home again, sick with regret and unthinkable pain, giving birth to a boy destined for Maud-Lucy's arms.

Viktor stole the butterfly and sold it for a nickel. She wished now that she'd hidden it, secreted it away for all these decades; she'd like to have given it to the boy. Perhaps it had been meant for him all along, for the spilling-over joy with which he'd have received it. And named it. And counted it. And kept it. No one she had ever known would have loved it more.

"Nothing fits," she called through the door. "I'll just have to wait."

Silence. "Do you want to borrow a nightgown?"

Time stretched and contracted; a flowery garment floated down over her head; she felt her arms being worked through silken straps. "You must have been a good mother," she remembered saying, before waking up in overstarched sheets, a Styrofoam cup of tea at her bedside. Belle was at the door, speaking to Quinn, who hovered just outside. Someone else, too: in the fog of waking Ona thought she recognized the sturdy corporeal architecture of the scoutmaster.

"I don't want trouble," someone was saying. Ona sat up, her normal clarity returning. She pulled the sheets over the slithery folds of Belle's nightgown. Yes, indeed: Mr. Ted Ledbetter, in the flesh.

"What's going on?" Ona said. "Why are all these men in our room?"

"Stop it," Belle said, and slammed the door. Outside, the men's voices rose and fell, fighting over a woman who wore butterflies on her backside. Ona fell back against the pillows, which had been fluffed—by Belle, presumably—into a virtual meringue. "For crumb-sake," she said, "are they planning a duel?"

"Amy told Ted where we were staying," Belle said. "Otherwise, he'd still be driving around Granyard looking for your car." She sat heavily on Ona's bed and stared at her little pink phone. "He would have searched forever. For me." Her hair hung in defeated hanks from her translucent skull, and she had on the clothes she'd been sweating in all day—all week, more likely. Ona felt a brief, blade-thin twinge of maternal alarm, a pang she hadn't experienced in well over half a century.

"So," Belle said. "You thought he had your birth certificate. That's all it was?"

Ona didn't know what to do with fragile people; she'd spent so much of her life around bullies. "Laurentas did beautifully without me for nine decades," she said, "and to think otherwise is to shoehorn me into the wrong story."

"Larry has six children," Belle said. "Four daughters, two sons."

"I recall that," Ona said.

"You have a great-great-great-grandchild." She paused. "Why weren't you thrilled to see him? Why weren't you upside down with joy?"

"You didn't know Maud-Lucy," Ona said. "A man with such a mother doesn't go looking for another one."

"I'm not talking about Maud-Lucy."

"Well, I am." All those letters, full of fib and blandishment. Not a word about the fire. And not one flittering peep about keeping Laurentas's origins a secret.

She jimmied herself up in the bed, pulling the covers with her. "It won't surprise you to know that I was a distracted mother, even an unwilling one. I was touchy and cross and too young and impatient much of the time. My boys were such a handful, I didn't have a single girlfriend, I'd married a man far too old for me and hated being his wife. Howard had delusions that weighed too much for our family."

"That part sounds like Quinn."

"Quinn is an optimist. Howard was crazy. For that I blame President Wilson. But my point: Mother of the Year I wasn't." When the telegram arrived about Frankie, her first thought was: *I deserve this.* "I wasn't like you," she said. "Your boy was lucky." She added, "If it makes you feel any better, I did love the sons I raised."

For a time, neither of them spoke. The room smelled of their own bodies and ancient applications of carpet cleaner.

"I don't honestly believe he's gone," Belle said. "I keep hoping he's here someplace, that he's only hiding from me." Slowly, reverently, in surrender and exhaustion, she pressed her unlined forehead to Ona's age-pebbled chest.

Without a single thought otherwise, Ona petted this weak and suffering soul the way she'd once petted Frankie. Before the army made a man of him—a dead man, it turned out, but Howard thought the boys needed beefing up.

"During the Battle of Saipan," Ona murmured, "my Frankie's job was to pull other boys from the tides. Boys who churned up and then fell apart in his hands. The very same shipmates he liked so well. His job was to remove their dog tags, weight down their remains in loops of chain, and return them to the seas."

"My God," Belle whispered.

"Twenty years old and his paid employment for the United States Navy was to wrap other mothers' sons in chains. How did my son manage a job like that? How does any son?"

She leaned back against the pillow and Belle leaned with her, her head heavy now against Ona's chest. Ona understood, after all these years, that as much as she'd loved Frankie, she'd have loved a daughter more.

"Howard suffered something awful after Frankie was killed," she said. "I remember he bought a toy jeep from Binny Morris at the Forest Avenue five-and-dime. Might have been one of your father's jeeps, now that I think of it, a pot-metal replica of the type of jeep Frankie had joy-ridden to his death. A morbid, infantile purchase, I always thought. He kept it on the mantel even though the sight of it gave me the woozies. That's when I decided to go back to secretarial school on the sly, just in case."

Belle's breathing had steadied. Perhaps she was asleep.

"You know," Ona said, "I've always had the strangest feeling. As if I was there with Frankie. Not when he died. When he did his job, returning some poor child to the deep. I can almost see it happening, like a vision or a daydream, as if I'm standing right there next to my son as he performs this unpardonable task." She ran her hand gently over Belle's thin back, the tiny knobs of her spine.

"I'm so sorry," Belle whispered. "So sorry."

"It takes about a year," Ona confided, "to get shut of that shocked-up feeling."

"I can't last a year," Belle said. "I really can't." She went very quiet, and Ona continued to caress her, withholding the news that the second year would be harder than the first. Instead, she whispered, "*Sha, sha, sha,*" her mother's old, soothing chant.

The men's voices had quieted, but they were still out there, warring blocs of testosterone radiating from the other side of the door. Why, she wondered, at this late date, had the Almighty deigned to drag her back into the fray? She'd been doing fine on her own. Just jim-dandy. Then he sent that boy, setting into motion a fireworks of *possibility*—that long-dead sensation of *possibility*—that she was simply too old to accommodate. And now this: where in her dwindling, circumscribed life was she to store this sweet, pitiful little draggletail who reminded her of things she'd rather forget?

"My friends have been so good," Belle said suddenly, lifting her head. "But they all have kids, and they hold on so tight. To their kids, I mean. They don't even know they're doing it. Tight-tight-tight. Right in front of me, like sudden death is contagious. There but for the grace of God, you know?" She took a long, juddering breath. "He took up hardly any space. Ted's boys, they leave everything everywhere. Finished with the sandwich, the sneakers, the math book, the backpack, drop it on the floor, in the yard, under the bed, let Dad get it later. My son wasn't like that. I pretended it was me. My shimmering influence. But, you know, it was just him. The way he was." She sat fully upright, crossing her hands over her heart. "Every day, I wake up stunned. I have this coil of ill will that stuns me, I want everyone to know how I feel, but there's only one way to know. And I want them to know anyway. Even though there's only one way." Her face flinched but no tears came. "Do you know how I feel?"

"Yes," Ona said. "I never knew Laurentas and I make no apology for that. It was my Frankie I wanted returned to me, my best and most beloved."

Belle regarded Ona for a long moment. "You would have liked me," she said at last. "I was a nice person." She tried to smile. "Ask anyone."

The men had started up again—an argument that Ona couldn't quite make out. How bracing it must be, she thought, to be so zealously sought after. One of them was tapping at the door but Belle ignored it. *Meilè*, Ona thought. Love.

"Your boy gave me a present," Ona said.

Belle leaned in. "What?"

"My mother tongue," Ona said. "From the moment I laid eyes on him, it's been coming back. Dribs and drabs. I can't explain it, unless he had some magic up his sleeve."

"He was made of magic." Belle gave Ona's hand a squeeze. "This tea's for you."

Ona had given her next to nothing, but as Belle moved through the soulless little cell toward the tap-tapping door, the room all but brimmed with her gratitude.

When she opened her eyes again, it was dark.

"How long was I out?" she asked Belle, who sat cross-legged on the other bed. She looked as if she, too, had gotten a little sleep.

"About three hours. It's nine o'clock." She flicked on a lamp.

"Are my clothes dry?" Ona's humiliation burned afresh: to have piddled like an untrained poodle in front of a young woman with a candy-pink bladder that could hold through a hurricane!

Belle turned her back as Ona dislodged herself from the flimsy nightgown and reclaimed her clothes. Her blouse was irredeemable so she took the shirt Belle had offered her earlier, red with little gold buttons. It smelled wonderful and looked so unlike anything she'd ever worn that it recalled the spirit of adventure with which she'd embarked on the long-ago beginning of this day.

"Is Mr. Ledbetter still here?" she asked.

"Uh-huh," Belle said. "I've been sitting here, thinking." She picked up a pen from the phone table and shook it to get the ink started. "I'm going to help you."

"I don't need any help."

"Oh, I think you do." She waved the pen momentously, her mood thoroughly transformed. "I can help you get your world record." Her expression filled with light. No wonder men dueled for her attentions. "Quinn didn't tell you where I work?"

"You're a librarian. You work, I presume, in a library."

"I work at the state archives, and if there's one thing on this earth I'm good at, it's tracking down information."

"That may very well be," Ona said, her hope redoubling despite herself, "but you can't get blood from a turnip."

"Too true," Belle said. The very air around her appeared to change color. "But you *can* get blood from a census."

Ona's stomach did a little *kerflop* as a bright image plummeted into her head: A young man at her mother's door. Suit and tie. Hair like a lit match. Maud-Lucy pattering down the stairs to translate, holding up her skirt to avoid tripping.

"Maine's census dates back to the seventeen hundreds," Belle said. She grabbed a notepad printed with the motel's filigreed logo. "Unless you were born before that, we're in business." She was writing now. "Where did you say you grew up?"

Ona stood up. Belle's blouse fit her beautifully. "Kimball, Maine."

"And when did you arrive there?"

"Nineteen-oh-four. I was four years old."

"It's amazing how much time some people get," Belle said, lifting her pen. "I mean, there's no rhyme or reason."

Her tone was ponderous, private, hard to read. Perhaps she expected Ona to blurt something along the lines of wishing she'd died in the boy's place. She wanted to believe she'd have agreed, had God asked, but in her secret heart she knew otherwise. It wasn't that she was selfish, or indifferent. Just too full of her own wants. She wanted to see her hydrangeas bloom come fall. To vote in another presidential election. To see the end of this war. And to find her name in a record book. She preferred life to death, that's all. Most people did.

"What was your address?"

"Wald Street. We didn't have street numbers."

"Your parents?"

Another downpour of words inside her head, words upon words, and then: *Aš esu lietuvis!* I am Lithuanian! This was her father's voice, a muffling despair from behind a shut door.

Then, nothing but the beaded sound of pen on paper. Timidly, she said, "A census is one doc." She was thinking: *Who am I? Who am I, really?* "I need three."

"Were your sons born in Kimball?"

"There's no record for Laurentas with my name on it. But Randall and Frankie, they were born in Portland."

Belle said, "Birth certificates record the mother's age."

Ona felt as if room 114 of the Apple Country Motor Court had just turned into a magic carpet; she experienced an agreeable sensation of flight. "I'm quite grateful," she said.

"Ditto." Belle jotted a final note and dropped the works into her satchel. "Let's grant that beautiful boy his dream come true."

Just then came another soft tapping on the door. Belle got up, futilely swiping a hand through her uncombed hair. "Ted and I are spending the night elsewhere." She turned around. "Unless—"

"I don't need a minder."

"Quinn's here, anyway," Belle said.

"I don't need a minder of any type."

Belle opened the door, and in stepped the scoutmaster, looking hale as a new recruit despite his unbroken hours in the car. Behind him, at the approximate distance one dog would keep from a rival dog, Quinn leaned against a porch stay, glowering. "You all right in there, Ona?" he called. His voice knifed through the warm evening air, straight to her fast-ticking heart.

"Of course I'm all right," she announced to one and all. "For crumbsake, why wouldn't I be?"

Ona followed Belle and Mr. Ledbetter outside, where Belle sliced Quinn with a new expression: sympathy, perhaps, or whatever else floated in the watery unsayable between two long-connected people.

"We'll be back in the morning," Belle said. "I'll drive you home."

"Quinn can drive me home."

Mr. Ledbetter said, "His license expired. Or something."

"I bought it back," Quinn said. "Ona wouldn't care even if I hadn't."

"Not a whit," she agreed, pleased to take sides. It had been so long since she'd embroiled herself in the business of human striving that she embraced all of it, even the parts that broke her heart.

"Are you going, or not?" Quinn said.

Mr. Ledbetter teetered with indecision. "We'll come back in the morning," he said. "Belle and I can follow behind, so if something happens"—here he zeroed in on Ona, with touching sincerity—"we can take you with us, Mrs. Vitkus."

"I don't need a goddamn police escort, Ted," Quinn told him. "Take your girlfriend and go."

The scoutmaster massaged his temples, not with rancor but with the resignation of a troop leader whose charges keep tripping up. "Mrs. Vitkus—"

"I mean it, Ted. Go find a B&B with pineapples on the curtains. Go *relate*."

"Quinn, don't be an ass," Belle said. She patted Ona's arm. "You're okay with this?"

"Perfectly," she said, switching sides again. "Get yourself some sleep in that nice man's arms."

"I don't like to leave you stranded, Mrs. Vitkus," that nice man said now. She'd refused the new boy—*I can manage just fine in the summer*—but resolved now to accept the Scout he brought come fall, no matter how objectionable the specimen.

"She's not stranded, Ted," Quinn snapped. "Jesus Christ, you see me standing here, right?"

"I'm not stranded, Mr. Ledbetter," Ona said. "Merely afield of my usual haunts."

Belle headed off toward the van, then turned back. "Feed her," she said—to Quinn, presumably. "Last time she ate was in Keene." It was fully night now, and she disappeared into it.

"All right, then," the scoutmaster said to Ona. "I guess . . ."

"She's fine, Ted. Go."

At last Ted Ledbetter turned to Quinn, his presumed rival. From a young woman's point of view it wasn't much of a contest, and in Belle's red blouse Ona gauged the men as Belle might have. Quinn: vaguely dangerous-looking, tall and slouchy, the lines on his face hard earned. Mr. Ledbetter: safe as gingerbread in his polo shirt and puckered elbows, a gangling Honest Abe, a guileless, wifeless family man in search of a family.

He turned to Quinn now, without malice. "I loved your son," he said. He betrayed not a pin drop of irony. This was no dogfight. This was a cry from a suffering man, and Quinn seemed to know it, so he backed down, thoroughly disarmed.

Mr. Ledbetter walked quietly away. They watched him get into his van and join the sparse line of traffic headed back toward the town of Granyard.

"You hungry?" Quinn asked. "The restaurant looks passable."

"I could eat." In truth, she was ravenous. Her run at immortality, doomed by a house fire, had been resurrected by an unstrung woman who'd horned in on her road trip. How could it be that Ona Vitkus, after so many years alone, had been netted by the maneuverings of lovers and interlopers, tangled into their grief and envy and clumsy efforts at peace? And oh, weren't they a show: their puzzling wants, their cross-purposes, their own mundane, ticking-down minutes.

* * *

This is Miss Ona Vitkus. This is her life memories and shards on tape. This is Part Six.

Go ahead. You pick one.

. . .

The Roaring Twenties? Let me see those. The Jazz Age? The Great Depression? I see where this is going. If you're looking for a history of the twentieth century you're better off with a textbook. Or a man. Tell your Mr. Whoozinwhat that people don't live in capital letters.

. . .

Linkman. Tell Mr. Linkman that Miss Ona Vitkus spent the Jazz Age washing diapers and reading *The Modern Priscilla*.

. . .

It's a magazine about keeping house. But I'll tell you one thing about the Great Depression. Two things, since you like lists.

One: Some people skated by just fine.

Two: You think you discovered recycling? We reused butcher paper.

. . .

First you soap off the juices.

. . .

From meat. Beef and pork and such. Then you smear vinegar over the whole works. Then you dry it up and use it again. We kept it in the store to wrap guitar strings.

. . .

Let's find one I can answer. Here's one: Influential People. Ask that.

. . .

Maud-Lucy comes to mind, naturally. In my girlhood. Otherwise, Louise. Louise was a ticket. Sometimes I see her, clear as a full moon.

. . .

Not literally. I don't literally see her, for crumbsake. But she's there, in my mind's eye.

. . .

Is that so? How long was he gone?

. . .

Five years is a long time when you're a young fellow. Not so much when you're my age. At my age five years is an eye blink. What happened when he came back?

. . .

My goodness. And how long did the second one last?

. . .

Do you like your mother's new fellow? This somewhat secret fellow who might be your father someday?

. . .

You certainly did mention it, however briefly. You're not the only one with a good memory.

. . .

He sounds like a very nice man.

. . .

Of course you love your father. I might point out, however, that it's no crime to love the other fellow, too, if he's a good man who's kind to you.

. . .

You're welcome. Now, where—?

. . .

Oh, Louise was something else: that queenly bearing, those snappy eyes—oh, my, just a stunner. Unfortunately, it brought out the mouse in me. I'd left Howard to become a professional secretary, so wouldn't you think I'd be twanging with confidence? But certain women, they command things and you obey.

. . .

Thank you. But I wasn't that type at all. I required filling out, and when you're the type that requires filling out, you go looking for stuffing, and there she was.

. . .

Except for me, and the Franco ladies who ran the kitchen, I was the sole female at Lester Academy when Louise blustered in like the last leaves of autumn. So, we were comrades of sorts, Louise and I. Lester was our desert island and I was starving and Louise had all the food.

. . .

They were good boys, I would say. Nothing like these boys today. Present company excepted.

. . .

You're welcome. They came from Boston, mainly. Tuition was no trifle, but what secretly kept Lester afloat was a fearsome woman named Mrs. Emmaline Simpson. She was the great-granddaughter of the founder. Mrs. Simpson grew up in Lester, where women aspired to nothing, but somehow Mrs. Simpson managed a Bachelor of Arts degree from Swarthmore College.

. . .

Oh, it's quite the fancy-pants place, in Pennsylvania, I believe. Every June she visited us, with her high white hair and mother-of-pearl combs and an eighty-pound dress you could convincingly hang on a curtain rod.

. . .

Her purpose was always the same: she wanted more lady authors in the English classes.

. . .

Something along the lines of Mistress Bradstreet. She'd make her so-called suggestion, leave the men to so-called decide, and then, at five sharp, return to school to deposit her annual check. On her way out she always gave me a box of sweets from Italy.

. . .

A lady poet from Colonial America. She wrote quite a bit about her wonderful husband.

. . .

That's all right, I'd never heard of her, either.

. . .

Well, Mrs. Simpson died. The trustees thought the old trickster might've left her money to a pack of homeless cats. But she did them one better, oh, she did. Her bequest was gargantuan—millions and millions!—but here's the hitch: the English department at Lester Academy for Boys would thereafter include a qualified woman.

. . .

Oh, I agree. Homeless cats would have been equally deserving. But can you imagine the hand wringing at the trustees' meeting? On they went about the Lester tradition.

. . .

On the contrary, it was kind of amusing. One man after another, gum-flapping about tradition, tradition, tradition. If they could *eat* tradition, they would have. They combed their *hair* with it. What a day that was. A woman on the faculty? Unthinkable. I took notes, which was my job, and some of the words I declined to take down were the type for which no shorthand yet existed.

. . .

Of course they did. Money talks, always does. Fall of 1954: enter Louise, a one-woman weather system.

. . .

Hmm. Smart. That's the first thing. Independent. But you really—you had to know her to see how she was. The war changed certain women. Note that down under World War II.

. . .

That's all right, I can wait.

. . .

Some women, correct. On the outside, I must have looked like one of them, one of those changed women. I'd lost poor Frankie;

I'd left Howard; I'd moved away from home and taken up another life. But otherwise I was the same bridled girl I'd always been, if you don't count my one bolt out of the barn at the age of fourteen, the consequences of which I have already committed to this little gizmo—under duress, I might add.

. . .

Don't apologize. You're a good boy. I am merely noting the ratio of your willingness to my willingness. But what I meant was that the war changed Louise, too—she lost her two baby brothers in a single day—but you got the feeling it made her more of what she already was.

. . .

Alive. Blazing. She was forty-two years old and looked thirty. I was fifty-four and looked sixty.

. . .

Oh, she worked out fine at first. They had a kerfuffle over Shakespeare, of all things. Mr. Shakespeare could be a naughty old teaser, and Dr. Valentine took umbrage at Louise's interpretations. So, a skirmish during year one, nothing fatal. Year two, also quiet, by Louise's standards. She taught mostly what she was asked to teach, didn't complain much. But by year three, she found her feet and started improvising.

. . .

We were well into the school year, I remember—the trees were *spitting* leaves. Here comes Louise, in this gabardine suit dress tight across the seat and so purple you'd swear it had a pulse. Until now she's been standoffish—"hello" is about all I've heard from her direct—so I've got her pegged as a stuck-up.

"Shall I tell Dr. Valentine you're here?" I ask her. Very politely, of course. It's my job.

"If you dare," she says to me.

. . .

Oh, she was. Very funny. Then she laughs that steamship laugh of hers and plunks her hind end right down on my desk, on a stack of unsent letters.

. . .

Dr. Valentine suffered from chronic regret so I saved correspondence for double-checking at the end of the day. I didn't care to ask her to move her backside, but I wasn't leaving her unsupervised with those letters, either. So I sat there. A hostage.

. . .

Doing like you're doing. Looking. Getting the lay of the land.

. . .

Here's what: Louise thinks she's in trouble over George Eliot—that's a lady writer from the eighteen hundreds. She's been working George Eliot's shadowy love life into her lectures. A mother called, then a father called.

. . .

But that's not why she's being summoned, and I don't know how to tell her, since she's gibbering on about George Eliot being a glutton for punishment when it came to men. I felt like a glutton for punishment myself at the time, for reasons I shall not go into here. "But oh," Louise says to me, "it made her writing so much more *lush*." She made the word *lush* sound like biting into Satan's apple.

. . .

Lush.

. . .

More or less. I'm a poor mimic. "Does Dr. Valentine suppose that great writers draw inspiration from dust?" Louise asks me. "From air?"

. . .

I'm sure I had no idea whence great writers drew their inspiration; I was trying to fiddle out whether to warn her that Dr. Valentine had summoned Louise Grady on another account entirely.

. . .

Well, there was a rumor afoot.

. . .

About Louise and the Hawkins boy.

. . .

A boy in the Senior Seminar. Quite a hale, strapping fellow who shaved twice a day. A freckle-faced eighth-grader got the story going and now, *bammo,* it was everywhere. Poor Louise, nattering on about George Eliot, when in truth she was being hauled in as a corrupter of morals. A *femme fatale.*

. . .

A schemer. A female schemer.

. . .

Somebody who connives to make people feel a certain way even when they don't exactly want to. There's no corresponding word for a man but there should be.

. . .

Scheming to, well, to make that boy fall in love with her.

. . .

I had no idea whether or not it was true, but I was worried.

. . .

Because she was the only woman I ever saw all day. I didn't want the only other woman on the premises to get fired.

. . .

I said, "Perhaps if you tamed your lectures you would cease to be such an attraction."

. . .

No, no. This was after we got to be friends. Louise liked being an attraction. She *was* an attraction.

. . .

Oh, but you will be. You just wait. Girls are going to line up at your door.

. . .

Yes, they will. You have the sort of handsome that girls don't notice until later.

. . .

Eighteen or so. Twenty-one.

. . .

It's not that long. You'll see.

. . .

Right, so there sits Louise on my unsent letters, expecting a bracing duel with Dr. Valentine. "Such sheltered little sticks, these boys," she says to me. "Exactly like their fathers. Have you noticed, Miss Vitkus?"

This, I should note for the record, was the first full sentence she ever directed specifically to me. And she keeps running her lip, even though by this time Dr. Valentine's door is open and there he is, not ten feet away, a portrait of electrified alarm, standing beside Mr. and Mrs. Hawkins, whose fire-breathing rage I can feel in the tingling roots of my hair.

. . .

Oh, my goodness, yes, I nearly died. But Louise has a sixth sense for an audience, so she removes her bottom from my desk—without so much as nudging a single letter—stands up, and before turning fully around says quietly to me, though everyone within earshot can make out her words, "If there's one thing the male animal cannot abide, Miss Vitkus, it's a female with secrets."

. . .

Wow is right. To this day, I don't know whether she was referring to George Eliot's secrets, or her own, or mine. In any case, I was burning—oh, I was *aflame*—because after she said that, Dr. Valentine stopping looking at Louise.

. . .

At me. He was looking at me.

. . .

Indeed I was. I was a female with a secret.

Chapter 16

He woke late, in a funk of self-reproach, trapped in bleachy motel sheets. After banging on Ona's door for ten frazzling minutes, he summoned the motel manager—same beaky kid from the night before—who unlocked the door on the mortifying sight of Ona emerging from the bathroom in a knee-length nightgown. Quinn yelped like a stepped-on cat.

"What are you doing in here?" Ona wailed. "Get out!"

Quinn clapped his hands over his eyes as the manager fled. "I knocked fifty million times, Ona," he said, turning his back. "I thought . . ." He faced the open doorway, the daylight beyond, the temptation of Ona's gassed-up car. He was done with good deeds. Ted's theatrical "rescue" had pretty much exhausted his appetite for goodness.

"Get *out*," she repeated. "I don't plan to expire for another eighteen years."

An hour later, over a wretched breakfast in the attached grease trap where they'd eaten once already, Quinn remained mute with embarrassment, sipping morosely at a cup of watery coffee as Ona polished off a three-stack of blueberry pancakes. Apples, it seemed, were not yet in season.

Ona took up the slack. "Wouldn't you expect a successful surgeon raised in the lap of loving kindness to come up with a happier ending than wheeling himself around a nursing home with a pair of binoculars?"

"People don't write their own endings," he said.

"Well, I'm planning to write mine." Despite the nightgown incident she was oddly perky, owing to Belle's impulsive offer of help, which she'd mentioned four times already.

"We could swing by to see your son again on the way out of town," he offered. "Not to put too fine a point on it, Ona, but this could be your last chance."

"Don't you worry," she said. "Laurentas has a good ten years left in him." She twinkled from across the table.

He said, softly enough that she might not catch it, "I was a rotten father."

Ona nodded, noncommittal. "There are worse things."

"Like what?" He really wanted to know.

"Being an adequate mother." She took a swig from her coffee mug. "Rotten fathers are a dime a dozen, who even notices? Whatever kind you were—and I'm sure you weren't as bad as you think—you probably did the best you could, and nobody expects much more out of a man."

"Belle did."

"I'll tell you, Quinn," she said gravely. Her use of his name startled him. "If you acted more like a grieving father, your lady might want you back."

In her face he saw fondness, so he surrendered: "What does a grieving father act like?"

She said nothing for a time. Then: "Like that Ledbetter fellow."

Stung, Quinn made no answer as a party of seven clattered in, high school kids in team jerseys, hooting like owls. They took the curving window station and spread out as if they owned the booth, the town, their own souls, all the joy and folly in the world.

"And I wish you'd stop calling her my 'lady,'" Quinn said, "when she obviously isn't."

"You asked me a question. I gave you an answer."

He thought about getting up and leaving her there. Let her figure out how to drag her Ledbetter-loving bones the two hundred thirty miles back to Portland, since the sainted scoutmaster hadn't shown up after all.

He waved away any further discussion, and they finished eating in silence. Ona plucked a napkin from her lap and dabbed at her chin. "I wonder if there's a record for most delicious pancakes."

Quinn observed her for a moment. "I can't figure out how he hooked you on this records kick." He drained his coffee. "You got reeled all the way in."

"One," she said, "it's not a kick. Two, he reeled me in with enthusiasm."

He kept forgetting essential facts about his own son: the boy had been an enthusiast, this was true. His laughter erupted out of nowhere, startling as a dog in the night; he had his delights well sheathed and brandished them at unexpected moments. Here and gone, here and gone. Unlike Belle, unlike Amy, unlike anyone with a soft spot for the boy, Quinn found this card trick of an inner life unsettling, even disorienting. A memory of the boy's recitations attacked him unannounced: the wiry voice; the lists; the counting; the motionless face and twitchy fingers. He'd been uneasy around the boy, troubled by the world in which he dwelled.

"Look here," Ona said. "Look who's here."

Ted and Belle: Ted hugging a lurid geyser of maroon and orange lilies, Belle in a fetching white sundress he'd never seen. The straps, trimmed in red, looked edible. Her hair shone. *Touché, Ledbetter,* he thought bitterly. *Well done.*

"I need a favor," Belle said. "Don't say no." Before Quinn could duck for cover, she lobbed the grenade: "Ted and I are getting married in half an hour and we need witnesses."

The high school kids applauded; Belle gave them a startled glance, then smiled. Ted grinned like a sunflower as Quinn's head filled with bees.

"A wedding?" Ona said. Her color bloomed. He could see how someone might take her for, say, ninety-five, in exactly the right light.

"We got the license this morning," Ted told her, "but we need witnesses to make us legal."

Belle said, "The town clerks weren't very friendly."

"That's just Vermont," Ted said. "They don't say much."

"Anyway, we wanted to have people we know." Belle turned to Ona. "I figured you'd still be here. Quinn hasn't gotten up before ten since high school."

"This isn't as sudden as you think," Ted said to Quinn. "We've been talking about it"—here he looked lovingly at Belle—"for a while."

Belle lifted her foot, from which dangled a white sandal decorated with gold rivets. "I picked these up at a Walmart. We've been up since six." She looked—not happy, no; but less doomed.

"I've got a gig tonight," Quinn said, head still buzzing. "We have to leave, like, ten minutes ago." He'd been smacked in the forehead with a baseball once and this felt worse.

"It's those religious boys," Ona reminded everyone. "They won't mind if he's a little late."

"It won't take five minutes," Belle said. "I don't expect cartwheels, Quinn, but if you care for me, then this is how you show it."

She gave him a look, spectral and large-eyed, that embraced the length and breadth of their history. This was all he had left of her.

She had looked this way on the night before the boy's third birthday, sitting Quinn down in their darkened house after he'd dragged in from a gig and set down his gear. "This wasn't my idea of family life," she said to him, snapping on a lamp. "Loneliness was the last thing I expected." It was one of those moments in which clocks seem to stop ticking. "I'd rather do this by myself," she said, "than feel resentful all the time. I'd rather have you be *actually* absent than *virtually* absent."

Bleary from an hour's drive on rainy roads, he fished the night's take from his pocket. "I'm making a living," he said. "I'm holding up my end."

"We need more than a living," she whispered. "We need a life."

He wanted his bed, his wife's warm body laid against his, and two or three hours of oblivion before being woken by their son, who was fearful of insects and dust bunnies and bulky coats and the color yellow. Every morning was the same: the same tremolo of panic scaling the octaves as Belle bolted out of bed and Quinn woke to a head rush of adrenaline.

"I thought we'd rise to the occasion a little better than we have," she said. But of course Belle *had* risen to the occasion. If there were a theoretical maximum height to which a person could rise to an occasion, Belle had reached it; she had scaled the craggy summit of occasion through icy winds, in bare feet, pursued by wolves.

"What?" Quinn said, alarmed by her expression. "Wait." Words harbored myriad meanings and he was a poor interpreter. He felt swimmy and cockeyed, though he'd been sober since the day the boy entered the world. Their son: fifth percentile in height and weight but bright to the point of unease, completing puzzles made for ten-year-olds and copying words out of books. Belle's aunts, who baby-sat in shifts, dotingly claimed that he wore them out just by existing.

"Here's what I want," she said now, unfolding a piece of paper. It looked like a long list. "I want you to fix the fence," she began. "I want you to like getting up early. I want you to take us to the park on Saturdays. I want you to quit gigging." She paused. "I want you to act like you love us." Her voice took on a harmonic understory, the sound of an old, wooden instrument, the same plangent voice in which she'd first revealed her pregnancy. She'd missed a pill—an unconscious act of will, they decided later—but at the time she could not fathom how such a thing had come to pass. *Now that it has, though, it's ours to embrace.* Then, as now, she'd emanated a slow burn of core belief. *You don't have to marry me, Quinn. A lot of guys wouldn't.*

"There's a studio starting up in Cambridge," he said carefully. "I know the guy."

Belle shut her eyes.

"No, Belle, listen, he's looking for session players." He took her hands. "We wouldn't have to move. I'll commute."

"Oh, Quinn." Belle sighed and covered her eyes. "All this was fine for us once. I liked getting sucked down the rabbit holes. But that was before."

"Belle, listen—"

"I loved your music," she said. "I thought—" She folded her hands on the cottony lap of her nightgown, where her list of requests made an ominous crackle.

"You thought what?"

"I believed you. I believed it all."

Her use of the past tense flooded him with grief. He flashed to her dorm room after his gig with the Benders in the quad, Belle a girl of nineteen, her walls pulsating with abstracts framed in pine. "I thought I wanted something different," she added softly. "I wish I could have wanted something different. Really, Quinn, I do. But it turns out I want the same things everybody else wants." Her voice retained that timbre, that wearified resonance. A voice made for singing, except that Belle couldn't carry a tune. He loved this about her: to Belle, all music was a miracle.

He said, "I wish I could've wanted something different, too."

"What I want"—she looked at him—"is another baby."

"Oh. No. Oh, Belle. I can't."

She nodded solemnly. "I know."

A small clang went off in his head. "There isn't—is there someone else?"

"No," she said. But he heard: *Not yet.*

He'd married her when to do otherwise would have been easier—proof, as if he needed it, that he loved her. He'd claimed their child. He hadn't blamed her for the missed pill. This slender sign of his own decency—his hope that he wasn't *a lot of guys*—guided him through their parting. There were ultimatums and slip-backs; long, anguished nights of lovemaking; promises made and broken; and many tears; but in the end Belle's heartfelt list amounted to one impossible task: become somebody else.

When finally he took to the road, he vowed to do just that, become somebody else, like the gold rushers and stake claimers of the

American West who chased the horizon and sent their money back home. He'd establish a presence in a good studio, become the flexible journeyman, the musician's musician, the go-to guy who showed up in liner notes and album credits. He'd prove to her how worthy was his dream.

The legal dissolution reached him in Chicago, where he read all the fine-printed paragraphs, every *whereas* reminding him of their history, so intricately woven it could be sundered only by force of law. Five years later, when he married her again — *Because I missed you, Quinn, and sons need fathers* — he said "I do" with such force and volume it made her laugh out loud.

But he meant it, that second "I do," even with his mysterious son standing by — staring, listening, counting something unknowable on his bonelike fingers. Was the boy counting Quinn's thoughts? Is that what he was counting?

He'd felt like a bulldog presented to a boy who had asked for a parakeet.

Did he try hard enough? He thought he did. A year later, numbed by a job assembling sound systems at Best Buy, Quinn was suffering the old, awful, needling itch of restlessness and Belle was talking once again about babies. His fingers ached from not playing, and the plodding months had dulled his shiny wish to restore Belle's happiness.

"He likes to list things," he ventured one night, washing the dishes as she dried. "Is that unusual?" For weeks he'd kept the question unasked, but it blundered out unbidden, spoiling their tableau of domestic calm.

Belle shrugged. "*One, two, three* were his first words." The words had not come till the boy turned four, one of countless troubling details Quinn had strung together since his return.

Amy, visiting for the long weekend, chimed in then: "They call it personality, Quinn." She tore off a piece of homemade gingerbread and offered it as compensation for trumping him, but his hands were wet and he refused it.

Carefully, he said, "It's just that the other kids don't seem so—"

He stopped, regrouped. "I wonder if there might be a concern. Some possible—concern."

Belle continued drying, though her body showed she was listening. "What do you mean by 'concern'?" she asked, confirming his belief that she planned to transmit information in orchestrated stages for fear of derailing the family reunion. His dismay was tempered by the pride he felt in reading her so well between the lines.

"One, he stares," Quinn said, using his fingers to make an additional, not-heretofore-mentioned point. "Two, his arms don't move when he walks."

Belle was watching him now, holding a filigreed saucer. She'd taken to serving coffee in old-fashioned vessels, which struck him as an overreach.

"He doesn't move like other kids," he went on. "His arms just sort of stay—put. Straight down. At his sides. Like somebody tied him up."

Belle's forehead crinkled. "Are you—you're not making fun of him?"

"No! God, no, Belle. I'm being a, an involved father." He shot a panicked glance at Amy. "I don't have experience with kids"—an eye roll from Amy here—"so I don't know what's normal and what . . . isn't."

Silence.

"Three," he said, "it's like there's a tape recorder in his head. If he hears something wrong the first time—somebody's name, say—it sticks there, like it's on a tape loop and can't be overdubbed with the correct information." He'd dug his hole now and decided to keep digging. "It just seems like there might be a couple of areas of concern. Possible—areas. In his social development or whatever."

"His vocabulary blows the doors off those other kids," Amy said.

"I know, he does, he has a great vocabulary. Stupendous vocabulary." He didn't understand where the boy got his words, or the often elaborate syntax into which he inserted them. "But, okay, how about the way he calls his teacher Mr. Linkman? I've corrected him fifty times, but he still says Mr. Linkman. I mean, he knows that the sixteenth president of the United States was Abraham *Lincoln*. He can tell you all about *Lincoln's* childhood home and *Lincoln's* wife's name and what play *Lincoln* was watching the night he was shot and the names of the men who made up the *Lincoln* cabinet and who built the *Lincoln* Memorial, but he still insists on calling his teacher Mr. Linkman."

Belle and Amy exchanged deflatingly knowing glances. "Maybe that's because his teacher's name is Mr. Linkman," Belle said. "Andy Linkman." The women burst into laughter, and the sustained tension of the conversation reached a chordal resolve that came as a relief to all.

"Gosh, Quinn," Amy said, "it's like you've got a *tape recorder* in your head."

"Leave him alone," Belle said amiably. "I like a man who worries."

"Obviously that was a bad example." But there were others: the boy called grasshoppers *grasshornets*. He called boundary *bondery*, gratitude *grabitude*.

The women laughed again, especially Amy. He let her have her moment—it was part of his campaign to be a better person—then said, "What I'm saying is that no matter how many times he sees or hears the word *grasshopper*, he's going to say *grasshornet*. And I'm wondering—if you don't mind, Amy—if that might be a problem. I'm wondering, as a concerned father."

Belle stiffened. "There's nothing wrong with him."

"You're not listening," he said, geared up now for no reason he could rationally name. "Can't his teachers help him?"

"I don't know, Quinn. Why don't you march on down to his school, if you can find it, and ask Mr. *Lincoln*? If you think you're in over your head, tell me now."

The moment, it seemed, had come. For a year and a half now he'd been watchful, his questions cautiously posed and artfully dodged as the boy went about his mystifying business. "I'm *asking*, all right?" he said. "As his *father*. He's in his room right now, doing what? Counting shoelaces or memorizing world bowling scores or arranging two hundred blank CDs into an indecipherable pattern or writing unexplainable items on a list. Why doesn't he have friends? Why the hell does he *count* everything?"

Amy sat up. *What CDs?* her eyes asked. *What do you mean, no friends?* Belle returned a look of helpless indignation. Did she decide to consider medication then? Right here, when Quinn intimated that the boy was damaged and Amy sat up, noticing?

"He's just who he *is*," Belle said, facing them both. "Our own funny little boy." Which was exactly the right thing to say—quintessential Belle. In one exquisitely calibrated sentence, she managed to round them up as a trio, beefing up Amy's responsibility while diffusing Quinn's.

Later that night, while Belle saw to the boy's elaborate bedtime ritual—ten sips of water, ten fluffs of the pillow, ten deep breaths—Quinn confided to Amy, "Shouldn't a nine-year-old kid be on a baseball team?"

"He's in Scouts."

"But he can't name a single other kid in the troop." Quinn had taken him to a den meeting that very morning, a humbling exercise wherein he watched Ted Ledbetter, his unbeknownst future rival, demonstrate his skill with children. "You don't think that's strange, Amy? From a list maker? That he can't name one kid in his troop?"

They were drinking Scotch in the living room—or, Amy was drinking Scotch; Quinn had a Sprite. "Actually," Amy said, "what's strange is that you told him fifty times that his teacher's name was Mr. Lincoln, and he knew it wasn't, and he didn't correct you."

Quinn took a long, unproductive guzzle of his fake drink.

"He's afraid of you, Quinn. You have to try harder." She set down her own drink, which quivered alluringly. "Sisterly advice? Belle thinks you never bonded with your own child, and whether or not that's true"—here she paused significantly—"making judgments about his basic and unchangeable nature just adds fuel to the fire."

Quinn despised the word *bonded*, which reminded him of liability insurance, and he suspected Amy of using it to goad him. But she was a little drunk, and they were otherwise getting along, so he gave her a pass.

"He's not an easy kid to bond with."

"What could be easier?" she said, without rancor. "He's a beautiful, beautiful child," she said. "I love him." Then she faced him with an expression so unguarded, so achingly helpless, that he couldn't muster the guts to hold her gaze.

Belle and Ted were waiting for his answer. He sensed the party of high schoolers watching from their corner booth.

"I've never been in a wedding," Ona twittered. "No one has ever once asked me."

"I wanted to get married at home," Ted said, "but this'll be just fine. Just perfect." He turned to his bride-to-be, unable to hide his bafflement. "My mother and the boys will be disappointed, though."

"We'll have a party eventually," Belle said. "Maybe even another ceremony." She slipped her hand into the crook of his elbow exactly as she'd once done with Quinn.

Oh, God, Quinn thought. *She loves the guy.* And why wouldn't she? Ted Ledbetter wanted a real wedding in which he rounded up his creaky mother and charming sons and all of Troop 23 and the other teachers at King Middle School and the women who'd known his angelic late wife; he wanted to assemble on a beach to proclaim his love over the music of gulls and cellos, but because Belle could not bear a meeting of dearly beloved—not now, maybe not ever—he'd agreed to repeat a few boilerplate phrases after a pokerfaced Vermont town clerk. He was committing to the crushed remnants of the woman he loved, to a lawsuit that would take years, to a sister-in-law who would engage him in a lifelong border dispute, to a father-in-law who would chew him up so hard there'd be no need to swallow.

Quinn tried to marshal his envy and resentment; instead, he dredged up a surprise: awe.

"It won't take five minutes," Belle said.

He couldn't smile. "I'd be delighted."

Ted edged in, smelling of peppermint, wearing the same shirt from the day before, a far cry from the wedding coat he'd likely kept for months in a dry-cleaning bag. "She won't regret me, Quinn, I promise."

Quinn didn't doubt it, much as he longed to. Ted was the kind of man Belle should have married in the first place. "Goddamn it," he said under his breath, "let's just go."

Ona got up. "I'm hardly presentable to attend a wedding, much less participate."

"Neither am I," said the besotted Ted, "but try and stop me."

The overfilled bouquet turned out to be two separate bundles, one of which he presented to Ona. "For the matron of honor." His smile lengthened and he seemed to relax, his happiness at last immune to Quinn's presence, to the functional ceremony, to his closest kin being two states away.

"I accept," Ona said, as if *her* hand were the one he wanted. Quinn shot her a punishing glare for so fluidly switching sides, but she merely opened her eyes wider, silently urging him to rise to the occasion.

"Good luck, you guys!" called one of the high schoolers, a girl in a pink baseball cap.

Quinn paid the bill and Ona took his arm as if they were in an official wedding party. Mac Cosgrove had always admonished Quinn to associate with "goal setters." Well, he was escorting one out to the car this very minute; she'd freshened her lipstick and smelled very nice.

"You're a gentleman," she informed him as he ferried her through the grease-printed doors. "You're doing the gentlemanly thing."

Despite her age, her infirmity, her lack of physical wiles, she managed to float on his arm in Belle's red blouse like the girl she must once have been, and her attentions flattered him. He found them improbably welcome. She looked up at him as if appraising a gem; the least he could do was stand up for the bride and try his best to shine.

PART FOUR

Draugas (Friend)

* * *

This is Miss Ona Vitkus. This is her life memories and shards on tape. This is Part Seven.

. . .

We were talking about Louise. And that awful rumor. Louise first landed on my doorstep very shortly thereafter.

. . .

I think it was October. Couldn't have been winter yet. But all the same I recollect her arrival as a wintry one, her cheeks afire with cold. Seems like a January night in my mind, now; the air had that midwinter crackle. You know that feeling, like the air might break?

. . .

Well. Weather was different back then. I'd just made one of my favorite suppers, and suddenly there was Louise Grady at my door.

. . .

Meat pie, with fried cabbage on the side. The secret is caraway, if you ever take a notion.

. . .

It's a seed. Possibly I had my mother in mind. She'd died over the summer and Papa had passed long before that. But until the summer of 1955 Mama was living on Wald Street, ninety-one years old and still minding her parsnips. She dropped right there in her garden on a hot July day, which struck me even at the time as an easeful way to go.

. . .

All those growing things must soften the blow, don't you think? A dressy row of carrots calling, "Don't be afraid! It smells marvelous under here!"

. . .

I know. Funny. So, there's Louise and her fiery cheeks in October. I invited her in for supper—couldn't very well avoid it, since she was standing there with a clear enough intention.

. . .

"Why, thank you, Miss Vitkus." That's what she said, as if my invitation was a big gift-wrapped surprise.

. . .

Oh, she could eat, that Louise. Plump equaled beautiful back then. You didn't see these half-starved coat racks prancing around in their underwear. Louise had on that purple suit dress.

. . .

Heavens, no. I wasn't the suit dress type. I had a closetful of shirtwaists. "What brings you out on such a cold evening, Miss Grady?" That's what I asked her after she'd shoveled into the pie.

. . .

She said, "Miss Vitkus, I find myself in need of an ally." Why she needed an ally I had no idea. The boy who'd loosened up the rumor—a scholarship boy, unfortunately, from a cannery family on River Street—he'd been expelled.

. . .

Because Louise confronted the little fellow right in front of the Hawkins boy and his parents, and when she finished she had Mrs. Hawkins in tears apologizing six ways from Sunday. The boys, too: both of them in tears.

. . .

It was over, yes, but Louise was taking no chances. Like me, she had no man to pay her bills. "How would you like to become a schoolgirl again, Miss Vitkus?" she asks me.

. . .

"I haven't been a schoolgirl since I was fourteen years old, Miss Grady," I told her. And I hastened to add, in case she thought me ill educated, that I'd had a brilliant tutor.

. . .

Exactly! Maud-Lucy Stokes, who schooled me like a countess.

. . .

She said, "Then you'll welcome the chance to reprise your studies, Miss Vitkus," and she invites me to take part in her Senior Literature Seminar. I would vacate my station from one o'clock to three o'clock every Monday afternoon, and apparently that was fine with Dr. Valentine. You have no idea what a radical proposition this was in 1955.

Has anyone ever told you—?

. . .

Your face. Not a single judging bone in it.

. . .

You're welcome. So I tell Louise, "I'd be honored to attend your seminar, Miss Grady." And Louise says, "Call me Louise."

. . .

Of course I did. Then I plundered my cupboards and found a bottle of sherry left behind by the previous tenant. I didn't have the right sort of glasses, but we toasted.

. . .

"Cheers," I imagine. I don't exactly recall. I remember clinking the wrong sort of glasses and wishing I had the *right* sort of glasses, and to this day I consider that moment—*clink!*—as the beginning of our friendship. I'm glad it made a sound.

. . .

I'll say we did! We went through half the bottle, and because I was unused to drinking, I may have mentioned Dr. Valentine more than once.

. . .

Oh, I adored him. He was so . . . accomplished. But Louise got an idea in her head.

. . .

As she was leaving my apartment she turned around and said, "How long, Ona Vitkus, have you been in love?" Her arms came around me. She smelled like violets even in that freezing night air. "He's your secret valentine," she said. "But Ona, dear, are you his?"

. . .

. . .

Excuse me. I forgot you for a second. You have this way of disappearing. Do you know what *unrequited* means?

. . .

U-n-r-e-q-u-i—. Never mind. You won't need that word, fine-looking boy like you.

. . .

You never mind about him. Poor man spent the rest of the term tippy-tapping around Louise, going so far as to let her tinker with the final modules of the seminar. That was Dr. Valentine's word, *modules*. I think he made it up, though by the time the sixties got into full swing everybody was using it.

. . .

The idea was to corral time in a fashion that took advantage of the boys' fickle brains. At the time it was revolutionary, but you know, Dr. Valentine wasn't a rebel. He was just a man in the wrong job. He liked his tea and muffin in the morning. Honestly, he was just a smarter, pleasanter, better-educated, handsomer, more enchanting version of Howard.

. . .

Right, so Louise was getting ready for the final module of the Senior Literature Seminar, which was supposed to get the boys all hepped up over Nathaniel Hawthorne and Walt Whitman and Henry Wadsworth Longfellow.

. . .

Long-winded gasbags from the nineteenth century. But Louise slipped in some lady writers with scandalous personal lives.

. . .

"These boys need a fuller immersion in the bracing waters of literature," she'd say. I thought she had a point, not that anyone asked me.

. . .

Oh, the boys were all for it. They found the notion of female rebellion hard to resist. And anyway, they were all half in love with Louise by then.

. . .

Because she listened. The way you're doing right now. Poor Louise had to scuffle for every book on her list. She took it as her duty to turn out future husbands with whom future wives could bear to converse over coffee and crumpets without plunging a butter knife into their own breasts.

. . .

Because Louise herself had divorced two imperfect men. No children, which left her with an excess of motherly inclinations. The boys' real mothers had fallen down on the job, is how Louise saw it.

. . .

I'm sure they did do the best they could.

. . .

Yes, I'm sure they did, I'm *agreeing* with you, but according to Louise it wasn't nearly enough. It was her burden, by default, not only to shine up the future husbands of the world, but also to prevent them from marrying batty-lashed simpletons.

. . .

By forcing the boys to read things like "Désirée's Baby"—that's a shocking story by a lady writer named Kate Chopin. A crusader, that was Louise. Her mother was an old suffragette from Philadelphia.

. . .

. . .

Sorry, I forgot you again. You know, one meets so many people, the years pass and pass, but there are certain times, certain people—

. . .

They take up room. So much room. I was married to Howard for twenty-eight years and yet he made only a piddling dent in my memory. A little nick. But certain others, they move in and make themselves at home and start flapping their arms in the story you make of your life. They have a wingspan.

. . .

I would say so, yes. I would say that you are a boy with a wingspan.

. . .

You're welcome. So, Louise brought in all these books for Dr. Valentine's approval. But she was a cagey one, that Louise. In they came, stack after stack, big sliding mountains of books. We had six chairs lined up along the wall outside Dr. Valentine's office, and that's where Louise deposited her books, on these straight-back chairs where boys were supposed to wait in a sweat after some absurd infraction.

. . .

One stack per chair. You never saw anything so comical, all those books sitting in neat towers, each one the height of a boy. You wanted to put hats on them.

. . .

Quite the opposite. Oho, Louise presented her books with the innocence of a candy cane. She had on this swirly red skirt and a bright white blouse with cap sleeves. Her shoes matched: red, with white piping. I haven't thought of those shoes for years: they practically *talked*.

"I'm considering these," she says to Dr. Valentine, "and these, and these, and these. Subject to approval."

Now, Dr. Valentine was handsome in his way, but a trifle gawky. Loosely jointed. He leaned over one stack, plucked up a book, leaned over another—like one of those long-necked birds you see in roadside marshes stabbing at tadpoles.

. . .

Not as funny as it sounds.

. . .

Because Dr. Valentine had elegance. So, we've got books on six chairs and Dr. Valentine is thoroughly flummoxed. Plus, Louise freighted the deck with such obvious outrages that her actual choices looked maidenly by comparison.

. . .

Dime-store paperbacks. Some Communist screeds. An account of a seventeenth-century lady of the night. In other words, some of her real choices slipped through unread.

. . .

You don't miss much, do you? It was *exactly* like watching a trick—a midway flimflam where you show the mark a talking magpie and pick his pocket while he's teaching the bird to say "Cincinnati."

. . .

You're right! Everything reminds me of birds today. Watch the window. I had a junco earlier. You might get number fifteen. In another couple of weeks you'll have your twenty and then some.

. . .

Thirty's not out of the question. You might get thirty.

. . .

Well, it took poor Dr. Valentine two weeks to poke through all the stacks. He missed "Désirée's Baby" and some other good ones, but he caught a book called *Mrs. Dalloway* by Virginia Woolf, who wasn't even American. That one he brought home for his wife to read.

. . .

It's about a lady who goes out to buy flowers for a dinner party. Which she didn't have to do.

. . .

Because she had plenty of money. She could have sent someone. Or had them delivered.

. . .

You know, I just recalled Dr. Valentine's wife's name. Sadie. She also gave dinner parties.

. . .

I was never invited. But Louise, she went to all of them. Sadie Valentine turned out to be a thorough reader, since she found the scene in *Mrs. Dalloway* where one lady kisses another lady, and she had to read quite a bit of the book to get to that part.

. . .

No, the dinner party happens at the end. The whole story takes place in one day; Louise made a big deal over that. The lady who's giving the party, she lives her whole wrong life, plus her other life that she might have had, in that one day.

. . .

Oh, no, Louise taught it anyway. I don't think Dr. Valentine ever found out. It's not a long book. Not my cup of tea, exactly, but Louise was a wonderful teacher. I hadn't studied with such ardor since I was a girl.

. . .

It *was!* It was *wonderful!* The truth is, people are replaceable.

. . .

They are. If you live a long time, you discover this. It took more than thirty-five years for Maud-Lucy's place to fill, but fill it did, with Louise, another brilliant woman willing to take on the burden of my education.

. . .

I'm no good at summaries. I suppose you'd have to say — if you had to, in one sentence — that the book is about being unthinkably lonely. Oops, there's your junco. That's fifteen.

MARRIED

1. Longest engagement. 67 years. Octavio Guillien and Adriana Martinez. Married at age 82. Country of Mexico.
2. Most times married to same person. 66 and counting. Lauren and David Blair. Country of USA.
3. Highest marriage rate. 35.1 per 1,000. Country of US Virgin Islands.
4. Largest wedding cake. 15,032 pounds. Country of USA.
5. Longest marriage. 86 years (1743–1829). Lazarus and Molly Rowe. Country of USA.
6. Most couples married in one wedding ceremony. 35,000. Country of South Korea.
7. Largest TV audience for a wedding. 750 million. Prince Charles and Lady Diana. Country of UK.
8. Longest train on wedding dress. 2,545 feet. Country of Netherlands.
9. City to hold most wedding ceremonies. Las Vegas. 280 per day. Country of USA.
10. Longest kiss. 30 hours and 59 minutes and 27 seconds. Louisa Almedovar and Rich Langley. Country of USA.

Chapter 17

According to the second hand on Quinn's watch, the ceremony—conducted in a beige second-floor office of the Granyard Town Hall—took six minutes and twenty-two seconds. The newlyweds headed homeward in Ted's freshly vacuumed van. Quinn bundled Ona into the Reliant and took the wheel. For about twenty miles the two couples caravanned, then Quinn lost patience, passed Ted's poky Windstar, and gunned the engine, Ona's matron-of-honor bouquet discharging festive clouds of lily pollen.

The wedding had given them much to ponder, so they didn't talk much. The drive was pleasant, the weather cooler, and he had the boy on his mind. During his five years away, Quinn had often felt as if he were orbiting the earth as real life went on far below him, barely visible. Upon reentry into the home atmosphere, he'd experienced a sweet sense of approach, and for months he cleaved to that feeling by force of will. The inevitable crash landing came in midwinter during a father-son "bonding" experiment embedded in a brief series of guitar lessons.

He'd taken a second day job teaching at a music store on Forest Avenue—Stanhope Music Company, the site of his future friend's past—and found himself an awkward teacher. The store owner deemed him "intimidatingly overeager," adding that many of the students (admittedly, the ones with no aptitude) didn't like him.

"This is different," Belle had assured him. He could still remember the way her lips formed the words. "He's your son."

For lesson six, Quinn once again invited the boy into the heated comfort of Belle's roomy garage, currently cleared out for renovation.

He arranged two facing chairs and neatened up a short, thoughtfully chosen stack of CDs.

"The longest distance marched by a marching band," said the boy, "was forty-six-point-seven miles."

Quinn plugged in two guitars. Belle jaunted in, left snacks, patted them both on the head, and retreated.

The boy took a single Oreo off a plate, a single parsimonious sip of ginger ale. "They marched from the town of Assen, country of Netherlands," he said, "to the town of Marum, country of Netherlands, on May 9, 1992."

Quinn presumed there was a manner in which one answered such conversational gambits; it's just that he could never think of one. He urged the boy to notice the salvaged soundproofing, installed since the last lesson, and the neatly assembled stash of equipment he'd scored from a local studio going under.

"It took thirteen hours and fifty minutes," the boy said. "Sixty marchers started and fifty-two marchers finished."

The floor problem—fissured concrete—remained unsolved, possibly unsolvable without overspending their budget. But giddy hope was the flavor of the season in his newly tooled household, so Quinn retained the mulish expectation that he'd have a studio up and running by spring.

"It was your mother's idea," he told the boy. "We'll bump out that wall, replace the doors, and rent out rehearsal space." He smiled zealously. "Plus recording services."

He said "we" to include the boy, to whom he'd already demonstrated his newly acquired setup—what boy didn't love machines?—but so far the boy had bared not a jot of interest. "I'll be the session player by day," Quinn said, patting the guitar in his lap, "and keep the home fires burning at night."

In response to the boy's stillness, Quinn added, "Do you know what *compromise* means?"

After another moment of solemn consideration, the boy said, "I don't think that will work."

What he meant was anyone's guess, so Quinn asked him to imagine the control booth beyond the wall, the performance space in front of him, a floating mic above his head, an open appointment book crammed with names, a humming empire that the boy, who had difficulty with spatial perception, could not envision.

"Never mind," Quinn said. "You'll see it for real soon enough. Did you listen to the songs I gave you?"

"Yes."

"Three times, like I asked?"

"Plus seven more times. Ten times." The boy looked terrified.

"This isn't a test. Try to relax. What did you think?"

"The songs have too many notes."

A terrible, unwanted thought crashed through the ceiling of Quinn's meticulously constructed caution, and not for the first time: this child couldn't be his. He just couldn't.

"They were supposed to inspire you," Quinn said. Physically, the boy was all Belle: all open-faced, belly-up innocence. The part that wasn't Belle—the part that resembled a secretive, burrow-dwelling animal—reminded him of his own father, who rarely spoke except to deliver pronouncements.

"Okay," the boy said, seeming to absorb Quinn's every unfatherly thought. How could he know? He did, though; Quinn felt cornered, caught, made to pay for his five-year absence. But he decided to take what was coming to him—not just now but forever.

You boys have to be men now, his father had once said. *Your mother's dead and that's all there is to it.*

The boy had put on his Scout uniform for the lesson, the logic of which surpassed Quinn's powers of deduction. Quinn regarded the costume's precise creases and attendant frippery, patches for everything except music. He placed a guitar—a Les Paul junior knockoff Belle had bought on sale—into the boy's arms and led him through a profoundly unsuccessful scale. "Don't think," he said. "Feel."

"Feel what?" said the boy.

Crying won't bring her back. Now let's get these things into the truck.

"Maybe ten times is too many times," the boy suggested. In his arms the guitar looked radioactive. Quinn wondered if it was possible for a human being to actually dislike music.

"Here," he said, arranging the boy's fingers into a first-position G. "We're going to try the one-four-five progression from last week, just to remind you what it sounds like. Then we'll review the other scale I taught you—remember the blues box?"

The boy's mouth made a perceptible downturn.

"Okay, then. Great. By the time you get back to school on Monday you'll have girls lining up to carry your books."

"I don't know any girls."

"You will if you play the blues."

"You said this was rock."

Quinn let out his breath, long and silent. "What is the foundation of rock-and-roll, the heart and core of all modern popular music?"

"Blues," the boy recited glumly.

"And what is the best blues solo ever produced by a nonblack guy, ever?" Quinn was getting heated up now and tried to hide it.

"'Sleepy Time Time,' by Eric Chapman."

Eric Chapman was Belle's across-the-street neighbor who washed his car every day and dried it with a leaf blower. Eric Chapman had once informed Quinn, from the wide-bottom seat of his lawn mower, that a man without a man's job had no business procreating.

"*Clapton*," Quinn said to his son, for the fiftieth time. "Eric *Clapton*. Clapton, Clapton, Clapton." He removed the guitar from the boy's narrow lap and laid it on the floor. "How about if we just listen?"

"I can listen," the boy said, apparently relieved to be divested of the guitar's metaphorical weight. Quinn was aware of the father-son dance he was conducting but helpless to improve his footwork.

It's time you pulled your own weight around here, mister. You want me to break that thing in half?

"Just relax your ears," Quinn said, cueing the music. He turned the balance all the way to the right; Clapton's notes rang through one speaker with the rhythm pulled into the background. The boy's huge, moonlike eyes took in either everything, or nothing. Who could tell? As the song engaged its reliable momentum, Quinn anticipated the arrival of Clapton's virtuosity, for the first time in his life, with dread. His head throbbed.

"You hear the solo coming in now?" he said, trying mightily to feel some way other than the way he felt. "Listen to that call and response." He shook his head in wonderment, as he always did, but it felt, again for the first time, like a learned gesture, and he was beginning to blame the boy for ruining one of his most trustworthy sources of bliss. "It's a conversation he's having with himself. You hear that? It's like something rising out of the goddamn *sea*. Just listen."

You sound just like the record, honey, his mother had marveled, standing at his bedroom door. One lasting memory: her gaunt fingers tapping on the doorjamb, keeping time. Her fingernails yellowing with illness. His mother, who loved music. Any music. But especially his.

The boy turned his head, at long last, toward the speakers, as the room filled with melodious joy. He appeared to be in physical pain, panting through parted teeth. Quinn stared into the ancient country of his son's unmoving eyes. Wrong song, wrong band, he realized. There was too much to hear, too many twining treasures, especially for a boy who didn't tap his feet or bob his head or otherwise betray the remotest affinity for musical rapture.

"Try to *receive* it," Quinn said now, referring to the sublime phrasing of Eric Clapton-Clapton-Clapton. "You hear the notes he's *not* playing? You hear that building pressure, building-building-building, and then *whammo*, he's off to some other spectacular place, but you hear the notes he left *unplayed*?" He hit STOP. "Those are ghost notes," he said. "You hear them, but they aren't there. It should take your breath away."

"Okay," the boy said.

"I don't expect you to play this way. You understand that, right?"

"Okay."

"This is about appreciating. It begins with appreciating."

"Okay." Rooted to the chair, the boy assumed the motionless carriage of a felon awaiting sentencing.

"Relax, my friend. It's only rock-and-roll."

"You said blues." The boy's lip quivered.

"I did," Quinn admitted. "I did say that."

The boy recovered himself—maybe he was tougher than he looked. Quinn picked up his own guitar and reproduced the solo in slow motion, note for note.

"What does 'their father's hell' mean?" the boy asked. "'Their *fa*ther's *hell* did *slow*ly *go* by'?" This was from "Teach Your Children," the song they'd given up on three weeks ago.

Turn down that noise! Don't make me come in there!

"I don't know," Quinn said. "You have to be a poet to know."

"I'm not a poet," the boy said. "Are you?"

"Maybe we should wrap this up."

The boy rose ceremonially to his feet. "I believe," he said dolefully, "that would be for the best." He picked up the cookie plate and glasses and headed for the breezeway door, where he turned around briefly. "One, the marching band from the country of Netherlands was called Marum, the same name as the town they marched to. Two, the world's largest playable electric guitar is forty-three feet and seven-point-five inches tall. Three, you play ten times more excellent than Eric Chapman."

Quinn nodded. "That's true," he said, thinking of psychotic, lard-assed Eric Chapman on his riding mower. "I blow Eric Chapman's doors."

He watched the boy disappear into the house, then played the famous solo again, grabbing all the notes but missing everything that composed its ferocious radiance—Clapton's tone, his phrasing, his inborn musical heartbeat—and it pained him to do this, it always had, and yet he loved this solo so much, the motion it accumulated, the comfort it offered, the place it visited, the story it made; he loved these things so much that he could not refrain from trying to enter that story, and he could not refrain from failing, again and again and again.

As they approached the Maine border, Quinn asked Ona, "When exactly *was* the last time you went to a wedding?"

"Nineteen sixty-seven," she said. "A boy from Lester married a girl from Henneford. They were nearly thirty, which was ancient then. What about you?"

"Hah."

"Oh, that's right." She looked at him. "You get jaded, I suppose, one wedding just like the next. I myself found the ceremony beguiling, especially when Mr. Ledbetter had to borrow the town clerk's ring."

"He'll have a diamond on her finger by nightfall."

"No doubt." She looked out the window. "I'd like to see the sister's face when your lady comes back with a husband." She was talking over the buffeting wind, which gave her speech an air of urgency, as if they were racing to prevent something that had already happened. "Her father, too," Ona added, shouting now. "I don't suppose he'll be pleased."

"Are you kidding? That crowd thinks Ted Ledbetter walks on water."

She rolled up her window. "He's a nice man."

"He doesn't walk on water, Ona."

"Not literally." A few miles ticked past. "Are you terribly disappointed?"

"That the scoutmaster doesn't literally walk on water?"

She pointed at him. "That the scoutmaster bested you in the game of love. That's what I meant."

"I know what you meant."

"Come to think," Ona said, "you haven't yet been bested. She married you twice. The score's two to one."

Quinn laughed out loud—a feeling like the first drink after a dry spell, a rolling, remorse-tinged relief. Inside that space he located the

flat, steady place reserved for Belle. She was too good for him: everyone but Belle had known it from the start. Despite the tepid reception
from her family (*Guitar playing's not a job*) and her girlfriends (*That
type doesn't want babies*), Belle had a useful knack for self-fulfilling
prophecy: she'd kept his hair trimmed with those narrow red shears,
asked him for sentimental songs at family functions—in short, made
him appear better than he was, which kept him from becoming worse
than he was.

"I was faithful," Quinn said, "in case you wondered."

"I didn't."

"Through the divorce and beyond, both times. In case she
changed her mind."

"A lot of men start canoodling the second they leave the premises," Ona said. "Or, in many cases, before."

"I didn't."

"I'm glad to know it," she said. "Mr. Ledbetter strikes me as the
faithful type, but that's not a point for him if you're the faithful type,
too." She smiled. "One for one. Even-steven."

In the waning hours of his good deed, Quinn tried to muster a
Scoutlike feeling of charity. Ledbetter was a kid-loving, wife-snatch-
ing paragon. And yet. Could Quinn dismiss how the town clerk's office glowed with Belle's grief and grit? Could he dismiss how her face
had filled with the fragile light of comfort?

"I suppose any woman in your lady's position would prefer the
domestic consolations of a man like Mr. Ledbetter," Ona said. "He
doesn't have the happy feet like you do."

"It's called work." Quinn took the next exit, pulled the car over
on a sleepy stretch of Route 1, and got out.

"What's all this?" Ona asked as he yanked open her door.

"Take the wheel," he said.

"Here?"

"You want to pass the test or not?"

"These are unfamiliar roads. How am I—?"

"You want the record or don't you?"

She waited a good thirty seconds. Then: "I do."

"Then show me what you got."

Ona shot him a lasered look and trundled out of the car. Quinn escorted her to the driver's side, adjusted her seat, then sprinted around to take the passenger side.

"Go," he said.

"I'll go when it's safe to go," she said, starting the car, putting it into gear.

"Check the rearview," he said. "And look over your shoulder."

"I'm not an imbecile," she said, pulling out. She drove in silence for a mile or so. "I've been driving for eighty years."

"You're twenty miles under the speed limit."

"Says the man with a hundred speeding tickets?"

Quinn laughed as Ona sped up. She was doing all right. Her confidence amazed him and he told her so.

"Your boy was an excellent teacher," she said. "He quizzed me on the written test while I went through my road paces. It took my mind off making a mistake."

"Keep your eyes a little farther ahead than—" Quinn stopped. "You let an eleven-year-old give you driving lessons?"

"He was very good. And far more patient than you, I might add. But you're not a bad teacher, Quinn."

"I'm a terrible teacher. Believe me."

After a few more miles, she said, "May I stop now? Have I proven I'm not a lost cause?" She pulled over. "I'm exhausted, if you want to know."

And suddenly—alarmingly—she looked it. "Jesus, Ona, why didn't you say something?"

She grinned. "Because I'm not past enjoying a good joust with a heedless musician."

"You did great," he said. "You are record-book bound."

He took the wheel, feeling oddly elated. By the time they reached Portland, Ona had nodded off, her knob-and-tube body crooked to one side, her small head bobbing against the shoulder belt. She appeared to have shrunk a size since yesterday. She woke as he made the final turn, a fresh set of flyers flapping on phone poles along her street. Through the open windows he could hear the loudspeaker at the car dealership summoning salesmen to their posts. Quinn had once worked as a Volvo salesman, but the signal system, which rang at a flat middle A, proved his undoing before he showed a single car.

At Ona's house, one of the flyers had blown into a cracked fence picket and stuck fast. He hopped out and opened her door, feeling courtly and pleased with himself. "Home, sweet home," he said. He'd done his bit, and then some. He'd more than fulfilled the boy's original charge; had, in fact, finished it with some grace.

Except. The place thundered with lingering projects: the broken picket, a detached gutter he'd promised to fix. Everything needed paint. He escorted her up the walk he'd de-weeded, over the steps he'd shored up. Ona carried Ted's overrunning bouquet, which showed no sign of wilt and obscured her entire body below the eyeballs.

"You should go to that neighborhood thing," he recommended, gesturing toward the stuck flyer. "Meet some people."

"Their children used to torture me something awful," she said, "and they never did a thing to stop it." She grunted. "I was the neighborhood witch, you know. I ate poodles for breakfast. Now I'm just invisible, which suits me fine." She lifted her nose above the bouquet, indicating the street. "There's a fellow in the green house down there, he's quite nice, but he's gone all winter. The couple next to him are passable. The woman next to them doesn't care for my yard keeping, but the man checks on me during snowstorms."

Quinn imagined the place in winter, feeling the wooze of responsibility: the number of things that went wrong in a house quadrupled in winter.

"Hello there!" came a voice from the street. A middle-aged woman capered up the walk in a pair of yellow clogs. Crisp shirt, pink chinos, sticky makeup.

Quinn lifted both arms, like acknowledging an advancing cavalry.

"We thought she'd gone!" The woman stuck out her hand.

"Shirley Clayton," she said. "Five doors down." She had the decisive grip of a newly licensed real-estate agent; Quinn suddenly recognized her doll-pink face from the plague of SALE PENDING signs on front walks throughout the city. "We thought she'd gone, but I had no one to ask, not a single contact number."

"I'm right here," Ona said, her eyes narrowed and mica bright. "Right in front of your face."

"Where are my manners?" Shirley said.

"I'm sure I don't know."

Shirley's gaze flinted back to Quinn, who felt like a bunny in a gun sight. Ona found her key and jammed it into the loose-fitting doorknob. A smart raccoon could jimmy the lock in eighty seconds — one more thing he'd neglected to repair.

"What yummy flowers," Shirley said.

"Don't touch them, please." Ona opened the door, where the forgotten overnight bag sat reproachfully in the foyer. "Where, exactly, did you assume I'd gone?"

"We *assumed*," Shirley said, inching toward the doorway like a cat hoping for a handout, "we *assumed* you'd gone . . . on a trip."

"On *the* trip, you mean." Color gushed into Ona's cheeks. She turned to Quinn. "This lady sold Louise's house to a pair of vampires with surly children and a malcontent dog."

"That wasn't me, Mrs. Vitkus, remember?" Shirley said. "You've confused me with a different Realtor." To Quinn, she said, "I didn't even live here when her friend's house sold. I was a homemaker in Albany back then."

Ona pursed her lips, leaving a pert starburst of wrinkles. "I know exactly what you're up to."

"All righty, I'll be off." She thrust one of the flyers into Quinn's hands. "Neighborhood Watch. Seven o'clock. You're more than welcome."

Ona stepped into her house and shut the door, leaving Quinn and Shirley on the porch.

"You her son?"

"No."

"Grandson?"

"No."

"People die and that's a fact," she said. "If you don't plan ahead, it can be months before anybody attends to the house, and in the meantime it goes to rack and ruin." She pointed westward, indicating the entire street, with the car dealership and the brand-new Lowe's looming over the rooftops. "This is a desirable neighborhood. Very friendly. Prices going nowhere but up."

In all of Quinn's visits here, not a soul besides himself, Ted Ledbetter, and the Meals on Wheels lady had breached the gate. He recalled the man in the green house—an older guy in a flame-orange cardigan who'd waved hello once—but Quinn had been wrestling a ladder at the time and didn't follow up.

Shirley eyed the peeling porch rails. "These oldsters are so naive about what they're 'sitting' on."

"I'm not related," Quinn said.

"I could sell this place in a week and get her a spot in assisted living. That's part of what I do for these people. My husband's a developer. There's a place opening in Westbrook, state of the art."

"I don't think she's much of a joiner."

"These people don't understand what a service we're offering," Shirley protested. "Sell your house and buy peace of mind with the profits. Frankly, we're concerned about safety. It's a neighborhood issue. These oldsters, they leave their burners on." She gestured toward the preserve. "That's irreplaceable land out there."

Unable to follow her leaps of logic, Quinn said, "I'm a friend."

"One street over? Mr. D'Angelo, ninety-one? I moved his place for ten times what he paid for it, and he's happy as can be at Eventide over in Falmouth." She accepted the flyer back. "Do you have sibs?"

"Listen to me," Quinn said. "She's going to outlive you."

Shirley sized him up, thought him over, then gave up at last and clogged back toward her sale-ready Cape—freshly painted, trimmed, and gleaming, as if the people who lived within could not contain their joy.

* * *

This is Miss Ona Vitkus. This is her life memories and shards on tape. This is Part Eight.

Where did you get this thing, anyway?

. . .

A financial writer? My. Your aunt sounds smart.

. . .

Louise? Again?

. . .

Well, yes. She was. A friend.

. . .

A good friend, yes. But you know . . .

. . .

It's just that—I've never had a true-blue friend.

. . .

Faithful. Through thick and thin. That kind. Where were we?

. . .

She left Lester Academy in the spring of '57, the end of her fifth year. We'd read dozens of books by then. All those writers, now *they* were my friends. What a pleasure that seminar was! We were *all* friends, after a fashion, even if I was the boring old guppy thrown into the fish tank.

. . .

You know how guppies bubble their mouths open, like this . . . ?

. . .

Don't laugh! That's exactly what I was doing, all but swallowing knowledge. I was so sorry to be fifty-seven; I thought I was so old! Even two minutes with Louise made me feel smarter.

. . .

For example, the difference between *convince* and *persuade*. The meaning of "To be or not to be." Louise loved Shakespeare, especially all those lippy women pretending to be men.

. . .

As a matter of fact, I just this week finished reading *Hamlet*.

. . .

It was like—it was like running into a pack of crazy folks I thought had predeceased me. Louise had a streak of premonition in her, I guess: she fixed it so I'd have company in my dotage.

. . .

Convince is for thought; *persuade* is for action. You couldn't *convince* me that taping my horrible old-lady voice was a good idea, but you *persuaded* me to do it anyway, didn't you, you little dickens?

. . .

Let's see; there's this dithery prince named Hamlet. His uncle killed his father. Hamlet's in a knot over the whole business, so he talks to himself a lot, which is where "To be or not to be" comes into the picture.

. . .

Because he's wondering if death, which is an undiscovered country, might be preferable to life, with its known drawbacks.

. . .

Like slings and arrows and outrageous fortune and what have you. Did I mention that Louise taught me to dance?

. . .

Right there in my parlor on High Street. These foolish things always happen in winter, when people are so sun-starved they don't know up from down. She brought over a book for me, as she often did, and I made a stew and bread. My apartment smelled like baking, which in winter is a marvelous thing. Louise came in, smiling. She had a new beau—Louise always had a new beau.

. . .

Not the kind you tie. The kind you kiss.

. . .

Paramour. Gentleman friend.

. . .

She always came alone. The table looked nice. I always put out cloth napkins for Louise, my really good ones, hand-tatted by my mother. Louise appreciated fine things; she was like Maud-Lucy that way. She dabbed her lips with the corner of the napkins just like Maud-Lucy. In all those meals we shared—I must have fed her a thousand times—she never actually soiled a napkin.

. . .

Not a speck. This night I'm thinking of, it had one of those skies where the stars look poured from a barrel. The cannery lights looked pretty, too, glowing on the river, like stars themselves, or the reflection of stars. Louise and I were chitchatting about her new beau—I wasn't even really listening, they were all more or less the same man—and it somehow came to light that I didn't know how to dance.

. . .

Well, I do now. Louise kicked off her shoes and led me into the parlor. I didn't have much in the way of music, so in the end we turned on the radio. I preferred Glenn Miller, but Elvis was all the rage that year.

. . .

Because he swiveled his hips and made goosy girls cry. This station Louise liked was playing Elvis. Three right in a row.

. . .

Oh. Well. Let's see. There was "All Shook Up."

. . .

One: "All Shook Up."
Two: "Jailhouse Rock."
Three: The hound-dog one.
Louise hears the first song and she says to me, "Do you know how to jitterbug?" Honestly, sometimes that woman could be so unhooked from the obvious. "Louise," I told her, "where in my squeezed-up life would I have learned how to jitterbug?"

"Here," she says. "Right here in your life. I'll be the boy," she says, "you be the girl."

. . .

Oh, I can't.

. . .

No, I can't.

. . .

Don't expect miracles. That's all I'm saying. Lower your expectations. My hip is acting up.

. . .

Step, step, and back-step. Good. Step, step, and back-step. You hold the lady's hands like this. That's right. Step, step, and back-step. You twirl the lady under your arm, like this.

. . .

That was my fault. I stepped on Louise's foot like you just—Wait a second. Whoo. I have to sit.

. . .

I'm perfectly fine. Just getting my breath. Whoo. We did laugh a lot. I can still see Louise's face, you know, clear as I see you.

. . .

Like an upside-down triangle, delicate but fierce. A fox face. Those snappy eyes. That woman could laugh. And she moved like warm water.

. . .

Oh, I know, listen to me! But it's true. Even in the parlor, just fiddling around, no audience, teaching me that silly dance. You could see why men thought so much of her. She had this way of making you feel . . . poetic. I was no good at all at the jitterbug, as I have just now demonstrated, but then this other song came on, a song from a movie.

. . .

"Tammy." About a girl falling in love. I haven't thought of that song for years. Debbie Reynolds sang it, in a voice that would put you in mind of maple syrup.

. . .

It was a waltz: *one*-two-three, *one*-two-three. Louise said, "May I?" and I said, "You may," and presto, we're waltzing, and Louise, you know she was really a very good dancer, even taking the man's part, because we waltzed the whole song through and didn't once blunder into the footstool. "Don't try to follow," she said, "just melt. You try to melt against the man and let him take you over."

Remember that when you get your girl.

. . .

Oh, yes you will. Handsome boy like you. At the end of the song—I just remembered this—I was awash. Just *awash* in tears.

. . .

Feeling sorry for myself, I surmise. Feeling alone in my world. Randall was a good son, very polite, dutiful, obliging. But indifferent, for all that. Howard and I, we were his obligation. He saw Howard on the second Sunday of every month and me on the fourth Sunday of every month. Like clockwork. Like notations.

. . .

Oh, but I'd never especially minded being alone. When you're dancing in the arms of your only girlfriend, however, and this dreamy song comes on the radio, sung in this dreamy way, you cry. You just do.

. . .

Of course you understand. Why else would I be telling you all this?

. . .

She stayed right where she was, in the waltz position. It was like being caught outside in a blizzard with nothing on but your slip. You'd have thought Louise was the snow itself, falling all around me, muffling the cold and the wind even as she was the source of it.

. . .

Actually, we never spoke of it afterward. We had our dessert as we always did, chatted a little more as we always did, she kissed my cheek as she always did, and went on home as she always did.

. . .

I don't recall. Cake, very likely. I still had Maud-Lucy's recipe for tomato-soup cake, kept through all those years. I made it all the time. As a matter of fact, the recipe came from Maud-Lucy's auntie, the same one she'd gone back to Granyard to care for in the summer of 1914. If not for that auntie, I'd never have run off with the midway show. I'd never have been reeled in by Viktor. I'd never have had my first son. For ninety years I've been making that silly cake.

. . .

No, really! Tomato soup. It's delicious. I'll make one for you. I'd be delighted to make one for you. Louise was flat-out mad for that cake.

. . .

You go like this. Other hand—that's right. *One*-two-three, *one*-two-three. Good. *One*-two-three, *one*-two-three.

Wait. You forgot to turn off the—

Chapter 18

On the way back from Granyard, whenever she began to nod off, Ona had been met by an image of herself and Maud-Lucy strolling past Shurtleff's Dry Goods, its window bright with silks and muslins. They're walking languidly in this memory, Ona twelve or thirteen, and spring seems the likely season: early springtime, a brilliant high noon, all the awnings on Mercantile Street rolled down in a gauntlet of colorful stripes. They're within shouting distance of the mills, if shouting could be heard over the din of the falls. Across the footbridge hundreds of men and women, her parents among them, are choking in the heat or burning their fingers or tending a machine at half-doze.

Maud-Lucy's voice rises at her ear, urgent and melodious: "You won't be going to work there. You were born for better."

All at once the memory snaps clear, the time and place precise: shoppers stalled in small, jostling herds to review the *Titanic*'s shocking fate, it's all anyone can talk about, so it is indeed spring—April 1912—and she is twelve, not thirteen, and her hair is swept up for the first time, a thrilling rite of passage, the whole shining mass held fast by four of Maud-Lucy's good combs. They are standing in the sunny doorway of Stanhope Music Company, where Howard Stanhope, her future husband and jailer and millstone, is polishing a piano.

"He belongs back in the city," Maud-Lucy confides to her, "among city people."

Howard hurries over, a portly businessman straightening his cuffs. His wife had been plump and sweet-faced, older than Howard by years, selling song sheets for a nickel apiece on Saturdays until her twinkling voice gave out to cancer. It was she who'd set up the floor plan—pianos in the front, Edison machines and Victrolas in the back, bright-buttoned concertinas half-mooned in the window as if ready to play themselves. Smaller items glimmer in a long glass case: mouth harps in three sizes; picks and bows; spoon sets with directions typed in four languages on Kimball card stock.

Ona will come to hate the sainted and savvy Mrs. Stanhope, whose design will be replicated in the Portland store eight years hence, down to the precise placement of the music racks. The first and best and irreplaceable Mrs. Stanhope, to whom Ona will be compared endlessly over a span of twenty-eight years until one day in 1948, when Howard—sitting in a cat-wrecked chair, listening to *Vic and Sade* on his beloved Crosley, business all but gutted thanks to his Tin Pan Alley dreams, attic bulging with unsold music sheets—*this* Howard Stanhope, this shucked shell, eyes sunk nearly to holes behind his greasy eyeglasses, *this* Howard will look up at Ona, the mother of his war-killed son, and say, "The first Mrs. Stanhope often looked into my eyes and burst into song."

To which Ona, out of rope, grieving Frankie, and secretly recredentialed in the secretarial arts, will reply, "Oh, Howard. Oh, dear Lord. I'm leaving."

On this day in April 1912, his ruin decades away, Howard greets the ladies and Maud-Lucy asks for a song. "Some gladness for my girl here, Mr. Stanhope," she says, knowing that Howard is famous for gloom.

He tries too hard, as he will always, plucking a sheet from the rack and swooping it theatrically. "It's a dark day for some, Miss Stokes," he intones, referring to the tragedy at sea. Taking a long, audible breath, he tenders his new ballad, penned for the Saturday shopping traffic, a mournful account of a motorcar somersaulting into the falls and hitting an ice floe and sinking into the black and hungry river. A few shoppers gather in the doorway, then a few more, tapping their feet to keep him tethered to the beat. Entranced and troubled, Ona listens. Despite his trimmed hair and immaculate fingernails, How-ard's desperation teeters on calamity. If she had money she would buy a song. She tries to picture him happy, younger, lying on a picnic blanket with Mrs. Stanhope's steadying hand laid across his forehead.

"A triumph," Maud-Lucy chirps, applauding. Ona hears the spar-kle of flirtation and in her three-gore dress and shimmering hair becomes fully aware, for the first time, of Maud-Lucy's overlarge fea-tures and dowdy shirtwaist. Howard adjusts his line of sight and aims it squarely at Ona, who all but catches fire. She lifts her chin to expose her throat, feeling brazen and amazed.

She's being appraised and appreciated and considered—by How-ard Stanhope, by old Mr. Drapeau looking to buy fiddle strings, by the Comeau boys knifing by with their newspapers, by Mrs. Farrar and her daughter Belle-May picking out sheet music. She melts in pity for Howard Stanhope and his droolsome ballad and castor-oil voice, never dreaming that a few years hence it will be her wifely hand on his big pink forehead, her shivering voice trying vainly to quell his fever for fame.

Then she catches Maud-Lucy, whose head turns on her thick neck, regarding Ona with possession and pride and something else that is not possession and pride. It looks like pain. It is envy.

As for the old Ona—her 104-year-old self stepping through the door of her house, leaving Quinn to get rid of that Shirley creature—the old Ona spied her beehive overnight case just where Quinn left it. Howard, at this moment, was both the portly store owner and the hound-eyed shell in the cat-ruined chair; he was everywhere and nowhere as the bouquet from Belle's wedding shed petals on the spotless floor. Reaching down to gather them, Ona received a sun-slanted glimpse of her hand, the spotted ruin that retained a gentle taper, an echo of girlhood, as if to lay bare the futility of physical beauty. Its brevity. Its useless invitations.

She'd sneaked a peek at Laurentas's hands, folded on his chair-bound lap. Her poor, foggy boy with his dissolving life. His hands were still beautiful.

If time did what we wished, Ona could have breasted the crashing waves, dragged herself to that distant shore, and shaken that goosy girl senseless. *You take all this for love?* Maud-Lucy's image burned with foreboding, a hint of betrayal, as if she were already leaving on the train with Laurentas in her arms. To whose memory did this image belong, the young Ona, or the old? Can memory be revisited to allow us to see now what we didn't see then? Old Ona, exhausted from her trip and searching her cupboards for a vase, yearned to tell young Ona, *Can you see the iceberg coming? No one will love you more than they love themselves.* But the young Ona can't see.

Shaking off the memory, Ona arranged Mr. Ledbetter's flowers in a glass vase, a present from Louise. The lilies gushed like the forward burst of fireworks. She closed her eyes, her head pattering, faintly confused. Memories of Kimball over ninety years past: an unfailing sign of heartsickness in the present. But she had not thought herself heartsick.

"Okay, Ona, gotta go," Quinn said, sticking his head inside the door. Oh. She saw it now: world's oldest goosy girl, left behind once again.

"Where are you spreading the Good News this time?" she asked.

"Actually, the God Squad got their guy back."

"The drugged fellow? He came back?"

"Sprung himself early."

"And you're out on your ear, *ding-bang,* just like that?"

"Like the beggar at the rich man's table. The boys called while you were sleeping. Phone kept breaking up, but I got the gist." He checked his watch.

"I most *certainly* was not sleeping," she said. "I may have closed my eyes for a minute."

"Anyway, I scored myself a happy hour that starts in forty-five minutes."

"Well," she said, "aren't you the worker bee."

"That's what they tell me," he said, checking his watch again. "So, listen. Take care."

"You're a good driver, Quinn," she said, "despite what I was led to believe."

He laughed. "Surprise." He put out his hand. "I'll call you."

"That would be splendid." Whether he would or would not call, she did not know. Something was ending, though; that much was certain. "Mr. Ledbetter will be bringing a new boy before long," she said. "I hope it's not that whiny one."

"Whoever it is, Ona, try not to scare him silly."

"Good luck with your music."

"Good luck with your record books."

She watched him trot down the street toward the bus stop and thought: *Laurentas would have loved me.*

By six she was ready for bed, nearly weepy with fatigue. She got into her own nightie and unpacked her unworn clothes, including a cotton-knit Sunday dress in glass green that would have been perfect for the wedding. She shoved it onto a hanger in disgust.

At six thirty she had tea and toast and listened to the news. At seven she brushed her teeth. At seven ten she turned down her bed, adjusted the bedroom shades, and opened her book: *Nicholas Nickleby* by Mr. Charles Dickens, a novel she'd last read in 1921. At seven fifteen, she fell asleep with the book on her chest.

Sometime later—full darkness—she snapped awake, a single word tapping against the inside of her skull: *pavojus, pavojus, pavojus.*

Danger.

She bolted up, the book crashing to her lap, the word fading as her quickening pulse apprised her of—what? Something. She cocked her head. A perception of movement. A wrongness in her house.

Thus alerted, rooted in place, she let her eyes adjust to the dark. Gradually, the darkness sculpted itself into air and object, the appointments of her room materializing as smoky shapes: a skyline of perfume bottles on her dresser; the skeletal rocker and its equidistant rails; a dark rectangle where the door opened into the deeper dark of the hall.

Listening above her breath, she sensed an alteration in the quality of the silence she'd grown used to. She understood, with a thudding dread, that she was not alone.

"Who's there?" she called out to her darkened room. Her voice crackled timidly; she might not have spoken at all. She rued her bad hearing and scolded herself, wishing she still had Louise to tell this to. *Likely a mouse. I'll have to get another cat, Lou.*

She slipped out of bed on trembling feet and approached the door. Again: something. For a brief, brimming moment, she thought: *It's the boy.* She cleared her throat, adrenaline rinsing through her, and called into the emptiness: "Is it you?"

All at once: a thundering on her stairs and deeply male barks of alarm—"Move out! Move out! Move out!"—in a calamity of smashed glass and slamming doors. Then, just as abruptly: a profound, sepul-chral silence.

"Go away, go away," she whispered, snapping her bedroom lock and flinching toward the window. Her heart made a froglike pumping in her throat. She clutched the sill and peered into the street where a fleet human silhouette, then a second one, ducked into a dented car. They made a three-point turn that shredded a chunk of grass, and sped away.

Ona pressed a hand to her throat, alone in her shrinking universe, trying to stay the aftereffects of fright. The streetlight brightened the edge of her yard along the fence, leaving the rest in shadow. A neighborhood flyer, still stuck to a fence picket, resembled an arrow shot from an enemy encampment. Everything looked like something else: the streetlamp like a tall angry man; the night-quiet houses like markers in a Monopoly game. She fixed on the houses; their nearness calmed her. She did not cry.

Instead, she worked out what she'd done wrong. The trip to Granyard had wound her up: when had she last lived so full a forty hours? Her head too full of heartache and surprise, she'd forgotten the porch light, her nightly precaution since the break-in down the street back in May—a lifetime ago, just as the boy exited her life and his father entered.

Breathing open-mouthed in the dark, she let her pulse relax. Only then did she dare switch on her bedside lamp; it was a little after three. She'd slept for eight hours. She put on her slippers and robe, unlocked her door, and peeked into the dark. In the empty hall she perceived nothing but the renewed skittering of her own breath.

One foot in front of the other, she told herself, quoting Louise in her final days. The memory calmed her. She flicked the switch for the stairwell and inched down the stairs. In the foyer she snapped on another light. Louise's vase lay shattered on the soaked floor, the flowers spilled and trampled. She bent to gather the pieces, thinking again of the boy and his miniature recorder. It was out there someplace, a whirring tape with her life affixed. Her paltry shards. She straightened up with a groan.

Then a man walked out of her parlor.

"Drop that, Granny," he said. His voice: even, relaxed.

The glass fell with an innocent-sounding *plink*. Not a man, quite. A big, greasy-haired teenager in a black mask of the sort used by Zorro in the old TV show. The mask was cheap and cracked across the nose. Through the holes in the mask his eyes showed pale and hazy and pink-rimmed. In his hand glinted a small and terrifying gun. He looked her over and laughed.

"You alone?"

She nodded, too scared to speak. He slipped the pistol down the pocket of pants so big they looked like a skirt. Behind him, in the parlor, she glimpsed Randall's sideboard, all its handsome drawers tipped out. Linens tossed into heaps. Chair cushions flipped over. She'd slept straight through the damage.

Awaiting instruction, she stood still.

"Where's the cash, Granny?" Calm as a very old cat.

"I have nothing but what's in there," she said, meaning her purse, splat on the floor with the wrecked flowers, wallet dismantled, everything soaked: a credit card, her expired license, her insurance cards, a picture of the boy in his Scout uniform, an ancient coupon for Meow Mix. She burned with shame to see her spilled things, exactly what a burglar would expect from an old lady's wallet. Her useless docs.

"Come on," he said. He beckoned with all his fingers. "Cookie jar? Flowerpot? Come on, Granny, give it up."

"I'm not one of those old people you see in the movies," she said, suddenly quaking with rage. "I keep my money in the bank, like everybody else." *I won't go out this way,* she told herself, *I won't.*

He pinched her shoulder and urged her up the stairs, where he dropped her, breathless and shivering, into Louise's rocker. Her hip twinged but she sealed her lips against the pain. "What're you, a hundred?" he asked, showing his awful teeth. His hair was wet-looking and dandruffy, and he had a peculiar smell, swampy and medicinal. His bone-white arm had been blackened with letters she couldn't resolve into a word. As he looked her over, her fear returned and all but melted her legs.

"There's nothing here," she said, gripping the chair rails. The floor felt movable.

"Stay," he ordered, jabbing her chest. The aftershock jangled in her breastbone. He hunted through her dresser and nightstand, pitching everything more or less bedward. The Guinness World Records pack slipped to the floor in a fanning sheaf. He found her beehive case and the emergency five that had lived in the silk pocket since she'd carried it out of the Woodford Street house in 1948. "See?" he said, waving the bill under her nose.

As her intruder pillaged her bedroom, Ona considered the lifeline button hanging from her neck, hidden beneath her nightgown and robe. She'd been told to test it periodically but had done so only once. After the initial bell and ninety seconds of silence, a woman's voice had come through the box in the parlor, calling her "honey" and asking if she was "A-OK." For all she knew, the batteries had run down.

"You got nothing," her intruder said. "Not a motherfuckin' thing." He pursed his lips as if deciding whether or not to blame her.

"Your friends left without you," she quavered.

He showed his teeth again. "They won't get far. Car's a piece of shit."

"Funny you didn't go with them," she said hopefully.

"I like a challenge. Not that you fuckin' count." He unzipped a makeup bag she hadn't used in forty years and dumped out a half-used lipstick. Her hip hurt from sitting so still but she feared the slightest shift might set him off. People like this either killed you dead when startled, or fled like bees, if she remembered correctly from the cop shows she used to watch before they got so violent. She fished the button from her bodice, made her decision, and gave the thing a squeeze.

Downstairs, the buzzer engaged, a high-pitched double blast. Amazingly, he barely flinched, and she realized he was in another world altogether. "Who's that, your boyfriend calling?" he asked, as she silently began to count. He got up, tossed the last of her doodads and pocketed the five, and leered at her through his sweating mask. "One thing, Granny," he said.

She made an involuntary peep, like a baby chicken, then sucked in all the air she had and roared it back out, loud and guttural: "*No!*"

He laughed. "Aw, you think I'm gonna what?" he said. "You think I'm gonna what?" He laughed again. "You waaay too ugly."

As she swallowed back a rising bile, he raised his hand, let it float a moment in midair, and then, almost gently, slapped her cheek. "Be good," he said, then sauntered down the stairs and left the house with a quiet click as a voice came over the intercom, ninety seconds on the dot: "Hey there, Miss Vitkus, you A-OK?" Ona rubbed the memory from her cheek and tottered toward the window, where she saw her intruder sprint into the night like a frightened squirrel. She had at least that satisfaction.

Minutes later, paramedics arrived; after that, two patrolmen. Then a detective showed up, followed by a loose knot of neighbors, shy and timorous, excepting Shirley Clayton, who looked maddeningly put together at three in the morning.

"Oh, my Lord," Shirley crooned. She forced a handshake on one of the patrolmen, who looked too young to drive. "I'm the neighbor. Mrs. Vitkus, who can I call?"

"Nobody. Go away."

"She has a grandson," Shirley said. "They just got back from a trip."

"What's your grandson's name, ma'am?" asked the detective, a young woman in a gray blazer. Ona had once had skin like hers.

"Please," she said. "I don't need anybody."

The pretty detective wanted a description of the intruders, but Ona remembered her tormentor not in physical form but rather as an embodiment of mockery. *Granny.* He'd made her see through his eyes: her age, her fright, her balding head, her piddly size. The only possible revenge would be not to mind.

But she did mind. She felt slight and ugly and gawked at: a trifling nobody. Just yesterday—Or was it this morning? Time had gone gluey and soft—Quinn had seen her in this light when he'd caught sight of her skinny, accordioned, eyeball-white legs. The greasy-haired intruder had confirmed her as a dusty, frightful, genderless shell, and she hated him for it.

"Bad case of the pinkeye," she said, remembering now. "And letters tattooed on his arm. The other two got away before I could get a look."

The detective asked her age, and as she proclaimed it a shock of sympathy rippled through a trio of neighbors who had inched into the house with Shirley. They were unrecognizable in their pillow-marked faces and thrown-on clothes. She was afraid of them, she realized; afraid of their goodwill, their outrage on her behalf, afraid she might have been wrong in her judgments; and she felt unaccountably stranded when the older patrolman urged them out of her house.

Out on the porch a middle-aged man in a bathrobe was waving a flyer at the younger patrolman, snatches of their conversation carrying inside. There had been a string of break-ins, she gathered—discussed at the neighborhood meeting she'd scorned. She was the first one caught at home.

The detective glanced around the kitchen. Did she assume the house always looked like this—turned inside out and smattered with glass?

"I'm an immaculate housekeeper," Ona said.

The first patrolman was back. "When we find these guys, Mrs. Vitkus," he said, "we're gonna kick their sorry butts from here to the moon." He put a hand on her shoulder, which ached from the intruder's grabbing fingers; she'd have a doozy of a bruise for sure. But the officer had a consoling face and her eyes filled without warning.

The remaining protocol required Ona to inspect the wreckage, now blighted with boot prints, and determine what had been taken. Nothing, as it turned out. Only Louise's vase was gone, in its way. "Money and drugs," the lady detective said, and Ona hadn't much of either. Her medicine chest contained nothing more alluring than aspirin and Metamucil, which the thieves had left behind.

"Can you keep this out of the news?" Ona asked. "I feel like a sitting duck."

They said they'd try and she had to believe them.

When at last the police left her in peace, Shirley came back to reassemble the furniture and wash up the fingerprinting dust and clear the front hall. "I saved a few lilies," she said to Ona. "Most of them got stepped on."

Another neighbor, a very young woman, returned with a generic frosted vase of the sort found in households accustomed to flower deliveries. Another woman—possibly Shirley's daughter, same pink roundness—put Ona's purse back together and offered her a cup of tea, which she meekly took. They were like Louise, these women, multiplied many times over: energetic people who enjoyed a crisis, who easily rose to righteous outrage, who revealed stores of affection at the least expected times. How had she lived here so long without knowing this?

By daybreak everyone had gone and there was no more night to get through. Ona decided to spend the day washing everything the intruders had touched, including her blankets and nightgown.

The young patrolman, who had a great-grandmother still living, had parked outside until his shift change, when another drove up to relieve him.

Once the day fully lightened—she'd been thinking of Laurentas wheeling through the jaundiced light of the day room—Ona turned on the radio for company and heard her story leading the commuter news, a brisk, affronted voice making much of the presumed frailty of the "victim" and the corresponding rottenness of the home invaders.

She suspected Shirley as the snitch. The phone began to ring and ring with local media wanting her "own words." But she had no words for these recent, dizzying hours, which had felt like the midway, filled with hubbub and confusion and homesickness and shame and conflicting desires.

How, she wondered, had an eleven-year-old boy talked her into wanting eighteen more years of this? Fatigue assaulted her from the inside out, slowing her blood and jellying her bones. She unhooked the phone and sat with her thoughts, replaying in her head the long, discouraging interview by the lady detective. Except for the bills lifted from her wallet and the five from her beehive case, the intruders—hard as they may have tried—had found nothing here of value.

COMPETITION

1. Jeanne Louise Calment. 122 years and 164 days. Country of France.
2. Shigechiyo Izumi. 120 years and 237 days. Country of Japan.
3. Sarah Knauss. 119 years and 97 days. Country of USA.
4. Lucy Hannah. 117 years and 248 days. Country of USA.
5. Marie Louise Meilleur. 117 years and 230 days. Country of Canada.
6. Maria Capovilla. 116 years and 347 days. Country of Ecuador.
7. Tane Ikai. 116 years and 175 days. Country of Japan.
8. Elizabeth Bolden. 116 years and 118 days. Country of USA.
9. Carrie White. 116 years and 88 days. Country of USA.
10. Kamato Hongo. 116 years and 45 days. Country of Japan.

Chapter 19

Her voice arrowed through the crackle of his cell phone, piercing the shroud of sleep from which she'd roused him. Seven o'clock: an hour for deer hunters and bird watchers.

"A speck of emergency," she said.

He sat up. "What kind of emergency?"

She said, "It's nothing." She said, "Would you come over, please, right now." She sounded like herself: solid and self-possessed. He figured: busted faucet, a bird-hit window.

He'd done his job, fulfilled his duty, dispatched his obligation, and then some. Perhaps it had never been possible to complete the sworn duty of an uncompleted boy. Seven charity visits—what could be easier?—had somehow led him into a fronded jungle of human entanglement.

Then she said, in a different voice altogether, "I've no one else to call," and he pulled on a shirt as he clicked off the phone.

He found her on the porch, inspecting the door.

"I was burgled last night," she told him. "I need to get this house buttoned up."

She looked small and translucent, like a baby turtle from a nature documentary. He fought an impulse to pick her up and carry her to safer ground. As she stood there, fading before his eyes, he extracted the details as if through an old telegraph, dots and dashes that he gathered into a story. When Ona trotted off to the bathroom—*The neighbors poured tea down my throat all night*—he called Belle from Ona's ten-pound rotary.

"I just found out," she said. "Ted heard it on the radio. Is she all right?"

"She says she is."

"Give her my best," Belle said. "Will you give her my best?"

"Right, I will, but I was thinking, this looks like more of a female thing to me." He should have changed the locks; they were ass-crap locks, he knew they were ass-crap locks, and he should have changed them.

"Ted's bringing over a lasagna."

"Right, but I thought you could maybe come over here. Seems like you two hit it off pretty well. She's acting like nothing happened but she's so white she looks invisible."

"I'm going back to work today, Quinn." She paused. "I won't take this burden from you."

"I didn't ask that."

"You did, though."

"She's not my burden anyway. I mean, she's not mine."

"Then whose?"

He glanced out the window at a cruiser parked at the gate. The grass was overdue for cutting; the new kid was in for a sweat. "The cops are watching the house," he said. "She's not alone."

"I have to go, Quinn. I can't be late on my first day back."

"Good luck," he said. "You can do it, Belle."

She paused again. "So can you."

He checked Ona's windows and put a fresh bulb in the porch light and changed her locks and, just because, replaced the batteries in her smoke alarms and paid for everything himself. Late afternoon, returning from Lowe's with a sign that said ROTTWEILER, he found her in the kitchen with Ted Ledbetter. They were eating lasagna on plates he hadn't seen—filigreed with tiny gold birds.

"Mr. Ledbetter brought me a big treat," she said.

How Ted had managed to teach a full day of summer-school math, bake a lasagna, and deliver it was another of his many mysteries. Quinn gave Ona the ROTTWEILER sign. "My," she said. "That ought to do it."

"The locks look great," Ted said. "Super job."

"Quinn's quite handy," Ona said. "You wouldn't think that about a musician."

He owed his father for teaching him the manly arts. *Your mother spoiled you boys rotten.* Brutal as the lessons were, poisoned by his father's disgust, Quinn had managed to learn a thing or two.

"I've got a gig, Ona," he told her. "Will you be okay?"

"I talked to her patrolman," Ted said. "They'll be watching the house for a few days."

Quinn had never been good at feeling two things at once. Knowing that the patrolman—and Ted—were on the job came as a relief, but he felt relieved in an entirely different way when Ona followed him out of the kitchen and stopped him at the front door. "He put *spinach* in it," she whispered. "If I had a real rottweiler I'd feed it under the table."

"*Bon appétit,*" he said, and she laughed.

He checked his watch. "Damn, I missed my bus."

"Why on earth is a man with your ridiculous musical schedule relying on the city bus to get around?"

"I'll get a car eventually. Right now I'm in savings mode."

"I took the bus for months after failing my road test. I didn't care for it. Too many ne'er-do-wells."

"I'm a ne'er-do-well."

"You're the opposite of a ne'er-do-well, Quinn. And you may borrow my car, is what I'm getting at. It's a good car. You said so yourself."

If he took the car he'd have to bring it back.

"I can't drive it for another week anyway," she said. "The police are watching me." She folded her scrawny arms. "You took me to Vermont, Quinn. It's the least I can do to repay you." Before he could answer, she added, "Please, Quinn. Take it."

So he accepted, promising to return the car the following week, after his shift at GUMS. She dropped the key into his palm, then laid her hand over his, as if she'd just conferred the key to her heart.

A week later, the cops nabbed the thieves—three hopeless junkies caught in someone else's house. "Straight to the clink," Ona said, undoing her shiny new lock. "That lady detective's a *ticket*."

Quinn thought she looked a little shopworn, but she pronounced herself fiddle-fit and in need of nothing. "They filched five dollars and broke a vase," she reminded him. "You'd think I'd been hauled off by the Russians."

A slight swelling in her consonants—reminiscent of the accent he'd detected when they first met—was her only residual hint of distress. Otherwise, she appeared unflapped, standing in her tidy kitchen, a pot of tea steeping on the sideboard.

"Your real-estate lady waved me down just now," he said. "She wants you to know she's praying for you. They're all asking God to take away your quote-unquote trials and tribulations."

"Well, I found an earring I thought I'd lost." She was wearing the matched set, ice-green droplets that made her eyes jump. "The burglars must've shaken it loose from a chair cushion."

Either despite or because of Ona's bravado, Quinn felt knee-weak. It was the weakness he'd felt as a teenager hearing his brother howl the news that Dad just called from the "place" and Mom was dead, the news tearing a hole in the day, exposing Quinn in his bedroom where he stood before a mirror practicing guitar poses. The news had been coming for months, and yet it toppled him, literally; he hit the floor, a six-foot fourteen-year-old dropping like a shot goose.

He was here to return the car. To close a door, gently. But he couldn't quite find his balance. The thought of those fuckers in Ona's house—putting their filthy hands on her things, on *her*—filled him with a sticky rage. "You must have been scared, Ona," he said. "Were you scared?"

"I'd like to have Louise's vase back. That's one thing." She opened a cupboard. "I've got supper if you're hungry." It was four thirty in the afternoon. She rustled two plates to the table—mismatched ones, he noted, and well used. "You might as well keep the car for now."

Quinn couldn't think, not while she was looking at him this way.

"The patrolmen have been so nice," she added. "I don't want to put them in the awkward position of pulling me over. I figure I'll lay low for another couple of weeks." She crooked her finger, remembering something. "Look here." She opened her microwave, an old-fashioned type with a dial. Inside was a stash of mail. "Strangers are sending me checks."

Quinn sorted through a dozen envelopes of different types—some printed with business logos, others smaller and flowery and handwritten. The checks ranged in amount, though fifty bucks seemed to be the going rate.

"Holy shit," Quinn muttered. "How much total?"

"Five hundred plus. Is this pity money?"

"At least they're not camped in the yard with candles." After the boy's death and a hysterical Sunday feature on Long QT Syndrome, Belle had returned over thirty checks with the same frigid note and typewritten signature.

"It's because I'm old. That's all it is." She scanned one of the letters. "It'll take me a good week to write my bread-and-butter notes."

"You're keeping the money?"

"I need a new roof." She inspected one of the checks. "You know, it was just my word, but people believed me anyway. My age, I'm talking about. They went on my word." She looked up. "I've something else to show you." She reached into the pocket of her sweater and handed over a "doc."

Quinn looked it over. "You got a learner's permit?"

"One of the church ladies gave me a ride to the DMV. Killed me to ask, but I passed the eye test in four seconds. I got ninety percent on the written test, too, and I'll have you know I studied my head off. I'm two-thirds back to legal." She tucked the permit back into her pocket. "What do you say to a couple of driving lessons in exchange for the use of my car?"

It would be so easy to give it back, just return the damn thing and beat a path out of this house, haunted as it was with his son, with the weight of obligation, with his huge and pointless regrets. Six weeks ago, five, and he would have: out like a man shot from a cannon. But that was before Ona thought him a gentleman and made him want to be one. "No time like the present," he said, and ushered her out the door.

"It's the parallel parking that gets me," she said, hands on hips, glaring at the innocent Reliant. "All the docs in the Western Hemisphere won't park that car for me."

Quinn set out her trash barrels, which were made of aluminum and made quite the clatter when hit—multiple times. A few neighbors came out to investigate, including Shirley Clayton, who called, "Everything all right over there?" Even her voice was pink.

"Doing my bit for safer highways, Shirley," he called back.

Lesson concluded, he followed Ona into the house, where she pulled a glass dish out of the fridge. "Leftovers, I'm afraid. I've got just enough left for two servings."

"You're giving me Ledbetter's lasagna?"

"I hate to throw food out."

"It's a week old," he said. "Plus spinach."

"You could use the iron, if you don't mind my saying. You look terrible, Quinn. Worse every time I see you."

"Would it kill you to give me one of those fancy plates?"

She smiled with her long, square teeth, and he realized he'd have to bide awhile, disconnect more gently, for she was fragile and alone and far less hardy than she seemed to think. He swung by every couple of days, running her to the bank or the grocery store or the library, often in the slim window of time between a GUMS shift and an evening gig. On one occasion she spotted his gear in the back seat and asked him to bring his guitar inside, where he recalled the chords for "Till the End of Time," a Perry Como classic he'd learned years ago for a wedding. "It's been rattling in my head all day," she told him, and she croaked out all the words, face aflush, after Quinn twice lowered the key.

In the meantime, coming and going, he passed Shirley Clayton's FOR SALE sign and fanatically trimmed hedges, realizing what he looked like: the caretaker. And when he found Ona inevitably at her door, or, sometimes, at the end of her driveway, looking for him, he felt more than ever like the thing he resembled.

By August she was cooking for him regularly, old-country recipes spooned onto the good plates: comfort food, shapely and aromatic, formed with root vegetables and cream. "You've gotten so thin," she said, and he felt like the opposite of the caretaker. He felt like the child.

Then Belle summoned him to her house, where, like a Scout reporting to his leader, he cataloged his good deeds. Lined them up like evidence.

"I'm glad she's all right," Belle said. "It's good that you're looking after her." She had a band on her finger, white gold with twinkly diamonds. He looked around pointedly, wondering about Ted, but felt he'd lost his right to ask.

"How's work?"

She shrugged. "Another false start. They're being wonderfully patient."

Curious absences—another table gone, a floor lamp—gave the room a feeling of undernourishment. He could make no story from objects kept versus objects cast away. She was holding a framed picture of the boy—same one Quinn had in his apartment.

"He'd be proud of you," she said. "He was so ridiculously fond of her."

"It's a little more than I bargained for," he admitted. "I don't know how to, you know, wrap it up."

She regarded him for a long, laden moment. "What you bargained for," she said, "is a friendship. You're not supposed to wrap it up." She set the picture on an ugly end table—a remnant from their first wedding, a present from one of her aunts. "I went through some more things," she said, opening a quilted box of the sort found in fairy tales. "I picked out some mementos. Just a few. For a certain few."

She lifted the cover but kept its contents secret, cradling the box like a kid determined not to be cheated from during the big test. This did feel like a test and his nerves curdled. At least he'd been chosen. He wondered what Amy had gotten.

From the frilly box Belle eased a perfectly appointed object: a stapled sheaf of papers on which the boy had pasted calendar listings from newspapers and broadsheets, three years' worth of time-place listings for Quinn's relentless employment. He leafed through the neatly arranged pages—hundreds of scissored clippings arranged into prim patterns—amazed to find himself so assiduously trailed.

"When did he do all this?"

"No idea," Belle said. "I didn't think he followed you at all."

Quinn's skin heated up as bars and clubs flitted past his eyes, school cafeterias and auditoriums, restaurants and function rooms, festival stages and town squares. Had the boy counted these things? The band names, the venues, the days upon days? There were so many, his every booking plucked from the pack and smoothed out and glued in place and weirdly sanctified and possibly committed to memory.

Fitted into this handmade book, Quinn's life should have looked small. But the opposite had happened. The boy had made his life look large. And productive. And worth something. So many pages, so white and clean and carefully made; hundreds of notices, over and over, in varying styles of newsprint. He recalled his own childhood book of stamps, a mess of curling corners and dripping glue.

He set down the sheaf, breathing through parted lips.

"And this," Belle said, producing a CD, one of dozens the boy had stacked into pillars.

"What's on it?"

"Nothing," she said. "They're all blank."

It felt light and cold, like the boy's own hand in his hand.

"You brought music into his life," Belle said. "I thought it might remind you." Her generosity—her willingness to find goodness here—struck him like a wall of water.

She closed the box and walked him to the door. When he tried to lay down the check she stopped his hand. "You don't honestly think this helps," she said, "do you?"

He shook his head. "It helps me."

"That's who I meant, Quinn. I meant you. You don't honestly think this helps *you*." She closed his fingers around the crackling check. "No more," she said. She took him by the shoulders and kissed his cheek. "Sooner or later," she whispered, "you're going to have to feel something." The CD was her parting gift, the clippings his consolation. Quinn was done here. He knew her painfully well.

The next day, Quinn led Ona through another parallel-parking drill. She hit only one trash can per try. To celebrate the improvement, Ona invited him in for cake.

"Wow," Quinn said, eyeing a dense, reddish cake festooned with nasturtium blossoms from the front yard.

"I haven't heard from your lady," Ona said, setting out the good plates. "How is she?"

"Married."

"I was hoping she could track down some docs," Ona said. "Do you think she forgot?"

"She's not really back at work yet."

"Oh." Ona shook her head. "Poor little thing."

"I hope it lasts," he said, helping himself to a piece. "Belle's marriage, I mean. Not the cake." He tried to mean it; he did mean it.

"Of course it will last," she said. "That Ledbetter fellow's a striver."

"I'm a striver," he said.

She cocked her head at him. "You're a dreamer." She switched plates. "Take this piece, it's bigger."

"It's good, Ona. What's in it?"

"That's a secret."

He guessed applesauce, some Depression-era substitute for butter. "Are the flowers edible?"

"Of course they're edible. Why else would I put them on a cake?"

He looked at her, his little squirrel of a friend. "Which are you?" he asked. "Striver or dreamer?"

"Striver," she said. "But I'm changing. Figure that, at my age." She took a dainty bite of cake. "Do you want the car for another week?"

He paused. Decided. "If you don't mind."

"I don't mind."

He had not loved his son enough. This knowledge lived like a malignancy on his heart. He wanted to believe that the boy, in a future now lost and impossible, would have forgiven him, would have taken their blundering history and found its logic and shaped it into items on a list. And that this—eating cake with Miss Ona Vitkus—would be one of those items.

"Ona," Quinn said, "what was he like?"

"Who?"

Quinn said nothing.

"I didn't know him long enough to say," she said quietly. "But I can tell you what *I* was like in his company."

He waited. "Well?"

"Dreamer," she said, and her eyes glittered beneath their melting folds.

Chapter 20

This was his life now: cramming his calendar, watching his money. The money had taken on nearly biblical significance, an ironclad symbol of rectitude, all his other choices porous by comparison. He would pay, in the parlance of his Catholic mother, "without a show." If Belle refused it, he'd leave the money to molder in a separate account, a mounting reminder of his fatherly failure. Child support with no child.

The night was cool, summer on the wane, lots of stars. He parked the Reliant in the back lot of Jailbreak, where the guys arrived en masse for their weekly gig. "Did you bring extra cord?" he called to Gary.

Gary sprang out of his Jag, all smiles. "Roger that."

Quinn lifted a speaker from the back of Rennie's SUV, idly wondering how long his back would hold out. Music could be hard on the body. He followed the guys into the fuggy warmth of Jailbreak, where they found another band setting up in their place.

"What the hell?" Alex said.

ROCK STEADY, read their sign, in horror-movie red paint. Two good-looking college types pulling cord across a riser, a teenage drummer fooling with his kit. The one off-note was a middle-aged shipwreck in a Sox cap tuning a vintage Strat.

The guys turned to him as one face. Quinn sighed. "I'll talk to Sal."

"You want me to do it?" Rennie asked. "You look like roadkill, I'm not kidding."

"Be my guest." Quinn had no energy tonight for Sal, Jailbreak's stingy, volatile owner.

"I'll go with you, Ren," Gary said, setting down a gear bag. "Watch our stuff."

Quinn nodded, queasy with fatigue, and parked himself against the far wall next to Alex, hundreds of staples from ripped-down posters needling into his back.

"Check out that guy's Strat," Alex said. "Nineteen fifties, bet you anything. I wonder where he got it." After a minute, he added, "Wonder if he'd sell it."

Quinn closed his eyes, trying to ignore the house music—Mariah Carey's moany-groany, three-octave pyrotechnics—adding and subtracting all the gear he'd bought and sold over the years. The numbers took on overbright, reproving colors.

The place was half empty but in another hour would be packed with people willing to dance for hours. Alex wore the same red Hawaiian shirt he always wore. Gary liked T-shirts with logos, and Rennie favored golf shirts in slimming black. They'd once sat with him in his motherless apartment on Sheridan Street, eating his father's store-bought biscuits and writing up their first set lists. They'd knocked their fists together for luck and over the years talked endlessly about gear, whole hours sucked into the pros and cons of modifying pedals or tracking down some Russian tubes, as if the Benders' dusty forty-song repertoire required a regular infusion of cutting-edge technology.

These guys had known and loved his mother. For this alone he stayed.

"Did you see this morning's paper?" Alex asked. "Big puffy story on that band you sub for? Hearts-and-flowers local-boys story, color picture of them with Mommy in their home studio, square footage off the freakin' charts." He laughed. "The mom's a babe." A pause. "You listening?"

"I'm listening."

"Okay, so they turn down a sweet deal from Warner Records, babe-Mom goes nuclear—"

Quinn popped awake. "They turned down Warner?"

"Oh, yeah. The lead singer—what is he, twelve?—goes on and on about God's work and all this other bullshit, like Warner is the epitome of godless commerce and they're gonna hold out for a megabucks record company that also loves the Lord. Can you believe that?"

"Yeah, if you're really asking." He felt a complex inrush of pride and envy.

"But that's not the story. You didn't see it?"

"I had a wedding in Bangor."

"Well, the story is they turn down a big, sloppy kiss from Warner and then lo and behold, guess what, there really *is* a megabucks record company that loves the Lord. How's that for luck?" He chuckled ruefully. "I mean, holy shit."

"Who'd they sign with?"

"Solomon. Biggest fish in the God pond. Your choirboys took the offer." Alex checked his watch, which must have cost him six hundred dollars. "Well, not all of them. Their lead guitarist quit. Decided he was an atheist."

This news settled like a stone in his stomach.

"If I were you," Alex said, "I'd get myself baptized. Rock your soul in the bosom of Abraham before the gravy train takes off without you. Oh. Wait." He knocked on the tattered wall. "I guess then we couldn't do, you know—this. Maybe Colin could fill in for a while." Colin was Alex's nineteen-year-old nephew, a geology major who played guitar like a girl.

The interloping band had begun its sound check. "What if we'd really buckled down . . ." Alex began. This line of thinking was a trope the guys resurrected every few years. But it was just talk. What they really wanted? Exactly this: to live Quinn's teetering life vicariously, once a week, while socking money into their IRAs.

Quinn said, "Go see what's taking so long."

Alex took the hint. "Watch our stuff."

Quinn nodded.

"Are you watching?"

"I'm *watching*."

Alex took off, joining the guys at the far end of the bar where a debate had reached full throttle, Rennie in his new Nikes and ass-flat jeans, Sal jabbing his finger at a schedule book. Quinn whistled out a long, irritated breath, deciding to run interference, but the middle-aged player of the trespassing band skittered into his path, face as white and starchy and expressionless as comfort food.

"You're Quinn Porter," he said.

Quinn ran into former bandmates all the time—they turned up sooner or later, often beyond recognition, lugging forty extra pounds and a degree in something sensible and a self-image readjusted to allow for their botched expectations.

"I'm sorry?" Quinn said.

The man's face ruddied up, then seemed to disintegrate in slow motion: a jelly-quiver to the cheeks, the small mouth working open, the eyes panicked and searching and shot through with blurry veins.

"You all right, man?"

The stranger spoke again, or tried to: Quinn couldn't make him out. Then he found the face beneath the face.

"Juke—?"

The man nodded wildly, his voice stuck someplace south of his larynx. It took another beat before Quinn understood that the man—Juke Blakely, who'd lived for eleven years inside the David Crosby story and now played a role in a different story altogether—was merely crying. "If you want to hit me," he gasped, "go ahead. If you want to tear me up with your bare hands, be my special guest." His mouth zigzagged with the effort of controlling his voice.

"Whoa," Quinn said. "Juke. Jesus."

"I wanted to tell you"—he sounded as if he'd been running hard—"you and your wife, I wanted to tell you—"

"Don't tell me anything. Really, Juke. Don't."

Juke's soft body pitched forward and back, a stutter-step of unstoppable weeping, his features chewed into mismatched pieces: eyes puckered shut, mouth undulating, forehead harrowed, the entire mess gone maroon with misery. At the back of the house his band-mates took notice, stalled amid their ever-proliferating setup. One of them spoke into the mic: "Check, one, two. You okay there, Juke? Check, one." Several patrons began to openly stare.

"Take it easy, friend," Quinn said.

Maybe it was the word *friend:* a sudden upshift in Juke's bawling introduced the possibility of a 9-1-1 call. Quinn led him outside to the grimy concrete slab that served as Jailbreak's service ramp.

"Listen, sit down," Quinn said, easing Juke to the ground. "Jesus, man. Get ahold of yourself."

"They told me not to talk to you," Juke said, his sheeting cheeks quavering. "Don't talk to the—family, like I was a machine they—could click on and off." He had a pick stuck to his sweaty palms.

Quinn leaned over him. "Breathe."

"The lawsuit was killing me," Juke went on, seemingly to himself now, stopping often to suck in more air. "I wanted to tell you how sorry—but they kept saying don't talk—to the family don't—say sorry don't—say forgive me." Quinn began to feel short of breath himself. "I spent my—savings on lawyers and point taken you know point—taken, mistakes have consequences."

Juke shook his head, his waxy nose sequined with sweat, his deep breaths accommodating more and more words. He wiped his hands on his pants and the pick clinked to the ground. "I had eight patients backed up and a cartload of charts and I was over my head and they warned me not to say forgive me but I can—say it now for what it's worth, forgive me, I'm saying it, I'm asking you, Jesus God, and I'm thanking you for calling off the dogs before I lost it all." He sat there, panting.

Quinn sat down next to him. "They're not my dogs."

Juke breathed in and out, for minutes, it seemed, until he recovered himself. His voice went quiet. "I watch myself writing out that prescription. I see it over and over. The ink on the paper. My hand on the pen. They said not to talk to you or your wife. But I can say it now, oh, my Christ, I'm sorry I'm sorry I'm sorry."

Quinn stared out at the squalid back lot, pitted with ancient frost heaves. Gary's Jag resembled a kid's toy, parked with two feet of clearance between Ona's dumpy Reliant and Rennie's SUV. A couple of pole lights bathed the whole mess in a vinegary sheen. How many hours of his life had he spent in back lots and alleys, guarding a heap of equipment? He thought of Belle's father, the disgraced toy magnate, going over and over—and over—the wrongful-death writs and briefs and et ceteras.

"I didn't call off any dogs," Quinn said. And then realized: Belle must have. Good old Belle. He experienced a transitory glimmer of joy: something decent had been returned to the world.

Juke ran his palms over his cheeks, leaving shiny tracks where he'd rearranged the moisture. The night air began to take effect. He took another tremoring breath: "It's like I've been crawling through this dark forest, calling and calling." He wiped his forehead with the sleeve of a lemon-green shirt patterned with regular-green bumblebees. Over that he wore the same leather vest he'd affected in the old days, though his expanding girth had shrunk it to the size of a doily.

"It was her father pulling the strings, Juke. Belle's not like that. I don't want you to think it was her."

"I deserved it," he snuffled. "I deserved to go all the way down."

"You really didn't," Quinn said, and he meant it. He silently thanked the God he didn't believe in for the near misses in his own life, the ones he would never know about because the one in a million was never him.

Juke's voice slid down half an octave. "I looked right into your wife's face and said, 'Why don't we try *this*?'" He mimed writing on a pad. "'Why don't we try *this*?'" He resumed weeping, quietly now, Quinn watching this spectacle of despair in a kind of awe.

"She's not my wife anymore," he said.

Juke uncovered his face. His eyes were nearly swollen shut.

"She married somebody else," Quinn said. "A good guy, actually."

The band had started up: a white-boy cover of "I Feel Good."

"Your guys must be wondering where you went," Quinn said.

"They're really a trio anyway," Juke said, wiping his face. "The blond one's my sister's kid; she made him ask me in. They think I don't know I'm a charity case."

One of the pole lights sputtered out. They sat a while longer, listening to the end of "I Feel Good" and the beginning of "Sweet Home Alabama." The lead guitar wasn't bad.

"Remember that night on the island?" Juke said.

Quinn nodded. "David freakin' Crosby."

"You ever—think about that?"

"Sometimes. Once in a while."

"I never told anybody." Juke sounded dozy now, like a man whose fever has just broken. "Not even my wife, because for a while afterward I sort of hoped he'd get in touch with me and I didn't want to jinx it. Idiot." He chuckled lifelessly, flooding Quinn with a confusing sympathy that included them both.

"You were good, though, Juke."

"Not that good." He shook his head. "Idiot."

Just then, Rennie gusted out the back door, tight-lipped and chafing and toting his gear bag. "Fuck *him*," he muttered. He turned to Quinn, red-faced, shouting, "We're *fired*." He jacked open the back of his SUV and shoved his bag inside, then sat disconsolately on the carpeted floor. Gary and Alex appeared then, heading toward Quinn, veering away when they spotted Juke's puddled face.

"Listen to me," Quinn murmured, close to Juke's ear. "Any other kid—I mean any other kid in the known world—could have taken those pills and done just fine."

"Oh, God," Juke whispered, face once again in his hands. "I have a son."

This time, Juke's remorse reached Quinn in a heretofore entombed place. He made a frantic, involuntary, interior leap away from his own pain but it found him anyway, knifing him with a clean, clarifying memory: not of the boy, but rather a photograph of the boy, the one sent by the boy himself to his rented room in Chicago. The effortful smile, the starched uniform, the fake backdrop of a barnyard fence. Women liked this photo (*Is he yours?*), thinking the boy beloved. He'd framed it and kept it and, in the end, carried it all the way back home.

"Your guys are looking for you, man," Gary said, appearing out of nowhere, peering down at Juke. "You all right, buddy?"

"He's all right," Quinn said. He stood up and then bent to Juke. "Get up, man. You have to get up."

Quinn helped the man to his feet—he was heavy and trembling—and patted his back. "Just go on back in. It's all right."

"Tell me, just tell me—"

"I forgive you, all right? I forgive you."

"Your wife—"

"Belle can forgive anything of anyone. It's the best thing about her. Go in peace, my man," he said, copping one of Resurrection Lane's most persistent benedictions. He watched Juke move toward the door, where heavily metered bass notes thudded from the darkness beyond.

Rennie and Alex were in the lot now, Rennie stalking over to the van to reload the equipment.

"What the hell was all that?" Alex asked.

"Nothing."

"Sal says his bartender left a message on your machine."

"I don't have a landline anymore, I have voice mail."

"Then your voice mail's not working, because we were supposed to be here *last* night, which Rennie couldn't have done anyway because of Kayla's recital, but Sal was an asshole about the mix-up, so Rennie kind of went off, and now Sal's really, really pissed off." He looked around, then added, "We're all pretty pissed, to be honest."

"You'll live," Quinn said.

"If you had an answering service—" Alex said, then shook his head. "We count on this gig, Quinn, is what I'm saying."

"Fuck you, Alex," Quinn snapped. "What Sal pays won't equal a single one of your billable hours."

"Hey, hey," Gary said. "Easy."

Quinn looked at Gary—reliably sweet-tempered Gary, who owned four dogs—and saw him whisper something to Alex, who then backed away. All summer Gary had put himself in charge of reminding everybody of their bandmate's "loss." In Amy's catalog of Quinn's moral failings, *prone to violence* did not appear, but he suddenly wanted to yank Gary's liver up through his throat. Gary, his friend of thirty years.

"I didn't mean money-wise," Alex said. "I meant—you know, fun-wise."

"Do I look like I'm having fun?" He stared at his friend's salon haircut, his beautiful watch. He shouted to the SUV—brand-new, ferociously waxed—where Rennie was still sitting, brooding down at his old-guy stomach. "You hear me, Ren? Do I look like I'm having *fun?*"

He headed inside—like walking through water—where Sal blamed the screwup on a new guy who couldn't manage a calendar. "No prob," Sal said, "except for Rennie's *attitude*." Sal said he didn't like *attitude,* and these rich guys could be surly as a goddamn *crow*.

Quinn agreed, sure, but they went back too far to end things like this, and maybe Sal could stop for a sec and imagine what Rennie had to put up with running that outfit of his, you want surly you should meet his day supervisor, and Sal laughed a little and wound up shaking hands and apologizing, then apologized again for not having said a thing about, you know, and how was the kid's mother holding up, and Quinn said don't worry about it, the kid's mother was okay, and Sal said Jesus friggin' Christ, though, what a thing, and Quinn said yeah, what a thing, and when he returned to the lot he said nothing. Something about their jumpy faces, their halted breath, it made him sick all of a sudden, because he understood it. He understood yearning. Walking into auditions with his shined-up guitar thinking, *This time, this is it,* he'd looked like them a thousand times over. Exactly like them. Wanting in. Thinking he deserved it just because he wanted it so badly.

So he said, "Sal's thinking it over," and helped them load the rest of the gear.

He drove home, mercifully alone, bidding good riddance to the howling of his fellow man, grateful for the use of a car so unhip that none of the guys cared to join him in it. The moonlit highway took on a recriminatory gloss, every fleeing mile reminiscent of previous flights.

If only the boy hadn't been born in the middle of the David Crosby story, Quinn arriving at the hospital humming with the memory of a star-lighted island, a draped gazebo, a sudden belief in possibility. When he and Belle finally brought their delicate, underweight baby back home, Quinn's imagined future felt like a shut door, but for one unexpected, mitigating high note: the baby had notable fingers. Long, squishy appendages attached to fists the size of a doll's eyeballs. Quinn's first thought: guitar.

The sensation that came to him now felt too dangerous to identify. Belle would have called it a memory of love. It felt like a haunting; a glimpse of the might-have-been. And it blazed by so quickly that it left nothing in its wake but a stabbing memory of light.

Just inside the city line, a cop pulled him over. The cop was young; by the book; a kid in grownup clothes. "Sir, may I see your license and registration?"

Fuck, Quinn thought. *Fuckfuckfuckfuck.* He found Ona's registration in a plastic sleeve, crisp and bright and beyond reproach, which was a hell of a lot more than he could say for his back seat, which looked like the aftermath of a music-store heist.

"Wait here, sir." The cop returned to his chuffing cruiser while Quinn stared into the Saturday-evening traffic of Brighton Avenue, this stretch of the artery clogged with chain restaurants and cut-rate motels. Up ahead glowed the big, bright Lowe's sign and beyond that the car dealership at the corner of Sibley. So close, so reachable, he could probably make a break for it, reach Ona's driveway in two minutes, bang on her door, scare her silly, much hue and alarm before Ona cleared him— *Of course he has permission, how else do you think he got my key?*—but surely not before the cop looked up Quinn's driving history.

The minutes ticked away. Quinn surrendered to what Amy liked to call "the karma of the hour," which was supposed to make you one with the universe, unless, as now, the karma sucked out loud and you ended up being one with your own ridiculous self. Juke's outpouring of sorrow returned as something growing beneath Quinn's skin, tumid and pulsing, and there wasn't a thing he could do at the moment except sit with it.

The cop was back, his face ballooning into the window. "Mr. Porter, the owner of this car is a Miss Ona Vitkus."

"I know that," he said. "She's a friend."

"She's a friend. Okay. Looks like you also had yourself a busy time last winter. I'm looking at three speeding tickets in January alone."

"I paid those," Quinn said. "I took the course, the driver's-ed thing."

"It's called defensive driving, sir. And then in May you were stopped for an expired registration—"

"I sold that car. I don't even have it anymore."

"—and speeding—"

Thirty miles over, a steep fine incurred on the night after the boy's death. He'd sold the car within two days and given the money to Belle.

"—at which point your license was suspended."

"I paid up. I'm all squared away with the State of Maine."

"All squared away. Okay." The cop flicked his flashlight over Quinn's license.

"You can see for yourself it's current," Quinn said.

"It does appear current, sir, that's correct. But sometimes appearances can be deceiving. And it doesn't explain what you're doing in a car owned by Miss Ona Vitkus."

"I have her permission."

"You have her permission. Okay. This registration is also expired, are you aware of that, sir?"

"What?"

"It was due in April, sir."

"Jesus Christ."

"Would you step out of the vehicle, Mr. Porter?"

"You can ask her yourself," Quinn said, getting out. "She lives four blocks from here."

"Would you place your hands right there, Mr. Porter, where I can see them?"

"I've got her on speed dial," Quinn said, spreading his palms on the roof. "Wait, scratch that, she's in bed, don't scare her." He expected a pat-down but the cop was still examining the license. "Listen, she's a friend. I repointed her foundation."

The cop aimed the light into the back seat. "This your stuff, Mr. Porter?"

"I'm a guitar player. I'm on my way home from a gig. Which is how I got those speeding tickets back in January."

"On your way home from a gig. Okay." The cop made a theatrical connection with his wristwatch. "Whereabouts?"

"Portsmouth."

"Portsmouth. Okay. That's what, about an hour away? I was in a band once myself, waaay back. I used to play a little bass."

Quinn thought, *Waaay back? When you were, what, six?*

"My experience?" the cop said. "Gigs usually start around eight, nine o'clock, and it's ten past nine right now."

"Scheduling mix-up. Long story."

"Long story. Okay."

Quinn breathed slowly. "I'm a professional musician. I pay taxes."

"On behalf of the State of Maine, I thank you for that, sir."

"Look, her house is right down there, Sibley Street. Just past the dealership. You can see it from here."

"Keep your hands where they are, Mr. Porter," he said. "I know where Sibley Street is. In fact, I personally happen to know the lady who owns this vehicle."

After a moment, Quinn said, "You the cop who watched her house after the break-in?"

"You the grandson she didn't want to call?"

"Her friend. I'm her friend. She did call me."

The cop shifted his flashlight beneath his arm. "Somebody should be taking care of her, sir. She's a nice lady."

"Somebody *is* taking care of her!"

"Keep your hands where they are, sir."

"*I'm* taking care of her! *I* am!"

"Relax, sir. You can remove your hands now." The cop handed back the license. "Now, I could arrest you right now, bring you down to the station, and have this car towed, because you're done driving till this registration is renewed and your license is reinstated."

"It's been reinstated for weeks."

"Sometimes our records don't match, sir. Once in a while that happens."

"That's what happened."

"You can call the state tomorrow and get it all straightened out, sir. In the meantime, seeing as how we're both of the musician persuasion, and seeing as how I'd hate to make that nice old lady's life any harder than it already is, I'm going to cut you a little slack."

The little slack turned out to be an elaborate series of phone calls—first to Rennie, who told him to fuck off, then to Alex, whose phone was off, then Gary, who had just pulled into one of his three garage bays and said he'd be glad to help.

But it was Ted—Ted and Belle—who showed up an hour later in Ted's minivan.

"Gary had some kind of crisis," Belle said. "Their dogs got out, so he called me." She was brisk and businesslike. "Officer Kelsey said Ted can take you home in Ona's car. We'll get it registered in the morning."

"I'll take the bus from here," Quinn said.

"Not with all your stuff." She hopped back into the van, leaving the men on the street. Rolling down the window, she said, "Don't make this harder."

He looked at her. "I saw Juke tonight. Richard Blakely. The PA."

A barely perceptible nod. "How is he?"

"A mess. One of the worst things I've ever seen."

"He'll survive," she said. "People do."

"I'm sorry, Belle. For all of it."

"I know you are."

"It's not fixable."

"I know. Some things aren't."

She reached through the window, briefly squeezed his hand. Then she drove away.

Behind the wheel of Ona's Reliant, Ted looked grim but forbearing, and as the karma of the hour melted into a puddle of unsanctified shit, Quinn regretted not having chosen arrest. He got in.

"Appreciate it," he muttered, adjusting the seat.

"It's the least I can do after what you've done for the troop."

"What I've done—?"

"The money was starting to pile up, so Belle had to tell me where it was coming from. She told me tonight, before we came out here."

Good old Belle. The knowledge lurched in, fully lighted: she'd been passing the money to Ted, who wittered on about expanded field trips and the future purchase of a sixteen-seat bus. Quinn listened, his face tightening, his fortitude wobbling like a spun quarter.

Ted stuck out his hand. "On behalf of Troop 23 . . ."

"Don't thank me," Quinn said. "Do not thank me."

"You can send it directly," Ted said. "Belle doesn't like being the go-between. And it's easier for the troop to keep a record."

"Right."

"I'll give you the address."

He felt like the mark in one of Ona's card tricks and nearly laughed—or cried—hearing his mother's voice drifting in from the misty past: *We don't choose our own punishments.* Or maybe it wasn't his mother. Maybe it was Ona. Sounded just like her.

PATIENCE

1. Longest time spent standing. 17 years. Swami Maujgiri Maharaj. Country of India.
2. Longest time spent adrift at sea on a raft. 133 days. Second Steward Poon Lim. Country of UK.
3. Longest time in full-body contact with ice. 1 hour and 6 minutes and 4 seconds. Wim Hoff. Country of Netherlands.
4. Longest time spent waiting on a hospital gurney. 77 hours and 30 minutes. Tony Collins. Country of UK.
5. Longest time to spin a coin. 19.37 seconds. Scott Day. Country of UK.
6. Longest square-dance calling. 28 hours. Dale Muehlmeier. Country of USA.
7. Longest time lived with bullet in head. 87 years. So far. William Pace. Country of USA.
8. Most airplane flights by a cat. 79. Smarty. Owned by Peter Godfrey. Country of Egypt.
9. Longest post-earthquake survival by a cat. 80 days. Country of Taiwan.
10. Longest time spent in space. 803 days and 9 hours and 39 minutes. Sergei Krikalev. Country of Russia.

* * *

This is Miss Ona Vitkus. This is her life memories and shards on tape. This is Part Nine.

. . .

Because suddenly I don't feel talkative.

. . .

I have a song stuck in my head.

. . .

"I've Grown Accustomed to Her Face."

. . .

It's from *My Fair Lady*. Louise was wild about that movie. She could recite it.

. . .

A-c-c . . .

. . .

Correct. In the movie, a gentleman sings it about a lady of whom he's grown fond, much to his surprise.

. . .

In fact, I was not thinking of Louise. I was thinking of you.

. . .

Because I missed you this week. Which led me to realize, in a way I had not realized for quite some time, that I live alone. And so, I don't feel talkative.

. . .

Answering questions about the Korean War would most certainly *not* improve my spirits. Your Mr. Linkman is obsessed with wars, does he realize that? You tell him all war is the same: lots of pointless killing and then broken people coming back home. Speaking of war, how are you faring with your enemy?

. . .

You know who. The one who kicks your desk and trips you in the hallways.

. . .

I know all kinds of things. I worked among young boys for two decades, remember?

. . .

Troy Packard. Right. How are you faring?

. . .

Hmm. You know, I watched a documentary about Eurasian eagle-owls last night.

. . .

You did? Wasn't it grand?

. . .

Do you remember the part about the Eurasian eagle-owl fluffing its feathers to appear larger than its normal size? To intimidate the enemy?

. . .

I don't see why a human boy couldn't do that. Stand up.

. . .

Straighten those shoulders, you tend to slump. Straighter. Now throw them back. Chest out. How do you feel?

. . .

On the contrary, you look enormous! Downright ferocious!

. . .

Stay like that for a sec. Shoulders back. Now, repeat after me: No!

. . .

Oh. All right. Mouth it, then. With a scary face.

. . .

Excellent! I'm frightened to death! Now, scarier. Ten times scarier.

. . .

There you go! How does that feel?

. . .

It took me most of a century to learn that. I'm giving you the great benefit of hindsight.

. . .

It *will* work. People like your bully run like heck from a fluffed-out Eurasian eagle-owl.

. . .

Pardon?

. . .

Why, thank you. I've grown accustomed to your face, too.

Chapter 21

After a fitful sleep punctured by phantoms—Juke (*Forgive me*) and the young cop (*You the grandson she didn't want to call?*) and Belle (*Don't make this harder*) and Ted (*On behalf of Troop 23*)—Quinn put the boy's picture in a drawer, sliding the frame beneath a shroud of T-shirts, intending to outpace his regret. He fished a newspaper from his neighbor's recycle bin, where he found a quarter-page color photo of Resurrection Lane minus Zack, the Christian-turned-coke-head-turned-Christian-turned-atheist.

He called Brandon. Then Tyler. Then the Jays. But it was too early to pick up; cleansed souls notwithstanding, they kept musician's hours. They were sorry to miss your call. They wished you a super day. They wished you the Lord's saving grace.

He got through to Sylvie while waiting for the bus, which was late, which meant he'd have to report directly to the floor and skip the cushioning ritual of free coffee in the GUMS lobby.

"Quinn!" Sylvie said. "For God's sake! I left you fifty messages."

"Something happened to my voice mail. The paper said Zack's gone. Is that true?"

"He was a sweetheart once upon a time, he really was. Now my thoughtful nephew's in Miami—drug capital of the Western Hemisphere—without so much as a fare-thee-well to the family. Broke my poor brother in two. That kid's been a heartache since the day he hatched and God forgive me I'm glad he's finally out of my hair." She sighed. "Listen, can you come out here? Like, this minute?"

"I'm on my way to work, Sylvie. *W-o-r-k.*"

"Are you giving me lip? Because I'm not in the mood. I get all the lip I care to get, thank you very much, from my sainted sons—who, according to that tweety-bird *putz* of a reporter, defied their quote-unquote overheated stage mother when they told Warner Records to take a hike."

Quinn laughed. "I heard."

"I'm not overheated. Or a stage mother. I'm a businesswoman."

"An overheated businesswoman."

A throaty vocalization—it sounded like the purring of a dangerous cat—emanated from the receiver. "Oh, God, Quinn. Doug's right, I'm in over my head, I need somebody to talk to, and if I had a phone number for Mr. Jesus H. Christ himself, you can bet your leather pants I'd have dialed it long before this. But absent the great Holier-Than-Thou, I'll stick with you."

"Sylvie? Are you growling?"

"I'm *smoking*. And for your information, you're speaking to the queen of *w-o-r-k*. I didn't inherit my nine acres from the king of fucking France." He heard a long, nicotined exhale. "You have no idea what they put me through, nattering on about 'artistic differences,' oh, my God, 'artistic differences.' And now, of course, they think it's God's will that they ended up with a decent deal from Christ Incorporated."

"And they're a man short. Right?"

"I've got a contract to sign, lawyers to consult, and Doug is being a complete ass, hiding out at the hospital, for all I know forcing people into brain surgery just to fill up his time. It's not that I can't handle it, Quinn, I just"—her voice dropped, and he realized she was not scared, as he'd once thought; she was terrified. "You're the only one I can think of in this business who isn't a shark with dripping teeth. We need you over here."

Hope flamed in his throat. "I get off at four," he said. "Relax, Sylvie."

"I can't relax! I wish my kids had never gotten on this train. They have this sense of—invincibility. Anything they want, presto, it happens." She paused. "Frankly, I blame you."

Even for Sylvie, this was rich. He said, "Whoops, I guess you for-got who bought them a Winnebago."

"I'll ignore that," Sylvie said. "I will just ignore that. I was refer-ring to your *example*. Your stellar, living-proof, inspirational *example* to these impressionable little — *marmots* that it's possible to make a life out of music."

Quinn went dumb. This was the kindest thing Sylvie had ever said to him, though she hurled it as an accusation. She hung up before he could say thank you. And before he could remind her that he did not wear — had not once worn, not even in the eighties — leather pants.

He swung into the GUMS employee lot, which was bordered by small, architecturally notable trees.

"Welcome, Porter," Dawna sneered, clipboard tapping at her hip. "What a pleasure to see you." She scribbled his name on the daily agenda, then handed him a job nobody wanted: hand-stuffing slip-pery, high-gloss inserts into four thousand brochures for a company that sold hiking gear. The hand-stuffing was a corrective measure that, according to Dawna, resulted from a slip-up on a shift last week, which *would not have occurred at all* had Quinn reported to his sta-tion *like he said he would*.

"I was helping a little old lady," he said.

Dawna laughed out loud. Quinn didn't care; he was internally re-peating every word of his conversation with Sylvie. *We need you over here.*

If there's a God, he prayed, *please let him be a guitar player.*

"I called in," he reminded her. "Rennie gave me the day off." But Dawna had a long, malevolent, photographic memory that would not delete the now-weeks-old road trip with Resurrection Lane, the first time he'd ever missed work — any work — without calling first. He re-alized belatedly how juiced he must have been, how eager to step into Zack's tainted shoes.

Around ten thirty, Rennie showed up, ostensibly to check the run. "Hey," he said, hoisting himself onto a worktable. The pockets of his pants poofed open like a girl's skirt.

"Sorry about last night," Quinn said.

Rennie looked around. He wasn't known as a ball buster and his presence on the floor barely registered. "Gary says I should apologize. Not that I'm saying it wasn't your fault. It *was* your fault, you're the one who's not supposed to let crap like this happen, but I feel like a jackass for losing my temper." He surveyed his noisy empire. "I don't know what came over me." He lowered his eyes. "Playing there is the only fun I ever have."

"Forget it, Ren."

"You get home all right?"

"Belle's new husband gave me a lift."

"Huh. Sounds civilized."

"Seems I'm buying his Scout troop a new van."

Baffled, Rennie looked away. "I know it's been rough," he said. "If I lost my kid I'd kill myself."

"I talked to Sal," Quinn said. "We're back, next Sunday, just like always."

"No way!" Rennie smiled all the way up to his eyeballs. "No freakin' way! Did you tell the guys?"

"You get the pleasure."

"I'll call them," Rennie said. Twenty years slid from his face. "Right now. I'll call everybody."

He hopped down, hitting the floor with an old man's *ooof*, then all but skipped off the floor. From the back, not counting the waistline melting like candle wax over his belt, he could still be the neighborhood kid from Sheridan Street, the band's cool black guy, albeit a black guy with flaming acne and high-water pants.

"That was your break," Dawna said.

She instructed him to feed the reassembled brochures to the ink jet, a machine that made sounds like indigestion amplified through a bad PA. The noise bothered him, even with earplugs, which Dawna told him was pretty ironic considering his normal line of work. She'd been married to a musician once and seemed to hold Quinn responsible.

As he stuffed the machine's gullet, Dawna brooded at the foot of the conveyer, catching the coded brochures and slamming them into the tying machine. She wore skinny jeans and a yellow top that looked like underwear. Despite her avian features, she wasn't a bad-looking woman. She sweated fetchingly, crossing her arms to wait for the next laggardly batch, rolling her heavily inked eyes.

"It'd be easier on your eye sockets to just tell me to hurry up," Quinn shouted over the machine.

Dawna raised her viciously plucked eyebrows. "Really?" She picked her way around the cartons and mailbags, her wiry, Nautilized arms impressively tanned. She arrived within two inches of his face, smelling of cough drops. "Hurry. The fuck. Up." Her lips made a little pop on the final consonant.

To nail her point, she hoisted a stack of brochures from the bottomless vat, counted them by feel, squared them up, flattened them onto the conveyer, and as they *shupped* into the machine she squared up the next batch. This job meant something to her. This job, and her gym membership, and maybe a new boyfriend, and probably a kid. A four-cornered life, one that she cherished.

"I've trained you twice," she said. "Are you too good for it, or just an ordinary, run-of-the-mill screwup?"

"Jesus, Dawna, can you give me a break already?"

"You had your break."

"I meant metaphorically."

"My ex was a big fan of metaphor. It came in handy when he was running up my Visa bill."

"*Touché*," he said, honestly hurt now. "*Touché* to you, Dawna the Supervisor."

"What is your *problem*, Porter?"

"Life is short," he said. "That's my problem."

"Tell me something I don't know."

"Literally?"

She challenged him: "Yeah."

"I'm sorry I screwed you up that time. And I'm sorry the brochures didn't get done last Friday. Because I just noticed that you pretty much run this place."

He had to shout over the shop noise, so the compliment sounded more fulsome than he intended. Stunned into silence, Dawna deliberated as the machine belched and gargled, empty of cargo.

He spent the lunch hour on the phone with the State of Maine, which, as it turned out, had no problem whatsoever with his driver's license and implied that any suggestion otherwise had been a misunderstanding—on Quinn's part, of course, not the officer's. When Quinn returned to the floor, Dawna was still there. They worked in silence for an hour, then two.

Then Quinn said, "Now you."

"What?"

He raised his voice: "Tell me something I don't know."

Dawna thought a minute. She plucked a brochure from the stack and said, "See this? Somebody's gonna get sued." At first he thought she said "soup." The machine made the kind of noise that mashed consonants.

"Look at this thing," she said, flapping it in his face. "Take a look at this guy."

Quinn saw nothing but a fake-looking image of children in adorable clothes hiking beneath a sky in which clouds spelled out SALE. "What guy?"

"*This sky.* Hello. Take a look at *this sky.* Are all musicians deaf? My asshole ex was deaf."

"What's your point, Dawna?"

She flicked the offending brochure. "I'm saying this looks exactly, *totally* exactly, like the Lands' End sale flyer from last summer. Exact same layout, exact same color, exact same cloud writing in the exact same sky. They want you to think their cheapo crap is from Lands' End."

Dawna was on a roll now, declaiming with the pride of experience exactly how the hiking-gear company was going to get its ass handed to itself in a lawsuit. As she scorned this outrageous rip-off, flapping *this color* and *this image* and *this font* and *this sky* at him, Quinn hatched a sickening realization about words.

For years it had tried to make itself known to him, but he'd tucked it away, refusing to see it or feel it or name it. He felt it now. Saw it now. Named it here, now, on the noisy floor of GUMS where Dawna was instructing him on the finer points of copycat marketing.

Her disquisition had made her looser, almost indulgent. "Shoot, it's almost three," she said. "Call it a day, Porter. I kind of shorted you this morning."

He made it to the lobby and pulled out his earplugs and took the landscaped pathway that led to the road that led to Lot C and the bus stop beyond. He began to hurry and then to run, and when he reached the road he was out of breath, knees on fire, the misheard words still pinballing through him, bright and electric.

Look at this guy!

An easy enough mistake—people misheard words like this all the time. This guy; this sky. Easy for a hearer to mishear. Especially if perceived through the lips of David freakin' Crosby and filtered through a gabbling outdoor crowd, a billion gallons of ocean smashing against a cliff, and your own grateful chords vibrating through a bank of speakers. Especially if these words were the very words your wishful ears most wanted to hear.

Look at this guy! Quinn had heard those words. He'd nodded, smiling, eyes on his own flying fingers. But they were not, not exactly, the words that had so giddily exploded from David freakin' Crosby's mustachioed lips.

Look at this sky! This sky's amazing! As it indeed had been on that magical evening, broad and high and midnight blue and flooded with stars. *I love this beautiful place,* ol' Dave had said. Meaning a real, geographical place. Meaning: This water. This cliff. This outrageous house. This amazing sky. This sky's amazing.

The bus pulled up and took him in and he sat in the back with his eyes shut, looking inward, surprised to find his mother there, his mother whose memory over the years had dimmed nearly to nothing.

I could listen all day, honey, she marveled, as his father snorted into his newspaper.

He had fast, nimble fingers, an ear for harmony, and spotless timing. *You must be quite talented,* Ona had said, and he was. But even talented people, sooner or later, cracked their heads against their own personal ceilings, as Quinn did now, and he nearly cried out against the seismic blow. He could improvise in the style of a hundred players, but musical invention, the kind that made listeners stop in their tracks—*This guy's amazing!*—was not Quinn's gift.

He was not a dreamer, no matter what Ona thought. He was a striver. A striver who loved music. All of it: the sublime inventions of his idols, yes, but also the two-chord folksongs, the hair-band medleys, the Delta blues, the Jesus music, the Gypsy jazz, the big-band horns, the classic rock, the Macarena, the chicken dance, the Electric Slide. He loved it with a sweltering, headlong, irrational affection, as if music—all of it, the best and the worst—were a child given over to his care.

"You all right, fella?" came a voice from across the aisle. A man in an orange bowling shirt, a regular rider. Small, rabbity, sympathetic eyes, and raging boils the length of his neck. Another regular sat just behind him, a misshapen wretch with shivering limbs. Down front, a young teenager nestled into the tiered misery of his own blubber. A busload of pilgrims today on journeys they never chose, having once believed themselves born for more than this.

He'd played a hundred songs, five hundred, a thousand songs that made people bite their lips and bob their heads, recalling a place they once lived, a person they once loved, a version of themselves they'd forgotten. "Rock of Ages" and "I Am a Rock" and "Rock Around the Clock." "The Long and Winding Road" and "Roadhouse Blues" and "Blue Suede Shoes." "Born to Be Wild" and "Wild Thing" and "Thing Called Love." Was it really so foolish to have loved it all? The muddy acoustics and pit-stained tuxedos, the flat-footed brides and their chubby husbands, the grannies and uncles-in-law jamming the dance floor? The sun-weary crowds at the county fairs, the kids at the prom in their cheap-shiny clothes, the corporate drones who clapped on the downbeat, the beer-swilling pub crawlers and their ribboning laughter?

He loved that they loved him. He loved the hollow he filled.

It was the boy who'd understood this. The boy, whose lists and lists filled his own hollow, the one his father had left behind.

A loosening in his chest, like sliding rocks, took him so abruptly that he doubled over, trying to hold it in.

The boy, of all people.

The boy, who listened to music in puzzlement and pain. The boy, with his razored clippings and neat beads of glue, dogged and watchful, arranging his father's story, preserving and tending it, page after page after page.

SUCCESS

1. Highest rank achieved by law-enforcement camel. Reserve Deputy Sheriff. Bert. Los Angeles County Sheriff's Department. Country of USA.

2. Highest jump by a rabbit. 18 inches. Golden Flame. Owned by Sam Lawrie. Country of UK.

3. Tallest snowman. 113 feet and 7 inches. Country of USA.

4. First father and son to finish first and second in the Daytona 500. Bobby and Davey Allison. Country of USA.

5. Last surviving giant tortoise. Lonesome George. Country of Ecuador.

6. Biggest snowflake. 15 inches by 8 inches. Year of 1887. Country of USA.

7. Oldest billionaire. John Simplot. Age 95. Country of USA.

8. First father and son to become president of the United States. John Adams and John Quincy Adams. Country of USA.

9. Farthest distance eyeballs popped out of head. 0.43 inches. Kim Goodman. Country of USA.

10. Most merit badges earned by one Boy Scout. 142. John Stanford. Country of USA.

*　*　*

This is Miss Ona Vitkus. This is her life memories and shards on tape. This is Part Ten.

How's the cake?

. . .

I knew you would. You and Louise.

. . .

I can't tell you that story. I don't like to dwell on it.

. . .

Did I not just now say I don't like to dwell on it?

. . .

She was fired. That's all you need to know.

. . .

Not a boy carrying tales. This time it was Mr. Finn, the librarian, who told a lie. Ugly, *ugly* man.

. . .

Imagine all his features snugged into the dead middle of a stupendously large face. He was one percent eyes-nose-mouth and ninety-nine percent face. If you turned a blown-up balloon on end, so that the knot was facing you? That would be a reliable facsimile.

. . .

A hateful troll, that's what. A rat in the weeds. He barreled into the office once or twice a day with some complaint or other.

. . .

Tardy book order. Chatty boys. Bottle of floor cleaner left behind by the janitor.

. . .

I didn't mean that librarians *in general* are rats in the weeds. I'm sure your mother is very nice. Most librarians are.

. . .

All of them, then. I'm a patron of that little branch over on Stevens, do you know it? They're all helpful. But Mr. Finn was another story. He kept his books clean-clean-clean. It killed him to lend them out.

. . .

The boys called him "the Kaiser" behind his back. They had names for all of us.

. . .

Sharpie. Now finish your cake.

. . .

Because they thought I was a card sharp.

. . .

Somebody who's good at cards. I did tricks for the boys who were waiting. Same ones I do for you. It took the sting out of the wait. They were good boys, most of them.

. . .

Now that you mention it, they *do* remind me of you. Not all of them. Some of them. One or two. One, maybe.

. . .

Good listener.

. . .

You're welcome. So. The troll. With the face. Our first dustup came on my thirty-ninth day of employment.

. . .

I *did* count! Before I ever knew you! It gave me a sense of accomplishment. I was so thrilled to be working. Anyway, the library was empty, except for Mr. Finn himself, perched on a ladder checking the shelves for fingerprints or God knows what.

. . .

What I wanted couldn't have been simpler: to borrow a book.

. . .

Bleak House, by Mr. Charles Dickens. I hadn't read it since Maud-Lucy, and I was looking for something sizable because I had a winter's worth of long evenings ahead.

. . .

Indeed he did *not* ask, "May I help you?" Far from it.

. . .

"*Who are you!*" Like that.

. . .

I know! The rudeness! Like a booming god: "*Who are you!*"

. . .

More flummoxed than surprised, I'd say. I could just make out his face above that balloony middle of his, and the bright bottoms of his shoes.

. . .

That gassy old weasel had seen me a hundred times at my desk. We'd spoken directly on at least two dozen occasions. And yet, in his precious library, he didn't recognize me.

. . .

Nothing. I was too startled to speak. The way Mr. Finn glared down from his book ladder, all those rungs, the soles of his shoes so shiny and judging. Did he think I was somebody off the street?

. . .

I'll tell you how I felt. Like a girl from the Kimball pulp mill, sorting rags in a room lit by windows so filthy you could hardly tell day from night. Maud-Lucy's tutelage counted for a big fat nothing—that's how he made me feel: uneducated.

. . .

I'll tell you what I *felt* like saying: "I can *read,* you egg-eyed bully! I am a professional secretary, you puffy old targer!" That's what I *felt* like saying.

. . .

Don't get the idea I was anything like Louise, despite that one notable whoopsie in my girlhood. I was Louise's opposite. I scampered away from Mr. Finn like a baby chipmunk on my little chipmunk shoes.

. . .

I didn't care for thundering exits. Louise would have pulled the ladder out from under him.

. . .

Me, too! I'd have bought a *ticket* to see that. Oh, and guess what? That night I dug out a carpetbag full of books I'd taken with me from the house on Woodford and guess what I found?

. . .

Bingo. In perfect shape. The very copy Maud-Lucy had given me.

. . .

It's about an orphan with a scandalous birth. And her mother, a great society lady who disgraced herself and pretended otherwise all her life.

. . .

You might. There's a cartload of dramatic deaths. One fellow bursts into flame for no reason whatsoever. Where was I?

. . .

Oh. The boy in question this time was the Morton boy. Another senior, a lovable redhead who grew into his looks too soon. And this time there was no talking the parents out of it.

. . .

Because Mr. Finn, for all his unthinkably bad qualities, was every bit as silver-tongued as Louise, and didn't he ever match her, word for word.

. . .

The *parents,* you never saw such people. Two doctors. "It's *Doctor* Morton," the wife says. She had this cultured, icy way of speaking. I thought my eyelashes might freeze clear off my face.

. . .

I was taking notes, trying to make myself invisible—as I was trained to do—while the most unseemly ruckus commenced.

. . .

It didn't matter one whit that the Morton boy denied everything, or that Louise explained to the trustees that Mr. Finn hated her guts and that his accusations took advantage of the previous incident, from which she had been thoroughly exonerated. Two of the trustees were there, prosperous men who loved Lester Academy more than they loved God.

. . .

One was a railroad man and the other one ran the bank.

. . .

I don't recall. Mr. Shiny Shoes and Mr. Silk Tie. One of them had overly large teeth. Dr. Valentine was there, of course, and Mr. Finn, looking thrilled with himself, and the Morton boy with his big green eyes, and the formidable Doctors Morton. Big donors, of course, which made a difference.

. . .

"We know what we know." That's what they said, over and over. I finally stopped writing it down.

. . .

Well over an hour. I thought I'd die of exhaustion.

. . .

At some point—I forget just when—everybody agreed that if Louise quit Lester Academy that very afternoon, her employment record could remain unblemished. That's the word I wrote down: *unblemished*.

. . .

Of course not. Can you imagine making a deal like that with a woman like Louise?

. . .

She—this is the part I don't like to . . .

. . .

Well, she grabbed me by the wrist, yanked me to my feet, and announced, "I think we can all agree on the unimpeachable character of Miss Vitkus. Miss Vitkus has attended my Monday seminar every week without fail for three years. Surely she can offer a word in my favor."

. . .

More than shocked. I was all bollixed up. In case you haven't figured this out on your own—you're a bright boy, I'm sure you have—everybody at Lester Academy regarded me as a piece of furniture. A well-constructed wooden chair that no person had ever sat in.

. . .

Thank you. But a *nice* chair is still a chair. Nobody but Louise knew a thing about me.

. . .

For example, on Lester's main lawn we had a granite slab engraved with the names of war-killed Maine boys, but nobody knew one of those boys was my Frankie.

. . .

I just said my Frankie prayer each day as I passed the names and walked inside on my chipmunk feet. Now all of a sudden here I was, center stage, Louise showing me off like a prize pig. "Miss Vitkus," she says, "persuade these people that I'm an upright woman and that Mr. Finn is a lying you-know-what. Persuade them, please!"

. . .

I noticed exactly the same thing! Ridiculous thing to notice, under the circumstances; but there I was, facing a wall of worked-up people who paid my salary, my spilled notebook all which ways, and the thought that sprang to my brain was that Louise Grady used *persuade* in place of *convince*. It was the best hint I had that beneath the bluster she was thoroughly undone.

. . .

First, Mr. Shiny Shoes looked down his snoopy nose at me. "Have you anything to add?" he asks me. I was supposed to say no. What on earth would a chair have to add?

. . .

They waited. Dr. Valentine and Mr. Finn and Mr. Shiny Shoes and Mr. Silk Tie and Doctor Morton and Lady Doctor Morton and the Morton boy. And Louise, of course. They waited and waited, while I stood there, dumb as a paving stone.

. . .

Because I was thinking of the day Louise read several sugges-
tive poems by John Donne—that's a dead English poet—while sitting on her desk with her legs crossed like Lauren Bacall asking
Humphrey Bogart for a light.

. . .

Movie actors from the forties.

. . .

To Have and Have Not, that was the first one, I think. And
Confidential Agent. That's two. I saw them all. *The Big Sleep,* of
course. *Key Largo.*

. . .

Well, that's four. You'll have to content yourself with four.

. . .

They just kept waiting. Especially Dr. Valentine.

. . .

I wasn't fast on my feet. I was turning over that Lauren Bacall
image in my mind.

. . .

Nothing. My mind was racing, but not one word came out of my
mouth. Not a word on behalf of my friend.

. . .

She left in a lather, as you might imagine. She steamed out of
there for good and ever. *Ding-bang,* just like that.

. . .

What I *wish*—? I wish I'd told those men, "You listen to me! Mr.
Finn is a big fat liar!" But I couldn't do it.

. . .

She came to my door that night. I thought I was in for a tirade,
but instead she sailed into my parlor without a word and dropped a
pretty box of chocolates on the chair. She'd been saving them for
me from a shop she liked in Portsmouth, New Hampshire.

. . .

Then she pointed to her cheek.

. . .

Well, I kissed it. It was very soft. We'd been talking in class just that week about biblical imagery, and the subject of Jesus and Judas came up.

. . .

The one who kissed Jesus on the cheek.

. . .

So the Romans would know which man to grab away. You don't know that story? It makes my hair stand on end. I kissed Louise like Judas kissed Jesus.

. . .

"I did nothing wrong," she said. "Don't you see what has happened here, Miss Vitkus? I have been hunted down by a posse of frightened men, and you helped them burn me at the stake."

. . .

She did have a flair for the dramatic, but I nearly died of grief. It was the "Miss Vitkus" that did it. I'd lost her, my only friend.

. . .

"You chose your secret valentine over me," she said. Those were her parting words.

. . .

I cried for days. I stayed out of work for a week. Which ruined my record of perfect attendance, you'll be interested to know. I cried and cried. For weeks. For years.

. . .

Because my secret valentine wasn't the headmaster. Oh, I should have stood up for my friend! I should have said something, and I didn't.

. . .

Because I was afraid.

. . .

Of Dr. Valentine. Afraid to lose his kind regard. He had hired me, respected me, relied on me. He made me feel indispensable, a feeling that trumped everything. I had never in my life felt indispensable. I loved that job too much.

. . .

But I *do* blame myself.

. . .

But I *wasn't* young. I was nearly sixty years old.

. . .

Oh. Maybe. I wasn't very practiced in the art of friendship. I might have been young in that one respect.

. . .

Just Maud-Lucy. Who turned out to be a not-very-good friend.

. . .

That was it. My goodness. Two friends in my entire life.

. . .

You've got lots of time. You'll find plenty of friends.

. . .

It *is* hard.

. . .

It *does* take time. From the day I laid eyes on her, I wished Miss Louise Grady could just once look at me and *see* me. For years I kept that twinkling chance like a jewel in a box. That's what *unrequited* means.

PART FIVE

Vakaras (Evening)

Chapter 22

Ona hadn't seen so much as one hair on Quinn's head for three whole days. The Reliant, back in her driveway like a relative she didn't want, appeared to be telling her something.

Nothing lasts.

The burglars had whisked Laurentas clean out of her head, but now, when she considered him again, she marveled that she could have held him so long at age forty-eight—a hale, square-jawed, boulder-ish fellow. The memory of the day room haunted her, her son's fragile mind as unhinging as the burglar's pinching grip on her shoulder.

A curious tenderness lived in the shoulder now, not pain. Perhaps the shock of seeing Laurentas required a bruised place in which to settle. Every time she lifted her arm she thought of him.

Mercifully, there remained the matter of her world record, a ballast against her sense of weakness. She hove into her old routine, designed by the boy:

1. Lift bean cans ten times.
2. Stretch arms ten times.
3. Stretch legs ten times.

The list went on, and she followed his instructions as if he were standing right in front of her, nodding saucer-eyed encouragement against her complaints.

In the morning paper she found another flown soul, 114 and relegated to an inch of type under "World Dispatches." Only a few names still correlated to the boy's original lists, and though she winced with pity while crossing off the departed, she enjoyed moving default winners up the ladder. The new record holder was a Dutch woman who'd kerplunked unannounced into the pool of contenders, her docs suddenly stamped or sealed or dipped in gold or whatever they did to anoint you. She went by "Henny," which put in mind a chicken racing around a barnyard. Who else lurked in the shadows, docs in progress, scurrying past her on the track to immortality? None of them still drove; there was that.

In the afternoon, Belle appeared, cleaned up if not quite gleaming.

"I've been wondering about you," Ona said. "How's married life?"

"Poor Ted." Belle trotted up the steps. "I should have come before now."

"Your man brought me a lasagna after my trouble," she said. "You haven't left him, I hope."

"I haven't *joined* him yet," Belle said. "Someone should have stopped him. He deserves better. Did you think I was in my right mind?"

"I hardly know you. How would I tell your right mind from a daffodil?"

"Quinn just stood there."

"You told him to."

"Did I?" She still looked underfed, but her air was light, considering. "It's sweet, the way you defend him."

"I'm not defending him."

"Don't deny it, enjoy it."

Ona felt like somebody's little sister, the way Louise had once made her feel. "I appreciated the card. Thank you for not including money."

"I was so angry about the break-in," Belle said. "Have you recovered?"

Ona regarded the folder in Belle's arms. "Is that for me?"

"Uh-huh. I finally went back to work. Fourth try. I didn't think I could do it, but it turns out I could."

An electrical sensation buzzed through Ona's middle and washed out toward her extremities. "I was afraid you'd forgotten."

Belle patted the folder. "This helped. More than you can imagine. It was like taking my little boy to work with me. Which I did once, on Take Your Daughters to Work Day. My God, he worked circles around those girls. Some people are *made* for research." She smiled, genuinely; a hint, perhaps, of her vanished self. "Anyway, here they are. Docs galore."

Disquieted now, Ona preceded Belle into the parlor where, like a magician preparing an illusion, Belle laid out her tools, arranging forms and certificates on the coffee table. They'd been printed from a microfiche machine on shiny paper, some in photographic negative, white on black; some handwritten; some bearing the woolly, carbon-copied characters of a heavy manual typewriter.

"Behold your trail," Belle said. She waved her hand over the lot as if sprinkling it with fairy dust. "It took me all day. Twenty-four hours, I mean." She squared up three of the documents—the docs, at last!—one by one, in chronological order. Ona scuffled her reading glasses to her face and examined them:

1. *Record of a marriage.* January 25, 1920. Ona Vitkus, age 20; Howard Stanhope, age 39. Bride's d.o.b.: January 20, 1900. Groom's d.o.b.: February 1, 1880.
2. *Record of a birth.* December 21, 1920. Randall Wilson Stanhope, 8 lbs., 8 oz. Father: Howard Stanhope, age 40. Mother: Ona Vitkus Stanhope, age 20.
3. *Record of a birth.* June 19, 1924. Franklin Howard Stanhope, 6 lbs., 10 oz. Father: Howard Stanhope, age 44. Mother: Ona Vitkus Stanhope, age 24.

Ona gathered her hands to her throat. Her voice had been snatched away.

"Ready for the big finish?" Belle asked, holding the final pages like the last card in a trick. She flashed that smile again, then produced a

horizontal sheet—three regular-size sheets taped together that un-
folded dramatically, a trick indeed. "This is the 1910 census for Kimball, Maine."

The information had been compiled into a table, dozens of sur-
names that told the tale of her immigrant town: *Fitzmaurice, Kaubris,
Murphy, Roche, Vaillancourt, Sinclair, Flynn.* Here before her, recorded in an impeccable hand, was her old neighborhood. Ona spotted the Donatos first, her parents' second-floor tenants. The Donatos,
yes: two short, dimpled people and their tall dog. Listed next: *Stokes.*
Maud-Lucy Stokes, queen of the third floor. The handwriting belonged to a young man whom Ona remembered in color now: ghost-
white face and a pompadour of orange hair, a chocolate-brown coat.
He'd made a roosterish bow when Maud-Lucy came downstairs to
translate.

She read *Burns, Masalsky, Doherty, Carrier.* She traveled back up
the page, and there, just above *Donato,* she found them.

Vitkus, Jurgis.

Vitkus, Aldona.

"*Sha, sha, sha,*" she whispered.

She saw their building, three sturdy floors financed with gold
pieces Aldona had sewn into her petticoats and the American dollars
they earned from their shifts at the mills. *Build good house, Ona! Ona-
my-love, what you t'ink?*

It's tiptop, Papa! said Ona at the age of six, her parents laughing
in return. *What you say?* They could not translate her American slang,
but they didn't mind, they held her hands and glowed, showing their
big, square teeth.

A moment kept for nearly a hundred years: on that lovely, sum-
mer-lighted morning, her parents appeared to her for the first time as
foreigners, even at the instant of their entry into the great American
enterprise—real estate. If there was a Lithuanian toast to such an occasion, little Ona did not know it. Not until Randall learned to talk
did Ona accept the full measure of her parents' sacrifice of assimila-
tion. Their love for her was too severe, and it cost so much—commu-

nication with their only child—that even now she could not imagine how they managed to pay.

"My goodness," she said, finding her own name at last. "Here I am."

Belle edged the paper closer to the lip of the table and read over Ona's shoulder. "'Nativity: Vilnius, Lithuania. Age: 10.' There's your proof. Ten years old in 1910. You should have asked me for help from the start."

"No, no," Ona assured her, looking up. "We so enjoyed the hunt." Ona peered at the other categories, nineteen headings soldiered across the top of the taped-together pages. The young census taker had filled each slot in a neat, forward-slanting hand (a Palmer Method boy for sure), much of it so fine as to be unreadable without her magnifier. "Where exactly does it show my age?" she asked.

"Right here." Belle pointed to a spot on the left-hand side of the sheet. *Position in Household; Age; Place of Birth; Marital Status; Rent or Own . . .* "Here's your father's information. 'Age: 49. Trade: acid cooker. Industry: pulp mill.'"

"My parents were old, for the time," Ona said. "I must have been a big surprise."

Belle continued: "'Aldona. Age: 45. Trade: rag sorter. Industry: bag mill.'" Ona tried to make out the words, to receive the words, as if words had souls. She followed Belle's finger as it moved across the sheet, category by category, until it stopped.

Belle said, "You had one sibling?"

"No. Only child."

"See this?"

Ona couldn't.

Belle hesitated. "It says, 'Number of children living: 1. Number of children born: 2.' It doesn't specify brother or sister."

"I didn't have a brother or a sister," Ona said, but all at once yes, yes, she did.

Brolis: the word had dropped like a single bead of hail when she opened her door and found the uniformed boy on her dripping porch. *Brolis:* the first word broken loose from its hundred-year repose.

He appeared to her as she closed her eyes, a flaring glimpse: a tree in bloom, a boy in the blooming tree, a gangly trickster grinning down through a foam of pink petals. His cheeks are pink. Pink knees poke through the holes in his stockings. Another flash: the same pink cheeks, and some kind of costume—but no, that was the other boy.

Vakaras. The word crashed in, heavier than the others. How could she know this now, a century later? But there it was, the name of her village. Not Vilnius, the decoy city, a lie to protect family left behind. *Vakaras.*

Ona Vitkus came from a place called Evening.

She stood up. She was starving. *Kopūstas, grietinė, bulvė.* She wanted to eat something sweet and squashy. Something cabbagey, with cream.

"Ona?" Belle said.

Ona held her drifty head. "I need my magnifier." She scurried into the kitchen, pulse banging in her ears. The magnifier lay atop her weekly stack of newspapers. As she reached for it, the word for *newspaper* plinked to the floor. She snatched up the magnifier, and down came the words for *read, word, book,* harder now. She clutched the oven door for balance, and *bam, bam, bam* came the words for *cook, boil, bake.*

It was like being struck repeatedly by lightning. She shuttled back into the parlor, zinged anew by *chair, rug, window.* Her every step unloosed an electrified word, and she spoke them aloud, pronunciations arriving in a faultless *pushka-pushka-pushka.* Her chest ached alarmingly, even as something else in her—something sweet and ancestral—came to rest.

"Are you okay?" Belle asked.

"Where is it?" Ona fumbled her magnifier over the pages. Her fingers tingled.

"Right here." Belle placed her nail-bitten finger on the spot. "Here."

Ona found him: her brother, lost forever and forever nameless. *Number of children living: 1. Number of children born: 2.*

She saw a wet door, a wet bunk, a wet shawl trailing down, a lacy tail she was too small to reach. She saw a wind-whipped deck and her weeping mother. She saw her own Frankie committing sailors to the sea, as if she had been there beside him. She saw the pink-cheeked boy from the cherry tree draped whitely in their mother's shawl, she saw the rocks their father kissed before placing them inside the shroud. She caught *don't cry don't cry*. She caught *my baby my baby*. She caught *brother, brother, brother*. She saw the net of arms, the letting go, the sinking swaddled body.

Brolis, brolis, brolis.

She heard the sea inhale as it received him.

Ona? she heard someone call, far away, a wallpaper sound like traffic or birds. Inside her head, by contrast, lived an exquisite, glassy clarity. She floated through her house, clear-eyed, touching everything, each connection of hand to object jolting loose another word, and in her mother tongue she spoke each word as it came. *Door. Banister. Wall.*

Ona? Birds in the distance, a scrim of noise. *Ona?*

She gained a sense of urgency, aware of magic afoot—magic to be scooped up quick before it vanished. At the same time, she glided into an increasing sensation of rest, of safety, of homecoming.

Outside her bubble of clarity lived a muffled chaos, a rising panic, a voice on a phone, but nothing reached her. Words zapped loose, first disembodied nouns, then white-hot adjectives, then a great spilling of fully formed sentences, like rabbits leaping joyfully from a bottomless hat. *My brother, my big brother with your tree-skinned knees. Where is your name? What happened to your name?* Fearful to break the spell—and what was this if not a spell?—she kept speaking, words upon words, every syllable a gift unwrapping.

In the kitchen again, she reached to steady herself. Her hand landed on the record-breaker pack: *What world record do you intend to break/set? When/where/how do you intend to break this world record? How do you plan to document this world record?* Inside her head she perceived a kind of brilliance, a lancing light that revealed both her actual life and the life she might have lived, a life in which she spoke the *pushka-pushka-pushka* of her parents. As she surrendered to this enthralling doubleness, another voice punctured her consciousness, a male voice, smooth and calm, *The scoutmaster is here,* his hands on her hands, *Ona dear, Ona dear,* his face a pleasant blur, and a woman's voice shouting again into a telephone, but no word came for telephone, no word for microwave, for radio, for blender. No word for electricity, none for refrigerator, but when she touched it *icebox* arrived, and *ice, ice man, milk, eggs.* And *cheese* and *goat* and *chicken* and *dog* and *cat* and *rat* and *bug.* And *brother,* my brother, *Let's go back, Mama, please let's go back, I want to go home, I want to go home.* Over and over now, that single phrase, and just before she walked or staggered or crawled or was carried to her bed, to lie down, to fully claim this feeling of perfect rest, to let the sweet rain of words soak through the pocked surface of her life, she wondered, and repeated, in English now, dreamy and resigned: *Where is home? Where is home? Where is home?*

*　　*　　*

This is Miss Ona Vitkus. This is her life memories and shards on tape. This is also Part Ten.

. . .

Hah! I'm afraid you'll have to settle for a *little* finale.

. . .

I saw Louise again.

. . .

Yes, I did! Many years later.

. . .

On this very street, in fact, two days after I moved in here. Randall bought a new house out in Cumberland—his lady at the time hated this one—so he moved me in here.

. . .

I love this house! Let's see somebody try to pry me out! So, here I was, cutting roses, minding my own business, when the oddest sensation took me over. I looked up to see what hit me, and there was Louise Grady, three doors down on the opposite side, clacketing up the steps of that white house. See that house?

. . .

Back then it was white. Louise had on this billowy white skirt and it looked as if she'd appeared from thin air, like a ghost stepping out to go a-haunting. This was twenty years after she asked for my Judas kiss.

. . .

Oh, you just can't imagine! She was seventy-three years old, but there was no mistaking that hip-twitchy walk. You could hear her grocery bags crackling, and after that, all other sound in the known universe ceased to be.

. . .

I waved my clippers over my head and yelled like a fishwife!

. . .

Like this: "Louise! Louise Grady!" I was afraid she'd vanish back into the air. Did you ever see *The Incredible Journey*?

. . .

That last scene where the dog finally—

. . .

Same thing: Louise sets down her grocery bags and then, *ka-boom kabang*, she takes up running straight toward me like that dog, home again after logging thousands of miles on her raggedy paws.

. . .

Well, I know. We'd parted on sorrowful terms indeed. But Louise could move reality around the way some people move furniture. There she was, standing right out here in Randall's yard, thrilled to see me, oh, how she'd missed me, on and on.

. . .

It was as if she'd forgotten about my Judas kiss. She made it disappear: *poof.* Gone. When I think of the tears I wasted.

. . .

I can only guess, because we never discussed it, but I suspect the intervening years had made her more like me.

. . .

A woman alone. And she was in poor health. Maybe she needed an ally.

. . .

Think of that. She chose me twice. I missed her so much after she went.

. . .

To wherever people go. To live with the Lord Almighty.

. . .

I meant—I meant to say she died. I missed her so much after she *died*.

. . .

Well, let's see, we went to movies a lot, sometimes with other la-dies. Louise liked Robert Redford, especially in his shirtless roles. Sometimes we stayed up late to rewrite the endings, Louise grab-bing a broom or a mitten or a saucepan and off she'd go. It was the exact same way she used to teach Shakespeare.

. . .

Excellent indeed. And in all my years at Lester, Louise was the only one who believed I was educable. Oh, and birds!

. . .

One time we drove to Texas for the spring migration. I paid for the trip but Louise did the driving, and when we got there we hired a handsome guide who showed us birds in dizzying numbers, and on the last day . . . My goodness, I haven't thought of this in years.

. . .

The guide stopped his car on a dusty roadside. Louise sat in front, fairly put out that this handsome fellow was treating us like old ladies. "But we *are* old ladies, Lou," I told her, to which she in-formed me, "Speak for yourself. I think this young man is quite smitten."

. . .

She *hated* getting old. She was sick already but we didn't know. She creaked along, cranky and stiff-legged and out of charm and yet she expected to be treated like the reincarnation of Cleopatra.

. . .

Well, the guide helped us out of the car and we couldn't guess what he was up to. This was the dullest piece of roadside you ever saw.

. . .

Post-and-wire fence and a pasture beyond, same view you see all over Texas, except that here you could see the Gulf of Mexico a few hundred yards away, behind a clutter of wind-beaten houses just begging to be flooded out. Our guide whispered something, but Louise's ears were gone by then and she couldn't make him out.

. . .

"Fallout." I thought it was a religious incantation. You never know in Texas. But then we looked where he was looking. We stood there with our mouths open. It was a fallout, all right.

. . .

When birds come back all at once, completely tuckered, so spent and parched and hungry they quite literally fall out of the sky. Not many people ever see this, but we did, right there on a dusty Texas roadside.

. . .

Hummingbirds! Hummingbirds everywhere! Panting on fence wires. Resting in the grass. Sitting in the dust. One of them lighted on the bill of the guide's cap and sat there like a jewel. The fellow froze there, hardly breathing, while more hummingbirds appeared, having cleared the perils of the Gulf and spotted their first dry land in five hundred miles. Out of the hundreds of wildflowers on that weedy roadside, not a *one* was missing a bird, drinking to its heart's content.

. . .

This is the sort of thing Louise invited into my life.

. . .

I don't know how long we stood there. It was like watching the creation of the world, it really was.

. . .

Not a miracle—just nature at work. The miracle is that I wasn't home in my parlor watching *The Price Is Right*, which is exactly what I would have been doing if the Almighty hadn't put Louise Grady in a house on Sibley Street in Portland, Maine, a good twenty-plus years after I thought she was gone forever.

. . .

They disappeared. As hummingbirds do. Here and gone, like a magic trick. Picture it: one thousand hummingbirds with ruby throats fell out of the blue and straight to us, two old ladies who couldn't believe their eyes.

. . .

Louise was the one who counted. She grabbed my hand and squeezed once for every bird that fell. My hand hurt for days afterward.

. . .

No, I liked it. Those hummingbirds seemed like something I dreamed, and the pain helped me remember it was real.

. . .

Two years later.

. . .

Bone cancer. She moved in with me after a real-estate woman made a bad deal for her house.

. . .

I did. I took care of her to the end. Right here in this house. And you know the funny thing?

. . .

I had to be quite stern with doctors and insurance men and official wet blankets of all stripes, some of them a hundred times meaner than Mr. Shiny Shoes.

. . .

I stood my ground! Then one day it struck me that I'd borrowed Louise's personality in order to care for her properly. I was the one saying, "No, *you* listen!" or "That won't do at all!" I'd waited all my life to stand my ground, and here I was, finally, doing just that.

. . .

Exactly like a Eurasian eagle-owl.

. . .

In January, just before my eighty-seventh birthday. A lovely snowfall outside, I remember. The kind of day when you'd want to go, if you were ready.

. . .

She most certainly wasn't. Louise kicked and scratched at life until the very end.

. . .

I gave her morphine.

. . .

It's a terrible thing, to control the comfort of another human being. She calmed right down, though. I was sitting on the bed next to her, watching her perform a pantomime, which is the effect morphine had on her.

. . .

She mimed opening a bottle, pouring wine into an invisible glass, swirling the wine, sipping it. So graceful and precise I could almost taste it.

. . .

It was sad, yes, I suppose, but it made me remember how enthralling Louise could be, how unlike this bone-thin creature lying against her pillows, sipping imaginary Chardonnay. Her eyes shone with the morphine, but also, I hope, with the light of her whole life. I was proud to be the one she chose to care for her.

. . .

She didn't say anything. But I said . . .

. . .

I said, "Lou, what do you suppose ever became of the Hawkins boy?"

. . .

It just popped out. I don't know why. The snow, I suppose, had put me in mind of Lester Academy, all those dark winter afternoons at my desk.

. . .

Nothing. She just lay there in her bed, looking around the room, preparing to go, I suppose. Memorizing the last moments of life. I was deeply moved by this, because she was memorizing a room in my house, where I had cared for her. And loved her.

. . .

I did. Very softly.

. . .

"I love you, Lou." Like that.

. . .

Her eyes cleared, as keen and haunting as I'd ever seen them.

. . .

She said, "Miss Vitkus, that boy was delicious."

. . .

I don't know exactly. It might have meant nothing. Could have been the morphine talking.

. . .

I thought about the boy who'd started the rumor. The cannery boy expelled for lying. I couldn't even remember his name.

. . .

She died that evening and left me, in Louise fashion, sitting in ten kinds of dark. I'd suffered mightily over my Judas kiss, as you know, for years and years.

. . .

I thought I'd betrayed a person who had given me so much. For *years* I mourned. It was hard to make friends because of that. But who was the betrayer?

. . .

We'll never know. I was eighty-seven years old, but I didn't feel like an old lady until Louise died. She beautified my life, and that's the truth. In time, I forgot the rest and remembered only that.

. . .

Forgiveness is a handsome thing indeed. Eventually I turned her back into Louise of the one thousand hummingbirds.

. . .

You?

. . .

You'll be the lovely boy who told my stories.

Chapter 23

Every enviable detail of the Mills family compound flared inside a chamber of Quinn's brain that stored untreatable desire, and he needed a moment, simmering in the rich sunlight of Sylvie's circular driveway, to absorb its complicated ache.

Sylvie flung open the door. "Good, you're here." She squinted far down the pink-tinged drive. Sylvie was fussy about parking.

"I hitched a ride," Quinn told her. "You're three miles from the bus stop."

She looked briefly muddled, as if he'd spoken in tongues. "Come in," she said, leading him through the house. "The kids are rehearsing." Her bracelets rattled as she opened a set of French doors on a lurid garden and paved walkway that connected the house to the studio. "I suppose you know it's been a snark-fest around here," she said. "Honestly, I'm so mad at those kids I'm spitting nails." She flashed him an enigmatic grin. "But I had a talk with them last night, and thank God there's one thing we can agree on." She pushed open the silently hinged studio door. "You can probably guess."

Relief warmed through him like lamplight, soft and golden, for he'd been guessing and second-guessing all day. He followed her into the studio, which was pristinely appointed and smelled of fresh plastic. Large equipment had been intelligently stacked, smaller gear tidied into open cabinets, miles of cable coiled onto color-coded hooks. Scanning this bounty, Quinn's entire history of gear—beginning with the lacquered Marvel amp from his mother—whooshed through his memory in the kind of cinematic flash reported by people snatched just in time from the jaws of death.

Sylvie gusted into the performance space, empty but for a few chairs gathered on the floor and a fifties-era, butterscotch-blond Telecaster resting in a guitar stand. The boys were gathered at the piano with their backs to him, discussing a marked-up music sheet.

"Everybody, listen up," Sylvie said.

Brandon whirled around. "Hey, it's Pops!"

"Hey, Pops! Listen to this!"

Over Sylvie's objections, he was being herded to the piano, the boys urging him to listen, listen to this, Pops, you're gonna love this, Pops, do you think we should record this, Pops, whereupon a quartet of jeweled notes from the boys' kissed throats ascended a sweet and percolating tide of sound, Brandon and the Jays singing with eyes shut, shoulders thrown back, fingers snapping, Adam's apples aquiver, Tyler bent over the keys like a monk at prayer.

Eight bars in, Quinn understood what he was hearing. Howard Stanhope's unpublished song sluiced down the decades and landed in a flood of harmony, a hybrid of Tin Pan Alley and hallelujah that sounded freshly made, the lilting lament of an unworthy man begging the Lord for a break.

"Whoa," Quinn said, genuinely impressed. "You guys have turned into first-class arrangers. When the hell did that happen?"

As the boys laughed—their faces peach-ripe in the glow of Quinn's approval—Sylvie zipped the sheet off the piano. "Who wrote this?"

"The husband of a friend of mine."

Ona had called Howard a dreadful songwriter, and she'd been wrong. If the man had lived another few decades—not so long, not really—he could have stood in Quinn's place and listened to his song and blubbered like a grateful fool.

"Says here, nineteen nineteen?"

"She's a hundred and four. He's been dead for decades."

"Pops thought we'd like it."

"It's old enough to be public domain," said Sylvie the business-woman. She glanced at Quinn. "But of course we'll pay. We'll draw something up."

"We could be, like, conservators," said one of the Jays. "Like Paul Simon when he brought that music back from Africa."

"You've got a friend who's a hundred and four?" Sylvie said.

"I do."

Sylvie peered at him. "Seriously?"

"Yes," Quinn said. "Seriously." He turned to the boys. Was he beaming? Is that what he was doing? "I think old Mr. Stanhope's been waiting all this time for you guys to show up."

"Great, great, they're musical geniuses," Sylvie said. "Can we get down to business here?" Despite her diminutive size, she looked entirely capable of wrenching a door from its hinges.

"I'm listening," Quinn said, the old-penny taste of adrenaline flooding his tongue.

The boys, too, came to attention.

"Here's the deal," Sylvie said. "I'm about to board a circus train with these kids and I'm sick and tired of playing ringmaster all by myself." A collective sigh from her sons and nephews; they'd heard this part already. Sylvie adjusted her bracelets and continued: "Especially when it turns out that my hard-earned counsel and advice count for exactly *zip* when it comes to the biggest decision of their career."

"Aunt Sylvie," said one of the Jays, "we took a good deal."

"You shut up." Sylvie pointed at him with a lethal-looking finger-nail the exact color of fresh blood. His head shrank turtlelike into his collar. "You took a good deal after turning down a *great* one — a deal I spent weeks finessing."

Brandon said, "Mom still thinks faith is a phase."

Sylvie shot her son a look that could bend spoons. "Your cousin walked the lane just great and he turned out to be an atheist."

Brandon regarded his mother with a lush and layered affection, and in her returning sigh Sylvie, too, betrayed the marshy depths of her love. They were ill matched, mother to sons; and yet here they

were, jumbling toward their twining future, come hell or high water
or the ten plagues.

"What exactly did they offer?" Quinn asked.

"Nothing we want," Tyler said.

"They offered you the flippin' *moon*."

"It's over, Mom," Brandon said. "Time to move on."

"You are so right, oh, my sage young sons. Oh, my wise young
nephews." She turned again to Quinn. "I have to get their contracts
zipped up, a schedule worked out, a thousand little things I don't
want to do alone." She clenched his arm. "I need somebody I can
count on."

"You do," Quinn said.

"Full-time, ridiculous hours—as you well know—but it's an opportunity I'm offering, Quinn. I know this sounds like Mom blowing
smoke, but these kids are going places."

A flood of inner light, a hyperawareness of the fresh equipment,
the seamless soundproofing, the spotless gleam on the control-room
window. All of it his now, in a way: the performance space with its
baby grand, its sleek, armless chairs—

The chairs. Something wrong about the chairs.

"We can negotiate your salary," Sylvie was saying. "You'll find out
I'm a pussycat. For now, all I need to hear is that you're onboard."

As Quinn realized exactly how the chairs were wrong, and what
their wrongness signified, Sylvie picked up a clipboard and said,
"What do you want for a title? Co-Manager? Operations Supervisor?
King of the Road?"

"Wait," he said, louder than he meant to. He sat on one of the
chairs, noting its careful placement—not random at all, as he'd first
thought. Four chairs side by side, one chair set apart, near the Telecaster, which was plugged into a practice amp.

"Wait for what?" Sylvie said. "This is a *promotion*. You're being
kicked upstairs."

They were preparing to run auditions. For a permanent guitar
player. One with a saved soul and—far more important—a sunny,

youthful visage that wouldn't fuck up the cover art. Of course they were running auditions. Of course they were.

"I'll call you Commander in Chief if you want," Sylvie said, begging now.

But he was a player: he wanted to play. His head began to pound, and an image blazed: Dawna the Supervisor's tanned arms going spotty and pale, her hard-won muscles deflating over the years. He saw her feeding the sorter decades hence, tagging catalogs for a type of baby shoe yet to be invented. He was the guitar-player equivalent of Dawna: dogged; good at it; replaceable.

"I need you, Quinn," Sylvie was saying. "*They* need you. You're a stabilizing influence."

This seemed, astonishingly, to be so: there they were, four boys, waiting for his answer. Banking not on his musical skills, but his fatherly ones.

"Quinn! Hello? I'm looking for a yes."

If Belle could only hear this: after all this time, in fulfillment of her father's barbed and oft-repeated wish, Quinn Porter had finally been offered "something in management." Quinn briefly considered dangling Howard Stanhope's song as bait—an exchange, a barter. But he didn't want to be the man in Howard's song, the guy who rued his trespasses against the Almighty but still retained the gall to put in a request. He wanted to be the man who was that man's opposite. He wanted to be—God help him—Ted Ledbetter.

"You're our only choice, Quinn," Sylvie said. "We agreed to keep it in the family."

"I'm not family, Sylvie."

"Close enough," she said, followed by a mollifying rumble of agreement from the boys. Not boys, men: four young men rock-solid in their hearts. Gone were the teenagers whom he'd once advised to untuck their shirts. As Quinn had been darting from gig to gig in a wheezing rush, they'd kept their eyes on a prize of their own design. Four tortoises to his hare. The knowledge came to him like a voice from the burning bush: he admired them.

"It's me, isn't it?" Sylvie said. "I know I'm a bitch on wheels, I know that. You don't want to work with me."

"Actually, Sylvie, I like you." He liked that she got up every single morning and set herself on fire.

"The job comes with health insurance. I'll add your wife and kids."

"I don't have a wife and kids."

"Oh." She blinked at him. "I thought you did."

Quinn got up from the audition chair, vainly checking his pockets for aspirin. His first task as Resurrection Lane's commander in chief would be to hire a guitar player. For the foreseeable future—the first foreseeable future of his life, really—he'd be watching from the wings, no longer playing and instead being played for. A foreseeable future of rehearsals and recording sessions and road trips, making suggestions and schedules and plans and money but not music.

"Say yes," Sylvie said. "Put me out of my misery."

"Yes."

A cheer rose up, a rushing in his ears like applause. Tyler and Brandon and the Jays high-fived as Sylvie jumped up and down and shrieked like a girl. An immoderate round of hugs, handshakes, and back-pats followed, along with a sensation of being cracked open. Quinn felt—there was no other word that came to him—loved.

An hour later, he hitched a ride back to town with the driver of a laundry truck, Howard's chummy melody looping through his head, the hummable pleasure of it cheering him unexpectedly. *Howard,* he thought, *I'll put in a good word with your lady.* He was let off at the corner of Sibley, where he loped toward Ona's dead end, intending to tell his friend that decades after the mortal end of his tortured life, Howard Stanhope had risen again to make a thing of beauty.

The melody followed him and he matched his stride to its rhythm, recognizing all at once the "glittering girl" so ill used by the repenter in Howard's song. He could see her grace, her dimples, her cherry-wood hair. *Howard,* he thought, *I've got your back, buddy.*

In her driveway was parked a familiar van, which released in him a baffling gush of jealousy. As he was deciphering its meaning—like a lover's pique, though it couldn't be—he noted that Ted had parked in a slapdash, un-Ledbetterly fashion; that Belle's car was there, too; and that a small knot of neighbors had gathered ominously near the porch.

He broke into a run, sprinted up the walk, and took the steps by twos, calling her name.

Chapter 24

He found her upstairs, tucked ghostlike into her bed.

"Ona," he said. Helpless, overcome. "Oh, God."

"Shh," Belle said, putting up a hand to block his way, but Ted moved aside to make a path.

"What happened?" he said. "What happened?"

"She's okay, Quinn," Ted said. "Paramedics just left."

"Ona, hey," Quinn whispered, drawing nearer. Her eyes were closed, her face motionless but oddly rosy, the way people sometimes looked in their coffins.

"You'll pardon me if I keep my eyes shut," she murmured. "I'm going to sleep."

"No, no," he pleaded. "You have to get your license record." He peered into the mystery of her face. "Not to mention the long-life one. Think of Madame What's-Her-Name. Madame French Lady."

She opened her eyes, perfectly alert. "Not the *big* sleep, you goose. I need a nap."

"Oh," he said, caught short by joy. "Sure. Okay, Ona. Take a nap."

"I *was* taking a nap," she said. "You woke me with your caterwauling."

"Excuse me for being sorry you were dead."

"I wasn't dead."

"Well, I know that now."

"Jeanne Louise Calment."

"What?"

"Her name is Jeanne Louise Calment," Ona said. "The French lady whom I plan to best in the game of life."

He glanced back at Ted and Belle, who appeared to find this amusing.

"Your lady and the scoutmaster have been here for hours," Ona said. "I've known only one other librarian well, and as a result, this level of generosity has somewhat laid me flat."

It was then he noticed the tea cooling on her nightstand, the industriously fluffed pillow, the clean nightgown. These signs of care made him careful. He wanted to be generous—not to appear generous, but to be so.

He knelt and took her hands, which were warm and bumpy. "There's something—" He turned to Ted, made eye contact. "Can I have a moment?"

Ted ushered Belle downstairs as Quinn tightened his grip on Ona's hands. "There's something you have to know," he said. "About Howard."

"Howard who?"

"Howard your husband. Howard Stanhope. Songwriter Howard."

"Howard wrote dreadful songs."

"No, he didn't, Ona. He didn't."

Her green eyes narrowed on him. "What on earth are you going on about?"

"I just heard one of his songs, the one you gave me. The God Squad did a kick-ass arrangement, Ona, wait'll you hear it."

"The religious boys? They liked it?"

"Loved it," he said. "But here's the thing, Ona. Howard wrote that song for you." Quinn had never been more sure of anything. "I think he wrote all his songs for you, Ona, for young and lovely you."

"Now you're talking foolish."

"He wrote them for you, and you refused them because he didn't know how to give them to you." How could he, living his shadow of a life, floundering in the sludge of grief and failure?

"Have you been drinking?"

"Listen to me," he said. "You're the glittering girl with the cherrywood hair. You're the angel's breath and sunlight."

"Oh, for heaven's sake." She sat up crossly, her tufted hair seeming to quiver. "Quinn Porter," she said, "I never took you for a romantic."

"Howard Stanhope loved you," he declared. "I thought you should know."

"Well, all right."

"I thought you should know, Ona."

"Thank you."

"People should know these things."

"Yes, indeed. Thank you." She patted his hand and his head calmed. "You're a good boy, Quinn." She shrugged what passed for her shoulders; the bedclothes sighed. "I've had myself a day," she told him. "My mother tongue paid me a visit."

"Really? What did it say?"

"It said the name of my original village, for starters."

"You mean in Lithuania?"

"Could be there's nothing left there but names in a graveyard." She sat up straighter, with little apparent effort. "I went my whole life without the slightest interest in my homeland, and now I regret that I'll never see it again, this place for which I have nothing but the blinkiest memories."

"If you went back I bet you could snag the record for oldest airplane passenger."

"I'd probably have to fly the plane myself. Nothing new under the sun." She shook her head. "No, where I'm going is back to see Laurentas. I was unforgivably rude to my own flesh and blood and would like to make my apology." She paused a moment, then: "The world's oldest airplane passenger was Charlotte Hughes, by the way. Age one hundred fifteen. You can look it up."

He laughed. "I'll take your word for it."

She patted him again. "I miss it. I'm suddenly homesick for a place I don't recall. If a stranger walked in here right now to read *War and Peace* in Lithuanian, I believe I'd get the gist."

He sat with her in silence.

"There's more," she said. "But for now I'd like to get some shut-eye." She shooed him away, and, reluctantly, he went.

The crisis—if indeed there had been one—was over. A quartet of paramedics had pronounced her fit and lucid, vital signs normal.

"What was it, then?" Quinn asked Ted, who was pouring tea out of Ona's good pot.

"Delayed reaction to the break-in, is my guess. The guy said that can happen."

"It was magic," Belle said. "That's what it was." She looked up at Quinn, as serious as he'd ever known her, and informed him that their son, their strange, departed boy, had returned to Ona Vitkus her language, her memory, and her lost brother.

"I guess she had a little mix-up in her head," Ted said.

For a second Quinn thought he meant Belle, who indeed seemed to have a little mix-up in her head. Did she believe their son had floated in from the sweet hereafter, bringing with him Ona's lost brother? Did she believe he *was* Ona's lost brother?

"A minor lapse of some sort, I'm guessing," Ted went on. "In the brain. That's the explanation, probably." He squeezed Belle's shoulder. "It's probably that, honey."

"I believe it all," Belle said. "I'm keeping this day forever." She looked so happy; Quinn tried as hard as he could to believe.

"I wish you'd called me," Quinn said. "Somebody should have called me."

"Quinn," Belle murmured, "when have you ever wanted to be called?"

"Now," he said. "I want to be called now."

She looked at him. Assessed him. They were in the kitchen, the very place where vanished things had reappeared, including his own sense of duty and willingness. He studied Ona's neatly stacked cards. Her pile of coins. Her quartered hanky. The boy, too, had studied these things. Belle noticed him noticing, and he wondered if she felt the boy's presence. As he did now. When he'd first told her this he'd been reaching—overreaching—and yet over time he'd managed to grab hold of what he'd placed beyond his grasp.

"She's going to be fine," Ted said. "The guy said she's got the pulse of a racehorse. She's a lot younger than her age."

Quinn met his eyes. This decent man who had bested him in the game of love. "Thanks, Ted," he said. "I appreciate the update."

"Sure." He turned to his wife. "I have to go. The kids."

Quinn watched Belle walk Ted to the door. She gave him a wifely peck that Quinn felt as a sting on his own lips. Ted kissed her in return; not ostentatiously, as Quinn might have done in his place. She hung on, her arms belting his waist, her face nuzzled into his chest. Then she let go. Ted nodded once at Quinn, then loped back to his van, which was likely grimed with dog hair and strewn with mildewed baseball cards and boys' shoes and, in the way back, a carton of fresh merit badges waiting to be earned.

It was now late afternoon, the flowers in Ona's perennial bed releasing a heady scent. "I mulched those," he said to Belle. "Back in May."

Belle took a seat on Ona's porch glider, where she observed the flowers. "I'm moving in with Ted tonight. He's been patient enough."

Quinn said nothing.

She invited him to sit. They watched Ona's birds flit back and forth from the freshly stocked feeders. "I'm taking a job," he said. He told her about Sylvie.

"I'm sorry," she said quietly. "I know you don't want—" She paused. "I know."

"You're the only one who does, Belle."

She nodded toward the feeders. "You the one still filling those?"

"She could fill them herself if she really wanted to."

They laughed a little. Belle surveyed the tended yard, the resurrected lawn, the righted fence posts. "You did so much more than I asked."

"For once."

"More than he would have done himself, I mean. That's saying a lot. He'd be glad."

She kept looking at him. Waiting. For what, he didn't know. She seemed so far away, the boy filling the fragile expanse between them.

"You could never see it, Quinn," she said. "He was so like you. So single-minded. His eye forever on the wrong ball."

In the distance, the Brighton Avenue traffic sounded like a long, steady exhale. "I know you wondered," she murmured. "But you decided to be his father anyway." She waited for him to look at her. She said, "He was yours, Quinn. You know there was no one else."

He recalled the baby: pale, translucent, a network of blue veins visible through his skin. His see-through boy, too unformed for the world that lay in wait. He said, "I'm sorry you had to tell me that."

"You were entitled to your doubts. We were on and off back then, but I was a faithful girl. Not the wild child you thought I was."

"Me too," he said. "Faithful as a hound."

"I knew that. I always knew that." She slid her hand beneath his and he held on. "I kept hoping you'd want what I gave you. I waited for you to fall in love with him."

"I did fall in love with him. I did. But not until after he was gone." His son, his undeniable boy.

In answer, she rested her head on his shoulder. He was struck by the strangeness of time, how the three months since meeting Ona could feel so open-ended and slow to unfurl while that same period, using the boy's death as the starting point, shrank to such a degree that the tragedy seemed like an event that had yet to happen.

For some time longer they sat side by side, not talking, like a long-married couple in a private twilight. "Ted's a stellar guy," Quinn said. "You picked a good man."

"His sons rip me up, straight to the core. But eventually, I know, they'll be mine."

"If you ever need me, Belle."

Softly, without a trace of malice, she said, "It's too late for that."

"It isn't," he said. "You'll see."

The sound of the coming evening fell upon them: beyond the last-call flurry at the feeders, human families could also be heard from down the street, opening doors, clattering plates out to patios and backyards, flipping on televisions, pulling cars into garages. For the moment this place—the house Ona still thought of as Randall's—felt like his. The yard felt like his yard.

"We should check on her," Belle said, rising.

"I'll do it. You go."

She gathered her things. "I always believed," she said, "that he was desperate to be born." Leaning down, she kissed him on the cheek, then started down the steps, heading toward the life she would live without him.

Upstairs, gaining strength by the second, lay Quinn's inheritance, left to the father from the son: an old woman suddenly missing home. The bequest felt both heavy and light, welcome and not. It came with ten conditions and ten more after that.

Belle turned around. "You won't disappoint her, Quinn."

"I won't," he said. "She's my friend." He nearly said, *I love her.* What did he mean?

He meant he loved her. That was all. It was simpler than he expected.

* * *

This is Miss Ona Vitkus. This is her life memories and shards on tape.
This is also Part Ten again.

Hello, this is Ona Vitkus speaking. I am one hundred four years
old. And one hundred one days.

. . .

Here is my—my list?—my list for—posterity?—for posterity. For
all posterity.

. . .

One: *Būk sveikas.*

. . .

I'm thinking. I guess there's just the one.

. . .

Very good! You've got a flair for accents.

. . .

I think it means "Take care."

. . .

Thank you. You, too, dear. You take care.

OLDEST

1. Oldest caged mouse. Age 7 years and 7 months. Fritzy. Owned by Bridget Beard. Country of UK.
2. Oldest shoe. Age 10,000 years. Country of Italy.
3. Oldest tree. Bristlecone pine. Age 5,200 years. CUT DOWN!!! Country of USA.
4. Oldest dog. Butch the beagle. Age 27. Owned by Mr. Gregory Duncan. Country of USA.
5. Oldest vomit. Age 160,000,000 years. Country of UK.
6. Oldest bowling alley. Age 3,400 years. Country of Egypt.
7. Oldest chimpanzee. Age 73 years. Cheeta. Country of USA.
8. Oldest musical instrument. Bone flute. Age 40,000 years. Country of Germany.
9. Oldest merit badges. The year 1910. Bee farming, taxidermy, first aid to animals, music, and 53 others. Country of USA.
10. Oldest fossilized child. Age 3,300,000 years. Country of Cradle of Civilization.

Chapter 25

After getting up in the dark (one) and using the toilet (two) and washing his face (three) and brushing his teeth (four), he puts on his pants and socks and shoes and shirt and jacket and cap (five, six, seven, eight, nine, ten). He steals out of the house (one) and into the garage (two), where he grabs his bike (three) and wheels it to the sidewalk (four). In the shadowy predawn, he commences his tour of the neighborhood, tape recorder secured in the deep, warm, silken pocket of his leather jacket.

He loves this jacket. The squeaky leather sounds to him like encouragement. It counts his movements. The dark unnerves him, but the jacket's weight feels like an arm slung across his shoulder, sanding the edges of his dread as he pedals up the street.

Because he has never listened for the morning chorus and is not entirely certain what it is, he doesn't know exactly how to go about finding it. Every few yards he stops (one), gets off his bike (two), and lays the bike down (three). He listens hard (four), withdraws the recorder from its hiding place (five), and lifts it to the trees (six).

He wishes for more trees. He wishes for more light. He wishes for the stillest shadows to move, and for the moving shadows to go still.

Yesterday, Troy Packard (puffy little targer; son of a gun; egg-eyed bully) received from Mr. Linkman a highly public A for writing a three-page life story of his boring seventy-year-old grandfather and turning it in early. Probably Troy Packard's mother wrote those perfect pages, but Mr. Linkman is slow about certain things. It doesn't matter. Not now. The other stories will come in on the appointed day, and nobody else—of this he is quite sure—nobody else picked a possible Guinness world record holder.

They recorded Part Ten last Saturday, but this part—music!—is his extra idea. All week he has gone to bed practicing how to present to Miss Vitkus her finished tape, from which he will transcribe for Mr. Linkman the required three pages of not-secret things, in immaculate penmanship and flawless spelling, earning an easy A+ unless he accidentally does something B or C+.

The tape itself is a secret. Normally, he doesn't like secrets. But this is the good kind. Miss Vitkus is his good secret.

He pedals again, stops again, lifts the recorder again. Strange, muffling noises drift in: a car idling one street over (one); a rustle in a juniper (two) that might be hornets; a hornetlike hum of traffic (three) from Washington Avenue, where he is not allowed to ride.

No birds.

The quality of darkness is changing, right before his eyes, a single, flimsy layer at a time peeling back, leaving a less dreadful darkness and in the eastern sky a miraculous intensity that can't quite be called light. More like the promise of light.

There. A single note.

He fumbles for the recorder and offers it again. Another note, two birds now, one responding to the other.

Tweedle, the one bird says. *Tweedle,* says the second. The boy's mouth drops open. *Tweedle,* he whispers. *One, two.*

A robin? A blue jay? His list has stuck fast at fifteen—fifteen winter birds, the spring visitors still holed up in Rhode Island or Florida or Costa Rica or beyond—but even fifteen is too many: he can't commit their voices to memory. The musical matches elude him, despite the CD his mother brought home: a patient-voiced man naming birds one by one, which then oblige him with a song. He's listened to this astounding recording ten times—imagining a man in a sound studio with all the birds in North America perched side by side on a clothesline, his father in the control room pressing buttons—and yet he can't identify the invisible birds singing here, now. The disappointment tastes like metal in his throat.

He keeps the tape aloft, his arm beginning to ache. Gradually, from an unseen perch in the shadow of a tree between two houses, a third bird chimes.

Then a fourth.

Then ten, and ten again, chiming from concealed spots above and between and around the houses and garages and parked cars and telephone poles and the light urges into this astonishing hour, each chime pecking a pinhole in the sheeted dark until the last layers shred completely and the light pours in and in.

The cold clouds of his quickened breaths flit into the brightening air, just like birds. Sixty birds, seventy birds, ninety birds, too fast now, uncountable. Their voices join and swell, and he swells with them. This is the morning chorus, this is the morning chorus, and a rollicking delight takes hold of his body.

He hears a creaking in the trees and remembers: *a sound like a rusty gate.* Then he sees them, gusting out of a single tree, a heckling flock of grackles teasing the brightness out of the dawn. Then he spots robins, six of them, standing on separate, exposed branches, singing their part, the color in their breasts spreading as the light spreads.

He yips his yippy laugh, and the feeling in his own breast spreads, a mysterious intensifying pressure, as if color is rising in him as well, as if he himself were a bird capable of making music. The feeling fills him until it resembles something like pain, as if he might explode with happiness.

You hear that? his father once said about Eric Chapman's ghost notes. *It's like something rising out of the goddamn sea. It should take your breath away.*

His breath is being taken away, his arm weakening, but he holds the recorder high, determined to outstay the tape's last sputtering revolution. This is the big finale, the morning chorus, which he will take to his father, who owns a magical machine with knobs and lights. God can't make birds sing lower, but his father can.

He will ask this of his father, who will say to himself: *You can't make a simple D chord, how do you know about changing keys?*

I listened, he'll answer, and his father will realize how ardently he'd paid attention all along, how carefully he observed, how hard he tried. He will tell his father that the morning chorus sounded like something rising out of the breath it took away.

To which his father will respond, *All right, then, my friend; let's make some music.*

The ten parts of Miss Vitkus's story will end with bird music in a key she can hear, a big surprise that he will present to her next Saturday, exactly nine months and twenty-six days before her actual birthday. Miss Vitkus will want to meet his father, who lowered the key of birds, and they will all become friends.

He cannot know that the thing he thinks of as his friend's amazing life, ninety minutes on tape, will momentarily break from his hand and slide down the street to be crushed beyond seeing by the first squad car at the scene. The unwinding tape will twist and flutter, catching the rising light. Over time, the tatters will work their way underground, save for a single, glinting ribbon picked up at day's end by a passing crow, which will carry its own voice to a nest high above the place where the boy, thankful for his father, waits with his whirring machine, certain that his friend shall hear once again the whole of the wakening world.

Chapter 26

From *Guinness World Records 2006:*
    RECORD: Oldest matron of honor
    RECORD HOLDER: **Ona Vitkus,** age 104, USA (wedding
      of Belle and Ted Ledbetter, USA)

From *Guinness World Records 2009:*
    RECORD: Oldest licensed driver
    RECORD HOLDER: **Ona Vitkus,** age 108, Portland,
      Maine, USA

From *Guinness World Records 2010:*
    RECORD: Oldest Lithuanian émigrée to revisit homeland
    RECORD HOLDER: **Ona Vitkus,** age 109, USA (escort:
      Quinn Porter, USA)

From *Guinness World Records 2011:*
    RECORD: Oldest multiple record holder
    RECORD HOLDER: **Ona Vitkus,** age 110, USA

Acknowledgments

Thanks first to my editor, Deanne Urmy, whose advice and friendship I cherish; this is our second book together, and I remain in awe of her grace and wisdom. The Houghton Mifflin Harcourt team—especially Michelle Bonanno Triant and Nicole Angeloro—has been a delight to work with. The production team of Martha Kennedy, Beth Burleigh Fuller, and Barbara Wood hit another homer for me.

My agent, Gail Hochman, and her crew—especially Marianne Merola and Jody Kahn—have been the mainstays of my professional life. Thank you, oh fair and noble ladies.

Special thanks to my friend Mary Berry (in memory), whose youthful spirit offered me a way to write about extreme old age; to Amy MacDonald, who so often provided both a literal and metaphorical refuge for this writer; to Patty Hopkins, who loaned me her family lore and Lithuanian tapes; and to Susan and Bill, and Jess and Bill, who loaned me space and time to write. For musical models and inspiration, I thank my brother, Barry, still a working musician after all these years; and Bob Thompson, my old friend and erstwhile music partner.

This book took so much longer to write than I first imagined and therefore required more than the usual amount of encouragement. Polly Bennell, life coach to writers in despair, offered inestimable guidance. And I'm especially grateful to Anne Wood, Patrick Clary, and Bill Lundgren for their pestering affection and refusal to take no for an answer; to Catherine WoodBrooks on general principles; and to Dan

Abbott, my husband and teammate, who lives it all with me. I owe you guys big-time.

Finally, a long-overdue shout-out to my friends at Longfellow Books in Portland, Maine, who over the years have offered me books, cats, free stuff, undeserved adulation, Phyllis's cookies, ridiculously high sales, enormous moral support, and true friendship. I write this in loving memory of Stuart Gersen.

Discussion Questions

1. In the opening pages, we discover that the boy of the title has died. And yet he is a catalyst for everything that happens afterward. How did you perceive the boy's role in the story—as an absence? A presence? A sort of invisible stage manager? Did you sometimes forget that he was gone?

2. When did you first notice that the boy was nameless? Why do you think the author chose not to name the boy?

3. For the first time in her life, Ona gives away her secrets—to a child. What is it about the boy that Ona instinctively trusts?

4. Ona observes, "People like Quinn, always running from themselves, loved the road." What does she mean by this? Is Quinn the only character "on the run" here?

5. How does the road trip reveal the varying motivations of Ona, Quinn, and Belle? Was meeting Laurentas a surprise to you? What were you expecting to find in Granyard, Vermont?

6. When Belle says, "I figured you must have worked," Ona is thrilled to have been recognized "as the employable type." Why is her career as a "professional secretary" such a badge of honor for Ona?

7. Discuss the various friendships in the book: Ona and the boy; Ona and Quinn; Quinn and Belle; Ona and Louise. What about Quinn's friendship with his bandmates in The Benders? Or with Sylvie? To what degree are all these friendships necessary to the people involved?

8. Early on, Quinn derides Ted Ledbetter as "a middle-school teacher and single father who claimed to love woodland hikes." And yet, near the end, he thinks: "He wanted to be—God help him—Ted Ledbetter." What has changed? How is it that we so often end up admiring our rivals?

9. Whom do you believe Belle should have chosen, Quinn or Ted?

10. Quinn is "uneasy around the boy, troubled by the world in which he dwelled." Why do you think that is the case? Why are Quinn and his son so ill matched?

11. Near the end, Quinn confesses to Belle: "I did fall in love with him. I did. But not till after he was gone." When and how do you think this happened?

12. The author has said, "If a writer can't make you like a character, she must at least make you understand him." Despite Quinn's flaws, do you like him? If not, did you understand why he behaves the way he does?

13. "I have deficiencies," the boy tells Ona. Does he? The author has said that she created the boy before the words "autism" or "Asperger's" entered the American lexicon. "He's just who he is," Belle says, bristling against labels. Is Belle right? Does it matter?

14. Before meeting the boy, "Ona had believed herself through with friendship." How does old age change Ona's ideas about friendship? Did reading the novel cause you to examine your own friendships?

15. At 104, Ona is young compared to the world's oldest citizens. This is a surprise to both her and the boy. Was it a surprise to you? Did meeting Ona change your presumptions about extreme old age?

16. The novel contains a large cast of major and minor characters. Who makes the most significant journey? Is there more than one way to identify "the main character"? To whom does this story ultimately belong?

17. Did you find the last full chapter satisfying? Was the sudden presence of the boy a surprise? Did you want to see him at this moment in his life?

18. The author has said, "In my novels I assemble families from broken parts." Is that true in this novel? Is friendship sometimes more powerful than family ties?

19. The Guinness World Records plays a role in the book. If you were to set a record, what would it be?

20. *The One-in-a-Million Boy* has sold in over twenty countries, from Brazil to South Korea. What, if anything, about this American story strikes you as transcending culture?